CRITICAL ACCLAIM FOR
KILLIN' TIME IN SAN DIEGO

"Anguished characters and desperate situations coil through this collection of uniquely creative plots—a fabulous anthology."
—Joe Ricker, author of *Some Awful Cunning*

"*Killin' Time in San Diego* is weird, gothic, subtle, illicit, and a riot concocted by crime writers at the top of their game."
—Jay Gertzman, author of *Beyond Twisted Sorrow*

"Another worthy addition to the Bouchercon legacy. Top writers on top of their game."
—Colin Campbell, author of the Jim Grant Thrillers

"Holly West helms another fine anthology, proving once again that short crime fiction is alive and well...and living in San Diego."
—Josh Pachter, editor of *Paranoia Blues: Crime Fiction Inspired by the Songs of Paul Simon*

"It's not enough that San Diego has great beaches, natural attractions, and the world's best climate. No, now it also has this terrific anthology of canny crime fiction."
—Albert Tucher, author of *Blood Like Rain*

"A powerhouse anthology boasting stellar talent in top form."
—Tom Mead, author of *Death and the Conjuror*

"Twenty authors present a delightful tapestry of tales that go from touching to twisty to amusing, populating them with a cast of characters you won't soon forget."
—R.J. Koreto, author of the Historic Homes mysteries

"Revenge and survival, sly cozies and twisty plots all confirm that fabulous weather is no barrier to bad behavior and successful sleuthing in *Killin' Time in San Diego*."
—Janice Law, author of the Francis Bacon mysteries

"*Killin' Time in San Diego* continues a decade-long tradition of absorbing annual anthologies celebrating the Bouchercon World Mystery Convention."
—J.L. Abramo, Shamus Award-winning author of *Circling the Runway* and *Gravesend*

"A criminally rich compendium of San Diego-set mysteries that entertainingly spans the city geographically and throughout its history."
—Andrew Welsh-Huggins, author of the Andy Hayes private eye series and editor of *Columbus Noir*

"Bookended by two of the strongest stories I've read in a long time, this collection is thoroughly fantastic. Seen through these eyes, San Diego is both more appealing and threatening now."
—Ryan Sayles, author of *Like Whitewashed Tombs*

"From chatty Canadian tourists, clandestine hitmen and (my favorite) a smelly killer whale detective, this collection of twenty criminally entertaining stories is the perfect companion when you're stuck in traffic on the I-5."
—Linda Sands, award-winning Georgia Author of the Year

"A superior collection of crime stories punctuated by comic tales of murderous merriment, this will not be your heaviest read of the summer but it will rank among the best."
—Rob Pierce, author of *Snake Slayer*

KILLIN' TIME
IN SAN DIEGO

BOUCHERCON ANTHOLOGIES

HOLLY WEST, EDITOR

KILLIN' TIME
IN SAN DIEGO

BOUCHERCON ANTHOLOGY 2023

DOWN&OUT
BOOKS

Down & Out Books
3959 Van Dyke Road, Suite 265
Lutz, FL 33558
DownAndOutBooks.com

The characters and events in this book are fictitious. Any similarity to real persons, living or dead, is coincidental and not intended by the author.

Cover design by JT Lindroos

ISBN: 1-64396-328-7
ISBN-13: 978-1-64396-328-0

TABLE OF CONTENTS

INTRODUCTION
Holly West

I attended my first Bouchercon World Mystery Convention in 2009. It was in Indianapolis that year, and by day, I sat captivated, listening to my favorite authors talk about their work. By night, I stalked them in the bar, where (among other wonderful happenings) Ali Karim introduced me to my idol, Sue Grafton. Fourteen years later, I'm still stalking my favorite authors at the Bouchercon bar, and though Sue Grafton sadly passed away in 2017, I'm thrilled and fortunate to call many of these same authors my friends.

So when the Bouchercon 2023 organizers invited me to edit this anthology, my fingers couldn't type "yes" fast enough. As a California native who lived in Southern California for over twenty-five years, the San Diego setting was particularly enticing—and appropriate.

"America's Finest City" has a more laid-back vibe than its larger neighbor to the north, but its natural beauty, urban landscape, and diverse population make it an equally compelling setting for crime fiction. Those "hot, dry, Santa Anas" Raymond Chandler wrote about, during which "every booze party ends in a fight" and "meek little wives feel the edge of the carving knife and study their husbands' necks," blow in San Diego, too.

What follows is a collection of twenty stories, most of which are set in, or adjacent to, San Diego. Seventeen were selected from

1

over 180 submissions via a blind process that included me and a panel of four independent judges, each chosen for their love of reading, diversity, and passion for crime fiction.

What strikes me about these stories is how different authors can take the same general backdrop and turn it into something wholly their own. From humor (Mary Keenan's "The Canadians," Richie Narvaez's "Shamu, World's Greatest Detective," Tim P. Walker's "Bidding War") to heartbreak (Emilya Naymark's "Girl of Gold," C.W. Blackwell's "Hard Rain on Beach Street," L.H. Dillman's "To Hell and Back") to historical (J.R. Sanders's "Dead Even," Jennifer Berg's "A Bayside Murder," James Thorpe's "Casualties of War"), each selection in this anthology, including additional stories written by Désirée Zamorano, Kathleen L. Asay, John M. Floyd, Wesley Browne, Kim Keeline, Victoria Weisfeld, Anne-Marie Campbell, and Kathy A. Norris, brings San Diego to rich and vivid life with complex characters, twisted crimes, and skilled storytelling.

The remaining stories were graciously contributed by three of this year's Bouchercon Guests of Honor. While these aren't set in San Diego, their settings are nonetheless as rich and layered as a reader might expect from such accomplished writers. The isolation of being in a boat on a river in C.J. Box's "Every Day is a Good Day on the River" delivers immediate tension, while Naomi Hirahara's "The Celestial" tells the story of a Gold Rush-era Japanese woman forced into sex work after her husband leaves her for another woman. Finally, Ann Cleeves's "Drowning" is the quiet but powerful story of a first meeting between two gay men and a painful confession. We're thrilled to publish "Drowning" here, for the first time, in the US.

I'm not exaggerating when I tell you that I loved every part of the process of bringing this anthology to you. Though we could only choose a small number of stories from our submissions, I enjoyed reading each one of them.

I'd like to offer my heartfelt thanks to our independent panel of judges (who have asked that their identities remain anonymous). I could not have done this without you. Additional thanks go out to Marie Sutro, who helped administrate this project. Your hard work is appreciated.

The pool of talent in our community is infinite. I'm grateful to be a part of it.

Holly West
Folsom, California

EVERY DAY IS A GOOD DAY ON THE RIVER
C.J. Box

The guide, Randall "Call Me Duke" Conner, pushed them off from the sandy launch below the bridge into the river and within seconds the muscular dark flow of the current gripped the flat-bottomed McKenzie boat and spun it like a cigarette butt in a flushed toilet. The morning was cool but sunny and there was enough of a breeze to rattle the dry fall leaves in the cotton-woods that reached out over the water like skeletal hands. There were three men in the boat. Jack, who'd never been on a drift boat before, cried out: "Is this safe, Duke?"

"Ha!" Duke snorted. "Of course. Just let me get at the oars and get us turned around. Everything will be just fine. It's a good day on the river. Every day is a good day on the river."

Duke stepped around Jack, who had the front fishing seat in the bow. The boat bucked with his weight. Jack reached out and grasped the casting leg brace in front of his seat and held on and slightly closed his eyes until Duke got settled in the middle of the boat and it stopped rocking. The guide grasped the oars and with two quick and powerful strokes—forward on the left oar, backward on the right—stopped the boat from spinning and righted it within the flow.

Duke said, "See, we're perfectly fine now. You can relax. It's Jack, isn't it?"

"Yes, it's Jack."

Duke nodded, then spoke in a pleasant, soft voice. What he said was well rehearsed. "This is a McKenzie-style drift boat, Jack, the finest of its kind. It was designed for western rivers like this. Flat-bottomed, flared sides, and a narrow-pointed stern, and extreme rocker in the bow and stern to allow the boat to spin around on its center like a pivot. It's not sluggish like a raft or a damned tank like a jon boat. We point the bow toward one of the banks downriver and keep the stern upriver and we use the power of the river to move us along. That's why it's called a drift boat! I use the oars to keep us in the right place for fishing. Hell, I can shoot this boat from side to side across the river like a skeeter bug to get you fishermen in the best possible position for catching fish, Jack. That's why we float at a forty-five-degree angle to the current, so both of you will have clear fishing lanes and you won't have to cast over each other. It's stable as hell, so don't be afraid to stand up in that brace and cast. Just make sure you keep balanced, Jack. And try not to hook me in the ear on your back cast!"

Duke had a deep laugh that Jack would describe as infectious if he were in the right mood.

Jack found out his fishing seat would turn on its pedestal. He released the leg brace and cautiously spun the seat around so he could watch Duke work the oars. The guide was a magician, an expert, and he could move the boat with a flick of either oar. Duke was tall, with powerful shoulders from rowing, no doubt. He had a big sweeping mustache and a dark tan. He wore a fishing shirt, shorts, and river sandals. His eyes were hidden by dark sunglasses fitted with a strap so he could hang them from his neck. Forceps were clipped to a breast pocket as were clippers strung from a retractable zinger. He had a big wolfish smile full of perfect white teeth. Jack thought, *He's a man's man. One of those men, like skiing instructors or firemen, who just seem to have everything they ever wanted in life.*

Jack watched as Duke turned around and looked over his shoulder at the other fisherman, Jack's host, in the seat in the stern of the boat.

Duke looked over his shoulder. "And you're Tim, right?"

"Yes," Tim said wearily.

Jack turned in his chair. Tim looked small and slight and scrunched up in comparison with Duke. Jack thought Tim looked like a wet mouse, even though he was dry. Maybe it was the way Tim sat, all pulled into himself, hunched over in his seat, his chin down against his chest. He wore an oversized rain jacket, waders, and a ridiculous hat with hidden earflaps tucked up under the band. Jack shot a look toward the northern horizon to see if there were thunderheads rolling. Nope.

Duke said, "So it's Jack and Tim. You guys seem like a couple of hale fellows well met. Did you say you've fished the river before?"

Jack said he was new to drift boat fishing, but he was willing to learn the ropes. Jack confessed, "I've never fished with a guide before. This is all a new experience. But when Tim asked me to come along, I jumped all over the opportunity. So just tell me what to do, I don't mind."

"That's a good way to be, Jack. We'll have a good time. What about you, Tim?"

Tim didn't answer. He stared at the water on the side of the boat as if the foam and bubbles were the most fascinating things he'd ever seen. The only sounds were the metal-on-metal squeak of the oars in the oarlocks and the rapid *lap-lap-lap* of the water on the side of the fiberglass hull.

Again, Duke said, "Tim, what about you?"

Finally, Tim looked up. There was something mean in his eyes and his lips were pulled against his teeth so hard they looked translucent.

"Duke, why do you say our names every time you ask a question, Duke? Is that so you'll remember our names, *Duke*? Is that one of your guide tricks, *Duke*?"

Then he added, in an icy tone Jack had never heard Tim use before: "Your name is Randall, but you go by Duke. I think I'll call you Randall, Randall."

Duke flashed an uncomfortable smile and looked up at Jack instead of over his shoulder at Tim. As if trying to get Jack to acknowledge that Tim was out of line. The silence between them grew uncomfortable until Duke finally shrugged it off and filled it.

"Someone wake up on the wrong side of the bunk this morning? Well, never mind that, Tim. Everything will change, Tim. Every day is good on the river. We just haven't caught any fish yet because we haven't been fishing. So let's just get you fellows rigged up. I'll pull over here into this little back eddy and drop the anchor and get you rigged up. Everything will be fine once you hook up with one of these monsters."

Tim rolled his eyes and said, "*What crap. Jesus Christ.*" Jack had never heard Tim talk with such sarcasm before, and he was a little shocked. He tried to cover for his host. Jack said, "Tim's been all over the West on all the famous rivers, right, Tim? The Bighorn, the Big Hole, the Wind, the Madison, the North Fork, and of course here on the North Platte. He always tells me about his trips. So when he invited me on this one, man, I jumped at the chance."

Duke said," You've gotten around, eh, Tim?"

"I'm not the only one, Randall."

Jack shook his head. Tim seemed so out of character, so bitter. He thought, *Something is going on here.* He wondered if rich men treated guides this way. If so, he didn't think he liked it.

Jack heard a heavy splash and he turned around in his seat again. He'd seen the anchor hanging from an arm off the back of the boat and now it was gone. The anchor was ten scarred pounds of pyramid-shaped lead. It was triggered to drop by a foot release under Duke's rowing bench. Jack could feel the boat slow and then stop when the anchor bit into the riverbed and the boat swung around the current.

Duke spoke to Jack as if he hadn't heard Tim's earlier statement. "We'll get you started with nymphs and an indicator. When we get rigged up, throw it out there and keep an eye on the indicator, Jack. If you see it tick or bounce, you raise the rod tip fast. Sometimes these fish barely lip the nymph. So if you see that indicator do anything at all, set the hook."

Jack nodded. "Okay."

"It's easy to get mesmerized by the indicator in the water, so don't worry about that. We only have one place on the river where it gets a little hairy, and that's the place downriver called the Chutes. You've probably heard of it."

"I have. Didn't somebody die there last year?"

"About one year, actually," Duke said, stripping lengths of tippet from a spool to build the nymph rig and tying knots with the deft movements of a surgeon. "There are big rocks on both sides and some rapids down the middle. But as long as you hit the middle squared up, there's no problem. I've done it a hundred times and never flipped a boat. That's the only place you'll need to reel in for a few minutes and you may get a little splash of water on you since you're in front. Otherwise, don't worry about a thing. Tim, do you want me to tie on a couple of nymphs for you?"

"I'll do it myself."

"Suit yourself, Tim."

"I will, *Randall*."

Jack really didn't know Tim well enough to claim they were friends. So he had been surprised when Tim called him at his construction company the week before and offered to host him on a guided fishing trip on the North Platte River. Jack had said yes before checking his calendar with his wife, Janey, even with the odd provision Tim had requested.

Later, Jack had told Janey about the invitation and the terms of the provision. She was making dinner at the stove—spaghetti and meat sauce—and she shook her head and made a puzzled face.

She said, "He wants you to make the booking? I didn't think you knew him that well."

"I don't. But yes, he asked me to use my credit card for the deposit, but said he'd pay me back for everything afterward, including the flies we use and the top. He wanted to make sure we were scheduled to go on the river with the owner of the guide service—somebody named Duke—and no one else. He said it was important to go with the owner because we'd catch the most fish that way. Who was I to argue? Tim wants the best, I guess."

"But why you?"

Jack shrugged. "I guess he remembers I was the only one who never gave him any shit in high school when we were growing up. Everyone else did because he was such a weird dude. And he was. You've seen that picture of him in the yearbook. But hell, I guess I always sort of felt sorry for him. For some reason, I liked him and I kind of sympathized with the little creep. His parents were real no-hopers, and for a while the whole family lived in their car. That car was just filled with junk—sleeping bags and crap. They'd drop him off for school on the street we lived on so nobody would know, but I saw him get out once. He was real embarrassed, but I didn't tell anyone I saw him. I guess he appreciated that. He told me once he never wanted to live in a car again. A high school kid telling me that, I don't know. I was sort of touched. Man, I sound lame."

She laughed and said, "You do, honey, but that will be our little secret. Then he invented that thing—what was it?"

"You're asking me? Hell, I'm not sure. Somebody explained it to me once but it didn't take. Something about a circuit for a wireless router or something. Whatever it was, it made him millions."

She pursed her lips and said, "And he moved back to Wyoming. I always thought that was strange."

"Yeah, me too. He coulda lived anywhere."

"Jack," she asked, while making a sly face at him, "if you made tens of millions, would you move?"

Jack snorted and rolled his eyes. "We won't have to worry about finding out. I'll never have to make that decision, so you better keep your job."

"Bummer," she said, and changed the subject. "And he got married to that bombshell. What was her name?"

He could see her in his mind's eye: tall, black hair, green eyes, great figure. A bit much, but that was the point, he thought. But her name? "I can't remember," he said.

She said, "I saw them together once. Beauty and the Geek, that's for sure."

"Maybe he wanted to prove something to all the jocks and high school big shots who used to pants him and hang him up-side down from a tree, like *Look at me, losers!*"

"But he asked *you* to go fishing with him."

"Yeah, and I want to go."

"Maybe he thinks you're his best friend. That's kind of sweet and pathetic at the same time."

"Oh, bullshit," Jack said, looking away. "I just want to catch big trout with a five-hundred-dollar-a-day guide. That's the big time, baby. Every man wants to fish with flies and catch a big trout. Here's my chance."

Jack caught two large trout before noon with the nymphs and missed at least five more. The fish he boated and Duke netted were a rainbow and a brown. The trout were big, thick, and sleek and reminded him of wet quadricep muscles that hap-pened to have a head, fins, and a tail. Both were over twenty-two inches. When the fish took the nymphs, it was as if an elec-tric current shot up through the line to his rod, as if they'd like to pull him out of the boat and into the water. He'd whooped and Duke dropped the anchor with a splash and reached for his big net. Jack couldn't remember when he had had so much fun.

Tim caught ten, but netted them himself without a word, and Duke simply shrugged and said, "Let me know if you need any help."

"I don't. I do things for myself."

The rhythm of the current lulled Jack. He stared at the indicator until the image of it burned into his mind, and its bobbing mesmerized him. At one point he looked up and thought the boat and indicator were stationary on the river, but the banks were rolling by, and not the other way around. There were bald eagles in some of the trees—Duke pointed them out in a way that suggested he did the same thing every day—and they floated by mule deer drinking in the water and a family of river otters slip-sliding over one another on some rocks.

Duke kept up a steady patter.

"River right there's a nice hole."

"Nice cast there, Jack."

"Don't forget to mend your line. There, that's the ticket."

"If you hook up again, use your reel. That's what it's there for. Don't grab the line. Don't horse it in."

"What a beautiful day. Every day is a good day on the river, ain't it?"

All of the land they were floating through was private, with just a few public spots marked by blue diamond-shaped signs mounted on T-posts. There were few houses or buildings along the shores and it seemed to Jack they were the only people on the river, or, perhaps, on the planet. There were no take-out spots anywhere, and the truck and trailer would be miles ahead by now, he guessed.

He thought: *Once you're on the river, you're on the river for the rest of the day. You can't stop and go home. You can't get out. There's nowhere to go.*

* * *

Although he was concentrating on the gentle bobbing of the strike indicator, Jack saw—or thought he saw—an odd movement in his peripheral vision from the back of the boat. When he turned his head and looked directly, he saw Tim pulling his arm back and jamming his hand into the pocket of his coat. There had been something black in his hand and his arm had been outstretched, but whatever it was was now hidden, and Tim wouldn't look up and meet his eyes. Instead, Tim made a beautiful cast toward the opposite bank.

Jack shook his head and rotated back around in his chair. What had been in Tim's hand? And why did he think it might've been a gun pointed at the back of Duke's head?

Then Jack thought: *Stop being ridiculous.*

Duke backed the boat to the bank and dropped the anchor on the dirt with a heavy thud and said, "How about some lunch, guys?"

Jack had already reeled in because he could hear the increasing roar downriver. The sound was heavy and angry. He asked, "Is that the Chutes up ahead, Duke?"

"That's it, all right. But we'll grab some lunch here first."

Jack was hungry and it felt good to step on hard ground and stretch his legs and back. Duke had said the camp was leased from a rancher exclusively for Duke and his fishing guides and it had a picnic table, a fire pit, and an outhouse. Tim headed for the outhouse first, Jack followed. Duke stayed back at the camp and started a fire in the pit and dug items out of his cooler.

When Tim finally stepped from the outhouse, Jack smiled at him. "I really want to thank you again for inviting me along. This is really special."

"Sure, Jack," Tim said. But he seemed distracted.

Jack hesitated, wondering how to put it. Then he said, "Is everything okay, Tim? I know we don't know each other that well, but, well...are you feeling okay?"

Tim looked up sharply. "*Why do you ask?*"

"Is there something between you and Duke, or am I just

imagining things?"

Tim looked hard at Jack, as if searching his face for something or wondering what he should reply. Jack said, "A while back, I looked in the back of the boat and I thought I saw something."

"Really?"

"Yes. But I might've been imagining things."

In response, Tim reached up and patted Jack's shoulder as he walked past him. He said, "I shouldn't have gotten you involved. I'm sorry."

"Involved in what?"

But Tim was gone, walking alone toward the river to the far right of the camp.

Jack and Duke sat at the picnic table and ate hamburgers. Jack ate two and half a tube of Pringles. He washed it all down with two cans of Coors Light. He said to Duke, "I can't believe I'm so hungry."

"Being outside does that to you."

"The burgers were great, thank you."

"You're paying for them," Duke laughed, then shouted toward Tim, who was still standing alone on the bank, watching the river flow by. "Tim, are you sure you don't want lunch? You've got to be starving, man." Tim didn't reply. Duke leaned across the table and lowered his voice. "To each is own, I guess. Is he always this surly?"

"No."

"I never got his last name. What is it?"

"Hey, I really don't like gossiping about my host, if you don't mind."

"Sorry," Duke said. "I should mind my own business. You're right. Oh well, I've had worse in the boat. Luckily, I'm a people person. You have to be a people person to be a guide."

"I guess you get some characters, eh?"

Duke laughed and shook his head from side to side. "You have no idea, Jack. You have no idea."

Duke packed up the lunch items and secured the cooler to the floor of the boat with bungee cords. Jack waited on the bank, looking downriver toward the roar. He said to Duke, "You say there's nothing to worry about, right?"

"Right," Duke said, chinning toward the Chutes. "I've done it a million times and haven't lost a fisherman yet. And right past the rapids is one of the deepest holes in the whole river. You'll need to be ready to cast out as soon as we clear the rapids. We'll for sure pick up some fish in there."

"Jack, I'll take the front this time."

Jack turned. He hadn't noticed that Tim had joined them. Tim's face was ashen, and he looked gaunt.

Jack asked, "Are you sure? Duke says it gets a little splashy in front."

"Yes. Please, Jack, step aside."

Tim shouldered past Jack and stepped into the front of the boat and took a seat. He swiveled it around so it was backward and he faced Duke, who was already on the oars. Duke ignored Tim and spoke to Jack.

"I'll swing the boat around so you can get in the back easy."

Tim had his hand in his parka pocket and when he withdrew it he held a snub-nosed revolver. He pointed it at Duke's face, not more than two feet away from him.

Tim said, "*Start rowing.*"

Duke's face reddened. "Hey! What the fuck are you doing?"

Tim said, "I said start rowing. Pull up the anchor. We're leaving Jack here. He doesn't need to see this."

Duke spread his arms, palms out. "Jesus, this is a joke, right? It's a joke?"

Jack stood on the bank with his mouth gaped. Tim spoke to him without taking his eyes, or the muzzle of his gun, off Duke.

He said, "I'm sorry, Jack. I'm sorry I used you and brought you along. But I was afraid Randall would recognize my name if I made the booking. I'm sure Amanda told him my name."

Jack noticed that the blood had drained from Duke's face. Amanda, that was Tim's wife's name. Amanda.

Tim said, "Right, Randall? Right? She told you my name. She called you and told you I was going on a business trip? Or a fishing trip? So you two could get together and humiliate me in my own hometown? Right in front of dozens of people who know me? I know all about it, Randall. Did you laugh at me when you were in my bed? Did you laugh because I was so stupid?"

"Look," Duke pleaded, "it was Mandy's idea. Really. We never laughed at you."

"Mandy, is it? She never asked me to call her Mandy. It's a stupid name. Like Randall. Or Duke." A few whisps of Tim's hair had dislodged from his scalp and hung down over his eye.

Duke said, "You don't have to do this. This is crazy. Look, I'll never see her again. I fucking swear it, man."

Tim's smile was terrifying. He said, "No, you'll never see her again. You're right about that. No one will ever see her again."

He let that sink in.

Duke moaned, *"Oh, God. No."*

"Yes," Tim said. "This morning. In that bed you know so well. She thought I was bending over to kiss her goodbye. And in a way, I was."

Jack didn't realize he was unconsciously stepping away from the boat until the picnic table hit him in the back of the thighs. The roaring in his ears drowned out the sound of the Chutes. Tim shouted to be heard over it.

"I'm sorry, Jack. I'm sorry to leave you here. But there's a ranch house a couple of miles away. You'll be fine."

Jack said, "Tim, don't do this. Please, Tim."

"Too late, I'm afraid. They laughed at me, Jack. That's the worst thing anyone can do to me. Remember how they used to laugh at me in school?"

"That was a long time ago, Tim. You're a big man now. You're a good man."

Tim said to Duke, "No one laughs at me."

Jack watched Tim say something else to Duke, and the boat slipped out into the current and was gone. Because of the heavy brush downriver, he lost sight of it quickly, but began to run parallel to the river, hoping he could catch them ahead on a bend. Hoping he could persuade Tim to pull the boat over before it picked up too much speed entering the Chutes and he'd lose them. And before Tim did something he'd regret.

Jack stopped when he heard the sharp crack of a shot. Then he lowered his shoulder and forced himself through the brush. Thorns tore his flesh and his clothing, and his face was bleeding when he broke through and stood knee-deep in the cold water.

The boat was a long way downriver. Beyond it, Jack could see the huge boulders in the river and the foam of whitewater. Duke was bent over the oars, his head forward, his arms hanging limply at his sides. Tim had swiveled his chair around, his back to Duke's body, to face the Chutes. Tim stood up in the fishing platform and braced himself. He tossed the gun into the water and reached up and clamped his hat on tight and then raised his chin to the oncoming rapids.

Jack shouted but couldn't even hear himself. The boat began a lazy turn sidewise.

"Every Day is a Good Day on the River" first appeared in C.J. Box's story collection, Shots Fired.

THE CANADIANS
Mary Keenan

Sam's shoes fell softly on the carpeted stairs, his fingers curling around the weapon in his pocket as he approached the hotel lobby. He was six foot two, dressed in chinos and a crisp, long-sleeved shirt open at the collar with a sweater over his shoulders, and he moved confidently with his back straight and his eyes forward. Nobody looking at him would know how long he'd waited for this day. Or how far he'd traveled. San Diego wasn't where he expected things to end, but he wasn't sorry. The weather and the sightlines were very much to his advantage.

He'd been trailing his old adversary, Richard Hart, halfway across the country. It was past time to settle their differences. Sam wasn't exactly the victim here: he'd stolen clients from Richard, exploded his car, beat him to the chase on more than one robbery. But Richard was the true aggressor. He'd cost Sam lucrative contracts. Smashed his knee so badly he needed a replacement. Scammed him out of his safe house.

The last straw was Richard's theft of the money Sam had stashed behind a dummy bookcase in his Des Moines apartment. He'd earmarked it to finance a fledgling criminal operation designed to set him up for life. When Sam saw the rubber chicken Richard left where the money had been, he knew he couldn't rest as long as Richard was breathing.

The morning was unfolding exactly as he'd planned. He looked like every other business traveler he'd seen in the hotel earlier, and those milling around the lobby on his way to the empty lounge. The pants, the shirt, the sweater. From the lounge's terrace doors, Sam watched the tail end of Richard's car in valet parking, beyond the faux-concrete columns anchoring the hotel's front gardens. He slipped his fingers back into his pocket. Closed them over the tube of metal that would separate Richard from everything he cherished in this world. Prepared to slip out unnoticed and—

A voice like a rusty bandsaw cut across Sam's thoughts.

"Haaaaarve."

Sam was still wincing when the whine resolved into words.

"Wouldja look at this cute little patio. I didn't see that when we checked in."

A morose voice answered the grating one. "It was pitch black. We didn't see anything."

"Well, I want to have breakfast out here tomorrow. I know the driveway's right there, but it's the same setup back home, a restaurant patio practically on the street, and the views are a heckuva lot better here. There's even palm trees right alongside."

Sam adjusted his stance to suggest he was simply testing the temperature or getting some air. His weapon was unconventional enough to attract notice, so he slipped his phone out of his pocket as though that was all he'd been reaching for. He could resume his plan once these two were gone.

They were a couple in their sixties, the man with a belly swelling the front of his untucked polo, the woman hiding hers under a tropical-print blouse. Their hair matched: white, short, and brushed up on top, though hers was tinted purple at the tips and had a few curls brushed forward at the sides of her face. She seemed less shy with strangers, too.

"Excuse me, sir. Are you another guest, or are you staff? It's hard to tell around here, and my husband Harve and I are looking for a good place to go out for breakfast."

Sam second-guessed his chinos, wondering if they were the

wrong color after all.

"I don't work here."

"You been to San Diego before? Heard of anything? None of our friends have ever been this far south in California, and the lineup at the front desk is something else. A nice lady from Tallahassee told us they all work for the hotel, in corporate. They're here for management training and those cute uniforms are so they don't lose track of each other on their scavenger hunt today."

Sam processed this information, which explained his wardrobe error. But he didn't dwell on it. He had a man to get rid of and not much time to do it. He modulated his voice to low. Smooth. Intimidating.

"I can't—"

The man, Harve, cut him off. "I'd like a diner, myself. Proper eggs and bacon and toast."

Sam recalibrated. He'd have to give these two something or he wouldn't get rid of them before Richard's car pulled away. "I passed a diner on my way in yesterday. It looked busy, so it must be good."

He gave them the name. He gave them directions. He gave them a look.

They didn't leave.

"We're from Cambridge. Not the one in England. The one in Ontario, in Canada. You been there?"

Sam made a point of not smiling.

"No."

She didn't pick up on his animosity. "It's nice and clean, but it's not warm like here. Except in summer. Harve and I both retired last July and we promised ourselves we'd get somewhere nice for January and February. It's plenty warm for us but boy, it seems like everybody who lives here thinks it's the depths of winter or something. I saw a lady with a jacket and scarf walk past just now, if you can believe it. I'd sweat to death if I..."

Richard's car pulled out from the curb and purred away, driving west.

* * *

Sam had slipped a tracker inside the wheel well of Richard's car, so it only took an hour to find him again. He would have worked faster if he'd shaken off the Canadian tourists before hearing their life story. Then he'd have seen where Richard went after he parked the car.

He should have guessed it would be a jewelry store. They'd long been Richard's preferred business for laundering his money. He liked the irony in all that shiny clean gold, and old habits die hard. About as hard as Richard would die once he and Sam hit a quieter stretch of sidewalk. Sam's aim was perfect, and he wanted the scene of Richard's death to match. He'd been patient this long. A few more minutes wouldn't hurt.

On his way to the corner, Richard stopped to look in the window of a pastry shop advertising café dining. Then he slipped inside. When he emerged again a few minutes later, Sam was close enough to see the deep lines on his face marking years of smirking and squinting. Richard was Sam's height, but he stooped at the shoulders, thinking it made him look less menacing until the moment he wanted to surprise someone. He certainly didn't look menacing now. He pulled a croissant out of the bag in his hand and took a bite as he crossed the street.

As good a last meal as any.

Sam picked up his pace, the heels of his shoes making a satisfying clip on the sidewalk. He reached the curb just before the light changed.

Then, he heard a familiar voice.

"Oh, wouldja look at that. Harve, it's that nice man from the hotel."

The Canadians had come out of the pastry shop and were blocking his path. Sam watched Richard move briskly out of view.

"Harve and I headed to the diner you mentioned, but then we spotted a restaurant selling cake. At this hour, no less. We decided, since we're on vacation, we deserve to enjoy ourselves, so we started to go in. But a lady on the way out guessed we were tourists too and tipped us off that the pastries are better over here. Boy, the people in this town are so friendly, aren't they, Harve? I can't speak for what was in the first place, but we sure ate well. We'll have to walk off breakfast clear through lunch."

"We're on vacation, Merle. The calories don't count." Harve winked at Sam, the movement slow and measured, like they were two old friends who understood each other.

"Either way, we need a park or something."

Sam saw his chance. "You should try the beach."

Richard would certainly not be heading to the beach. The further the Canadians were from wherever Richard went, the better.

Merle shook her head. "I gotta admit, I'm not one to put up with sand in my shoes. I was thinking maybe that Balboa Park. Or an oceanside running track or something. Which one's closer? Maybe we need an Uber. Harve, you get that map from the hotel lobby?"

Harve reached leadenly into his pocket and dragged out a fresh-looking map, the motion implying that another ten minutes would evaporate as he unfolded it.

Richard had disappeared entirely. Again. But when he returned to his car, Sam would be waiting in his own rental a few car lengths back. The traffic on this street was easy enough to merge into. And the Canadians would be well out of the picture.

Sam had tracked Richard to a small house in the Mission Hills area. There weren't enough palms or other plantings to cover him as he executed his plan—and Richard. He pulled over to the curb and waited, watching Richard stroll between two segments of a retaining wall and up some steps toward an abbreviated porch. A woman with long, copper-colored hair glanced in either direction as she held the door for him. Sam recognized her. Richard had used her as a decoy once on a job that ended in Sam's favor. She'd been a brunette then.

Sam considered how long they might be occupied. It depended on the reason for the visit. With Richard, it could be business, or pleasure, or both. He hedged his bets and pulled out to make a U-turn and circle the block. No point in leaving his rental car in full view, ready to be recognized if Richard happened to look outside. Around the corner, he spotted an alley running behind the target house. It was too quiet there to risk driving. He'd have to walk, but there were worse ideas. He might see Richard and the woman through the back windows of the house. And if one of the windows was open...

Sam parked and got out of the car, adjusting the too-hot jacket he'd swapped for this morning's sweater. Then he crossed the street. The temperate air slipped between his skin and his shirt at the collar, tangible against his damp skin. A slight breeze ruffled his hair.

The alley was littered with irregularly placed garbage cans, board fences, and stucco garages. He knew the secret to blending in, even in this unlikely spot, was to hold his body like he belonged. Sam focused on looking like he lived here. Just a local, moving from A to B, as though he wasn't mindful of the security cameras and the way he appeared to them. He'd counted the homes as he retreated down the street, and now he counted them in reverse until he reached the one Richard was inside.

The back wall of the house had been painted a pale linen. Coral shutters framed the windows. Some of the windows were open. Richard's head was plainly visible beyond one of them, and, more importantly, his neck.

Sam reached into his pocket. It was a casual movement. His fingers closed around the metal tube and began a measured slide to open air. Then he—

"Harve, I can't believe it. It's our friend from the hotel."

Sam whipped the kazoo from his mouth and rammed it into his other pocket.

The Canadians. How had the Canadians found him here?

Sam smelled a rat. Richard must be on to him. If he'd hired these two as bodyguards they couldn't be more effective. Sam had to assume he'd done exactly that.

Harve appeared at the back gate of a house fronting the other street. "You're right, Merle. I don't believe it."

Sam kept his manner relaxed. Unsuspicious. "I thought you wanted someplace to walk. How did the map get you to Mission Hills?"

Merle showed him a matching set of dimples. "It wasn't the map. It was the *weather*. It's so perfect, and our waitress at breakfast says it's like this all the time here. Another guy who was near us at the cash register heard us talking over whether we should stay longer, and he told us about this house in Mission Hills we could get as one of those short-term rentals. He got the address wrong, I guess, but the people were nice and let us check out their backyard to see what grows around here. You know, even on vacation, I love working in a garden. I told the guy that when he was recommending the place. Anyhoo, Harve's been noodling around on his cell phone and he found us another house a block over. I don't know if I want to be in this neighborhood, though. It's kinda far from a nice coffee place and going to a nice coffee place every day is one of my favorite things about being retired. Pretty great otherwise though, eh? Good area, clean views."

Harve chipped in with his monotone seal of approval. "The hills make for a good workout."

Sam should have guessed Richard would spot him at the hotel, then follow the Canadians to the café and decoy them to his next stop, knowing they'd talk him half to death if they ran into Sam again. Or maybe he'd hired them to intercept Sam at the hotel, then gave them fresh instructions at the café.

No matter. Sam needed to get away from them. Quickly, before Richard escaped again. And preferably without his face registering on the nearby security camera. But he couldn't plan a strategy to outmaneuver them. Not with Merle's voice etching defeat into his thought process.

"I still think we should look at that other place you found, Harve. The one in Normal Heights." Merle giggled. "I get such a kick out of that name. I wonder if it'd be on the mailing address, if we took a place for a month and had friends write us there from home. I'd frame an envelope with that on it for our front hallway at home, for sure."

Sam risked a glance at the window where he'd seen Richard. Gone again. He'd have to rely on the tracker and start all over.

For now, though, he'd play along. "You could do worse. I hear it's a good area too."

"See Harve? I'm not the only person who feels it's smart to look around. Thanks, stranger. Maybe we'll see you later."

Sam shook his head. "Oh, I think three times' the charm."

Merle laughed, showing slightly crooked front teeth and a significant bridge.

Harve stuck an affectionate elbow into her side. "He's got you there, Merle. Three times we've run into our friend now. Still don't know his name, though. What is it?"

Sam's answer came smooth as silk. "Fred." An old alias, and a good one. "Fred Friedman."

Then he made his excuses and left them to it.

Whatever it was the Canadians were really doing.

Sam found Richard's car parked on India Street, in Little Italy, but he didn't dare park his own and get out to look for him. It was nearly lunchtime now. The sidewalks were getting busier. Better to wait till Richard came back and moved on. Sam couldn't guess what he was doing here, but he'd bet his last ten dollars he wasn't picking up pizza.

Sure enough, when Richard sauntered back to the car, it was with one hand in his pocket and the other wrapped around his phone, which was holding all his attention. Perfect. He hadn't seen Sam. Didn't know he'd been caught. Didn't have any idea—

"Harve, isn't that Fred over there?"

Sam froze in his seat. Merle's shout had attracted Richard's attention.

"Yoohoo! Fred! Looks like three times wasn't the charm, was it?"

She was crossing the street now, Harve in tow.

"Fred? I'm over here, Fred."

Sam had sunk low in his seat so Richard wouldn't see him. He'd looked over, then squinted at the sun's glare off the windshield. And now he was driving away.

It might still be all right, thanks to the tracker. But the Canadians—was he to be forever cursed by the Canadians? Sam resolved to check his wheel wells the next time he got rid of them. He must have a tracker on his own car somewhere.

Merle was at Sam's window now. He straightened up, pretending to have collected something from the floor.

"Hello again."

"I'll say. We must stop meeting like this." She guffawed, then slapped Harve's arm. "Funny, eh? Say Fred, we heard there were some good places here for lunch. Care to join us?"

"I have a meeting in a few minutes. I only stopped to pick up some paperwork."

"Well, all right. But tell you what. I'll save a piece of pizza for you in my bag. We'll probably run into you again somewhere today, and maybe you'll be hungry."

"Maybe."

Harve waved at someone on the other side of the street, where they'd been when Merle spotted Sam.

"Looks like our table's ready, Merle. See you around, Fred."

The Canadians were definitely Richard's bodyguards.

Sam tracked Richard to the park in Old Town San Diego. It was full of sound and color and tourists carrying bags of goodies they'd display as evidence of their travels: the last place he'd expect to find Richard. He was more the upscale restaurant type, with muted walls, a glass of good wine, and a beautiful companion. There had to be some deal going down. Something he needed this innocent cover to conceal. Something worth a lot of—

"Hey."

Sam froze. For once, it wasn't Merle's voice. It wasn't even Harve's.

He turned slowly, locked eyes with his new companion, and gave a curt nod.

"Richard. We meet again."

Richard flapped his shirt collar in a way Sam recognized as a substitute for a ruder gesture, unsuitable for their surroundings. "Quit the theatrics. What's with you, anyway? Following me around all day like this. If you want to meet up, why not just call?"

Sam gritted his teeth. "I'll never call you."

"That sounds...not threatening. Did you mean to sound threatening? If it didn't work with those teenagers who mugged you in Sacramento last week, it isn't going to work now."

"I wasn't in Sacramento."

Sam had totally been in Sacramento.

"And Vegas, when that dog pissed on your shoe and you went after its walker."

Ditto.

"What do you want from me, Richard? Why are you even talking to me?"

"Because I want to know what you're after. It's much easier for you to tell me if you're within three feet instead of twenty. So. What is it?" He waited through Sam's silence. "I've only got a few minutes. People to swindle, buildings to torch. You know the drill."

Sam didn't speak.

"Nothing? No insistence on justice, or a *you'll get yours,* uttered while you impotently shake your fist?" Richard waited again, for two beats. "I didn't think so. If you don't mind, I'll be on my way, and you can take those brand-new shoes you bought while you were shadowing me in Seattle and—"

"Toss me in a giant birthday cake and strike a good long match."

Both men turned to look at the spiky-haired woman in a tropical-print shirt stamping toward them. Sam noticed Richard's face echoed the horror on his own. Maybe he hadn't hired the Canadians after all. Or maybe it was an act.

"Harve? It happened again, but with that nice man from the café, too. That's gotta be a sign. San Diego's welcoming us. Boy, this is some business trip you're on, Fred. They let you go to all the best places. If I'd had a job like yours, I wouldn't have retired." Merle shoved her hand out to Richard. "I used to work at the University of Guelph, myself. In Ontario, up in Canada. Excellent agriculture program, not that I was a professor or anything." She snorted a laugh and prodded her open hand at Richard. "Don't be shy. I won't bite. Any friend of Fred's, amiright, Fred? Like I was saying, I was in administration. Oh, here you are, Harve. It was Harve who was a professor. That's how we met. I was doing some of his overhead slides back in the '80s, before we had real technology. So, what are you two up to? Anything Harve and I might want to try?"

Richard looked at Sam. "Think we should tell them, Fred?"

Sam looked at Richard, his jaw clenched. "It'd be a shame not to, Richard."

"Richard. Ha. I thought you looked like a Richard." Merle didn't wait any longer to shake Richard's hand, which she was now doing vigorously. "So, what is it?"

"It's ice cream." Richard had turned to her with his sweetest smile. "The best ice cream in San Diego. We've had ours, but you can find the shop down that way."

"Ice cream. We are living it up today, Harve." Merle leaned toward Sam and spoke in a confiding tone, her voice piercing less of his eardrum. "We heard the Mexican food in here was pretty great, so we wanted to try that, but I can wash down anything with ice cream. Boy, cake and café au lait for breakfast, pizza for lunch like you suggested, Richard, and now this...it's like traveling the world in one city."

Merle took Harve's arm and the two of them marched off in the direction Richard had sent them.

When they were nearly out of sight, Sam gave Richard the evil eye. "The ice cream's the other way."

"I know. I thought we'd enjoy ours more if we didn't have your pet weirdos hanging around."

"My pet weirdos? You mean yours. It was a little too neat, the way you've set them on my trail."

"What, you think I hired those two to protect me?" Richard laughed, the sound more abrasive than the Canadian woman's voice. "I saw them talking to you in the hotel lounge while you were getting ready to annihilate my car with your death stare. Figured I'd goose you a little so I followed them to breakfast, knowing you'd follow me, and then playfully suggested a reason to hit my next two stops. They spot you there, too?"

Sam struggled to keep his fists at his sides. "They might have. I wouldn't know."

It was all over. It had to be. Months of stalking his prey and now Richard knew all about it. He'd even bought Sam a cone with sprinkles on top before waving goodbye and striding back to the parking lot. There was no way Sam could kill him. Not without getting caught.

He sat in his car for twenty minutes, watching the tracker ping Richard's trajectory. Maybe getting caught was worth it. He turned over the engine and left Old Town.

Sam followed the tracker to Presidio Park—specifically, the public lot near the Witch's Tower. He parked his own car close to the entrance and pushed his driver's door open, closing it again as quietly as possible once he got out. It was a weekday afternoon with nobody in sight. Sam considered where Richard might have gone. If he'd been meeting someone in Old Town, and Sam had spooked the other party, they might have arranged to meet here instead. In that case, they'd want cover. Shelter. Privacy.

Sam went cautiously to the wall of the Witch's Tower and inched around the corner, looking for Richard. Then finding him.

Sam's mortal enemy was standing alone at the top of the tower, waiting. Looking out over San Diego as if he owned it.

It was time.

Sam reached into his pocket. He pulled out his weapon and lifted it toward his lips, his eyes trained on Richard's unmoving body. He took in a deep breath and—

"Oh. My. God. A kazoo! Fred, I was a star on kazoo back in band, in high school. But you're holding it like one of those blow pipes. Here, hand it over. I'll show you how to work it."

Sam's fingers scrambled in midair, looking like a furious eggbeater, but he couldn't stop Merle from snatching it away. She lifted it to her mouth, pointing the business end right at him. With the height difference, the target would be his heart. Then she lowered it again, seeming to weigh it in her hands.

"Say, maybe it is a blow pipe. What're you doing with this, Fred?"

Harve leaned in to look at the kazoo. "Seems like a lot of trouble to take, when you could throw a rock."

Merle met her husband's eyes. "Think we should test it out on him?"

Harve considered this, in his slow, methodical way. "Better wait a few minutes, Merle. See what he has to say for himself."

"Nah, just do it." Richard had come down from the tower and made his way around the corner. "He won't have a good story no matter how long you wait. I hear the poison works fast—two minutes tops."

Merle cocked her head. "Maybe we should try it out on you.

You're both in a lot of trouble anyway."

Richard smiled, but it wasn't the self-satisfied grin Sam was used to seeing on his face. Sam guessed he didn't know what to make of the Canadians either. He must really not have hired them. Maybe they were working for Tony, the crook in Chicago who got hurt in their crossfire a couple of years back.

Merle pulled out a cell phone. "But the reward's better if we call you in alive."

"No. Wait. We'll pay you. Whatever you want." Sam and Richard spoke together, their pleas and their accusations of who pulled off which job so mingled, they were impossible to tell apart.

They'd named five high-profile heists and a bombing by the time Merle broke in, sounding confused. "What are you two going on about? We're just pulling your leg. Had to get you back for that ice cream trick. You guys sent us all the way in the wrong direction, right when I got a taste for a vanilla swirl."

Harve nodded. "Nothing makes Merle madder than getting crossed over ice cream. You shoulda seen her when she was visiting her sister in Toronto and they closed the Dairy Queen early. Or the time in Kingston. Or the one in Ottawa, right out there on the canal when the ice cream guy ran out of butterscotch topping. Sorry if we upset you, following you here to prank you. When we saw you sitting in your car back in the Old Town, Fred, Merle figured it was what the universe wanted."

"I don't think there's anything in here anyway." Merle raised the kazoo to her lips, as if testing it out, then coughed suddenly. The force was not insignificant, and it was helped by modifications to the inside of the kazoo. A dart whizzed through the air. It hit Sam's leg, the point puncturing his chinos.

"Oh God, it's all over." Sam grabbed at the dart and tugged it out with his last ounce of strength, then rammed it into Richard's arm.

"What, you want me with you through eternity?" Richard pulled a face at the pain from the dart. "You think I didn't know you were trying to buy a modified blow pipe to use on me? The guy you got it from loaded up the darts with tranquilizers. You'll have a nap, that's all."

Sam didn't hear him. He was already out.

"Well whaddaya know." Merle's face shone with delight. "I knew retirement would be a hoot, Harve, but I never expected this. And to think we'd be walking off calories right now if these two hadn't messed with us and sent us to the back of beyond instead of the ice cream stall. This'll be a great story to tell back home."

"The Canadians." Richard's words were beginning to slur. "I should never have underestimated the Canadians."

HARD RAIN ON BEACH STREET
C.W. Blackwell

"If I hear that song one more time, I'm gonna shoot someone," says Danny.

He sucks his inhaler and watches a white Camaro trundle through the parking lot, a Bee Gees tune cranked so loud you can hear the fenders rattle. The Camaro's packed tight with sunburned teenagers belting lyrics with their arms dancing out the windows, hands snaking the warm night air. A clown car of tube tops and hairspray. They hook left onto Beach Street and Danny follows the car with his eyes.

"You're watching the wrong car," I tell him. I tap at the wristwatch hanging from the rearview mirror. "Stay focused on the Oldsmobile. Should be five minutes, now."

Danny flicks the radio on. Some rock station from the college.

I flick it off again.

"Eyes up," I say. "This is important."

The Oldsmobile idles beside the main ticket booth, below the bright and twisting track rails of the Giant Dipper. We listen to the roar and clatter of the roller coaster, screams pitching and fading as ride cars swoop around the bend and dip out of sight. We've only ridden the Giant Dipper once since we came to town. Neither of us admitted it was much of a ride, even though you could see the fear in Danny's eyes when we took the first big drop. He's been that way since we were kids—a tough guy with eyes that said otherwise. I never tease him for acting so tough. When you grow up as sick as he did, you do what you can to keep the bullies at bay.

At eleven fifteen, a bald man slips out of the ticket booth with a blue duffle over his shoulder and knocks on the Oldsmobile's trunk. When the lid latch releases, he sets the duffle inside, closes the trunk lid, and climbs into the back seat. The car idles for a minute longer before easing across the walkway and onto the road.

I flick on the headlights, wheel off the curb, and follow.

It's almost never muggy on the Central Coast, but tonight it is. The streetlights hang in orange halos over the river. I can feel the sweat beading on my forehead. It feels good to be moving with the windows down, even though the air smells bad. The locals have been talking about it all week. A school of sardines got trapped in the harbor and went belly-up, bringing a frenzy of seabirds and foul air. You couldn't escape it.

"Now can we listen to the radio?" says Danny. He's got the dial pinched between his fingers, watching me like I'm the pain in the ass. It's the same look he's given me since he learned how to give looks.

"No," I say. "I need to concentrate."

"That's the problem," he says. "Your nose whistles when you concentrate. I'm tired of hearing it."

"Look who's talking, wheezy." I plug a nostril and blow my nose out the window. "It's this goddamn stink in the air. It's affecting my sinuses."

"The radio'll take your mind off it."

He sucks his inhaler and doesn't take his eyes off me.

"Fine," I say. "Just keep it low."

The college station comes on again. This time it's a Zeppelin tune. Louder than I'd like, but I'm no longer in a fighting mood. I follow the Oldsmobile across the San Lorenzo River, left on Laurel, right on Front Street. There's plenty of cars on the road, traffic backing up at the intersections. Mostly kids headed home from the amusement park. At the Bank of America on River Street, the Oldsmobile slows and wheels into the parking lot, then it loops around and parks with the front end pointing at the street.

I pull next to a shuttered taqueria, and we watch from the shadows.

The driver steps out. A tall man with a neatly-trimmed mustache—the kind you see on TV cop shows. Danny calls him a *rent-a-cop*. He's plainly dressed, but he doesn't wear the clothes well. Like he's trying too hard to blend in. He circles the bank on foot, taking his time, spinning the car keys on his finger as he goes. When he reappears from the back of the building, he unlocks the trunk, moves to the night drop window, and gives a signal to the bald man.

"That's your cue, baldy," says Danny.

I shush him, but he's right about the timing. The bald man exits, retrieves the blue duffle from the trunk, and makes his way to the bank drop box—the tall man standing watch all the while.

"I say three bags tonight," says Danny.

"I say four, easy."

"No way. A dollar says three."

We shake on it.

The bald man unzips the duffle and removes a plastic deposit bag with black scrawl on the outside—account numbers and other bank info. The bag is fat with cash. A green tick, ready to pop. The drop box groans as he tilts it open and shoves the bag into the slot, then another. We watch intently and count five bags.

Danny whistles.

"Tomorrow there'll be more," I say. "America's birthday, but me and you will get all the presents."

Danny opens the glove box and stares at the leather slapjack and the loaded .38 resting inside. He pretends to pull out the revolver, makes a shape of a gun with his hand instead. He cocks his thumb and bends it twice.

"Bang bang," he says.

He blows the phantom gun smoke from the tips of his fingers with a wheeze and a cough.

"Bang bang, little brother," I say.

We came out West after the Hooker Chemical Company dumped twenty thousand tons of poison into our water supply.

Before that, we had it pretty good.

Pop was a union plumber, Local 22. He rode the postwar boom straight into a three-bedroom house in a new neighborhood called Love Canal, with a wife and kids and a shiny blue Chevy sedan in the garage. Mom was a librarian at the high school and hustled Avon on the side. I played little league and rode a paper route for the *Niagara Gazette*. It was heaven until it was hell. The stench off the canal drove us all indoors, the water oozed black. Mom passed before we even knew she was sick, and Danny hasn't taken an easy breath since his fifth birthday.

So we quit Love Canal for the clean ocean breezes of California.

But the damn poison followed us.

It followed Pop, anyway.

"Heads up," says Danny, nodding with his inhaler aloft. He takes a noisy hit and gestures out the window as we're turning onto our street. There's a blue and white strobe popping against the apartment buildings.

We both know it's not for us. It can't be—not yet, anyway.

"I bet you Pop's up to his old tricks," I say.

It's a good guess. I pull to the curb and spot the old man as soon as I step out of the car. He's standing in the neighbor lady's front yard in his tighty-whities, waving his arms and demanding that Richard Nixon come out. Thing is, our father just calls him Dick, and there's no blaming an old woman for calling the cops on a half-naked man dancing on her lawn and screaming about Dick.

The city cop sees us coming. He's a middle-aged man with a

gray mustache and black hair coming out his ears. He's relieved, and it makes his hard brown eyes look friendly.

"This your father?" he says. He's got his arms stretched out in front of him like he was about to wrestle the old man to the ground.

"Yeah," I say. "Just a touch of the old-timer's. We'll keep a better eye on him next time."

The cop lifts his hat and wipes the sweat from his forehead. He gives a stern look, warning us with his eyes. Then he throws a nod to the neighbor, who's watching from her kitchen window, a cup of tea in her hand. Big round curlers in her hair. I give an apologetic wave, but the curtains shut quickly and that's the end of it.

I slip off my jacket and wrap it around the old man's shoulders and guide him across the street, back to our low-rent, two-bedroom apartment.

"Come on, Pop," I say. "Gerald Ford's on the telephone."

Danny shoots me a dirty look, shakes his head. He doesn't like when I poke fun at Pop. Their relationship always had a softer touch, something sweeter between the lines. I try not to take it personally and chalk it up to him being the baby of the family—*the meatball,* as our mother called it.

Danny takes the old man by the elbow.

"Come on, Pop," he says. "I'll fix you a drink and put you to bed."

"When's Mom gonna be here?" asks Pop. "It's getting late."

"She's on an airplane," says Danny, without missing a beat. It's his standard reply. "Probably looking down on us right now and waving."

The old man tilts his head and squints into the fogged-out sky as if he might catch a glimpse of her passing overhead.

Next day, I go to the hardware store and buy a second dead bolt for the front door, and I install it so the thumb latch is on the outside. Just something to keep Pop from bothering the neighbors while Danny and I take care of what needs taking care of. It isn't something I'd mention to the landlady, and certainly not the fire chief—but it's temporary. I keep reminding myself this whole town is temporary. Just a pitstop on our way down the coast where an armful of amusement park cash will stretch far.

The air is stifling, worse than yesterday. And by the smell of it, the sardines in the harbor still have a collective death wish. It almost reminds me of the summers back home—although I'd take the smell of dead sardines over whatever Hooker Chemical was cooking up any day.

We park in the same place, watching the roller coaster rise and fall. Rock-O-Planes wheeling at the dark sky. The teenagers are all dressed in stars and stripes, waving sparklers and lighting bottle rockets on the beach. Girls spin in the street with hot pink roller skates, laughing and twirling—maybe a little drunk, a little high. Maybe it's the joy of youth. I can tell Danny wants to go talk to them, and I wish he could. He wants to be a teenager on a hot summer night, too. But I've got to keep him focused.

"No radio tonight," I say. "So don't ask."

I sense Danny rolling his eyes in my periphery.

"When we get where we're going, I'm buying my own radio," he says. "I'm gonna listen to whatever I want. *Whenever I want*. Zeppelin, Sabbath, whatever."

"That so?"

"Oh yeah. I'm gonna answer every DJ trivia question and win a truckload of concert tickets. I'll take a different girl to each concert."

"I won't stop you, big guy."

"What are you gonna do with the money?"

"Buy headphones so I don't have to hear all the caterwauling on your new radio."

Sometime before midnight, I spot lightning forking over the bay. Soon there's more of it. They call the ride cars in and a few minutes later, a hard rain starts to fall. Everyone comes running out of the amusement park, laughing and shouting. Nobody's brought an umbrella. Some are gathering under the blue and red eves of the carousel. A blonde slips in the street and her friends stop to help her up. Danny rolls his window down and sticks out his palm just to watch it get wet.

"I didn't think it was supposed to rain here," he said.

"It's not. Not in the summertime."

"Maybe we brought the New York weather with us?"

I tap Danny's leg and point out the windshield.

The bald man is rushing from the ticket booth with the blue duffle held low. It looks heavy. The Oldsmobile is waiting for him, tailpipes gently smoking. In all the excitement, neither of us saw it pull up. He lumbers over the open trunk and dumps the duffle inside. Then he shuts the lid—nearly slipping as he opens the rear door, scrambling into the back seat.

I start the car and put it in gear.

We follow close behind, closer than I'd planned. I figure the driver's paying more attention to the weather conditions than who might be following. Besides, the car windows are gelled with rainwater. It's like we're driving through the surf at high tide—all I can see is the red glow of the taillights and a vague Oldsmobile-like shape ahead of us as we forge the slick and steamy streets toward downtown.

By the time we reach the Bank of America on River Street, the downpour has lightened to a steady, easy rain. I stop the car on the Water Street Bridge and let Danny cross on foot, just like we'd rehearsed. He dons a plastic Uncle Sam mask and gives me a salute with his black leather slapjack as if to say *I WANT YOU*, then he hustles down into the alley behind the bank. I continue on behind the taqueria and park there, watching as the Oldsmobile circles the bank lot and comes to a stop facing the street. The timing is perfect. The rent-a-cop with the thin mustache exits the driver's door with a folded newspaper over his head. He glances around the parking lot and starts along the side of the building to walk his perimeter, only this time he's hustling to avoid the rain.

I take the .38 from the glove box and check the cylinder, slip on my own Uncle Sam mask. A lone car passes, tires hissing on the wet road. I watch it veer left over the bridge and disappear in all the static.

"Come on, big guy." I whisper, dancing my fingers on the steering wheel. "Just like we practiced. Two or three hard whacks."

It takes Danny longer than it should.

When he finally pops out from behind the bank, he's stumbling in the parking lot, holding his gut. My own gut tightens. He looks like he's been shot, but I know that can't be true. I would have heard it. Baldy would have heard it, too—as far as I can tell, he's status quo in the back of the Oldsmobile.

Danny raises one hand over his head and dangles the car keys, and I hurry across the street, gun in my waistband. He gives me a thumbs-up with his other hand like everything's fine, but I can tell he's hurt. I can hear his breath over the sound of the rain. Gasping, wheezing. But I take the thumbs-up at face value and continue with the plan. I throw open the driver's door and level the .38 on the headrest so it's pointed at the bald man.

He watches me with hateful little eyes.

"We saw you following us," he said. If his eyes looked hateful, his voice was loathsome. "Down on Beach Street. We almost changed things up."

"Don't be so hard on yourself," I say. Danny has the trunk open, and maybe it's my imagination, but I can feel the Oldsmobile rise up a little when he lifts the duffle. "I want you to lay down in the back seat and count to three hundred. You understand?"

"Yeah, I get it."

"Good. Now we both have something in common."

"What's that?"

"We'll both be doing a lot of counting tonight."

Again with those wicked eyes.

Danny shuts the trunk and knocks twice, and I flick the gun

at baldy, who reluctantly curls up on his side and closes his eyes. There's something infantile about it, like he's waiting for us to leave so he can suck his thumb or sing himself a lullaby.

"Three hundred," I remind him and shut the door.

I take the car keys from Danny and hurl them onto the roof of the building, then I shoulder into the duffle and we start across the street toward the car. I've got one arm around Danny—he's leaning into me hard, feet shuffling on the asphalt as he goes. He finds the inhaler in his jacket pocket and draws a hit as we near the car and climb in. I'm about to ask what happened when someone starts shouting.

"Oh God," says Danny, coughing and pointing. "He's coming."

I look.

The rent-a-cop comes staggering along the side of the bank, face bloody, jacket off. He looks like a car wreck survivor, like someone trying to flag down a ride to the hospital. His shirt is torn and one pant leg hangs in ribbons. He yells again, but I'm too busy getting the car started to make out what he's saying.

"Hurry," says Danny. "He's got a gun."

A shot rings out and a spark dances across the hood of the car.

A spider's web blooms on the windshield.

I drop the car in reverse, and we go backward down a dark, lampless one-way street. Another shot—*and another*. It sounds like he's wasting bullets now, firing blindly, angrily. When the road tees off with Pacific Avenue, I hook the car a little too hard and we spin a quarter turn over the slick asphalt. The car stalls, but it's nothing fatal. The ignition kicks right back up, and a moment later we're zipping through downtown streets toward our little apartment on Blackburn.

"What the hell happened in the alley?" I say.

Danny holds his gut with one hand, the inhaler with the other.

"I couldn't knock him out," he says. "I must have hit him eight times with that silly stick. He hit me, too—knocked the wind out of me." He doubles over as if his gut suddenly recalled the blow.

"Man, it just turned into a wrestling match."

"Why were his clothes torn up?"

Danny scrubs his face with his hands. He looks haunted.

"I gave him a really hard whack and it finally stunned him. He didn't pass out, just sort of had a dopey look on his face. Then I dragged him to the levee and rolled him into the river."

"Into the river?"

"Yeah, straight down into the river scrub. I didn't know what else to do with him. That was one tough son of a bitch, I tell you. He kept grabbing at his ankle, and now I know why. He had a piece down there. *He could've shot me.*" But there's something else, now—a little curl at the corner of his mouth that could be a smile.

"All right, what's that look for?"

His smile broadens into something sweet and childlike.

"I looked in the bag," he says.

"Oh yeah?"

"Yeah." He holds up eight fingers.

"Eight bags?"

"Eight bags."

"Goddamn," I say. "We're practically rich. What a haul."

Police lights erupt on Laurel Street, just a block from home.

A single cop car parked ahead of us on the side of the road.

This time it could be for us, and we both know it.

I tuck the .38 under my thigh as we draw near. All I want to do is flip a U-turn and haul ass the other direction, but it's too late to turn around without drawing suspicion.

"Try not to look like you just got your ass kicked," I tell Danny.

He sits up straight, folds his hands in his lap.

"What if it's Pop again?"

I'm about to tell him it's impossible, the reverse dead bolt is foolproof.

But then I see him.

Pop is sprawled on the road shoulder, looking up at the sky, working his arms and legs as if making some kind of crude, urban snow angel. This time, at least, he's clothed—but the clothes are soaked through, and his hair is drenched and filthy. I can't tell if he's injured or just caught in the webs of his disease. Danny jumps out of the car before I can pull over. He runs to Pop and kneels in the gutter, hands all over his face, trying to get a good look at him. I place the revolver under the seat and come over quickly. I spot the city cop talking on the police radio—it's the same cop as last night with the gray mustache. He cradles the receiver when he sees me, straightens his uniform, and heads toward us.

"An ambulance is on the way," he says, coldly.

It's stopped raining now, just a slight drizzle, and there's a sour smell of pitch coming off the road. I ask what's happened to Pop, but Danny already has the old man sitting up, looking him over. He doesn't look hurt, just confused. Body shaking. I take off my jacket and shoulder it over Pop and he looks at me unknowingly, like I'm just a good Samaritan. He thanks me with a small, frail voice.

"No need for the ambulance," I tell the cop. "We'll get him home and warm him up."

"He'll have to go to the hospital," he says. "You had your warning, pal. This time I'm writing it up."

"Really—" I try to insist, but the cop won't have it.

"He could have died out here," he says. "He's hypothermic. Whatever you're doing isn't good for anyone."

"He'll be fine."

"Look at him. He could have caused an accident out here, lying in the street."

Danny's already walking the old man to the car.

"Please hear me out," I say. I'm trying to stall and trying to hurry at the same time. I know once Danny gets the old man into the car with the heater cranked up, we'll be home free. He's not going to pull us all out of the car again. And we desperately need to get off the road. "We've got a live-in nurse starting next week. It's the last time, I promise you."

"A live-in nurse?"

"That's right."

The cop's blood pressure is rising. I can see it in the way his hard eyes glower, the way his jaw tightens—and that's when the chatter comes over the radio. It's loud and urgent and bureaucratic. The dispatcher yells out call signs and locations, giving a litany of code violations. Other cops respond with their own call signs, barking their locations, sirens howling in the background.

It's the kind of chatter that might fit a couple of guys like us.

I let him worry about the radio and ease back to the car. Danny's already got the old man in the passenger seat with the heater cranked up. All I've got to do is duck behind the wheel and spin off into the night. Forget the apartment, all the junk and trouble we brought from our old life. All that matters is the three of us and the mountain of cash in the trunk.

"Hold up," said the cop.

His whole demeanor shifts from agitation to a keen, deadly interest. He's got his thumb on his duty weapon, giving our car a heavy dose of eyeball. The cracked windshield. The bullet hole in the hood. He peers through the windows to get a better look at Danny, who's still fiddling with the heater from the back seat.

I stop, slowly turn around.

"Where were you both tonight?" says the cop.

The radio is giving descriptions of two young males.

"Nowhere. Just watching the fireworks."

"Nowhere isn't a place."

The cop unclasps the radio and announces his location. Laurel and Blackburn.

Two young males and an elderly man in a Ford LTD.

Code three backup.

I hear a siren down the street. Maybe four blocks, maybe closer. It could be the ambulance, but I can't be certain. What I know is that any second, they'll ID us all—and that big blue duffle will be laid out on the hood along with the next ten or fifteen years of our lives.

Gunshot.

The cop reels back against the trunk of the police car.

Danny stands by the rear passenger door of the LTD with the .38 in his hands, and now the sour smell of pitch coming off the road is mixed with gun smoke. I scramble for the driver door, but the city cop's not finished. He fires back—one hand grasping his bloody gut, the other squeezing off rounds at the car. Danny ducks into the back seat as the windshield whitens and glass chimes over the dash. I put my foot into the pedal and make a skirling U-turn in a cloud of heavy white smoke.

Something's not right.

Danny's trying to tell me something, but I can't hear what he's saying over Pop's urgent questions. The rear door is ajar—swinging loose in the night air. Danny's writhing against the seat with his hand clasped over his neck and the sounds he's making aren't anything an inhaler can fix. I ask him if he's hit, ask him three or four times as I take the turns, zagging through downtown streets, praying that each turn I make isn't full of blue and white lights. Across the bridge, another hard left on Dakota. The rear door slams shut with the force of the turn. I cut the lights and weave through San Lorenzo Park and stop the car between two humongous redwood trees. The park is dark and quiet, but police sirens haunt the rest of the city—maybe sirens always sound haunted when they're screaming your name in the dark of night.

Danny isn't trying to talk anymore.

I flick on the dome light.

The cream-colored seats are painted red.

I climb back and try to sit him up, but it's no use. I'm sobbing, telling him it's going to be okay even though it's a lie. I tell him it's not so bad. Pop is crying, too. Danny's hand falls by his side and his eyes fix on something far away, something I can't see. He's staring through the roof of the car and up into the crowns of the redwood trees. There's a grisly bullet wound in his neck and it's still weeping blood even though I know by now his heart has stopped.

We leave the LTD in the park and set Danny up on a bench so he's facing south toward the bay, where fireworks are still blooming over the old amusement park. I leave the key in the ignition, the radio tuned to the college station. Pop and I choke out goodbyes while the music plays, both of us sick with grief. I hope for his sake they don't play the Bee Gees, but I know it doesn't really matter.

The river is low, and we walk along the scrub in the dark. I've got the duffle slung over my shoulder, and one hand on Pop's back, guiding him along. He's quiet, and that means he's lucid, even though I wish he wasn't.

"We're just going to leave him there, huh?" he says, looking back over his shoulder, wiping his wet eyes with his arm. "Just leave him for dead?"

"Yeah, Pop," I say. "We have to leave him. He's already gone."

"I'm not too old to carry him," he says. "I'm strong enough."

"I know you are, Pop. It has to be this way."

"Where are we going?"

"South. Maybe San Diego."

"Why?"

"Because things didn't go as planned."

We quit the river and hike up to a dirt overlook, where I spot a white Chevy coupe sitting under a cypress tree. Inside, there's a couple fooling around, radio loud, suspension groaning. They're listening to the college station and my first thought is I wish it were Danny inside, making out with one of those girls from the amusement park, her tube top and hot pink roller skates scattered over the back seat. I rap my knuckle on the foggy window and tell them to open up in my best cop voice.

The door creaks open and a naked young man peers out.

He sees the gun and his eyes clock wide.

Danny's blood is all over my clothes.

"It's all right," I say. "Get dressed. We just need the car."

Ten minutes later, we're on the highway heading south. Pop starts humming and I know he's checked out again—and for once, I'm jealous. I wish I could check out, too. The harbor is close by, and the smell of dead sardines pours through the heater vents. Pop notices it, and the stench seems to bring him back to center.

"This town's gone bad," he says, wrinkling his nose. "Time to pack up and go where the air is cleaner."

"Yeah, Pop. That's a good idea. We're driving out now."

"To California?"

"We're in California, heading south now. We'll start a new life."

He looks into the empty back seat.

"What about Mom and the boy?"

"They're taking a plane," I say—and I'm quick, too. *Just like Danny would have been.* "Probably looking down on us right now and waving. We'll meet them at the airport."

The old man gazes thoughtfully out the window. It's clearing now, stars marbled around the tattered gray clouds. There's an airplane passing low, wingtips blinking, maybe watching the last of the fireworks extinguish along the edge of the continent. I can still see faint bursts coming and going, lighting up the sky, and I wonder how many families like ours came out to escape the slow demise of the American dream, only to find it dying everywhere else, too.

"You know, by god, I think I see them," says Pop, waving at the sky.

DEAD EVEN

J.R. Sanders

I didn't think much of Pooter's girl. I met her at the Buscadero, the bar my pal Dusty Vanner ran with his old buddy Pooter. It was a watering hole for B-movie Hollywood cowboys, mostly day-playing extras, which was what Dusty and Pooter were when they weren't tending bar.

The Buscadero really wasn't my style, but Dusty had invited me to a little shindig they were having to celebrate their sixth month in business. And that was where Pooter introduced me to his "little gal." The name was Cassie Plumm. He'd met her on a film set, where she had been a fellow extra. Even before he introduced us, I'd noticed her—she was a girl you'd notice—but I'd thought she was just one of the usual chippies you'd find in any Hollywood bar. She'd made the rounds, dancing and flirting with every cowboy in the joint, and it was stacked ceiling high with them. She'd pranced and giggled and batted her eyes all evening. She was the kind of girl who was cute and knew it, and who was determined that, before the night was out, every man in the place would know it, too.

It came as a surprise when Pooter introduced her to me in terms that made it plain they were a pair. Not that Pooter was a bad-looking fellow, if a fair bit older than the girl. But I knew he had one other attraction that might draw women of a certain type. Unlike the usual day-playing cowboy living hand-to-mouth,

Pooter was rich. He was the only son of a family that owned half the oil wells in north Texas. And though you'd never have guessed that from Pooter's appearance or behavior, it was no secret among his crowd.

So being by both profession and disposition the suspicious guy I am, and being no fan of little dollies who behave as if the spotlight is—or should be—forever trained their way, I wasn't inclined to have a high opinion of Cassie Plumm. Neither was Dusty, from what I saw. And I didn't detect the least sign that her opinion of me was any higher.

Which made it that much more surprising when she showed up in my office the very next morning.

After the usual meaningless pleasantries, Cassie came right to the point.

"I need your help, Mr. Ross."

"You might as well call me Nate, since Pooter's a...well, a friend of a friend."

"Nate, then." I noticed she'd winced at the name "Pooter."

"And how can I help you?"

"First of all, Gerald," she said, Gerald being Pooter's given name, "mustn't know I've engaged you, or even that we've spoken."

"Engaged me to do what?"

"There's a man. A man from my past. He's menacing me, and I want him to stop. But Gerald can't know."

"A former boyfriend?"

"Yes." There'd been just enough shift in her eyes and hesitation in her response to make her doubt her answer. But I nodded as if I bought it.

"I see. And Poot—*Gerald*—can't know because you don't want him to know about the menacing, or about the man?"

She didn't like the question much. "Both," she said through pursed lips. "He doesn't know about Thane—that's his name—

and if he knew anyone was menacing me...well, I assume you know Gerald's temper."

Pooter and I weren't exactly bosom pals, but I'd been around him enough to know that he didn't have a temper. Not that I had ever seen. I'd never encountered the guy when he wasn't smiling and cheerful. But I decided to let that go for the moment. She knew Pooter in ways I didn't, so it was possible she knew a side of him I didn't. Instead, I shifted the talk.

"When you say this man's 'menacing' you, what do you mean exactly?"

"He's been following me, showing up at my door, making threats."

"What kind of threats?"

She dipped into her purse and fished out a wrinkled sheet of paper. She smoothed it on her knee and handed it over. It was hotel stationery from the King Edward. Scrawled across it in third-grade handwriting was a penciled message:

You broke our bargain. Come through or pay the price. -T

"I found that slipped under my door when I got home last night."

"And you're sure this is from him?" She nodded. "T for Thane?" She nodded again. "Is that his first or last name?"

"First. Thane Decker is his name."

"Okay. What bargain is he talking about?"

"He had some silly notion we were engaged. We weren't. He never asked me, and even if he had—"

"So by 'come through' he means—?"

"I guess he does."

"And by 'pay the price'?"

She bit her lip. "He's a dangerous man. He's done time in prison, back in Missouri. That's where we met—Missouri, that is, not prison."

"So you think he means what?"

"To kill me." She went weepy at that and pulled out a handkerchief to mop at her face. I'd been around long enough to know crocodile tears when I saw them.

"And what about Gerald?" I asked.

She blew her nose and looked at me. "What do you mean?"

"I mean, what are the chances that it isn't you he's threatening, but Gerald?"

She stowed the hanky. "Oh, no, I'm certain Thane doesn't mean Gerald any harm."

"How can you be sure?"

"A woman knows these things, Mr.—Nate." She gave me a smile that was supposed to make me hear violins. I heard alley cats scrapping. "Will you help me?"

"What exactly is it you'd like me to do?"

"Why, get rid of Thane," she said with a look, and in a tone, that said I might be the king of all idiots.

"Get rid of him how?"

She winked. "That's up to you." With that, she went into the purse again and pulled out a huge roll of bills. She peeled off a few and looked up at me. "Is two thousand enough?"

Against my better judgment, I ended up taking three hundred. This was only after I explained that I wasn't the sort of private investigator who hired out "to get rid of" people the way she was suggesting, and after she pretended she'd never meant anything of the kind. I told her I'd talk to Decker and try to convince him he should take his loss on the chin and move on down the road. She was dead-set against involving the police in any way, but that didn't mean I couldn't threaten the guy with cops if it came to it. I was pretty sure it wouldn't, since I didn't buy two words of Cassie Plumm's story. I only took the job out of curiosity about what she was really up to. Maybe I should have felt guilty about that, but Pooter was a pal. More or less. I figured I could always give her money back.

First order of business was to get a line on this Decker bird, and for that I did need the police. Cassie had said she had no idea whether Decker was living in L.A. or just staying, and in either case she didn't know where. The note paper was from the King Edward, but that meant squat. Anybody could walk into a hotel's writing room and filch a little stationery. If Decker had done time in the Missouri pen, there was a good chance he was on parole. If so, they'd have an address. It wouldn't be an L.A. address—if he'd left the state, he'd probably jumped his parole. But if he had, maybe they already had somebody on his trail. That could save me some time and shoe leather. I picked up the phone.

"Homicide, Queenan." He sounded more harried and hostile than usual.

"Captain, Nate Ross here."

"I knew this day was goin' too well. All right, where do I pick up the body?"

"Nothing like that today, Cap. Just need a small favor."

"Blah. Ain't no small favors when you're involved. Well, spill it—I don't have all day to shoot the lemon with you."

I knew it would cost me. Favors from Carl Queenan were never free. We had a sort of running tab between us—if I didn't owe him one, he owed me. But at the moment the books were dead even and I had no marker to call in.

"It's a simple one," I said. "All I need's a parole check on a con out of Missouri." I gave him Decker's name and the description Cassie had given me.

"I ain't even going to ask why you want this. I figure I'm safer not knowing." He took it all down with the usual grumbling noises, but there was a little glee in his voice when he said he'd get back to me. Much as he hated doing me favors, he always enjoyed me owing him one in return. And he always collected.

I put in another call to the King Edward. I doubted Decker was actually staying there but I at least needed to rule it out. When the desk clerk answered I asked for Manny Garza. Manny was the house dick there and an old pal from my days with the sheriff's department.

"Garza here."

"Manny? Nate Ross."

"Nate! How's the boy?"

"Doing fine, pal. You?"

"Ah, you know. I got a pretty soft job here." There was a pause. "You aren't calling to mess that up, are you?"

"Not to worry. Just checking to see if a certain party's registered there." I gave him Decker's name and what particulars I had.

"Okay, hold the line a minute." He wasn't gone more than thirty seconds. "Yeah, we got him. Been here going on five days."

"All right. See you in half an hour."

The hotel was a few miles southeast of my office, and with the late morning traffic, I made it in twenty minutes. The kid on the front desk said Manny had gone upstairs to check on something and he hadn't seen him since. I didn't feel like waiting and wasn't likely to need Manny's help, anyway, so I asked the kid for Decker's room number.

I rode the elevator to the fourth floor. The kid had said room 418 was at the opposite end of the corridor on the right. When I approached, I noticed the door was ajar, and when I got close enough to knock, I heard a groaning noise from inside. I nudged the door open for a peek. On the far side of the bed, I saw two legs sticking out—gray trousers, blue socks, and brown shoes.

I pushed my way in and went over to see who owned the legs. Manny Garza was stretched out on the floor, half-conscious and moaning. His hat was lying crumpled in the corner and he was bleeding on the carpet from a gash on the side of his head. A short-barreled .38 was on the floor beside him.

"Manny, what the hell?" I helped him up onto the bed and fetched a clean towel from the bathroom. There was no one else in the room.

He came out of his daze slowly as I mopped the side of his

head. Scalp wounds bleed so much they always look worse than they are. The cut was small—probably wouldn't even need stitches. The skin was already puffy and puckered around it and his hair was matted with drying blood.

I got him a glass of water, and once he'd taken a sip or two, his eyes seemed to focus.

"What happened to you, pal?"

"Somebody hit me."

"Yeah, that much I can see. Decker?"

He shook his head. "No, his key was on the rack. George at the desk said he left an hour or so ago."

"So what brought you up here?"

He looked sheepish. "I could tell from your call this guy was some kind of trouble. Just thought I'd give the place the once-over before you got here, in case he was back by then. Used my pass key. I didn't expect to find anybody here."

"Who *was*?"

He drank more water. "Maybe I'm loopy from the knock on the head, but I'd swear it was a cowboy."

"Cowboy?"

"Yeah. Big hat, boots, dungarees with the cuffs turned up." He ran a hand across his mouth. "Big gray mustache. He was even carrying one of those big horse pistols like in the movies. That's what he whacked me with."

I'd stopped listening after "mustache." I had a pretty good idea who had laid Manny out but I kept it to myself. I picked up his gun and laid it on the bed table then made a quick pass all through the room. There was nothing much to see—this guy Decker traveled light.

Manny had come around and insisted he didn't need a doctor, so I'd left him in the care of the desk clerk and driven over to the Buscadero. It was still early, and the cowboys were probably all out on one film set or another, so the place was deserted.

Dusty had his sleeves rolled up and an apron on and looked pretty much like any other bartender in town, except for the ten-gallon hat I'd bet he slept in. He was polishing beer mugs with a rag and doing his best to look casual and innocent. I knew better, so I got right to the point.

"Manny Garza at the King Edward sends his regards."

His eyes flickered at the hotel's name but he kept a poker face. "Garza, you say? Don't believe I know the man."

"About my age, not quite as tall, black hair, has a half-inch cut along here." I raked a finger above my left ear. "Of course, the cut's new—he only got it about an hour ago." He avoided my eyes. "Some cowpoke with a ridiculous mustache hit him with a stag-handled Colt."

He took a deep breath. "Friend of yours?"

"Yeah. And he's the house detective."

He stopped polishing. "Aw, hell, if I'd knowed that I would-na hit him."

"That's good to know, Dusty. What the hell were you doing there?"

He threw the rag aside. "I've been keepin' an eye on...Pooter's girl." He couldn't even say her name. "I seen her talkin' to this fella I didn't recognize on the street yesterday, so I followed him to that hotel. I watched this mornin' and when he left, I went into his room for a look-see. Just got started when this other gent come sneakin' in with a gun in his hand. I didn't know who he was—what was I supposed to do?" Before I could come up with a snappy answer, he gave me the dog eye. "And just what were *you* doing there?"

I didn't see the harm. Cassie had said she didn't want Pooter to know anything, but she never mentioned Dusty. I told him about my talk with her.

"I'm telling you, Nate," he said, "That gal is all wrong, and I aim to find out what the hell she's up to."

"I'll admit I have my suspicions too. But let's see if we can't go about finding out without putting the hurt on any more innocent bystanders."

"'We'? Does that mean you're going to help me?"

"Only if you promise not to cold-cock everybody we come across. Cassie paid me to talk to this Decker, get him to leave her alone. First, we have to find him. If we learn a few more things along the way, so much the better." I looked around the place. "Pooter's gone, I take it?"

He nodded. "Out on a shoot. So's *she*." He spat the last word out like it had a bad taste. Coming from Dusty, who liked everyone, it meant a lot. "But I can close the place up," he said. "Nobody's gonna come in until the crews knock off today, anyway."

We drove over to see Queenan. On the way, I filled Dusty in on what Cassie told me about Decker's past.

Queenan was shuffling files and grumbling to himself when we walked in. He didn't look any happier when he looked up at me through his cigar smoke haze. His glance landed on Dusty. "Well, if it ain't Gabby Hayes." He looked back at me. "Wait, don't that make you Roy Rogers? Your spangly shirt at the cleaners or what?"

"Hello, Cap." If he was giving me the razoo he was in a good mood, so I was content to grin and bear it. I was there to collect a favor. "Just stopping by to see if there's any word yet from Missouri."

"Oh, yeah." He shifted his cigar to the corner of his mouth. "Grab a seat."

We took chairs while he rummaged through the stack on his desk until he found the folder he wanted. "Them boys out in God's country are plenty helpful," he said. "They wired me Decker's whole prison file—mug shots and all."

"So he *is* on parole. Is he in violation?"

"He would be if he was still breathin'." He ran his finger down a page. "Accordin' to this he was killed, let's see...five months ago."

"Killed? How?"

"Shot going over the wall. Him and his old partner in crime cooked up some harebrained escape plan. Or maybe not so harebrained, because the partner's still in the wind. But Decker's sleepin' under the Missouri sod."

"Why the hell escape? What did they get for burglary—a few years?"

"Burglary?" Queenan's shaggy eyebrows lifted. "These boys were in for murder. Lifers, both of 'em."

"Murder?"

"Yeah." He closed the file. "And that bein' the case, and me bein' a homicide copper, this is where you tell me why you're lookin' for this bird."

Leaving out Cassie's and Pooter's names, and Dusty's assault on a hotel dick, I gave him a quick rundown.

"So somebody's using this dead guy's name," he said when I'd finished. "You know what your guy looks like?"

"Just a basic description." I pointed a thumb. "But Dusty's seen him."

"He look anything like that?" Queenan handed over a wire photocopy of a prison mug shot—a shaved-headed guy with blank con's eyes.

"Hair's grown out some," Dusty said, "But that's the fella I saw at the hotel."

"Milt Logan," Queenan said. "Decker's partner. If you know where this guy is, I'll send somebody out to reel him in." He grinned. "We'll show the 'Show Me State' how it's done in L.A."

"King Edward Hotel, Room 418," I told him. "Registered as Thane Decker." I turned to Dusty. "Meanwhile, we should check on the girl in case he's making another run at her." I looked back at Queenan "You'll let me know if you boys find him there?"

"Sure, sure." He gave me a warning look. "And you keep me informed."

I nodded. "And, Cap," I said. "A fugitive murderer? If you do get him, this makes us even, right?"

He bit hard on his cigar, waved a big mitt in the air. "Blah. Get the hell out of my office."

We drove back to the Buscadero, but it was still shut up—Pooter and Cassie were apparently still on the set somewhere. Dusty didn't know what shoot they were working on, so he started making phone calls to find out. After the third try with no luck, I put a call back in to Queenan.

"Well, your info turned out to be right for once," he said.

"You got Logan?"

"We got him, all right. He'll be on the next train to Jefferson City, but he'll be ridin' in the freight car."

"He's dead?"

"He decided he'd rather not go back to Missouri, I guess. Waved a .45 at my boys and they showed him what a mistake that was. Hotel's gonna need some plaster work and new carpet, but nobody got hurt. Nobody who counts, that is."

"Well, I guess that's that."

"Maybe," Queenan said. "Did you say there was a dame involved in all this?"

"Yeah, why?"

"I just got another batch of stuff from Missouri. Arrest and court records. Turns out it wasn't *a* murder these mutts were jugged for; it was *four* murders."

"Yeah?" I didn't like where I thought he was headed.

"They had a nice little grift going three years back. Logan, Decker, and Decker's wife."

"Wife?"

"Well, common law. We're talking Missouri, remember. Anyway, it went like this—the broad would glom onto some nobody, turn on the hootchie-cootchie 'til she got the poor sap to fall for her, then marry him. She'd take out a life insurance policy soon after, then—what do you know?—hubby would have an accident or some sudden ailment, and the grievin' widow would cash in. Then on to the next. Worked like a charm until they got a little sloppy with the arsenic."

"The woman go to prison, too?"

I could hear the smile in his voice. "No dice. She boo-hooed on the stand and convinced the twelve numbskulls in the box that the men forced her to do it. Hasta la vista—free as a bird."

"What was her name?"

I heard papers rustle. "Figg—like the fruit, but two g's. Cassandra Figg."

Like the fruit. Like a Plumm.

We went back to the bar, but still no Pooter or Cassie.

"Why do you suppose she set you after this Logan fellow?" Dusty asked when I repeated what Queenan had told me.

"Well, I'd like to say she was done with that life and wanted rid of him."

"But?"

"My gut says she figured she'd hit the mother lode with Pooter and she didn't want to cut Logan in. *That's* what his note was about, not the bullshit story she gave me."

Dusty pulled at his mustache. "Well, much as I hate to do it, we gotta tell Pooter. Before it's too late." He got back on the phone and in two more calls found out where Pooter and Cassie were. Only they weren't on any movie set.

"That dadgum knothead!" He slammed the receiver down. "He's fixin' to marry her." Dusty had talked to Mac McLemore, one of their day-playing cowboy clique, and Mac informed him that Pooter and his intended were heading straight from the movie shoot to Union Station, where they planned to catch the three o'clock train to Las Vegas and wedded bliss.

"We gotta stop 'em," Dusty said. He disappeared to the back room and came back out, tucking his big Peacemaker into his belt.

"Whoa, now, Tex," I said. "We'll try and head them off, but

let's not go shooting up the train station. I doubt this girl is packing heavy artillery."

I wasn't sure he heard me. He had a look in his eye I'd seen too many times to mistake. When he got that look, it was best to give him some room.

The traffic on the way to the station was heavier than usual. It would be. Dusty sat forward—on point, like a bird dog—his nose not six inches from the windshield.

"Damn it, Nate, can't you go no faster?"

"Dusty," I said, trying to keep my voice calm in the vain hope it would settle him down. "I can break every traffic law on the books, but the laws of physics I can't do much about."

He continued to mutter and curse under his breath. Meanwhile, I did my best to weave in and out of the traffic down Sunset and shot through every red light I dared. As we crossed Main and came up on Alameda and in sight of the station, Dusty looked at his watch.

"It's two minutes past three."

The words had no sooner left his mouth than we heard the long, piercing wail of a train whistle. Dusty gave me an accusing look as I bounced into the parking lot and slid into the first available space. We bailed out and made for the entrance at a dead run. I was amazed at how fast Dusty was in cowboy boots; I had a tough time keeping up. We tore through the ornate, high-ceiling main terminal and headed for the gate and platform for the Union Pacific. As we got nearer, I noticed that all the people we saw seemed to be coming the other way. We reached the platform to find only an empty track with a handful of stragglers wresting their suitcases.

Dusty ran up to an elderly porter pushing an empty baggage cart who looked him up and down with some alarm. "Train to Las Vegas?" he panted.

The old man pointed east down the track. "Gone, friend."

He waited, uncertain, and when Dusty didn't say any more, wheeled his cart away.

Shoulders drooping, Dusty walked over to me. "Well, shit," he said, scratching at his mustache. "You reckon we could catch a plane and beat 'em there?"

"We can check the schedules, I guess." I doubted it would do any good. It was the middle of the week, and I didn't think there would be many flights going that way. But Dusty had such a hangdog look I didn't have the heart to say so.

It was a moot point, anyway, because when we started back down the long corridor leading from the main terminal, the first person we encountered was Pooter. He greeted us with a knowing grin and a wicked twinkle in his eyes.

"Howdy, boys. Fancy meetin' you all here."

I hadn't often seen Dusty at a loss for words, but he just stopped and stared, his mouth hanging open under the big handlebar. "What in the..." He looked back as if he expected to see the train returning for his friend. "Where's..." He still couldn't bring himself to say her name. "Where's your gal?"

Pooter grinned even wider. "I expect she's still sittin' in that private coach, wonderin' why I'm takin' so long in the john." He looked from Dusty to me and back again. "I don't guess I need to ask what you two jaybirds are doin' here. Come to save me from the bonds of unholy matrimony?"

"How'd you know?" Dusty managed to get out at last. "About the girl, I mean."

"I ain't too proud to say I didn't at first," Pooter said. "Pretty little thing like that. But when I called my ma back in Texas to tell her my intentions... She's near eighty but still plenty feisty, and as protective over the family fortune as she is her baby boy. She hired one of Nate's cohorts back there to do some checkin' on Cassie and found out she was in the professional widowin' business. So I just bided my time until Cassie brought up the notion of runnin' off to Nevada." He waved an arm up the track. "I couldn't think of no better way to get shed of her."

He laughed. "Hell, I'll bet she's halfway to Barstow before she figures out she's travelin' solo." He threw an arm around both our shoulders and steered us toward the terminal. "Ol' Pooter can look out for himself," he said. "But it's sure nice to know you boys care. Let's go open up the bar and empty us a bottle."

Before we left the station, I went to the pay phone and called Queenan. He said he'd get right on the horn to the police in Las Vegas. Cassie might have a lonely train ride out, but she was sure to find a warm welcome waiting.

PLYMOUTH WEST
John M. Floyd

Susie Nelson, her purse in hand, stood outside the police station, checking her watch every ten seconds. Finally, she saw her friend Mona Carter round the corner of Broadway and 15th and pull up to the curb in her ancient blue Cadillac. Susie headed that way, weaving through the smattering of pedestrians on the sidewalk.

"It's about time," she said, dropping into the passenger seat.

"Not there," Mona said, shrinking back and holding up crossed forefingers as if fending off vampires. "Back seat."

"What?"

"Flu season," she said. "You want me to drive you, you ride like Miss Daisy."

Grumbling, Susie got out, shut the door, and climbed into the back.

"Stay in the far corner," Mona called.

"Okay, okay. Glad to see you're in a good mood."

Mona snorted as she turned the Caddie west on E Street. "You call me out of nowhere on Thanksgiving Day, ask me to drive all the way downtown, what kinda mood you think I'm in? I got my own problems, you know."

Susie almost smiled, and would've if she wasn't so tired. This bickering was nothing new; she and Mona had known each other since childhood. Their daughters, Andrea and Katie, had been roommates at San Diego State. "I know all about your problems," she said and added, in a pretty good imitation of Mona's voice, "Does this outfit make me look fat? Hurry up, or I'll miss *The Bachelorette*! What women's magazine should I read next?"

"Don't make fun of women's magazines. And FYI, I'm under more stress than you are."

"What's so stressful?" Susie asked.

"Well, for one thing, Katie wants to marry a drug dealer."

"Really? Is she having any luck finding one?"

Mona looked up at her in the rearview mirror. "Jokes? You call me from the police station and you're making jokes?"

"Couldn't resist."

Mona sighed and stopped for a traffic light. "Look," she said, "you gonna tell me what happened, or not?"

The question forced Susie back to reality. She sagged backward in her seat. "You remember Vic Hollister?"

"The guy you put out of business? The one who swore to kill you?"

"Hard to forget that, right? Even if it *was* a long time ago." Susie paused, remembering. "Did you ever meet him, know what he looks like?"

"No."

"Me either. And by the way, I didn't put him out of business," Susie said. "I just opened up my restaurant shortly before his closed. Is it my fault diners seemed to like my place better than his?"

"Whatever. What about him?"

Susie let out a sigh of her own. "We had Thanksgiving dinner together."

She'd met him at the marina a week ago, although he'd told her his name was Ernie Weathers, the teacher of a master chef's class at SDSU. He was a little older than Susie and a bit short, with dark hair thinning on top, but had a ready smile and an easygoing nature. Nothing that gave Susie the slightest hint that he wasn't who he claimed to be.

The two of them hit it off right away, talking about cooking and baking and grilling. So far they'd been meeting each day.

Then, two days ago, Susie had taken the leap and invited Ernie Weathers to lunch on Thanksgiving. After all, she was alone and idle—her daughter was at Susie's ex-husband's place in L.A. for the holiday, and the restaurant Susie owned and operated had been closed for several days to repair a roof damaged in a freak windstorm this past weekend. Actually, the work had finished Tuesday and she was scheduled to reopen this Saturday—so her spur-of-the-moment plan had been to open the place today for only a few hours, just for her and her new acquaintance.

Ernie agreed, but only if he could prepare their meal himself. Fine with her, she said. They wound up meeting at the restaurant this morning around ten, with him bringing the turkey (he'd done some precooking on it earlier, he said) and all the fixings. He'd made her promise to stay out of the kitchen and let him have it all to himself.

He also informed her that he was something of a historian as well as a chef and had discovered that the original Pilgrims had eaten turkey and cranberry sauce and pumpkin pie when they dined with the Indians on that first Thanksgiving. So that's exactly what he and Susie would be having today. They'd be reliving history, right down to the tall black hat Ernie was wearing, with its big silver buckle on the front. The hat was, as the lunch would be, authentic in every way, he told her—even though they *were* on the wrong coast. "Think of it as Plymouth West," he said. "Only four hundred years later." Both of them laughed. The fact he looked silly in the hat pleased her even more.

She gave him a quick tour, and he seemed impressed. "The Lazy Susan," he said, pointing at the tall restaurant sign visible through the front window. "Named after you?"

"Why not? I built the place."

"Are you lazy?"

She grinned. "You must be thinking of my friend Mona."

"Very funny," Mona said. "You want to get out and walk?"

"Sorry. It just sort of popped out."

They were clear of town and headed south now, under a sky the color of late afternoon. The warmth of the sun on her right cheek was making Susie drowsy despite the churning of her stomach as she related to her friend the ups and downs of the day. After a pause, Mona said, bent over the wheel like an old woman, "What does all this you're telling me have to do with you being at the police station? If he was really Vic Hollister and was stalking you, why aren't you dead? Did you brain him with a skillet and escape?"

"He'd banned me from the kitchen. And I still didn't know who he was at that point."

"Good grief," Mona said. "Okay. You've met him at the restaurant. Keep going."

Susie and Ernie had finished the tour and were standing in the dining room, looking at each other.

"It occurred to me," he said, "that since this'll technically be Thanksgiving lunch instead of Thanksgiving dinner, we should go out again tonight. Maybe just for a snack."

"A snack?"

"I've made reservations for two at the Coachman, on East Harbor. Eight o'clock."

"Pretty fancy place, for a snack."

"We'll order something light."

"Wait a minute," she said. "Didn't they close for good a while back?"

"They reopened," he said, and added, with a look around. "A lot of that going on, apparently. Anyhow, they have a special private-dining area. Come on, it'll be fun."

"Why not," she said. It'd be a chance to check out some up-scale competition.

On that note, he headed for the kitchen to put together the feast and Susie began tidying up the dining area, setting the table, arranging everything just so, even sweeping and polishing and dusting a bit. She and her staff hadn't yet restocked the kitchen—that was an all-day job set for tomorrow—but the power and water were on. She didn't really want to think of all the business she'd lost after being closed for this long.

On the other hand, she'd probably needed a break anyway. For now, today at least, she was happy.

But something was bothering her, something at the back of her mind. Something Ernie had said. The joking question he'd asked, about her being lazy? No. Something else. Even while the two of them spent the next hour calling to each other between the kitchen and dining area, even after the first delicious aromas began floating through the swinging doors between the two rooms, it was needling at her.

Then she remembered. Frowning—and a little worried, now—Susie paused the through-the-door conversation with Ernie long enough to look up some information on her cell phone and then make a quick and quiet call.

By the time she was done, the food was ready. Ernie stuck his head out the door and told her to sit, that he would bring everything out himself. He watched her take a seat at the huge table she had suggested they use (it had been designed to accommodate twelve), then ducked back into the kitchen. Seconds later, he reappeared bearing a tray with a pitcher of iced tea, two plates already heaped with turkey, sweet potatoes, cranberry sauce, and two large dishes of pumpkin pie. The only thing Susie had forgotten were napkins, which she asked him to pop back into the kitchen and grab for them before he sat down. He fetched those, and they sat, looking across the table at each other.

The meal was grand. It took them almost an hour to clean

their plates, consume two glasses each of tea, and discuss the problems of the world. When at last they were done, Susie's watch said 1:05.

They sat for a moment in silence, studying each other. Susie's gaze wandered to the front window and the sign beyond it and the parking lot, empty except for their two cars. The day was sunny, and the palms lining the street beyond the lot made the surroundings look like a 1960s color postcard. For a while, she watched the traffic flow quietly past, as if in a separate world. But mostly, she was thinking about what Ernie had said earlier—and what she'd found out on her phone.

Finally, she turned to find him staring at her from his seat at the other side of the table.

"Anything wrong?" she asked.

"Not at all. Just wondering if you feel okay."

She forced a smile. She felt anything but okay. "I'm fine. Why?"

"No reason," he said. He patted his stomach. "I enjoyed that."

"Me too. You're a wonderful cook."

"Are you hiring?"

Both of them grinned.

"We'll have to stay busy this afternoon," he added, "to work up another appetite. Remember our date, at eight."

Susie nodded, thinking. "I need to talk to you about that."

"Excuse me?"

"I tried to call the Coachman on my cell just before we sat down to eat. They are indeed closed, Ernie. I double-checked on Google."

He said nothing. His face was frozen as still as a painting.

She took her napkin from her lap, dabbed at her lips, and put it on the table. Her heart was pounding. "Apparently, you weren't planning to take me there after all."

Ernie's eyes narrowed. Several seconds dragged by.

He cleared his throat. "Why, exactly, are you looking at me like that?"

"I was just wondering if *you* felt okay," she said.

He didn't seem to know what she meant. Then, as she watched, his face changed. Beads of sweat broke out on his forehead.

"How do you feel now?" she asked.

His cheeks were reddening; his breathing sounded labored. He glanced down at his empty plate, then up at her. She felt surprisingly calm.

"What have you done?" he whispered.

"What I've done is, I've been wondering about something you said to me. And put two and two together."

"*What?*"

Holding his gaze, Susie gripped the edge of the table in front of her and gave it a sideways push. Both of them watched the round tabletop rotate a few inches, smoothly and quietly. Then she moved it back to its original position.

"The table revolves," she said. "Lazy Susan, remember? After you'd brought our food, and when you went back to the kitchen to fetch the napkins, I spun it halfway around. Your plate ended up in front of me, mine in front of you." She leaned forward, eyes locked with his. "You ate the food you intended for me."

His face was no longer red. It had turned gray in the overhead lights.

"Not feeling well after all?" she said.

He grabbed his throat and gagged. Veins stood out in his neck. His eyes bulged.

As she watched, he toppled forward, as if in slow motion. His forehead slammed into his empty plate, shattering it. Then he lay still. Though he hadn't known it at the time, Ernie Weathers, aka Victor Hollister, had cooked his own last meal.

"Watch the road," Susie said.

Mona Carter snapped her gaze down from the rearview mirror, steered the car back into the correct lane, and focused on the windshield. Outside her window, Susie saw her own street; she was almost home. A minute later, the old Cadillac eased into

Susie's driveway and stopped. Mona switched off the engine. Pale and wide-eyed, she turned in her seat to look at her friend.

"So you killed him?" Mona whispered.

"He killed himself, in a way. Dead as that turkey we ate for lunch."

"And that's why you were there. At the station."

Susie nodded. "I called the cops as soon as he keeled over. I told them everything, start to finish, even told them about the revolving-table switcheroo. I could see they had their doubts, but the forensic team did a preliminary autopsy and found enough strychnine in Hollister's tummy to kill an elephant. The bottle was still in his coat pocket, with his fingerprints all over it. None of mine. They also contacted the restaurant I'd called—The Coachman—and verified that it was closed and agreed that my lunch companion apparently had no intention of taking me out for dinner tonight. Why would he, when I was supposed to be dead?"

Susie fell silent then, sitting there in the car in the short driveway of her home on the quiet-for-a-change suburban street. She glanced past Mona to see birds playing in the drooping foliage of a pepper tree, watched the glow of the setting sun on the closed door of her garage, heard the wind sighing through the taller trees behind the house. Even in the closed car she could smell the fragrance of someone cooking an early supper, next door.

In a low, stunned voice Mona said, "How did you know?"

Susie shook her head. "I didn't know, for sure. But I suspected. I felt I had to do something, and I had nothing to lose: If I *was* wrong, and nothing had been poisoned, nothing would happen. We'd just wind up eating out of opposite plates."

"Okay, then—what made you *suspect* something?"

Susie paused, thinking. "It was a story I'd read a while back, about the first Thanksgiving, at Plymouth. Everybody thinks the new settlers had turkey, cranberry sauce, potatoes, pumpkin pie. That's a myth. They had fish, venison, duck, that kind of thing. Cranberry sauce and pumpkin pie weren't even around yet, and they hadn't grown any potatoes. And the tall, buckled hat? Buckles didn't show up until the late 1600s. The Pilgrims arrived in 1620. I Googled it on my iPhone, to confirm it." She paused. "He might've been a chef—but he damn sure wasn't a historian."

Mona said, still a little pallid, "And if you lie about one thing—"

"You'll lie about others." Susie rubbed her eyes, really tired now. "And that got me to thinking about chefs, and how few of them there are around here, and that I'd heard somewhere, back during all the death threats, that Vic Hollister was short, and dark, and balding..." She shrugged. "So, after 'Ernie Weathers' brought out the already-full plates, it occurred to me to take out a little insurance. Just in case."

"And turn the tables," Mona said. "Literally."

"Yep. And that's that."

Another silence. Finally, Susie sighed again and opened her door. "Thanks for the ride home, Monagirl. I'll call you tomorrow."

"One more thing," Mona said. "That stuff about the Pilgrims and Thanksgiving. You said you saw all that in a story. Where, exactly?"

This time Susie did grin, for the first time since noon.

"A women's magazine," she said.

WILDFIRE

Kathy A. Norris

A comedian once riffed that California has four seasons: earthquake, flood, drought, and fire. I can't speak to the first three, but as an arson investigator for the Los Angeles County Fire Department, I'm a fire expert.

My name is Jessica Cole, but everyone calls me Jessie. In 2002 the county hired me as a firefighter II because I checked all the affirmative action boxes, plus a few more:

> African American
> Female
> Minimum eighteen years old
> California driver's license
> Certified Paramedic

It didn't hurt that I come from a family of firefighters. My grandfather was a founding member of the Stentorians, the fraternal organization of African American firefighters, and both my grandfather and my father were assigned to historic Fire Station No. 30, one of two segregated fire stations in South Los Angeles between 1924 and 1956.

Firefighting is in my blood.

Keep up the good work, Station Chief Tom Curry tells me, and I'll be the first African American woman to lead the L.A.

County Fire Department.

I'm wide awake at four a.m., unable to sleep because the hot, dry Santa Ana winds buffet my Marina del Rey bungalow all night long. I push clammy bed sheets to the floor, exposing both me and the man sleeping beside me to the stifling air. I'm reconsidering my refusal to install air-conditioning when my cell phone rings. I assume it's my Aunt Ruth, so I answer without checking caller ID.

But it's another woman's voice I hear on the other end of the line. Younger. Angry.

"Put my husband on the phone," the woman says. She's got the imperative and possessive thing down cold.

I pause, glancing at the naked man planted facedown in my bed. Technically they're separated, so does the term "husband" still apply? An image of my Aunt Ruth, the morality police, pops into my head. Aunt Ruth rolls her eyes.

Thin as a whip, skin the color of walnuts, and a crown of wispy white hair, Aunt Ruth is eighty years old. She still takes the bus to her midnight janitorial shift at LAX. She likes to keep busy. She also likes to point out the error of my ways.

"Hel-lo?" the woman says.

"You forgot to say the magic word," I say, scanning the man's body. Long legs. Trim waist. Nice ass for a man in his early forties. Women frequently mistake him for Denzel Washington in his prime. He pretends to find this annoying.

It occurs to me that Tom Curry checks off most of the boxes Aunt Ruth has warned me against:

> Married
> Young kids at home
> My boss
> Emotionally unavailable

The woman hangs up.

"Who was that?" Curry mumbles.

"Your soon-to-be-ex. Or at least that's what you told me eight months ago."

Curry grimaces. "What did she want?"

"To interrupt our sleep."

"It might be the kids..." He searches for his cell phone while looking at me through half-closed lids. I see myself through his eyes, the height, the curves, the smooth brown skin, and the large, almond-shaped eyes. My hair is buzz cut, the better to showcase the elegant shape of my skull. Strong and lean, I could be a member of the Dora Milaje, the women who serve as bodyguards to the king of Wakanda in the comic book series *The Black Panther.*

"How did your soon-to-be-ex get my number?" I ask, arms crossed.

Curry sighs and pulls me close. "I've got kids, babe." His voice grows quiet. "They need to reach me if there's an emergency."

"But your wife—"

"Bunny crossed a line, I know. I'll talk to her." I inhale the pocket of scent where his neck meets his collarbone. All men should smell this good.

A cell phone rings, Curry's this time. His features sharpen as he listens to the caller. "We've been called to the Coastline fire," he says, hanging up. "All hands on deck." My own cell phone rings with the distinctive ring tone I've programmed for dispatch: "Fire" by the Ohio Players. Dispatch instructs me to report to the Coastline fire too.

Curry and I throw on clothes and run to our separate cars. He heads to the station to pick up a department vehicle. I decide to go straight to the scene; I keep an extra set of turnout gear, the fireman's bulky yellow coat and pants, and steel-toed boots, in the trunk of my car.

My gunmetal gray 1965 Ford Mustang makes short work of the Pacific Coast Highway, CA-1, to Pacific Palisades. I bought the car with my own money when I was sixteen years old. Dad and I restored it together. Now, all four hundred thirty-five horses of the five-liter V8 engine scream as I rocket toward the upscale beach community.

I see flames along a hilltop ridge as I near the fire. I park my BabyStang and flag down one of my colleagues.

"Who's in charge?" I ask.

"Price."

I stifle a groan.

Battalion Chief Price taught in the fire academy when I was a new recruit. The second week of training, he cornered me in his office and made a clumsy pass. I fended him off with a takedown straight out of the WrestleMania playbook. I can still feel the small bones of his hand crunch beneath my boot. From the look on his face when we pass one another in the hallway, he can too.

Stephanie, my mentor, laid it out for me day one. "Most of the guys are okay," she said, "but firefighting is a boys' club. Honestly, you'd think some of them had never seen boobs before. Handling their juvenile bullshit is part of the job."

My father and grandfather, knowing the harassment female firefighters faced, trained me to defend myself at a very young age. I still have the tiny gi I wore to Karate for Kindergartners.

When I walk into incident command, Price is standing in front of a giant monitor showing a map of the surrounding area. There are four men with him, two top brass and two firefighters in turnout gear.

Unlike Curry, Price is an older guy who looks...old. He could've retired years ago. Then again, why should he? He gets paid big money to give orders and doesn't have to carry them out. A good thing, given his bulging waistline.

I recognize one of the firefighters standing next to Price: Bob West, or "The Boy Wonder," as we call him. Tall, white, and clean-cut, West has raised ass-kissing to an art.

The BW is in the middle of a status report to the brass while Price looks on, beaming with pride at his protégé. My stomach clenches.

"The brush fire is of unknown origin, impacting 2,135 acres," the BW says. "The winds are too strong to use airtankers to drop fire retardant, so we're deploying one of our UH-1H Super Huey helicopters instead."

"How many engines?" asks one of the brass.

"Fifteen so far, along with three dozers and five water tenders. Logistics is setting up support for ten crews."

"Cause?"

"Possible arson. We've found cigarette butts at the point of origin."

Price steps in. "I'm turning this over to one of our best fire investigators." He speaks to the brass but looks at me out of the corner of his eye.

I step forward for my introduction, hand extended. I'm a senior fire investigator and have been lead on several big fires, including the Flamingo fire that destroyed twenty homes in Laguna Niguel. The regional chief himself commended my performance on that one.

"One of our best young firefighters," Price says. "Bob West."

One of the advantages of dark skin is that people can't see you blush. I step back and lower my hand, but not before making a small choking sound that draws everyone's attention. Price turns to the BW. "Bob, why don't you take our visitors on a tour of the incident command system?"

"Yes, sir," Bob replies, all but saluting and clicking his heels as he leads the men away.

Now it's just me and Price. His eyes sparkle: getting the best of me has made his day, petty son of a bitch that he is.

"It looks like Bob's got this under control," Price says. "Curry's going back to the station, but I'm sending you to Glendora."

"Glendora?" Glendora is a small bedroom community about forty miles inland. About as far from the action as you can get.

"We've had a fire out there, put out after an acre. You're to investigate and prepare a report."

"Glendora isn't even in our service area," I begin, confused.

Price fixes cold eyes on me. "Firefighter Cole. I'm ordering you to report to the Glendora fire. Immediately. Have a written report on my desk by end of shift. Understood?"

"Yes, sir."

I decide to exchange my car for a county investigation vehicle before heading to Glendora, and park next to Curry in the underground garage.

Inside the station, Curry pulls me into his office. This brings me face-to-face with the framed photograph of his family on the wall behind his desk. My beautiful Black boss with his beautiful white wife, bookended by two beautiful kids. Smiles all around. Their dentist bills must be enormous.

"What's up?" Curry says.

I tear my eyes away from the photo. Why do all the good brothers end up with white women? "Price assigned me to the Glendora fire," I say instead.

"I need you here. I'll give him a call—"

I put my hand up. "No, leave it." The last thing I need is for Price to connect the dots and figure out we're seeing each other. The L.A. County Fire Department has a policy prohibiting managers from dating subordinates, and I report directly to Curry.

Suddenly, one of the firemen starts yelling. "What the fuck?" Everyone in the station turns to the sound of his voice.

On the monitor, a woman wearing sunglasses and hair hidden beneath a baseball cap enters the staff-only garage. Her men's button-down shirt is tied at the waist over spandex tights. Her long legs eat up the concrete, adding momentum to the baseball bat swinging from her right hand. The camera's resolution is high enough for me to read the logo on the bat: Louisville Slugger.

"Who's that?" someone asks.

"She looks pissed," someone else adds.

The woman stops in front of my Mustang and assumes the classic batting stance.

"What?!" I yell at the monitor.

Her feet, hips, and shoulders are aligned, and she keeps her balance as she swings the bat against the driver's side mirror of my Mustang, knocking it off with one blow.

"Noooooooo!" I scream, running for the elevator to the garage. The other firefighters race behind me. By the time we reach her, the mystery woman has bashed in both headlights, smashed the front windshield, keyed my custom paint job, and spray-painted the words "CURRY'S CUNT" on the hood of the car. She's plunging a knife into the tires when Curry restrains her.

"Dammit, Bunny, what the hell are you doing?" he says. Curry's strong, but he has his hands full trying to restrain her. My coworkers exchange sly grins as they add 2 + 2 and come up with Jessie boinking the boss.

"Stay away from my husband!" Bunny screams.

"You're divorced, Bunny!" I yell back.

"Not yet! I'm going to kick your ass."

"You can try."

Two firefighters, knowing the impact a fight with a civilian while on duty would have on my career, to say nothing of sleeping with the boss, hold me back until I cool off.

It doesn't take me long. According to Aunt Ruth, only fools fight over men.

As much as I want to drape myself over the hood of my BabyStang and weep, I need to get my ass to Glendora. I arrange for a tow truck to take my Mustang to the body shop and reserve a loaner. Only then do I hop into a department SUV and head to the scene.

The Glendora fire burn area is small as they go, only an acre of blackened landscape. The steep hillside is bordered to the north by homes and to the south by railroad tracks and power lines. There's a news van on scene when I arrive. A reporter hops out and introduces himself.

"Pedro Salazar, Noticias Telemundo," he says, handing me his card.

Pedro Salazar looks like a telenovela star. Just when I think he's too good-looking to be real, he removes polarized Oakleys to reveal a lazy left eye. The difference between his eyes only heightens the perfection of his porcelain skin, his thick dark hair, and his lush eyelashes, longer than my own.

He scans my dark blue uniform, my badge, and the Los Angeles County Fire Department patch on my left shoulder. "Are you here to investigate the fire?"

"How did you hear about it?" I say, dodging the question.

"Over the police scanner. Thought I'd check it out."

His deep voice belies his slight build. I can tell by the way he rolls his r's that he's of Castilian, not Mexican, descent. A buttery soft leather jacket matches the color of his loafers. I give him two points for style and one for hustle. Chasing police scanners is a smart rookie move.

"And you are?" he asks.

"Fire Investigator Cole. This may be a crime scene, so I need you to stand back."

"You don't mind if I tag along, do you?" Pedro waves his cameraman over. I smile to myself as I head up the hill. He's persistent. In his line of work, he has to be.

"How long have you been a firefighter?" Pedro asks. His breath comes in gasps as he tries to keep up. Silently I prescribe him more cardio. Sprints, maybe, or interval work on the treadmill.

"Fifteen years. Ten fighting structure fires and wildfires, five as an arson investigator." I could add that I graduated top of my class at the fire academy and was awarded the Firefighter of the Year award after crawling through a burning house to rescue an eight-year-old, but don't. Modesty is the color of virtue, according to Aunt Ruth.

I stop at the top of the hill and survey the burn scene. Groves of trees border the east and west. A rocky embankment splits the burn area in half, the rest covered by dry brush and chaparral.

"What are you looking for?" Pedro says.

"The point of origin. Most fires have a characteristic V-shape, starting small and growing bigger and hotter as they expand. We're standing at the widest part of the burn area, the top of the V. The point of origin is somewhere below."

I start walking again, Pedro and the cameraman behind me. I stop by a burnt tree and snap off a low-hanging branch.

"Why are all the leaves pointing in the same direction?" Pedro asks.

"As fire gets hot, it creates a vacuum that draws the air toward it. Everything in that air stream moves toward the fire. Like these leaves. They get crispy, and don't flex back." I hold the branch out to Pedro. "What direction do you think they're pointing?"

Pedro examines the branch. "Down. The leaves point down the hill."

"More evidence that the point of origin is downhill."

"Did you get that?" Pedro asks the cameraman. He nods.

At the bottom of the hill, I narrow the search to twenty feet around one of the power lines. I crouch down and sift the dirt and ash around the bottom of the pole. The camera films my every move, including the moment the dirt flows through my fingers to reveal a small bundle. A strip of paper wrapped around a cigarette butt and matchsticks, secured with a rubber band.

Pedro's eyes lock on mine, his reporter's antenna bristling. "What's that?"

"Evidence." I drop the bundle into an evidence bag.

"Arson?"

"If the fire was set with malicious intent, it's arson. Arson is a crime. But we haven't established intent yet, and it's important not to jump to conclusions."

Pedro opens his mouth as if to disagree but thinks better of it.

* * *

To my surprise, Price is in Curry's office when I return to write up my findings. Not only in Curry's office, but in Curry's chair behind Curry's desk. A wave of foreboding rolls over me.

Price waves me inside. One of his flunkies is sitting in the corner and begins taking notes as soon as Price opens his mouth.

"Firefighter Cole," he begins formally. "The purpose of this meeting is to inform you that, effective immediately, you are suspended for violating the department's sexual harassment policy."

My stomach sours. Suspension, not administrative leave. That means no pay.

Price drinks in my dismay like a vampire then snaps his fingers. The flunky leaps forward and hands me a clipboard bristling with paper. I flip through the stack. The complaint was filed today. Price must have called in some heavy markers to get this processed so quickly. Curry's name features prominently. My accuser is not identified, but I imagine Bunny giving me the metaphorical finger.

"I need you to sign the first page indicating I've given you a copy of this notice," Price says. Price's own signature in black ink, approving the suspension, writhes against the white paper like a snake. I stare at him, motionless.

"Your signature does not admit guilt, only receipt of the personnel action," the flunky adds. His voice comes from a long way away, as if he's underwater.

They don't need my signature. They have the flunky as a witness. This is just another one of Price's power plays.

I rip the pages in half and walk out without another word.

I leave the station on foot, walking blindly along the street with no destination in mind. Curry pulls up in his SUV, but I don't notice him until he honks his horn.

"Get in," he says.

I keep walking.

"How else are you going to get to the rental car agency?"

I say nothing.

Curry holds up a Starbucks cup, "I got you a venti, skim, extra-shot, extra-hot, extra-whip, sugar-free caramel macchiato."

I get in the car.

Riding in Curry's Lexus is like being wrapped in a cocoon, the suspension smoothing out any bumps along life's road, the thick glass dampening the sound of traffic. Soft chimes from the GPS announce left and right turns, and the hot coffee warms my hands. I take a sip.

"You've been suspended too?" I ask.

He looks at me quickly. "Admin leave."

"What?" An employee on administrative leave is assigned to a different work location with full pay during the inquiry. I, on the other hand, have been suspended and sent home without pay. My laugh is bitter. The boys' club is alive and well.

"This will blow over." Curry reaches for my hand, but I pull away. He sighs as he drives into the rental car parking lot and shuts off the engine.

"We need to talk," he says.

I narrow my eyes.

"I think we should take a break."

"A break," I repeat.

"It's not you, Jessie, it's me." His face bunches. "Bunny's more emotionally fragile than I thought. I can't leave her and the twins right now. Plus, with the formal complaint—"

"Stop right there." I hold up my hand. "I swear, if you utter one more cliché—"

"This isn't a cliché," he says, indignant. "Believe me, this hurts me more than it does you."

I'm angrier with myself than with Curry, I realize as I stare at him. My Aunt Ruth warned me that a man with kids will always put his kids first. That's the way it should be.

I tip all twenty-three ounces of my extra-hot macchiato into his lap anyway.

I get out and slam the car door shut. "I'll Venmo you the bill for my car repairs," I call over my shoulder as I walk away. Curry's howls follow me all the way to the lobby.

By the time I pull into my driveway, my muscles are trembling. I keep an unopened bottle of Uncle Nearest's whisky for days like this. Then again, has there ever been a day like this?

> Suspended without pay
> Lost plum job assignment to rival
> BabyStang destroyed by married lover's wife
> Dumped by aforementioned married lover
> Sacrificed one venti caramel macchiato

Ah, well, I think. Things can't get any worse.

I'm wrong. As I approach my front door, I see a body sprawled on the porch. A black woman, elderly. My Aunt Ruth.

Adrenalin floods my system as I drop instantly into paramedic mode. When I shake her and call her name, Aunt Ruth stirs, eyelids fluttering. I check her carotid pulse—it's faint, but it's there. No need for CPR.

I sit her up and place her back against the wall.

"Where am I, Jessie?" she says. She knows who I am. Thank God. No amnesia.

"At my house, Aunt Ruth. Smile for me, please."

She tries, but the right side of her mouth droops. When I ask her to raise both hands over her head, her left arm stays up, but her right drifts down. Classic stroke symptoms. I look at my watch. It's 7:08 p.m.

"How long have you been out here, Aunt Ruth?"

"I don't know. I came by to see if you wanted some turkey eggplant casserole." I notice the broken casserole dish on the porch for the first time. My Aunt Ruth and I usually eat around five if we're eating together. She's been out here two, two and a half hours. Time is of the essence. Stroke treatments work best if they're administered within three hours of the first symptoms. I dial 911 for an ambulance.

At the hospital, I hold Aunt Ruth's hand while she waits for her brain scan. She dozes lightly. With her eyes closed and facial muscles relaxed, she looks like her younger sister, my mother. Both my mother and father died in a car crash. "You're all I have left," I whisper to Aunt Ruth as I drift off to sleep in the visitor's chair.

The doctors decide to keep Aunt Ruth overnight for observation after I raise a big enough stink. Outside the hospital, night has fallen. Out of habit, I start to dial Curry's number, then stop. The only man I can count on tonight is Uncle Nearest.

The next morning, while pulling my turnout gear out of the trunk of the rental car, I come across the evidence bag from the Glendora fire. Price suspended me before I turned in my report. I might as well do it now. It would be just like Price to write me up for insubordination for failing to file the report, even though he suspended me. I glove up and open the evidence bag on the kitchen table. The bundle of paper wrapped around the cigarette stub rolls out.

Suddenly, I remember a case study from the fire academy and call Curry. Before he has a chance to speak, I say, "Tell me. Did you get a look at the evidence from the Coastline fire? Any lined yellow paper in addition to the cigarette butts?"

"Yes," he says. "But listen, Jessie. Price wants your head on a platter. You can't talk to me or anyone else in the department without getting all of us in hot water."

My grip on the phone tightens. "Never mind," I say, and disconnect.

I don't like going outside the chain of command, but fires are a matter of life or death.

There are goosebumps on my arm as I retrieve Pedro Salazar's card and dial his number. The phone rings for what feels like an eternity. I hear someone muttering, "Come on, Come on—" and realize, with a jolt, it's me. Finally, Pedro answers.

"You remember the cigarette butt we found at the Glendora fire?" I say.

"Who is this?"

"Fire Inspector Cole. Keep up."

"You said it was no big deal—"

"It's a very big deal. And it's going to be a very big story. Are you interested or not?"

Pedro pauses a beat. "Why are you giving the story to me?"

"What's the shortest distance between two points?"

"A straight line."

"Let's just say you're the straightest line to broadcasting information that could save lives."

"Fire away," Pedro says. "No pun intended."

"There's a famous case we studied in the fire academy," I say. "Back in the '80s, a serial arsonist named John Leonard Orr set fires with an incendiary timing device. He made it himself using a lit cigarette and three matches wrapped in ruled yellow writing paper tied with a rubber band. He'd light the cigarette and be long gone by the time it ignited the matches and started the fire. One of his devices, set in a hardware store, killed four people. You can look it up on the CalFIRE website. It's known as the South Pasadena fire."

"The evidence from the Glendora fire uses the same materials," Pedro says. "Cigarette, matches, paper, and a rubber band." I hear his fingers fly over the keys.

"Not just the Glendora fire. The Coastline fire's still under investigation, but they found cigarette butts and lined yellow paper near the point of origin too." I pause a beat. "Yesterday was the forty-year anniversary of the South Pasadena fire. To the day."

Pedro whistles. "Are you saying we've got a copycat serial arsonist on our hands?"

I close my eyes. Go big or go home.

"Yes."

* * *

Epilogue

Forensics finds a fingerprint on the Glendora evidence that allows the L.A. County Fire Department to identify a suspect. The suspect confesses, eager for his fifteen minutes of fame, even if it costs him fifteen years in prison. Go figure.

I feel good about the lives Pedro and I theoretically save by capturing the copycat serial arsonist. But it feels even better to see the expression on Battalion Chief Price's face as he pins me with the highest honor the L.A. County Fire Department offers, the Medal of Valor, at a big splashy ceremony. Pedro ensures the awards ceremony makes the news.

Funny thing, all charges against Curry and me are dropped. Curry moves back with his family the next day. Did Curry bargain with Bunny, offering to return home if she dropped the charges, thereby minimizing the damage to my career? I like to think so.

Rumor has it Price put in his retirement paperwork, which means there's an opening for battalion chief. Curry looks good for it, and I look good to backfill Curry as station chief.

Once the BabyStang gets out of the shop, I take Aunt Ruth on a drive along Pacific Coast Highway. Both the Mustang and Aunt Ruth look good, the Mustang in a new midnight blue acrylic paint job, Aunt Ruth in a new wig that brings to mind the singer Nancy Wilson. I put the top down and we cruise, the shoreline on our left, the sun warm on our faces.

A Dodge Challenger sporting a hemi engine pulls up next to us at the red light at Sunset Boulevard. The driver lowers his sunglasses, looks at me, and revs his engine. I raise a questioning eyebrow to Aunt Ruth. The light turns green.

"Drop it like it's hot," Aunt Ruth says, looking straight ahead. "Go for it."

I do.

BUY THE FARM

Kathleen L. Asay

"She owns a *cemetery?*" I repeated. "Sorry. It's just so unexpected. Like you having relatives in a town like Honeyman."

I made a broad gesture to include Frances Chen, my sun-loving friend behind the wheel of her Lexus as we wound northeast out of San Diego.

Fran smiled enigmatically, just a quick turn of her head, then away. "She's not a blood relative, Nicole," she said. "It's a Chinese thing, an honorary title. June was my grandmother's dearest friend, so she became my mother's auntie and then mine. Auntie June."

We were on our way to Honeyman, California, to visit Fran's Auntie June who, I had just learned, owned a cemetery outside of town. We had left San Diego's low clouds and traffic over an hour ago and were slowly navigating a two-lane road that went nowhere else.

April. Inland temperatures in the sixties, bright sunshine, high cirrus clouds, both of us taking a much-appreciated day off from work. Frances was a paralegal for a high-profile law firm in town, while I was a columnist for *The San Diegan* newspaper. Longtime friends, we spent time together a couple times a year.

While I did not know June, I remembered her husband, Ray Abbott, Uncle Ray, another honorary. In fourth grade, Fran brought a stuffed bunny to school to show the class. The small rabbit had been a pet, briefly, before passing away for some forgotten reason, and Uncle Ray, a taxidermist, had stuffed the animal for Fran.

"Oh, my God," I said. "How could I forget? It was freaky."

"Some kids thought it was cool," Fran said. "I don't know who I hated more at that moment, those kids or Uncle Ray for mounting the poor thing."

I stifled my laugh, but Fran's giggle bubbled up like tiny church bells caught by a breeze. Early forties and Chinese, Fran was smart, empathetic, and often funny.

I was taller, curly-haired, and Caucasian, both edgy and suspicious. You get that way after eighteen years writing for a newspaper.

"All right," I said as she slowed for a narrow turn in the road, "Auntie June owns a cemetery, and Uncle Ray is a taxidermist. Why are we visiting them?"

Fran sighed. "You're here because I wanted company. But Uncle Ray died about a year ago, so it's only Auntie June we're visiting. She's a bit peculiar, and she insisted I come without telling me why."

"If I owned a cemetery and had married a taxidermist, I'd be peculiar, too."

"I know. I even wondered if she'd had Ray stuffed and wanted to show him off."

I closed my eyes against the image. "*Please—*"

"Sorry." She sniffed back another impending giggle. "Anyway, she lives at the cemetery. She's ninety-three, and she lives at the top of a small hill surrounded by graves."

"Oh."

"Here's Honeyman," Fran said at the same moment I saw the weathered sign in the shrubbery at the side of the road. *HONEYMAN, CA*, painted over in freehand, *elev. 1238, population 162. Speed limit 30.* Fran slowed. "I haven't been here often, but it looks worse each time."

I saw rustic houses, many of them abandoned. Then a few

worn commercial buildings, a city hall and post office, a gas station, a café.

"Lunch," Fran added.

I looked reflexively at my watch: 11:25.

Fran's phone rang in the dashboard. She pressed a button, said, "Hi."

The voice that replied blared like a cheap horn. "Where are you?"

Fran did not appear surprised. "We've just come into Honeyman."

"Meet me at Ham's." Click. Call ended.

"Auntie June?"

"As ever."

"And 'Ham's'?"

"It's Hamilton Honeyman's café."

"Ah. Do Honeymans still own the town?"

Fran turned right at the next corner and again into an alley where there was barely room for the car and a walkway to the café's rear door.

"What's left of it," she said. "There isn't much. You should know that Auntie June is a Honeyman, the last of her generation as far as anyone knows."

A thickset man wearing a gray apron over a black T-shirt and blue jeans held the door open before we got to it. He offered a wide smile and pointed a finger at Fran.

"Sally's daughter," he said.

Fran tossed her sleek black hair. "Sally's granddaughter."

"Would be, I guess," he agreed. "Ham." His hand shot out to shake ours. "June is coming into town, so we've been looking for you. Not you, just someone from some other place."

Fran led through a narrow hallway, past a kitchen redolent of fried onions then into the public space of the café. All six customers stared in our direction. They nodded, smiled among themselves. Ham set menus out at a table notably removed from the others.

"Sally's granddaughter," he said aloud for another round of smiles. "Having lunch?" he asked us. "The food's all good, if I do say so myself."

"Doesn't matter if it's good," a voice said. "It's the only place in town."

Guffaws followed and a question: "How's Sally?"

Fran bowed sweetly to the room. "Still kicking ass."

We pulled out chairs and sat down amid the laughter. Everyone then had a suggestion from the menu. In a friendly game of one-upmanship, they shouted across the room, more to each other than to us. All except a man who sat in a far interior corner and watched. He had a large mug in front of him and an empty plate. No visible newspaper or cell phone. No expression on his face though it was a nice enough face. Fran and I reviewed our menus.

June arrived about ten minutes later, a small figure beneath a wide straw hat, well-known to everyone in the café except me. The chatter let up as heads quickly bowed over menus or food.

"June!" said Ham, stepping out from the kitchen to catch her with a hug at the door. She resisted the hug, but he took no offense, words tumbling out. "Good to see you. Your guests are here. What'll you have?"

Before answering, she approached our table, looked it over, and nodded. She spoke to Ham, "We'll have three ham-and-turkey on rye. To go."

"But—"

"To go. And three iced teas. Put it on my tab. Ernie's missing. We can eat at the house and look for him. Go, Ham, and make the sandwiches."

Ham slunk away. June took our remaining chair, sweeping off the hat to reveal a pink scalp only partially covered by a fine mat of white hair. Shrunken features, weathered skin, large eyes, pursed lips. That horn for a voice. It carried to all the corners of the dining room and possibly the kitchen as well.

Fran smiled at her auntie and introduced me. I got a quick,

assessing glance and a short nod. "You'll do," she said.

Then to Fran, "Thanks for coming. Ernie will give you a tour when he returns, then we'll talk business."

"Business?"

"Price, contract. I want to live out my life here, but I need someone to take over the operations, finances. You'll keep Ernie, of course. He's never been anywhere else, and he knows it better than I do."

"Wait," Fran said. "What are you talking about?"

"The farm. I need you to buy the farm. You're the only person I trust and the only person I know who can afford it."

"But I—"

"I saw that pretty car. You make good money, you and your husband. And you won't cheat me, like some might. It's all set. I waited to call until spring because it's prettiest in the spring. Here's Ham with our lunches." She pushed back her chair and stood, surprisingly spry. "You girls take the food. My old wagon feels every bump. Our drinks could spill."

Fran and I looked at each other. My in-control friend might have been bushwhacked. Maybe she had. The word seemed to fit. I would have laughed, but I thought I knew how she felt and was glad I wasn't in her shoes, pretty as they were. We were slow getting to our feet.

"June." Deep male voice, nice voice. The man from the corner had joined us.

"Clint," June said impatiently, as to a misbehaving child. "What do you want?"

"I overheard you. If you're selling the farm, I'd like to buy it." Quiet and sincere, but with an urgent undercurrent.

Fran's frown eased, June's deepened, and I—I no longer felt like smiling. After years of interviews, I prided myself on recognizing a lie and a liar. Was that it? Nothing wrong on the surface but something dark underneath? We resettled ourselves at the table, stared up at him. He was tall, pushing fifty, with a square face, regular features, clean brown hair. He wore a plaid shirt with narrow-fitting jeans, low boots. He pulled over a chair from a nearby table and straddled it.

"I have the money," he said, focusing on June. "And I'm a Honeyman. This woman's not." Ninety-three against fifty, I expected Auntie June to shrink in comparison. But no, she bristled. The frail but determined chin rose, and the blue eyes met his.

"I've told you before," she said, "when I'm dead and gone."

He rolled his shoulders back and stood. "That may not be as far away as you'd like," he said and left. Fran and I sat there in a moment of stunned silence.

"Who—?" Fran asked finally.

"A cousin," said Auntie June, her voice lower than when she arrived. "Not close. He was born here, grew up here, then he got the idea he could make something of himself if he went to the city, San Diego. He was gone for years then came back with no explanation. His family had moved away. He works for the county, hangs around."

"Can he make trouble for you?" I asked.

"Threaten my business license."

I pulled out my phone and did a search for Clint Honeyman, found him in the county license bureau. He'd been there nine years.

"How did he know you'd be in here today?"

She drew herself up straighter. Her eyes went from one to the other of us. "Ham told him. Clint has something on all the Honeymans, so it's tell-me-or-else. Ham would tell; he'd be afraid not to."

"Nice," said Fran.

June scowled. "Let's go. We're wasting time here."

She was striding toward the front door before Fran and I had the lunch bags gathered up. We waved as she went out the front door and we turned toward the rear.

Fran quickly led the way through the kitchen out to her car. In minutes, the Lexus was on the road behind a classic Cadillac, sky blue, white wall tires, tail fins.

"Auntie June?" I asked.

Fran nodded. "Her pride and joy. Uncle Ray gave it to her. It must have been used when he bought it, but she doesn't care. She'll drive it until she dies. Or until it dies."

"And Clint? What do you know about him?"

"I've seen him once or twice, that's all."

"I don't like him."

"You think I do?"

When a feeling struck me as hard as it had with Clint Honeyman, I wanted answers. I shaded my phone so I could see what I was doing and called my office in the city. After a dozen rings, I reached an intern. Perfect. I gave the name, locations, Honeyman and San Diego, and approximate dates. The connection was scratchy but adequate. I decided to wait on hold. Three and a half minutes later she had him, the same listing I had found at the county, plus Honeyman.

"Good," I said. "The next part may be a little harder. Take the month and year he started with the county and scan back, say, one to six months, and see what you can find in San Diego. What happened then? Anything unresolved? Suspicious? Especially anything near to where he lived, if you can tell."

"Um—" said the intern.

I turned to Fran. "How long before we're at the farm?"

She shook her head. "Seven minutes?"

"You have ten minutes," I said into the phone. "Call me back at this number." To Fran, "Pull to the side here to wait so June won't see us."

"Yes, ma'am."

She rolled the car into a spot of shade and turned off the motor.

"I don't—"

"It's a feeling. You get them sometimes, don't you? Well, I scratch mine." I stretched out my legs. "While we have time, what can you tell me about Ernie?"

"Oh, Ernie's a dear. He's about sixty, and he's been working at the farm since he was a kid. He keeps up the graves and the grounds, and his kids help sometimes. He's the one who should buy the farm, but he doesn't have the money. It takes money."

"You're sure you don't want it?"

"Positive."

"Too bad."

Ten minutes on the dot, the intern called back. Apologetic. "Not enough time," she said. "I mean, I think you want just one or two events. I found lots. I need more time to check them out."

"Okay. Thanks for your efforts." I sat back, shrugged. "So, all we know for certain is that Clint works for the county. Better than nothing, I suppose. Let's see that farm and cemetery."

Six minutes later we rounded a curve, and a low hill rose up on the right. It had an iron fence, then a gate over a driveway. Above the gate, an arch carried the words *Honeyman Hill Farm* in an elaborate scroll. The gate was open. I studied the scroll work on one half as we entered: was that an animal? A dog, then another, and a cat, a rabbit, birds. *Cemetery*, the gate said.

"It's a *pet* cemetery!" I shouted. "It is, isn't it? A pet cemetery."

Fran grinned. "It is!"

She slowed to take the big car through the gate then stopped to give me the opportunity to look around. A two-lane roadway gently curved ahead of us as it climbed the hill. There were spring flowers and gnarled trees, gravestones, and monuments. The monuments were smaller than in a human cemetery, notably pet-size, and the stories they told were of affection and adventure, a dog with its paws in the air, a cat curled on itself. Was that a bird riding a dog's back?

"This is Honeyman Hill Farm," Fran said. "Or it was. It was an apple orchard for a hundred years. The Honeymans sold apples and other crops to towns between here and San Diego.

"But the story is that they wanted to make Honeyman a real town, and there weren't enough Honeymans to go around, so they offered land cheap, and more people came. Honeyman became a town, though small. Auntie June might have left, but Ray Abbott showed up. He was an animal-lover like she was; in fact, he loved animals so much, he'd gone into taxidermy. But what could he do with that? The Honeymans decided to give June the Hill Farm, which came with a house and an apple crop so she and Ray could afford to stay here.

"Ironically, Auntie June and Uncle Ray did not need the apples. They built a workshop for Ray, then traveled the countryside drumming up business. When not everyone wanted Fido preserved, someone suggested they create a pet cemetery, and that was all it took. They visited pet and human cemeteries, and Auntie June plotted out how and where to put the pets. The rest, as they say, is history. It must be forty-fifty years now."

I rolled my window down for a better view as we slowly drove up the hill. Dogs and more dogs, all kinds in all manner of poses. Cats, rabbits, a pony. A small animal mausoleum with a gate I'd have to stoop to enter.

A black Scottie dog stood in the grass about fifteen feet from the road, ears pointed, tail up. He might have been alive and sniffing at the nearby wildflowers dancing in the breeze. The flowers were spring volunteers, but the blossoms in grave cups spoke of grieving pet owners' continued devotion.

"It's quite wonderful," I said, searching for the right word to describe the emotion I felt on that hill. Grief, certainly, but love, comfort, cheer. How many? One hundred, two, probably more rested on a hillside decorated with flowers and visited with love. I thought I might not stop smiling. Until another thought struck me.

"What would a man like Cousin Clint want with a pet cemetery?"

Auntie June waited for us at the top of the hill wearing a frown as deep as the one she had given Clint. When we approached, she indicated a parking area in front of a low, rambling, wood-sided house. Some distance back stood another building, plain stucco, no windows, the "workshop," I assumed. June walked from the shade of the house to meet us, followed by two black cats and a yellow dog.

"I had to take a call from work," I said before Auntie June could ask why we were ten minutes late on a seven-minute drive.

She shook her head, not interested. Not angry either, she was worried. She shooed away her animals then stood so she blocked Fran's door.

"I still can't find Ernie," she said into the car. "His truck's here; he knew you were coming. He was supposed to give you a tour, but he's not answering the damn phone." She held her cell phone aloft to show us how he was not answering.

"Maybe he's having lunch," Fran suggested.

"He'd still answer the phone," June snapped. "And he couldn't leave without his truck."

"Then he's here somewhere. We'll find him. Climb in."

June gave a brisk nod before climbing awkwardly into the spacious back seat.

"Which way?" Fran asked.

"Take the road behind the house," June instructed. She leaned forward to look over Fran's shoulder. "He's not down here. We'd have seen him."

"Okay."

Fran backed the car out, so we were on the road uphill again. We quickly ran out of the cemetery, and dead apple trees and weeds lined the terraced hillside. Eventually, the road curved back downhill, where we met a black stone Labrador guarding a circle of graves. Then, a flock of parakeets perched on a head-stone. I spotted dogs and several cats. We were back alongside the house. Here the ground was filled again with grave markers, walking paths, spring bulbs, and gnarled trees. A fence marked the boundary of the cemetery to the outside world. Tall shrubs lined the fence.

"There," I said. "Something dark in front of those shrubs."

Fran hit the brakes, put the car in reverse. We scanned, stared. June scrambled across the back seat, mewed when she saw what I had seen.

We clambered out onto a gravel walking path. Fran reached for June's arm but was too slow. June broke away with a long stride for someone so small.

"Ernie, Ernie." Her voice strained by emotion, exertion, "Oh, Ernie."

She dropped to her knees beside the dark pile on the path. A man lay facedown, the back of his head thick with blood. Blood had run down and pooled beneath him. Hours ago. June put a hand on his shoulder.

I crouched beside her. "Don't move him," I warned. "He's alive, but he needs help *now*."

June's eyes widened on me. I flashed a rueful smile. "You have your phone? Call for an ambulance, and you might get a sheriff up here, too. This doesn't look like an accident."

I got to my feet. Fran, looking pale, helped Auntie June rise then held her for the phone call. That done, June knelt again beside Ernie, took his hand in hers and said his name. Again. Then, "I can't live here without you."

I looked around. From where I stood, I could not see the cemetery gate and only the roof of the house through the trees. Had chance brought Ernie here, or something else?

Peering down, I read the markers, various sizes of bronze or stone etched with pet names, dates, and outlines to illustrate what lay beneath. Mindy, beloved cat, seventeen years. Cleo, another cat, six years. Tyger, by the looks of him a pit bull, eight years old.

I did a double take. I'd skimmed over the pets' dates without thinking, but Tyger's caught my attention: Tyger had been buried in the approximate month and year that Clint had returned to Honeyman. I brought out my phone, no messages. Swore. Photographed the marker and poor Ernie.

The paramedics arrived first. Being only from the next town, they knew June, knew the farm, knew Ernesto, Ernie. While they worked, I checked in with the paper, reached the intern, gave her the date from the grave. Fran watched June watch over Ernie until the medics had him on a stretcher and into the van. In minutes, they were gone, and Fran had wrapped her auntie in a hug which was only reluctantly accepted, June anxiously scowling at the world in general.

"If he doesn't survive—" I said to Fran.

Fran may have said, "He will," but her words were lost in the arrival of another car. Not a sheriff.

Clint Honeyman, who hadn't needed directions to find us.

He drove a late model Nissan sedan that slid quietly up the hill with barely a sigh from its engine as it settled in front of the Lexus, blocking our exit. Clint looked at us, then walked to his trunk, popped it open, and drew out a midsize shovel.

"I passed the ambulance," he said as he approached. "Siren going. I guess the old guy's still alive."

My chest froze, but purple rage suffused June's face. She struggled against Fran's tightening arms, eyes blazing at Clint.

"You—!"

Clint smiled calmly, unafraid. "No need to get worked up," he said. "We won't be here long."

"'We'? But I heard them, too. One vehicle, two. Clint leaned on his shovel and waited. Ham Honeyman came first, still wearing his apron. He glanced down and hurriedly removed it. Two more men emerged from the next car. Beneath their matching Padres ball caps were similar grins of anticipation. June seemed to shrink as she watched.

"Franklin, Theo," she said bitterly. "Honeyman. Cousins. Where's Win?"

"He'll be here."

"A cop should be here, too," I said, which made the men laugh.

"That's Win," said Ham. "He had another call." He moved closer, took the shovel from Clint. "Sorry, Junie, we're going to mess up your pretty farm."

"There's still time to take me up on my offer," Clint observed. "But I guess you don't want to do that, even after seeing what happened to Ernie. Shame. Ernie thought there was a real dog buried here. The fool."

"Step aside," Ham said to me. He put the shovel into the ground. The others drew closer, even June with Fran protectively behind her. The men gave them room to watch.

I backed away, brought my phone up high enough to see it with head bent. The intern answered. I told her to lower her voice.

"I think I found it," she said. "Bank robbery. Inside job. Guard killed and one of the robbers. Two others got away. Twenty-six million dollars stolen. They knew what they were doing."

"Let's see if they still do. Get this on speaker."

Ham had begun digging. Eager. I let him get up momentum then spoke over the sound of earth moving. Held the phone at my thigh.

"Twenty-six million?" I asked the men. "I hear two people died, a bank guard, and someone else. Are you missing a cousin?"

All movement stopped.

"Benjamin." June's horn-like voice struck a low wail. "*Benny*. He died in a bank robbery. But that was you, wasn't it, *all* of you? He'd have done anything for you, and he worked in the bank. So, he told you when the money would be there. Ham, Clint, Win— *Why?* Why rob a bank?"

Ham leaned on the shovel. "Town's dying, June. We thought we would buy it back, make it all Honeyman again. But it's going down too fast. Nobody wants to live here anymore. And we're getting too old. I just want out of here before it's too late for me. Lie on a beach somewhere."

"With five million dollars each?" I asked.

"Yeah. Why not?" The cousins nodded in unison.

"Okay," I said, earning glares from Fran and Auntie June. "Let's see that twenty-six million."

Ham went back to work. Dirt flew onto the next grave. A pile formed. The hole deepened. About two feet down, he flagged, and his energy turned to frustration. Still, he kept at it.

Three feet down, he hit something hard. The men smiled with satisfaction. Clint took the shovel from Ham.

"I'll finish," he said. But before he started, another vehicle arrived, a tan county sheriff's van that parked alongside Fran's car. The driver could have been Ham's brother, even to the fleshy middle, except he wore a uniform, badge, and weapon.

"Started without me, I see." His cop's eyes took us all in. "And June's here and friends of hers? Win Honeyman, and you are? Frances Chen, Sally's granddaughter. Of course, come here to buy the farm. Buy the farm, get it? We could sell you a plot, but you'd need three or four. They're kind of small. So, Clint, what do we have?"

Clint growled at him. "Get out of the way, and we'll see."

Thud. Metal shovel on wood. A coffin for a pit bull or a carton containing a bank bag? Dirt flew. June trembled with anger. Fran held her again, for both their sakes. I remained motionless, hoping my phone was still receiving.

Someone grunted. Clint bent into the hole, drew up again, then allowed Ham to assist. A wooden crate emerged only to be dropped heavily onto the footpath. Ham and Clint looked it over, then Clint walked back to his car. He returned with a hammer and a pry bar. Impatient. The crate gave way in a shower of splinters. Inside—? Well, inside was a pit bull taxidermy.

The remains of a real dog. No money. No opening where money could be stashed inside. The Honeymans swore; they kicked at the lifelike corpse. Clint swung the pry bar like he was attacking a piñata. When that didn't produce the prize they sought, Win grinned, drew his gun, and aimed it at June and Fran. Fran cringed, but June took a half step closer, squared her shoulders.

"Winston Honeyman," she scolded, "you put that away."

Win, still laughing, flicked his wrist and fired a bullet into the dead dog's shoulder. June cried, "No!" but her voice was lost in the rush of five men to dig inside the dog.

Nothing.

"That's Ray Abbott's work," Ham said. "He said we could

trust him. Give him a crate and watch him bury it. Put a marker on it with a picture of a pit bull called Tyger. No one will open that, he said. No one opens any of the graves. All we had to do was pay him each year. He'd keep watch on it. Didn't even ask what was in it. Nice guy, Ray Abbott. Not greedy. He wanted that car for his wife, and he wanted a small payment each year.

"But we're here today because you want to sell the damn farm. Where's the money, June?"

Win waved his gun again at June, barely five feet distant. She took another irritated breath, but I didn't feel so confident. I raised my hand holding my cell.

"Before you think about shooting anybody," I said, "you might consider that your conversation has been received by my office and recorded. In a few minutes it will be forwarded to the FBI. You have a brief head start before real cops are here. Stay or leave. Your choice."

"Who the hell—?" Clint.

I smiled. "Nicole Clark with *The San Diegan*."

Fran and I met for lunch six weeks later in a favorite restaurant overlooking San Diego Bay. By then, *The San Diegan* had reported that the long-missing bank money had been found buried in a pet cemetery in the small town of Honeyman, California. Honeyman had also been home to the perpetrators, including one man who was killed by police during the robbery. Two others were now under arrest, and three more were being sought. It was believed they were all related.

Ray Abbott had indeed been as good as his word. Worried about the contents of the grave, he'd dug it up, found the money, and reburied it in three new graves leaving complete details where June later found them.

As for buying the farm, June took Fran's suggestion and accepted the bank's reward as a down payment from Ernie. He had, after all, nearly given his life for it. Ownership would provide him and his family with a home and income for generations. Meanwhile, Ernie and a son were running the place with June and her pet menagerie watching comfortably from the house at the top of the hill.

And Honeyman, the town? When the COVID-19 pandemic hit, a surprising number of desk-surfing Southern Californians remembered the town with the pet cemetery and decided to try living and working remotely up the two-lane road that went nowhere else.

TO HELL AND BACK
L.H. Dillman

Hollywood—March 26, 1997

There's nothing quite like the stench of old vomit and stale urine baking in the midday heat. Val Baxter covered her nose and mouth with her hand as she made her way up Devon Alley. This was by far the smelliest case she'd worked on in the ten months since she'd opened Baxter Investigations—worse, even, than the stake out of the gentlemen's club in Pacoima. But at least she'd found *that* woman. She'd been looking for Jeannie Chatham in the greater Hollywood area for four days, going on five, with nothing to show for the effort.

"Miss?" The speaker was a sunburned man sitting cross-legged on the asphalt, his back pressed against a cinderblock wall. "I just have to say, miss, you're lookin' fine today, real fine!"

"Thanks," she said, her BS meter on high alert. She'd put on minimal makeup, pulled her brown hair tight into a ponytail, and hidden her blue eyes behind Wayfarers. Her clothes were likewise intended not to attract attention: old jeans and a loose gray T-shirt disguising the bump of the Glock holstered on her hip.

A leer spread across the man's face. "You look like a girl can spare some cash."

There were two schools of thought on panhandlers: one, be

generous if you can because they need help; and two, don't give them money because they'll spend it on booze or drugs. Val knew a little something about chemical dependency, so she empathized with those afflicted—except when the panhandler was rude. Like this guy.

"Not today," she told him.

He grabbed his crotch. "Well, fuck you very much."

She ignored him and continued at her own pace to Sunset Boulevard. It was just after noon on Wednesday, and she'd been on the hunt since nine that morning. She'd checked two bars, a dozen tents, two SROs, three liquor stores, a needle exchange, and the big blue Church of Scientology. No one had seen or heard of Jeannie Chatham.

"Hey, you! Wait a minute!" The voice belonged to a woman waving from the other side of the road. She stepped off the curb and jogged across the street, dodging cars like an expert.

"What's up?" Val asked when the woman reached her side.

"You going to the event at the Hollywood Forever Cemetery?" The woman had blond hair bleached brittle by the sun and a face as weathered as an old saddle. "It's a few blocks south a here. I can show you." Her smile revealed several missing teeth. "Or you want one of the movie-star tours? I know the best one. I can take you."

"I'll pass, thanks. I'm looking for someone." Val showed her the high school graduation photo that Jeannie's mother had sent. "She's older now, nineteen. Brown hair, hazel eyes, average build. Have you seen her?"

"My name's Donna. What's yours?"

Val gave her name and shook Donna's hand, noting how dry and rough it felt against her own skin. "Have you seen her?" she asked again. "Name's Jean Marie Chatham; goes by Jeannie."

"She's pretty. She your sister?"

"No." You had to hand it to Donna: the lady had game.

"I think I seen someone like this, 'cept with longer hair."

"When?"

"A week ago?"

"Where?"

"Nearby." Donna glanced over her shoulder.

"Was she by herself or with someone?"

"You know, my memory works a lot better when I'm not hungry."

At last, the ask. Realistically, there was a less than fifty-fifty chance that Donna had seen Jeannie, but Val was low on leads. She reached into her pocket, extracted a ten-spot, and handed it over.

"Thanks," Donna said. "I'll meet you back here in fifteen minutes."

Right. Val swept her gaze up and down the boulevard, worried she might never find Jean Marie Chatham in this jumble of tourists and hustlers, dealers, and buskers. She herself was a mother, but the pain she felt over not being allowed to see Matty more than once a week had to be minor compared to Jeannie's parents' anguish over their daughter's total disappearance. Well, almost total: Jeannie had finally phoned her folks two weeks ago to let them know she was living and working in Hollywood, but that was all she'd been willing to tell them.

Val turned east on Sunset to continue the search. She showed Jeannie's photo to everyone who was willing to stop and sober enough to focus. At the appointed time, she returned to the corner where she'd last seen Donna, but the woman didn't show. Val ducked into a sundries store, one of those shops where business is conducted through a bullet-proof shield, and a six-pack of malt liquor costs less than a gallon of milk. The cashier, a heavy-set woman with spiky red hair, followed her every move in mirrors. Val sped past the beer and wine without a glance. Twenty months in, she still had to think about it.

She chose a bottle of Fiji water, brought it to the cashier, slid a fiver into the tray, and held up Jeannie's photo. "Have you seen this young lady?"

"I got a string of girls passing through every day," said the red-haired cashier, ringing up the purchase. "I only remember the ones who try to steal."

Val pressed the image against the clear shield. "How about this one?"

"Ain't seen her. Looks like trouble, though. What'd she do?"

Jeannie Chatham hadn't done anything other than run away from home some twenty months ago. Thousands of teenage girls did it every year in America, but few of them had parents who could afford to hire private investigators to track them down. Apparently, Cindy and Ron Chatham had money. They'd paid Val's thirty-five-hundred-dollar retainer by credit card, and they'd agreed to pay two hundred dollars per hour for her time, including the time she would spend transporting their daughter to San Diego, assuming she found her. Jeannie didn't drive. She *couldn't* drive; she had something called "Stargardt disease" that had stolen her central vision.

"She's an adult," Val had said over the phone. "What if she doesn't want to come home?"

"Oh, she'll want to come home once she hears about her brother," Cindy had said. "Jimmy was missing in action in Iraq, see, but they found him, and he's finally back. They were really close, those two, so I think she'll put aside her disagreements with us. We'll start with a clean slate. I'm ready to forgive everything."

What was there to forgive?

According to Cindy, Jeannie had been a good girl until she started hanging around a band in Sonoma back when the Chathams lived in Northern California. She grew distant and sullen; her grades tanked; all she wanted to do was write songs, play guitar, and sing. She left home the day she turned eighteen, and her parents had been worrying ever since. They feared that she couldn't survive out there alone, given her vision problems. And they detested the rock and roll lifestyle she aspired to—who wouldn't, what with the drugs and promiscuity and piercings and tattoos?

"We only want Jeannie to stay pure of body and spirit," Cindy said.

Good luck with that. Every teenager dipped at least a toe into the pool of impurity. A little experimentation was normal. A little rebellion was a part of growing up, according to something Val had read. Of course, she might feel differently once her own little boy reached puberty.

"Our faith means everything to us," Cindy continued. "And I know Jeannie will appreciate our path once she sees the good it's done us."

"I'll do my best to find her."

"I know you will, and please hurry. We're going to have a little party for Jimmy on Sunday. It'd be wonderful if she could make it."

Sunday had come and gone. Since then, Val had met all sorts of characters and witnessed all sorts of craziness—more bizarre, even, than what she'd dealt with on patrol for the Santa Monica Police Department—and now she could add the red-haired cynic to the long list of oddballs who hadn't seen Jeannie Chatham.

"She's actually a good kid," Val told the cashier. Then she pocketed the photo, collected her change, and left.

Outside, heat radiated off the asphalt in shimmering waves. Val stuck to the margin of shade close to the buildings. A block later, she spotted Donna jogging her way, the soles of the woman's old sneakers flapping like clown shoes. Did she have news, or was she back for more money?

"Guess what?" Donna said when she landed next to Val. "I think I found your girl. She's got herself a job stringing guitars."

Five minutes later, Val and Donna entered Sammy's Guitar Center, around the corner from Sunset, on Highland Avenue. Sammy's was a small shop and, thankfully, air-conditioned. Donna had a spring in her step as she escorted Val down the aisle. It dawned on Val that the woman fancied herself a tour guide.

"This is Miss Baxter," Donna announced to the acne-scarred young man at the cash register. "Here to see Miss Chatham."

The cashier, whose name tag read "Emil," turned toward the open doorway behind him. "Jeannie, they're here."

A moment later, a young woman with long brown hair came through the beaded curtain. Definitely the girl in the photo, but older and with a discreet nose piercing. She was petite, almost fragile. Turning her head slightly to the left, she regarded Val with her right eye.

"Yes?"

"Hi, Jeannie. My name's Valentine Baxter. I'm a private investigator—"

"My mom sent you?"

"Right, and—"

"What happened? Is Dad okay?"

"They're both fine. They asked me to find you because your brother is back."

Jeannie took a sharp breath. "Jimmy. Oh my God. Where?"

"With them in San Diego. If you want, I'll drive you there."

Interstate 5, Southbound—March 26, 1997

"Mind if I have a cigarette?" Val asked as she merged the Mazda onto the freeway. "I'll blow the smoke out the window."

"I don't mind," Jeannie said. "As long as I can have one too."

Val would not have pegged her passenger as a smoker. Jeannie looked like one of those all-natural types, with her long, air-dried hair and the absence of makeup and nail polish. The young woman's only adornments were hoop earrings and a tiny turquoise stud in the side of her nose.

Val reached for her pack of Parliaments. "Terrible habit," she said, offering Jeannie a cigarette. "Wish I'd never started. How long have you been smoking?"

"A few months." Jeannie lit their cigarettes, then took a long drag on hers and blew out the smoke. "I only do it once in a while. It's bad for my voice."

Val cracked her window. "Why'd you start?"

"Everyone smokes where I work—not at the guitar shop; at Lamont's. It's a club on Cahuenga. I'm the opening act Thursday and Friday nights."

Val had heard of it. "You must be really good."

"Hope so. It's tough, though, you know? 'Cause there's a zillion singers trying to make it." Jeannie took another drag. "But I had an audition yesterday, and I think it went great. It's a regular gig in Silver Lake, and it pays more. So, yeah, getting there."

"Your parents don't know how well you're doing, do they?"

"They wouldn't be impressed. They hate my kind of music."

"But the fact that you're supporting yourself?"

"Barely supporting, but yeah, they *should* be impressed. They didn't expect me to get anywhere because of my Stargardt."

"I'm glad you followed your dreams."

Jeannie ground out her cigarette. "I was going to wait and visit my parents in, like, five years, you know? After I made it? But since Jimmy's back..."

"Just curious," Val said, looking at the turquoise dot in Jeannie's nose. "You're leaving that in?"

"Absolutely."

"Good for you."

Jeannie stuffed her jeans jacket between her headrest and the window, relaxed into the makeshift pillow, and dozed off. For the next hundred miles, Val kept her eyes on the road, taking an occasional look at her passenger. Jeannie's skin was flawless, her features soft, her breathing slow and regular. She seemed younger than her nineteen years. Childlike. She made Val think of Matty—now eight—and how he'd fallen asleep while she drove him to his dad's place last weekend after a jam-packed visitation day. She remembered the lightness of his little hand in hers as she walked him up the front steps, the ache she felt as watched him enter the house, and her roiling rage when her ex shut the door in her face.

When Jeannie woke up, the sun was a red-orange orb clinging to the horizon. Off to the right, beyond the sand dunes of Camp Pendleton, the Pacific Ocean stretched westward like a blanket of sapphire.

"Wow, so pretty," Jeannie said, admiring the view with her peripheral vision.

"You've been down here before, right?" Val asked.

"Never. My parents were living up north when I left. I wonder if their new place has a view of the ocean."

"They're probably too far from the coast." Based on the Thomas Guide map, Val had estimated that Cindy and Ron's home was five miles inland. "Let's try calling again." She'd phoned the Chathams twice that afternoon, once after locating Jeannie and again as they began the drive, and got the answering machine both times. "Hopefully, they'll pick up." She tapped "redial" on the car phone. After a pause and a click, the line went dead. No answering machine, nothing.

Jeannie sighed. "Maybe they're busy with Jimmy."

Val frowned. She'd figured that, busy or not, Cindy and Ron would stay in touch. Surely they weren't mad about Val delivering their daughter later than they'd hoped. Surely they'd be thrilled to see Jeannie no matter when she arrived, which should be just after dark, depending on traffic.

Unfortunately, traffic came to a halt near Carlsbad.

Val lit another cigarette. "Are you excited to see your brother?"

"Yeah," Jeannie said. "It's been, like, over four years. He enlisted after Desert Storm."

"Out of patriotism?"

"Out of a need to get away from our parents. They were already weird by then."

"Weird how?" Val asked, blowing a stream of smoke out the window.

"Super religious. They joined this church back when we lived up north. Kind of Christian mixed with New Age. It was all about, like, reaching your human potential, getting to the next level of consciousness. Stuff like that."

Val shot her a sidelong glance. "What's this church called?"

"The Total Overcomers," Jeannie said with a snort. "As in, 'overcome whatever's holding you back.' They thought the church could cure Jimmy's stuttering and my Stargardt. Maybe stuttering, but Stargardt? I mean, I *wish*. All the doctors they took me to said it was impossible. This was back when they went to real doctors, before the church got hold of them. Anyway, if I've gotta choose between Ci and Ro and—"

"Ci and Ro?"

"*Ci*-ndy, *Ro*-n, nicknames the Overcomers gave 'em. So, yeah, I'll listen to the doctors rather than my parents, even if the news isn't great."

"I get it." Val thought The Total Overcomers sounded more like a cult than a religion. On the other hand, many well-established faiths required their members to believe things that simply couldn't happen under the laws of nature. Christians, Muslims, and Jews, for instance. All religions had some element of fantasy, didn't they? They all seemed a little wacky if you didn't belong. Who was she to say which were legit and which were not? Val was being paid to transport Jeannie, not to judge her parents.

"Jimmy's way out was to join the Navy SEALs," Jeannie said. "I just left."

An unpleasant possibility occurred to Val. "Does the church have a branch in San Diego?"

"No, it's too small to have branches."

That's a relief, Val thought. The Mazda continued to idle. She put out her cigarette.

Restless, Jeannie shifted in her seat. Her peripheral sight landed on a plastic action figure wedged next to the console. "You have kids?" she asked.

"A boy. He's eight."

"I bet he plays sports. Soccer? Little League?"

Val shook her head, no. Matty still couldn't run. Two years after his leg was broken, his bones still weren't strong enough, and Val still couldn't talk about it without crying. Time to change the subject. "Hey, check them out." She pointed to a group of people gathered on a hilltop near the freeway, their shapes silhouetted against the evening sky. "Can you see?" Jeannie was having trouble, so Val described the scene for her. "They're all standing there looking up. I bet they're watching that comet."

"Oh, yeah. Hale-Bopp, right? Some people are really obsessed over it."

Traffic started to move again. Five minutes later, they exited the interstate onto Encinitas Boulevard and headed east toward the upscale San Diego suburb of Rancho Santa Fe.

Rancho Santa Fe—March 26, 1997

It was dark when Val and Jeannie turned onto Colina Norte Road. They passed stately homes and dramatically lit landscapes. Gates and fountains and palm trees aplenty. A better term for the driveways would have been "approaches."

The address Val had been given belonged to a Mediterranean mini-mansion perched on a hill. The Mazda chugged through the open gate and up the drive. The house was two stories tall, with a red-tile roof and a portico over the front door. There had to be seven or eight bedrooms. Val understood the Chathams were well-off, but this was multi-millionaire territory.

"Your parents must be doing okay."

Jeannie smiled wryly. "I should ask them for a new guitar."

"Or two or three."

Val parked and cut the engine. They unloaded Jeannie's duffle bag and guitar case, walked to the front door, and rang the bell. No one came. The home was totally quiet, and yet they could see light through the curtains. Val banged on the door. No response.

She returned to the Mazda to try to reach Cindy on the car phone, but there was no cellular reception. On instinct, she grabbed the Glock from under her seat, checked the magazine, and slipped it under her shirt into the back of her waistband.

"You sure this is the right place?" Jeannie asked when Val returned.

"Why would they give me the wrong address? Let's check the back. Leave your stuff."

They followed the steppingstones around the side of the house to the rear. The tennis court lights were on, the fountain gurgled, and the patio was illuminated by crisscrossing strings of overhead lightbulbs. Someone was getting ready for a party, maybe the celebration of Jimmy's return.

Except there was no sign of life.

The French doors were locked, and the shades were drawn. At the far end was a plain wooden door that was ajar. Val headed in that direction, with Jeannie following close behind. They were a few steps away when all the outside lights went off.

Val froze in the darkness. "Shit."

"Look!" Jeannie pointed up to the sky. Half of a yellow moon emerged from behind a cloud, and, to its left, away from the haze, was a streak of white, a smudge among the stars. "The comet! It's really bright. Even I can see it. So cool!"

No, Val thought, this is not cool, not cool at all. "Why don't you go back to the car and wait."

"Why? I want to see Jimmy and my parents."

"I just think—"

"I'm worried about them."

"All right but stay behind me." Val nudged the door open, stepped in, and flipped on the lights. It was a storage room with a door at the far end.

And it smelled awful.

She'd encountered that stench once before.

"Go! Get out! Get in the car, Jeannie, and lock the doors. Hurry."

This time, Jeannie didn't argue. As she turned to the exit, Val took the Glock from her waistband. When Jeannie's footsteps faded, Val opened the door to the next room. It was empty save for a forty-ish man with pale skin and red-rimmed eyes standing five feet in front of her.

"Who are you?" She aimed the pistol at him.

He raised his hands in the air. "Rick Ford."

"You live here, Rick?"

He shook his head.

"Anyone else here with you?"

He shook his head again.

She asked if he was armed. He said he wasn't, but she patted him down to be sure. The guy was small and weak, and he was trembling.

"You a cop?" he asked in a near whisper.

"Private investigator. I'm looking for the Chathams, Cindy and Ron. You know them?"

He nodded. "We were in the church together. This place belongs to the church."

"The Total Overcomers?"

"They changed the name to 'Heaven's Gate' when they moved down here."

"You're not in the church anymore?"

"I quit. They wanted all the men to get castrated. There was no way."

"Jeezus. So where are the Chathams?"

"I didn't have anything to do with it," he pleaded. "I just got here, I swear. I came to find my friend—"

She raised the gun. "Where are the Chathams?"

"Upstairs with the rest of them."

"Dead?" She knew the answer; she'd known it as soon as she entered the house.

Rick nodded. "But they didn't think they were gonna die; they thought they were gonna ride the comet to paradise." Now the tears began to flow.

120

"Jeezus," she said again. "How many?"

"Thirty-nine," he said wiping his eyes. "I counted."

"Show me the Chathams."

She followed him across a two-story foyer to a grand staircase. As they started up, Rick told her he'd received a letter from one of his Heaven's Gate friends the day before saying that Hale-Bopp was close, and everyone was preparing to depart, with Do overseeing the arrangements.

"'Do' is the leader," Rick explained. "His real name's Marshall Applewhite. A very weird guy. Had everyone believing he was God's messenger. Anyway, I hitched a ride over here to try to talk my friend out of it, but I was too late."

The higher they went, the more putrid the air. How long had the bodies been decomposing?

"What was the postmark on your friend's letter?" Val asked.

"I don't remember. Three days ago, maybe?"

"Have you called the police?"

"The phones don't work."

The staircase brought them to a wide hallway with closed doors on each side. According to Rick, there were six to eight bodies in each bedroom. "I'm pretty sure which ones are Ron and Cindy," he said as they walked down the corridor. "But it's kinda hard to tell."

"Why's that?" Val imagined the worst.

"You'll see." He opened the last door on the left.

Instead of a pile of rotting corpses, she saw bunk beds and mattresses and cots, each holding a body lying on its back dressed in black with a purple cloth draped over the head. Most had their hands folded on their chests, and all wore a shoulder patch identifying them as members of the "Heaven's Gate Away Team." There was no blood, no sign of trauma. But the stench hit Val like a firehose of sewage.

"The Chathams...?" she asked, fighting off nausea.

Rick pointed to a double mattress that held two bodies lying side by side. A man and a woman, judging by the shapes. Val felt obliged to take a look, so she held her nose and carefully lifted the purple shrouds. So these were Cindy and Ron Chatham—white, middle-aged, and ordinary, except their skin was cold to the touch and bluish, their eyes were half open, and their mouths gaped like caverns.

"What about their son, Jimmy?" Val asked. "Is he here?"

"Jimmy died in Iraq years ago."

"How do you know?"

"Ron told me."

So Cindy had lied. "Reuniting with Jimmy" had been a trick—bait to lure her daughter. The deceit didn't surprise Val so much as it disgusted her. That woman had no right to claim the mantle of motherhood.

Val replaced the cloths and was about to step away when she noticed something under Cindy's hands: a small, folded piece of paper. Along the edge, written in pencil, was the name "Jean Marie." Val's training told her not to tamper with evidence or disturb a crime scene. She'd traipsed through too many rooms in this house already. On the other hand, didn't Jeannie have a right to read the note without waiting months? And what difference could one little message from mother to daughter make for an investigator trying to understand the deaths of this many people? While Val debated, Rick took off. She let him go. A moment later, listening to her heart instead of her head, she pulled the paper from under Cindy's hands and dashed downstairs. She paused in the foyer to read it, then ran out the front door to the Mazda. Jeannie was waiting in the passenger seat, wide-eyed and shaking.

Ten minutes later, Val found herself parked outside a gas station dialing 9-1-1 on the car phone. She had to repeat herself three times. The dispatcher had more questions than Val had answers, so she hung up.

"They're sending someone," she said.

"Oh. Good." These were Jeannie's first words since she learned the truth about her brother and read the note from her mother.

Val stared at the Super Lotto Plus sign in the gas station window, thinking about the abuse of faith and the power of charisma, wondering whether Marshall Applewhite had killed his thirty-eight followers or convinced them to do it themselves. How had he attracted them to the cult in the first place? What had happened to their will to live? To their minds? Had it ever dawned on any of them that they might be making a mistake?

The blinking lottery sign said the jackpot was $39 million—a million dollars for each member of the Heaven's Gate Away Team, Val realized. She squeezed her eyes shut and counted to ten, but when she opened them, the jackpot hadn't changed. If this was the universe reminding her that evil was real and bad things happened to good people, it needn't have bothered. Val had seen plenty of treachery and tragedy in her career—even in her personal life. It was what you did about it that mattered. As a cop, a P.I., and a mother, it was her duty to protect the innocent from harm. Mostly, she'd gotten it right, which was more than a lot of people could say. But she did have some regrets. She should have turned the car around as soon as she heard about The Total Overcomers—which she would have if she'd followed her instincts instead of focusing on finishing the job and getting paid. And she regretted not recognizing her own sickness sooner, not owning up to her weakness, not swallowing her pride in front of her ex: she should have let someone else drive Matty to the ballpark that evening, someone who hadn't been drinking.

Life was a series of lessons, some of them devastating.

Jeannie started to cry. "They lied about Jimmy."

"I'm really sorry," Val said. "About your brother, and about your parents."

"You saw what they wrote? That I'd be better off in another world than living in this one with Stargardt? If we'd got here two days ago, they'd have tried to force me—"

"I wouldn't have let them. I'd have protected you."

"I know you would."

Sirens wailed in the distance. Swirling red and blue lights appeared down the highway. Seconds later, a column of police cars, ambulances, and fire trucks sped past the gas station in the direction of Colina Norte Road.

Val squeezed Jeannie's hand. "You're going to be okay. You have your whole life to live. Good things are going to happen, I promise."

Jeannie nodded and wiped her eyes. "Thanks. You must be a really good mom."

"Working on it." Val started the engine. "Let's go back home."

Author's note: The mass-suicide tragedy of Heaven's Gate was unprecedented in San Diego history—in any civilized history. Thirty-nine people killed themselves in three waves over a three-day period in late March 1997 by ingesting phenobarbital mixed with applesauce and vodka. The cult leader, Marshall Applewhite, known as "Do," had convinced them that the Hale-Bopp comet, one of the brightest comets ever seen, would transport their souls to a better state of being and that to prepare for the trip they needed to depart their earthly "containers." On March 26, an anonymous tipster—later identified as Richard Ford—sent the San Diego Sheriff's Department to the Heaven's Gate house. Applewhite had left a video statement explaining, "We do in all honesty hate this world."

SHAMU, WORLD'S GREATEST DETECTIVE
Richie Narvaez

When Charles "Chick" Hennessey arrived at SeaWorld on a Thursday in April, he tried his best to hide his shock. He was pretty good at it, and little wonder. Having dated four linebackers, two catchers, and one golfer, I knew that athletic types, even retired-and-gone-to-seed ones like him, didn't like to show genuine anything to anyone. Everything was always hunky-dory with them. But even the best poker faces have a tough time with Shamu.

It's the smell.

I imagine it's because killer whales are so aesthetically pleasing on the outside, people expect them to be pleasing in general. Think of the scent of garbage piled outside of a seafood restaurant after a very long, very hot day. But a thousand times worse.

Shamu emerged from her tiny pool onto the slideout and called to me, via the thought-activated loudspeaker slung above us. "Angie! By my calculations, it is almost time for lunch. A bit late for callers, is it not?"

"There's just the one, then you can chow down. For your lunch bucket today, Jürgen will be serving frozen salmon and gelatin. Yum."

"Yet again? How shall I contain my joy?" said Shamu, who then eructated loud and long, clearly meaning to astonish our guest. "Very well. I am famished enough to punt a porpoise. Proceed swiftly, Mr. Hennessey."

Hennessey, his nose twitching above a rather ostentatious handlebar mustache, turned to me, "How did it know who I am?"

"*She* watches a lot of TV." I used my head to indicate that he should speak directly to the orca.

"Mostly entertainment news," said Shamu. "The real news is far too depressing."

Hennessey, still looking at me and now pointing to his head, said, "So there's an implant?"

"Basically," I explained for the jillionth time. "Five years ago an interface was implanted into Shamu's brain that translates her thoughts and allows her to communicate with us bipeds."

I almost added, "And she hasn't shut up since."

"Mr. Hennessey," Shamu said, "there are few things in life I tolerate less than being late for lunch. To hurry matters, please understand that I already know you are the owner of the San Diego Padres. You are a former player yourself, have an ex-wife and two children, are worth $826 million, own three homes and a yacht, and that you recently ate a pretzel with mustard."

Hennessey looked down at his mustard-stained tie. "Hah, that's pretty good," he said, still looking at me. "A very overpriced pretzel." (Did this guy not know what prices were being charged at Petco Park?) "But how'd you know about the money and houses and stuff?"

"Shamu's also connected to the internet." I nodded again to my boss, and Hennessey finally got the picture.

He turned to her and said, "Okay. Here goes. Month ago I traded with the Yankees for a new outfielder named Freddie Lopez. He's a good kid, did well in his first few games. But now, suddenly, I can't find him. He's not in his digs, won't answer his phone. I'm the kind of guy who goes to the best when he wants things done, and my contacts say you're the best, so I'm here."

Shamu slapped her tail on the water. "Have you asked the police to locate Mr. Lopez?"

"Nah. Guy like me goes to the cops, it gets all over the news. I don't need that kind of publicity."

Shamu abruptly slid back into the pool. "Thank you and good day, Mr. Hennessey. Lunch awaits!"

Hennessey's bald head, already red from the sun, turned crimson. "What the hell does that mean?"

I tried to clarify things. "That means Shamu will not be taking your case, sir."

"This is bull. You think I'm an idiot? You got some nerd behind the curtains doing all this smartmouthing?"

"I assure you that is not the case."

I was prepared for what happened next. Hennessey should've worn a wet suit. Shamu launched herself out of the pool and bellyflopped, soaking us both in whale-scented water.

"Lunch!" she said.

Mr. Hennessey made more off-color declarations and threats before leaving in a huff.

I turned to Shamu, still submerged except for her tail, which was waving a wet goodbye at the millionaire.

"Why didn't he make the cut?" I said. "I don't have to note that Hennessey is filthy rich, and working for him could get you closer to that coastal sanctuary you're always moaning about."

"Correct. You do not have to note that."

"Was it the nerd insult?"

"Hardly original."

"The mustache?"

Shamu surfaced and spouted water. "The very thing. He reminded me of a sea lion with whom I once shared billing. An unapologetic ham."

Jürgen arrived, and I helped him feed Shamu and then went off to feed myself some fish tacos. They were delish.

I didn't think about Freddie Lopez at all, not until the next week when Inspector Didi McCall showed up in her usual blustery fashion.

"Boy, you really fry my eggs, Shamu," said the curly-haired (bottle) brunette. "How a captive animal gets her fins involved in all my cases is what I'd like to know."

Shamu ignored the remark. "As always, it is somewhat of a pleasure to see you, Inspector. May I ask to which case you are referring?"

"Freddie Lopez, new outfielder for the Padres. He's been murdered. I hear Chick Hennessey was here recently asking you to fish around—"

"Careful, Inspector," I said.

"Yeah, yeah. Like I said, asking you to *find* Lopez."

"We didn't take the case," I noted.

"Maybe that was too bad. Who knows if you and Charm-Free Willy over here would've been able to save his life. I just wanted to let you know it's a straightforward investigation, and there's no need for you or your partner here to waste any of your valuable time."

"Very kind of you to come out here and tell us," I said.

Shamu shimmied onto the slideout. "Agreed. Your persiflage may not be welcome, but you always are, Inspector."

"Have I just been insulted?"

"Don't ask me," I said.

"Since the investigation is, as you say, straightforward," continued Shamu, "and since you and your stalwart team will solve it imminently, perhaps you can tell me more about the circumstances of the murder. I ask only out of professional curiosity."

McCall shrugged. "I might as well because it'll be over in a day or two. Lopez had just ordered a beer at the Chee-Chee Club when he received a call and walked outside. Someone shot him point blank, right there on the pavement. He was taken to Scripps Mercy and underwent emergency surgery but didn't survive his injuries.

"Witnesses say Lopez had been talking to an older gentleman at the bar. Beard, glasses, wearing a suit. Dude fled the scene, but we've got a description and are on the lookout for him. Should pick him up in a few days. Like I said, straightforward. We've got plenty of witnesses. Just a matter of time before we hook the perp. Sorry! 'Arrest,' I mean, 'arrest the perp.' Didn't want to trigger you."

"Very considerate," Shamu said. "And I do thank you for the information. Even though, as you have generously noted, my involvement is unnecessary."

"Yeah, yeah," said the inspector. "Just keep your wet nose out of it!"

That really seemed the last of it. Until two weeks later. A young woman named Molly East, with pretty curls and hazel eyes, came in looking flustered and upset. I would have ushered her in, but it was 9:50 in the morning and I told her she had to wait.

"It won't be long. Every a.m. between eight and ten, Shamu maintains her Sims account. She has an Italian baroque villa populated entirely by Hemingway cats."

"Oh. That sounds—"

"Nuts, I know. Why would a four-ton toothed whale create and maintain an Italian baroque villa populated entirely by Hemingway cats?"

"That's interesting," she said, but she was just being polite. She had something serious on her mind. We gabbed for another few minutes, and then the world's greatest detective herself leaped from the water to ring the bell above the pool. Business was open.

I did the introductions.

"I hope you don't mind my saying, Ms. Shamu, but I've always loved you since I was little."

Neither Shamu nor I bothered to tell Ms. East that "Shamu" was a stage name and that there'd been seventeen other Shamus before this one, and that no doubt little Ms. East had been enamored of one of the earlier incarnations.

She continued. "Well, the thing is, someone killed my brother, and the police haven't been able to come up with any answers. He was a baseball player. His name was Freddie Lopez."

The whale looked at me and I looked at the whale.

Shamu said, "When was the last time you spoke your brother?"

"A few weeks ago. I could tell he was upset about something, but he didn't want to say anything."

"How could you tell he was upset? Did he hint at anything?"

"No, he's not like that. But, well, my son, Jeremy, he's in high school and hoping to get a scholarship to U of C because we can't afford college. A friend of his offered to hack into the school system to change Jeremy's grades, and before I could say that my son refused to do it, Freddie went off on a tear about how he hated people who cheated and that nothing was more important than being honest and fair in this world. That it was more important than winning."

Shamu shocked me by saying, "Ms. East, I promise we will find out who killed your brother."

"I will pay you, of course."

"Yes. Angie will discuss those particulars with you."

After Ms. East left, I said, "Any particular reason for the change of heart?"

"She called me 'Ms.' and she said, 'Please.' Manners are to be appreciated and encouraged, Angie. Now, I would like you to find out as much as you can about Mr. Lopez."

"Well, as a matter of fact, after our last visit from the inspector, I took a moment and already did some research."

"Very proactive of you, Angie."

"I think so." I opened my phone and read from my notes. "'Recently traded from the Yankees.' Seems Hennessey got the better end of the deal. Both players Lopez was traded for were 'injured or missed games for health reasons.' Lopez had a batting average of .280. A decent fielder. One sports reporter called him 'an up-and-coming star.' No wife, no kids. Nor any scandals, I might add. Like his sister intimated, kind of a Boy Scout."

"A Boy Scout, you say. Even a Boy Scout has secrets. And the ones who know best are his fellow scouts and his scout leaders."

"So you want me to visit the Padres bullpen and poke around?"

"The sooner the better, Angie."

Two pieces of good fortune happened that afternoon. First, it wasn't a game day, so I didn't have to park a mile away from Petco Park, wade through the encampments of unhoused in the East Village, and then get crushed by bug-eyed tourists looking for something to do between SeaWorld and the Gaslamp Quarter.

Second, after I couldn't get ahold of Chick Hennessey, I was able to reach an athletic trainer I'd dated a couple years back. He said he'd be more than happy to sneak me into the clubhouse.

"Angie Gomez. Sexy as ever," he said to me, giving me a warm, lingering hug.

"Drake Parker. Shy as ever," I said.

After some catching up, I asked Drake if he had any intel on Lopez.

"In shape. Seemed like a nice guy."

"Any secrets you know of? Steroids? Gambling? Girls? Boys?"

"Not that I'm aware of. But you better check with Reno and Britt. They hung out with him. You know who they are?"

"I know who they are."

He walked me to the locker room and before he opened the door, he said, "Mind you, you might see a lot of nude dudes."

"Well, since you're their trainer, you should be able to tell me which ones to avoid, so I don't trip over anything."

We agreed to dinner soon, and he gave me another long hug, topped off by a lingering kiss.

In the locker room, I was greeted by even more rampant masculinity, solid funk mixed with cologne, and predictable hoots and catcalls.

In the corner, second basemen Reno Raines and outfielder Britt Pollack were playing what looked like gin rummy.

I told them who I was and asked, "Can either one of you tell me anything about Lopez?"

Britt shook his head. "What's there to say? He was new in town. We took him out to a few places."

"Like the Chee-Chee Club?"

"Nah, wouldn't be caught dead in that dive. Ooh, sorry, I didn't mean that. He seemed like a cool dude. Then last week he stopped showing up to practice and no one could get him on the phone."

"Listen, the cops already talked to us," said Reno. "We told them all we knew, which ain't much. They seemed to think it was a random killing, and Freddie was just in the wrong place at the wrong time."

"That sounds like them," I said. "Which reminds me. Now I know you two are strong, handsome, intelligent ballplayers. But even the best people who get interviewed by cops can feel put on the spot, and it's only afterward they remember something they forgot to mention. Did either one of you have one of those?"

Right then Reno smacked Britt in the arm. "The app!" he said.

"The app?" I asked.

"Um, yeah. We forgot to tell the cops, but we thought about it later but then forgot again, like you said. Didn't seem important. See, Freddie was new in town and he needed a little spending cash, so he was starting doing one of the fan-interaction apps. I was gonna do it, too, but I never got around to it. What was the name of it?"

"Fandr, I think it was," Britt said. "Yeah, Fandr!"

I called Shamu to give her an update. She said to go to the Fandr HQ ASAP. I was already on my way.

"So how does it work?"

Fandr was created by an app dev outfit called QuasiMobo, one of the tech companies gentrifying the northeast East Village. After a few transfers and holds, I was shunted off to their head of PR, Jude Foster, who agreed to meet. Their open space office was in a warehouse of concrete floors, twenty-foot-high ceilings, and a coffee station every ten feet. Foster was all scraggly facial hair and expressive eyebrows.

"Ah! Fandr allows fans to interact with their favorite celebrities. Each movie star, music star, or star athlete sets a price and fans pay for brief interactions with them. Get a recorded message or enjoy a live video chat. Available now. Upload for free at the App Store."

"Thanks for that thorough pitch," I said. "So, Freddie Lopez signed up to meet fans on the app?"

"Yes."

"I know this is virtual, but do any fans get to meet the stars live and in person?"

"Wellllll, they're not supposed to. Connections can be made, of course. Stars are people too. We advise against it, and we make sure to tell the celebrities that."

"To make sure you're not liable."

Foster's eyebrows went up and he smiled. It made him look dumb but cute.

"Can you give me a list of the names of the fans he interacted with?"

"Um, some are listed on his page. But that's only if they've chosen to share that. There may be some who choose to remain private, and we cannot release those names."

"Nice. Privacy is important."

"Indeed."

"Indeed. At the same time, it's possible one of your users was involved in murder."

Foster's eyebrows crashed together. Even dumber and cuter.

I gave him my best smile and put my hand on his forearm to press the point home. "You want to make sure your company's good name is kept clean."

The eyebrows melted. He turned around to his laptop and did some quick clicking. "Lopez wasn't on for very long, but he was popular because he was with the Yankees, so... Yeah, he interacted with more than nine hundred fans."

"Whoa. That much? Can you narrow that down to fans who live on the West Coast, San Diego area?"

"Just a minute."

"Thank you, Jude. Can I call you Jude?"

The eyebrows danced. "Please do. Seventy-five."

After a shared single-origin coffee and an invite to dinner sometime, I brought the list of names back to Shamu. It was feeding time, so there was no discussion of business. Afterward, we looked through the names on the list together.

"This will take a long time to sort through," I said. "We could give it to the cops and let them do the work for us."

"We could, Angie, but then would we be doing due diligence for our client? I think not. We need to get a better look at all these suspects, the local area ones first."

"You think one of these might be our shooter?"

"Possibly. Or he or she may be able to give us information that will bring us closer to the shooter. In any case, we do not want to tip our hand. The killer may feel he or she is free and clear of the police, but if we sniff around too closely, he or she may flee."

"What's the plan then? I know you have one."

"We offer free tickets to see the star of SeaWorld! I will put on my old show."

"Really? You think that will work? Everyone in town has likely seen you ten times already."

"And an eleventh time would still be a privilege! But I comprehend your implication, Angie. Very well. Then say I am announcing a secret prize!"

"What kind of prize? It can't be more free tickets to see the star of SeaWorld."

"Very well then. Cash!"

* * *

Shamu has some pull with the park's owners, so we were able to rope off a section for the seventy-five locals on the list.

Shamu did her old, well-honed, jump-and-jive routine, which dazzled the crowds.

I scanned the roped-off seats and understood immediately why Shamu had wanted to see them. I noted not one, not two, but five older gentlemen with beards and glasses. I knew that Shamu, despite her performing her heart out, had sharp vision and would no doubt have noticed the five as well.

One of them might have been the person who went drinking with Lopez that night and ran off before talking to the cops. With five possible leads, it was helpful that we'd had each of the suspects, I mean, *guests*, sign forms and sit in specific seats.

I was about to confer with Shamu about our next steps and—

—and that was the moment Inspector McCall showed up with stiletto heels, a megaphone, and a platoon of cops.

"Okay, everyone. Show's over!" She pointed her goons toward the seventy-five. "Round those people up."

So much for not showing our hand.

I stormed over to her. "Inspector, you can't do this."

"Can't I? I told you and your blubber-filled boss this investigation was off-limits."

"That's not exactly what you said. You said that the investigation would be over in a couple of days. And here we are more than two weeks later and *pfffft*."

Shamu splashed her tail for attention. "Inspector! If I may beg your indulgence, we are at the moment of crisis in this case. If you would just give me a few more minutes, we might have it solved."

"No can do, Moby-Doo. We just heard about that app thing, and I appreciate your bringing these suspects together. Be grateful I don't charge you for withholding evidence. But that's only because I don't have cuffs big enough."

So all seventy-five guests were herded into cars and taken to the station for questioning.

If you've never heard a whale curse like a sailor in a computerized voice for a few hours straight, it's not something I recommend.

After trying, mostly unsuccessfully, to calm down Shamu, I knew I needed a break. For the moment, it looked like the case was out of our hands. We had no more leads, and since there was nothing left to do, I decided to call up Drake Parker.

"I'm glad you called," he said. "There's something I want to talk to you about."

"If this is about my safety word again—"

"No, no. About the case. I have something to show you."

We made a plan to go back to our favorite joint, the Bali Hai on Shelter Island. After what Drake said, not only was I hungrily anticipating crispy calamari and frosty piña coladas, I was also eager to see what the heck he was talking about. Given that Shamu was not in the best mood, I decided not to tell her until I knew what was what.

I put on my sexiest skinny jeans, an Eddie Vedder T-shirt, and ankle boots. It was a lovely night in San Diego, but aren't they all? As I pulled into a parking space, I spotted Drake getting out of his hybrid.

I parked, opened my door—and then a sound like a firecracker rang out. I ducked and rolled, checked my myself for wounds. Nothing.

More shots. The sound of breaking glass. Then a gasp and something hitting the ground.

Under the cars, I saw Drake was down.

I ducked and rolled some more. There were enough SUVs between Drake and I that I had good cover.

When I reached him, I saw his wound would be fatal if he didn't get medical attention ASAP.

The shots seemed to have stopped. People were running. I heard the crackle of a walkie-talkie.

I kept myself low to the pavement, got my phone out, called for an ambulance.

Tapping off the phone, I looked down to see Drake holding his car keys up with bloody fingers. Before fading out he said, "My backpack... Read the files."

After a trip to the hospital with Drake—he was going to be okay, but would be laid up for a while—I chatted with some detectives who were polite for a change. I told them about the gunfire but didn't mention the files I'd gotten from Drake's car. Those I kept in my bag. Later, I went back to the park and filled Shamu in on everything.

Despite the lateness of the hour, Shamu immediately called the inspector and put her on speaker.

"Inspector McCall?"

"Ah, look what the tide brought in."

"Cease your flummery. It is eleven o'clock in the evening, and you are still at the station. I imagine interviewing seventy-five suspects will take at least until the morning and beyond. How will you get your beauty sleep, Inspector?"

"What do you want already?"

"I can solve this case in time for you to get home and rest your minuscule human brain. Could you please bring the following suspects to the pool as quickly as possible?" Shamu named the suspects.

"Just these five? Why?"

"When you gather them together, the answer to that question will be painfully obvious. While you might be tempted to proceed on your own from there, please know that I also have some evidence that I would like to share with you, in the interest of justice."

"Justice, uh huh."

"And would you also please locate Charles Hennessey and bring him with you. I'm sure he would like to be here as well."

"How the hell do I convince a millionaire to come see a whale?"

"Tell him the fate of his franchise hangs in the balance. He will come."

Meanwhile, I called Molly East and Jude Foster and invited them to come down as well.

By midnight, the area around the slideout was filled. Shamu emerged from the water, the nighttime spotlights giving her the dramatic entrance she loved.

"Freddie Lopez was a very good baseball player, a potential star. But more importantly, he was an honest person. And when he inadvertently became tied up in a deception, he balked and fled. Ten days later he was found murdered."

Shamu turned to the five bearded and bespectacled suspects McCall had hauled in and asked each of them to describe what they had discussed with Lopez.

The ophthalmologist had always dreamed of becoming a ball player, and from the sound of it, he grilled Lopez for twenty minutes straight about the possibilities of an ophthalmologist "in pretty near top condition" becoming a professional baseball player at thirty-seven years of age.

The waiter said he was just checking out the app and that Lopez was the cutest and the cheapest celebrity on there.

The sales rep said he was so high when he chatted with Lopez he didn't even remember downloading the app.

The security guard said he was a diehard Padres fan (bless his heart) and that he wished Lopez the best of luck.

The lawyer's name was Rick Simon (né Sidransky) and he came from the Bronx. That clicked something with Shamu. Her eyes closed and she gently swayed her tail under the water.

"... at first we just talked about the old hometown," said Simon, "reminiscing about Yankee Stadium and good deli. But then when he found out I was a lawyer, he said he was in a bind and asked me if he could talk to me in person, as he was unsure of the security of the app. He wanted legal advice. We made an appointment to meet somewhere out of the way, where no one was likely to recognize him."

"The Chee-Chee Club."

"Exactly, but before we got to talking, he got a text that seemed to spook him. He ran outside without another word. I waited, then I heard a shot. A bunch of us ran to look, but the shooter was gone. I was afraid I'd be implicated, so I bolted."

"Thank you, Mr. Simon. Now the question surfaces: Who texted Freddy? Who and what would grab Freddie's attention so forcefully that he would end this secret rendezvous so quickly?"

McCall spoke up then. "We traced the number of the last text he got. It led to *nada*."

"As I would have expected," said Shamu. "Mr. Foster!"

His eyebrows flew way up. "Yes?"

"Your company prides itself on the privacy of its apps. But in the case of Fandr, what part do the franchise owners have to play?"

"Now wait a minute!" Hennessey seemed even redder at night. "I don't like where you're going with this."

"Noted. Answer the question, Mr. Foster?"

"The franchise owners are involved in the contract process."

"So Mr. Hennessey knew that Mr. Lopez was on the app. Did he ask you to give him recordings of the interactions?"

I leaned in. "Be honest, and you might wiggle out of an accessory rap."

I can't quite describe what his eyebrows were doing, but it was vigorous.

"Yes! Yes, he did."

"When did he ask for these? What date?"

"Oh, April 15! I remember because of tax day."

"Three days after I refused to find Mr. Lopez for him," Shamu said. "Mr. Hennessey, I have in my possession medical records for players on the San Diego Padres baseball team."

I handed the records to McCall.

"These records show that for the last several years, since Mr.

Hennessey's ascendancy to team owner, there have been two sets of medical records for the players. One for internal use and the other for industry consumption, in an attempt to come out ahead in trades. The latter was remarkable for its omissions and understatements. Mr. Lopez somehow found out about these records; it offended his admirable sense of fair play. If these records were revealed to the public it would cause a great scandal for you, would it not, Mr. Hennessey? Which would further decrease the already lagging ticket sales, hurting your business empire considerably. No doubt, hiding these records made it worth your while to stalk and kill Lopez and then also to shoot Mr. Parker?"

Hennessey looked apoplectic. "I ain't talking to a fish. I want a lawyer. All you got is circumstantial."

"Not merely. A quick check of your hands should find gunpowder residue, regardless of how well you washed them. But, rather more dramatically, you failed to note the amount of security cameras now placed at the marina."

A video suddenly appeared on the gigantic display above the pool, and it showed, briefly but, yes, dramatically, Hennessey running through the Bali Hai parking lot holding a gun.

McCall took him away without so much as a thank you.

To no one's surprise, blue skies ruled over San Diego the next day. I was doing laps with Shamu and it was almost time for her to zone out with her Sims.

"I gave Molly East the discount you told me to," I said. "You know that means your retirement is a little farther off?"

"Her brother's character prompts one to be charitable." Shamu turned and exposed her white belly to the sun. "In any case, it is more important to be honest and fair than to reap profit. I will see my dear ocean soon enough, all in good time. Besides, I signed up for Fandr and have already earned a considerable sum from my devoted fandom. Now, Angie, to my kitties!"

DROWNING

Ann Cleeves

I first met Matthew at a conference. It was one of those events, thrown together quickly when the council finds a bit of cash at the end of the financial year, or a politician needs to show that they're doing something about a social problem that's just hit the headlines. This time, the subject of the moment was the insensitivity with which the law treats adults with learning disabilities. One case had sparked outrage. A middle-aged woman had gone through the whole process of arrest and being held in custody without anyone realizing that she was so severely learning disabled that she had no speech. The officers had thought she was drunk or drugged, or just being difficult. In fact, she was a victim. Not of a violent criminal, but of the system that forced her to sleep on the streets and shoplift for food.

The press got hold of the story and then it was all over social media. She was miraculously assessed and found a place in supported living, but there were recriminations and questions in the House. Hence the conference and my invitation to speak. At the time, I managed services for adults with learning disabilities in North Devon, and I was considered some sort of expert. It was before we developed the Woodyard as an inclusive arts and day center, before the grand plan that changed my life.

Matthew was working for Avon and Somerset Police in Bristol then, but the conference was held in my patch, in a large, white Edwardian hotel on the river in Barnstaple. It was late January, so there were few tourists, and I suppose the authorities got a good deal on the accommodation. It was grey and rainy, and though I had a room at the front, the visibility was so poor that I couldn't see over the bridge to the former timber yard, which would become the place of my dreams.

I'm not sure why Matthew was there. Perhaps his bosses thought he would have a special interest in the subject, as if being gay was some sort of disability. Certainly, Matthew wouldn't have had the confidence to question the decision at that time. He still finds confrontation with his superiors awkward, embarrassing.

Our first session was held in the main lounge, an old-fashioned space full of chintz and polished wood, with pictures of hunting scenes on the wall. There was an open fire and the place was surprisingly comfortable. It was after dinner on the first night, and we were served coffee by the young staff. It had the air of a country house party.

The person in charge of the conference was Felicity, a soft, fleshy woman who reminded me of a rag doll. She had no sharp angles and had a preference for floral print dresses and thick, colored tights. She was an academic in the school for social work in a regional university, and she was passionate about the subject. I grew to like her over the weekend, but at that first meeting, her enthusiasm seemed naïve. I thought the sector needed proper funding, not warm words and imaginative ideas.

Felicity made us pull our chairs into a circle. There were twelve of us, with different backgrounds, from all over the south west. She began her introduction. She said that the solution to the problem of people with learning disabilities becoming lost in the system was better communication between agencies. There had to be a formal structure to provide for that, but informal relationships were important too. There was too little trust between, for example, police officers and social workers, and sometimes that turned into overt hostility. The object of the weekend was to break down those barriers and to understand each other's roles.

I was listening to her words, but my concentration started to lapse when I saw Matthew, sitting opposite to me. You must realize that I had no ambitions then to form a permanent relationship. I liked the irresponsibility of my personal life, the freedom to form friendships, to hook up with whoever took my fancy. My adoptive parents' marriage was tense, joyless, and I wanted none of that. I wanted fun, spontaneity. But there was something about Matthew, even then, which pulled me in. He was lovely, certainly, but I know lots of lovely men. It was his stillness, his restraint, the sense that even sitting in a circle he had built an invisible wall around himself. I suppose I saw that as a challenge, but I admired it too. His self-possession. I wanted him as a friend, even if not a lover. He would be, I could tell even then, totally loyal. Totally dependable.

When he told us that he was a detective, though—Felicity did the thing of making us go round the circle and introduce ourselves—I dropped the idea immediately. I dislike the notion of being told what to do and I'd always considered the police an arm of an authoritarian state.

In the final session of the evening, Felicity split the group into pairs.

"Find a quiet corner, have a drink or a coffee. Get to know each other. Tell your partner something you've never told another person. Let's start building bridges here."

It was all quite predictable, I thought. Later, we'd be asked to do role play, to put ourselves in our partner's shoes. I wouldn't mind that. I've always been something of a performer. Nothing I like better than an audience.

"Jonathan and Matthew, would you like to work together?"

It wasn't a surprise when she paired us up. We were such obvious opposites that it seemed somehow inevitable. Matthew was wearing a suit, and despite the weather, I was in shorts and a sweatshirt. My style has always tended more toward Glastonbury than the office.

"Shall we go to the bar?" I asked. I'd sensed it would be for me to make the first move. He seemed diffident, shy. I'd never known a shy cop before. Did I know he was gay at that point? Oh, I think I did. I just wasn't sure he'd be prepared to tell me he was. He'd be very careful about giving anything of himself away.

"I don't drink much."

"Just a glass of wine." By then, I really needed one.

He nodded. Our colleagues had had the same idea and were in earnest conversations at small tables. I bought a bottle of Malbec—I knew one drink wouldn't be enough—and we took it and a couple of glasses to the first floor, where there was a small sitting area looking out over the river. It was dark by now and the rain was lashing at the tall windows. Our space seemed very intimate, cut off from the rest of the world. We could have been in a boat, or a shack on the beach.

"I once killed someone."

Again, I was the person to speak first. The words came out as soon as we sat down. I think I'd known from the start that this was the tale I'd share.

There was a moment of silence. "I'm sorry?" He apologized a lot, but this wasn't really an apology, more an expression of shock. He'd expected some form of confession, but not this. Not something that might relate to his work.

"That's the thing I've never told anyone," I said.

"You'd better give me the whole story." He sounded quite calm now. He would be, I knew, a very good listener. Focused. He didn't warn me that anything I said might be passed on to his colleagues in the region. He didn't have to. I could tell he would stick to the rules.

"I was sixteen, unhappy." I topped up my glass. His was still three-quarters full. "A bit wild. I was adopted and really, I had nothing in common with my parents. They're hill farmers, grafters, and they expected a boy who'd love dogs and tractors. Instead, they got me..." I looked at Matthew and he nodded to show that he understood, to encourage me to continue. "I mean," I gave a little smile, "there's nothing wrong with dogs and tractors, but I had wider horizons. I wanted to travel. To play music. To have sex with men."

He nodded again. Not shocked this time.

"At weekends I ran away to the coast. There were a bunch of us who'd meet up at Saunton Sands on a Friday afternoon. We'd walk as far as we could be arsed away from the village. Surfing wasn't commercial in the way it is now. We were school kids playing at being part-time beach bums. We'd build fires on the shore, smoke weed, play music. Then roll up in a blanket and sleep under the stars."

There was a moment of silence. "It sounds..." he said, "...uncomfortable." He gave a little smile and I could tell he was mocking himself for being so uptight, so old before his time.

I laughed. Perhaps that was the moment I realized that I might come to love him.

"Go on," he said.

"One night we were joined by a group of boys. They were from a posh public school doing a residential Outward Bound course in a center on Baggy Point and they'd escaped. They were already pissed by the time they got to us. They were my sort of age. Sixteen, seventeen. They all had these voices. Loud. Opinionated. They treated us as yokels. Or more, as an alien tribe, as if we were pygmies or cannibals. There was no aggression between us though. We were chilled. It was our space and they'd have to be back in the center by morning. We let them shout and show off, and we were happy to drink the cider they'd brought with them."

I paused, and for a moment, I was young again, lying on the sand, still warm from the day's sunshine, all the edges blurred by the smoke from the fire and the booze. There were girls in our group and a couple of them started flirting. The school group provided new company. The boys were exciting, different. They had the money and confidence that we lacked. I wanted to tell the girls that these lads weren't worth the effort, but I was too idle. Besides, was it really my business?

"Someone suggested skinny dipping," I said. One of the girls. Lisa. She played guitar and had the sweetest voice. "There was a moon by then. Perfect and round. And the waves came rolling ashore, in those long, lazy lines, breaking white in the moonlight."

Matthew nodded as if he understood. "Saunton's always been my favorite beach."

"You grew up round here?"

He nodded again but volunteered no more information. "Go on."

"We stripped off and ran into the sea. It wasn't such a big deal for us, but the others were inland boys. Their school was somewhere in the Cotswolds. This was a great adventure for them. The girls made a lot of noise, splashing them, giggling. I hated to see it. It was as if the posh boys were celebrities they needed to impress."

"You were jealous?"

"No, not that," I said. "I thought the girls should have more pride. They shouldn't demean themselves."

By now Matthew had emptied his glass and I topped it up. It was still raining. Occasionally a car would drive along the street and the headlight beams were reflected in the rain on the window.

"There was one boy," I said. "He was quieter than the others. Anxious. He'd not had so much to drink. He'd be more like you, a keeper of rules. I thought he regretted being there, that he'd been forced along with them, because he'd not wanted to admit he was scared.

"He was skinny and dark and his name was Angus. Something about you reminds me of him. A wave took him by surprise and knocked him over. He was being dragged under and was gulping water. He wasn't used to the pull of the tide. I got hold of his hand and pulled him to his feet.

"And when a cloud went over the moon and it was dark for a moment, I put an arm around him and led him to the shore.

He was shivering and his skin was cold and I could feel the bone and muscle beneath it. We were a little way from the others and nobody saw.

"The others were still messing about, but we got dry and left them to it. We found a sheltered spot in the dunes and we talked." I looked at Matthew. "You know how intense you can be at that age. We talked about music and poetry and our fucked-up parents. His father was a government minister. A right-wing Tory, who believed the '50s had been a Golden Age. I thought Angus might become the love of my life."

"What happened?"

"His bloody friends happened. We fell asleep, our arms around each other." I looked up at Matthew. "I didn't seduce him. There was nothing like that. We'd shared addresses, phone numbers. We knew something might develop, but it was friendship. Nothing more. Friendship and comfort. Then just as it was getting light his pals found us. We woke to the blanket being pulled back. One of them was taking a photo and then there was the noise of their laughter. It was cruel and hard. They were like the hounds their parents hunted with, baying for blood."

Matthew didn't say anything then. He wasn't a man who wasted words.

"Angus killed himself." I tried to keep my voice even. "It was my fault. If I hadn't taken him into the dunes, if we hadn't slept together, it would never have happened. They'd have been found out, of course, for escaping the center, given a rollicking, but boys will be boys and the teachers would have forgiven that. They'd have admired the adventurous spirit. What really freaked them out was that Angus had been pictured lying almost naked. With a pleb, a farm boy. That the photo was circulating around the school, and his father was going crazy about the lack of supervision. How could Angus deal with all that? The spite and the hate."

"It wasn't your fault." The words came out slow and separate like stones thrown into a river.

"He drowned himself," I said. "He cut his wrists and sat in the bath at his parents' house and slipped under the water."

"You never heard from him again?"

I shook my head. I couldn't speak. This time Matthew poured more wine. His glass was empty too. He put his hand on mine. We sat in the dark, with the rain-like floods of tears on the window.

"I read about it in the paper," I said at last. "The sympathy was for the family. Nobody cared about Angus. But I did. I cared."

"I can tell." Matthew was staring into the darkness. "I'm so sorry."

That was when Felicity found us. We could hear the footsteps of her flat wide shoes on the stairs. I expected Matthew to pull his hand away, but he didn't. A real act of courage.

"All okay up here?" Her voice sounded very normal, a little loud. Perhaps we'd been whispering. "We're just getting together back in the lounge to plan for tomorrow, if you don't mind making your way down." She disappeared again without waiting for an answer.

"I haven't shared my story," Matthew said. He sounded anxious. Even now, he was a little dismayed not to have carried out her instructions to the letter.

"Never mind." I finished the wine in my glass. "There will be plenty of time for that."

"Yes!" There was a note of surprise in his voice. "Yes, I think there will."

"Drowning" was first printed as Waterstones exclusive content in the UK in 2022, and first published in the US in this collection for Bouchercon in 2023.

29 PALMS

Wesley Browne

If there was one thing I hated about being on probation, it was not being able to leave Nevada. If there was a second thing I hated about being on probation, it was falling for a girl in 29 Palms, California and not being able to leave Nevada. Let's be real though. There were way more than two things I hated about probation. Pissing in a cup, pissing in a cup with somebody watching me piss in a cup, supervision fees, home visits, not being able to possess a gun, and on and on, but I digress.

I had three years to kill and I couldn't leave the jurisdiction, so working as a bar back at Whiskey Pete's Hotel and Casino in Primm, Nevada seemed like as good a way to do it as any. I couldn't stay in Vegas because, well, let's just say that the people I got mixed up with that led to me being on probation weren't real excited about the deal I cut to get probated. Not when it led to them doing real time. And the people who weren't real excited about my plea deal had a lot of friends in Vegas who knew what I did, and I was none too excited about running into any of them on the regular.

If you lived in Vegas and were into what I used to be into, there wasn't a lot of reason to go to Primm. So Primm it was. Right on the state line and literally just off I-15. There are only so many jobs you can get in a casino when you're on probation, but bar back is one of them. That's how I met Sienna.

She was working as an apprentice to a dog groomer in 29 Palms and the place was busy. She wasn't making much money and didn't get many days off, so when her friend's bachelorette party came to Primm, she cut loose. So much so that I didn't find out any of this until the next day.

We had a regular named Logan who worked at the women's prison ten miles away in Jean and I'm telling you, he was a fucking creep, but he was a good tipper. When Sienna got to our bar that night, she was slurring so hard she had to point at the cocktail menu to place an order. She kept saying something that was a little hard to make out, but eventually, it became clear: "I lost my friend." She had on a tiny T-shirt that read, *That Bitch's Friend*, which led me to believe a *That Bitch* T-shirt was also somewhere in Primm. Once Logan noticed the state Sienna was in, he was on her like ants on a dropped lollipop. Should Randy—our bartender—have served her? Hell no. But once he knew Logan was buying her drinks, he also knew he'd catch a Benjamin, so he went on with it.

I was crouched down when Logan said, "I'm gonna hit the head real quick, then what say we get out of here?" Sienna didn't say anything because she hardly could. She'd had at least three more after he started buying and she was already verging on incoherence. Logan winked at Randy, "Bill it to my room." Then, standing behind Sienna before he went to the bathroom, he bent both arms at the elbows, made two fists, and executed the international sign for humping her.

I don't know why she pulled at my heart strings, but she seemed so helpless that I couldn't watch what was happening and not at least try to intervene. I got up from where I was stocking pint glasses on a lower shelf and said, "What's your name?"

I thought she said "Sarah" but it was hard to tell.

I said, "Sarah?"

She shook her head exasperated and said, "Sarah," again.

"Sounds like Sarah to me. I'm going with Sarah." She threw her hands up as if to say she didn't really care. I said, "Sarah, do you want to go with that guy? I'm pretty sure he's planning to have sex with you. Is that what you want?"

She shook her head no again but even more emphatically. She mouthed big without actually saying the word "No."

Randy realized what was happening. He came over, took me by the arm and pulled me a few feet away and said real low, "What're you doing, man?"

"Making sure something bad doesn't happen here tonight."

He pointed a bottle of Jack at me with the pour spout on it. "We ain't the fucking morality police. You're fucking with our money. You're fucking with *my* money."

I shrugged. "If there's one thing I've learned lately, no money's worth your soul."

Logan was headed back our way, smirking. There was heat in Randy's voice now. "Speak for yourself. That fool's in here every week splashing money and I've never seen this girl in my life and probably never will again. Consider the consequences."

"That's the thing," I said, "I did."

Logan came up behind Sienna and took her by the arm. "Come on, honey. Let's do this before you pass out."

I stepped up closer and put a hand on her other forearm. "Hold up, Logan. I'm Sarah's ride."

Logan double took. "You're what?"

"Yeah, man. She's my friend. I'm her ride home. She's waiting here for me to get off. I need her to stick around."

He scoffed. "She's your friend? Okay. And you let me buy her drinks and didn't say a fucking word?"

"She likes to party, man. What can I say? Like, it was just drinks. What'd you think you were buying? Something else?"

He still hadn't let go of her arm with his one hand but he stuck a finger in my face and looked at her. "You know this guy?"

Sienna nodded blearily.

"And he's your ride."

She kept nodding.

"And you want to go with him instead of me?"

More nodding.

Logan's jaw rippled and he turned loose of her arm at once. "Fine. Go home with this fucking dipshit." He went into his pocket for a fat roll of cash and peeled off just one dollar bill and smoothed it flat on the bar. "You just lost a regular."

"Aw man, don't say that," Randy pled with him. "It's just a misunderstanding."

Logan huffed out a breath. "Yeah. A misunderstanding." He shoved the rest of the cash back in his pocket then jabbed his finger at me one more time for emphasis. "I won't be back."

I said, "See you around."

Sienna put her head down on the bar and slept until my shift was over. I kept hoping her friend would turn up and take her away but she never did. All she had with her was a tiny wristlet wallet but there was no room key, just her California driver's license, a couple credit cards, five bucks cash, and an obsolete Starbucks rewards card. She had no phone on her. I looked at Randy trying to figure out what to do with her but he was unsympathetic. "You broke it, you bought it."

I managed to ger her just awake enough to walk to my car with a lot of support. I took her back to my one-bedroom apartment at Desert Oasis. It was the only housing in Primm and I was only allowed to live there because I worked at the casino. I was lucky to get it. If I hadn't gotten in there, I would've had to find something in Henderson and that was like forty-five minutes away.

I managed to get Sienna up two flights of stairs and into my apartment. I put her in my unmade double bed and managed to get her wedge heels off. She was snoring before I was back from brushing my teeth. I left the light on in the bathroom. I changed into some sleep clothes, swiped one of the pillows from the bed, took a blanket from the hall closet, and went out to sleep on the couch.

I woke up around five to the sound of her puking in my toilet.

I went in and she had her head in the bowl. "You okay?" I asked her. She gave me a thumbs-up without raising her head and kept puking.

Once she was done, she came out to where I was in the kitchen waiting on a pot of coffee. Sienna was understandably bewildered about how she came to be in my apartment. She said the bachelorette party was actually at Primm Valley Resort and Casino but the bride-to-be had talked her into taking an Uber over to Whiskey Pete's with her and some guy she met, then disappeared. "She probably fucked him."

"So she really is that bitch?"

Sienna shrugged. "Yeah, but the guy she's marrying's kind of an asshole. He cheats on her too. It's so toxic. The wedding should be a good party though."

We wound up going over to the IHOP at Whiskey Pete's to get some food in her stomach and kill time before I drove her back to her hotel to find her friends. Over breakfast she thanked me for what I'd done the night before and I said, "Anybody would have done the same thing," and she said, "No they wouldn't," and I knew she was right but I didn't say so.

She asked me how much I'd charge to drive her home if we couldn't find her friends or her phone. I decided to just go ahead and tell her I was on probation so I couldn't. Honesty—to a point—was part of how I was trying to change. She said, "For what?" and I said, "For making money the wrong way," and she said, "Well, I don't know if you've noticed, but I apparently have a little problem with alcohol, so nobody's perfect."

She had a piece of waffle on the end of her fork. She looked me over. "I need a date for this wedding and I'm not going alone. Why don't you come with me. It's in three weeks."

I eyed her back. She grinned at me before she popped the waffle in her mouth. I said, "Let me ask my PO."

I asked my PO about the wedding but I gave him the wrong date on purpose. I gave him a week too early. He said no. I figured if he said yes, I could tell him later that I got the dates mixed up and change it. Sure enough, he did a home visit on the fake date I gave him. The next weekend, I went to the wedding.

The California state line is basically at the bottom of the on ramp from Primm headed south on 15. I wasn't five minutes from my house before I had violated the terms of my probation. All I passed on 15 aside from desert was solar panels, a golf course, and some kind of agriculture station. If I had stayed on 15, I'd have eventually wound up in Los Angeles.

Instead, I exited and wound up in the Mojave on a series of some of the most desolate side roads I'd ever been on in my life. In over a hundred miles I passed maybe a dozen buildings. The closest thing to a town was a place called Amboy on a stretch of the old Route 66 where the train tracks crossed. Aside from that and a few moonscape-looking dry lakes mined for road de-icer, there wasn't much to speak of until I started seeing Joshua Trees like an army of wraiths in the desert as I neared 29 Palms.

29 Palms wasn't much different than suburbia anywhere else except it came up out of nowhere in the desert and it was attached to a huge marine base. It's funny how development in the desert has a way of looking more like a scar than anywhere else.

Sienna had expressed shock and dismay when I told her I'd never eaten at a Foster's Freeze, so she asked me to meet her there. It wasn't much more than a white and blue block building with a big covered front patio and a swirled ice cream cone man sticking up out of the top of the roof.

Sienna was already on the patio and strolled into the lot with a bemused grin. She didn't kiss me or anything because we weren't really there yet but she did pat my arm. "You made it," she said. Then she started singing "Breaking the Law" by Judas Priest.

Inside, the place smelled like nothing but grease, which I kind of liked. We ordered some burgers but she said we should wait to get ice cream. She wanted to eat outside, which surprised me because it was hot as balls.

She was kind of cheerful but at the same time kind of distracted. I ate my burger fast because I'm a slob like that but she was taking her time. She was only halfway done when she set it down and got all serious. "I need to tell you something."

My first thought was that she was going to say she had a kid. Or kids. These single women with kids always act so weird about it. You'd think they're going to tell you they're a prostitute or something. What she said instead was, "My ex is going to be at the wedding."

"Okay."

"It might get weird."

"What do you mean weird?"

"Just, like, it didn't end well. And Derek's in the military. He's a marine."

I jutted my lower lip. "So, is he gonna want to fight me or something?"

"I didn't say that. He won't fight you. I just—you know how it is. Sometimes things get weird. I didn't want you to be blindsided."

"I can handle weird."

"Good." She put her hands to her chest. "I just didn't want it to be this big thing. So now it's out there." She picked up her burger and took another bite. I started trying to picture this military man who wouldn't want to fight me but who might make things weird. Sienna went on like a weight hand been lifted. She was all smiles when we went back in to get dessert. After we'd had our ice cream, I followed her back to her apartment so we could rest up and get ready for the wedding.

I knew the wedding was going to be outdoors, and since it was in 29 Palms, I knew it would be in the desert. But there's the desert, like Vegas, where it's hot as hell but all concrete and buildings, and then there's the desert. This wedding was in the real ass desert.

We drove to the Indian Cove Amphitheater, six miles southwest of town, with nothing around but cacti, scrub, and rock formations. Sienna had given me the lay of the land both literally and figuratively. There was nothing out there but the amphitheater and a campground. *That bitch* was named Melinda, and Melinda worked at a bank. It turned out that Melinda worked at a bank because her family owned it. But they didn't own just one, they owned a lot. And her family would be in from San Diego for the ceremony. "She lives kind of trashy but she's rich." That meant even though it was going to be a small ceremony, it was a high-dollar affair.

Melinda had reserved the entire campground as well as the amphitheater. They were trucking in luxury RVs for the bridal party and their families, a mobile catering kitchen, bar, tents, air-conditioned bathrooms, you name it.

Sienna drove because I had a couple beers at her place. She had decided to wait to get started as she was hoping to avoid a repeat of Whiskey Pete's, although she did say, "At least whatever happens tonight will be consensual," before laying her first ever kiss on me. I'd be lying if I said that didn't spur a little movement in my Netherlands. I didn't expect any quid pro quo for breaking my probation or rescuing her from Logan, but it was certainly nice to know she was thinking of me.

I've never seen so many Jaguars, Mercedes, and Audis parked in a place without a valet anywhere in my life. Mixed in there were a few other cars comparable to Sienna's Hyundai, but not many. When we got out, I stood in the open door and said, "You weren't kidding, were you?"

Sienna enunciated the phrase, "I was not."

The sun was still up but in the area near the RVs at the campground there were a couple white tents festooned with hanging lights not yet lit. The tables, the bar, everything was draped in white linen. A smiling young woman wearing all white came by in a white golf cart and drove us to the amphitheater.

We arrived at the amphitheater to the sound of a female

string quartet dressed in all white playing a classical song I recognized but couldn't name. The place was surrounded on three
sides by rock formations that were mostly tan with bits of bronze
and black. There was a stage surrounded by benches made of concrete dyed to match the rock. The back sections of benches had
been cordoned off so that the fifty or so guests were all collected in
the first few rows. I'm not one to be easily impressed, but even I
had to concede, the place was striking.

You know how you can tell people who have money by their
clothes even when they aren't real dressed up? Everyone in attend-
ance was kind of casual but there were all these linen shirts and lin-
en pants that screamed expensive, and the dresses were much the
same. The only tuxes were the white ones worn by the groom and a
couple groomsmen who were seated on the stage. Some kind of
minister dressed in a white robe was up front near them. I was beginning to feel like I'd walked into a boy band video.

Then I saw this guy on one of the benches in regular old kha-
kis and a polo with running shoes whose hair was high and tight.
He held my eyes just long enough to let me know he was looking
before he looked away. Sienna had taken my hand after we got
out of the golf cart and I leaned and whispered, "I found Derek."

She looked his way. "Yes, you did." She squeezed my hand a
little tighter and pulled a little closer.

That handsome sonofabitch had a jaw like a granite slab and
the woman next to him was maybe no prettier than Sienna but
in a different sort of way. Sienna had a not immodest girl-next-
door way about her that may have had something to do with
why I had worried about her back at Whiskey Pete's—although
I'd like to think I would've intervened for anyone. Derek's date
looked more like one of the showgirls I sometimes rubbed elbows with doing my old job in Vegas. We chose seats as far
away as we could in the last open row.

Folks sat chatting. A bird flew loops up above us. The strings
kept playing and the hum of an engine grew closer from a distance. Sienna would gaze around and then I would notice her

eyes had landed on Derek. Then she would look away again.

I started checking out watches. The thing about watches anymore is you don't really have to wear one because everyone's phone is basically a pocket watch. So if you do wear one it's more of a fashion statement than anything else. It might as well be a bracelet. These bastards had some nice bracelets. I saw two Patek Phillipes that I knew for a fact were mid six-figures just from my seat. And then there was the actual jewelry. I could typically tell real from fake, and the rocks on the rings and necklaces and earrings all around us were not costume items. I'd seen countless pieces in Vegas, I had acquired them, but I couldn't ever remember seeing so much out in the wild like that.

I checked the time on one of the watches situated near me, and it was past half past the hour, which is when you start weddings because of something about the upswing is good luck or some shit. This thing was supposed to have started. The strings would stop and kind of look around, then play something else. The engine I'd heard earlier had drawn close and then stopped. I heard some voices rise over near the parking lot and campground. That was my first inkling that something was up.

A four-seat UTV came roaring up the path to the amphitheater with three men aboard dressed in regular clothes but with their heads covered in black balaclavas, and they had the bride in the back. The string music came to an abrupt halt. The one in the front passenger seat had an assault rifle hanging out pointed at the sky. "Nobody move! Nobody move! Phones away! Phones away!" Shock ran through the crowd. My heart rate ticked up a beat and I got a little shot of adrenaline, but it was nothing I hadn't felt before.

Sienna buried herself in my side. "Terrorists," she said.

I held her hard and said, "No. If these were terrorists, people would already be dead. We're just getting robbed."

"Oh my god."

Coming down the path behind the UTV were all the caterers, the bartender, the rest of the bridal party, and a disarmed US

Park Ranger. There was another man behind them carrying an assault rifle with his face obscured. He was also dressed like a caterer except for the balaclava, so I gathered that he had embedded with the wedding staff, which is just how I would have done it. He prodded that group to the stage with the groomsmen, the minister, and the musicians.

The three men from the UTV got out, two with assault rifles and another with a big olive-colored canvas bag. They directed the bride to the stage with everyone else. One of the men wore a dark green, long-sleeved compression shirt and he was the one doing all the talking. "I want to start by saying, everybody just stay calm. We don't want to hurt anyone, so please, don't touch your phones. Just leave them be. If you have a gun, drop it now. You're hopelessly outgunned. We're here for your wallets, and your purses, and your jewelry, and your watches. We're going to take your phones and your car keys too, but we'll leave them behind, so you'll get those back. You folks will be able to go on and have your wedding. Food's hot, drinks are cold."

I scanned the crowd and one man in the back reached behind him, withdrew a handgun, and tossed it away. The man in green said, "Thank you, sir," as one of his colleagues went and picked it up.

"Derek has two," Sienna whispered. "He always carries two."

I watched him hoping he'd give them up. His shoulders were tensed, his feet were flexed and bouncing. He didn't give up anything. I said, "Shit."

This kind of robbery, it has almost no real consequences. The people who get robbed have money to spare and then some, and they're insured anyway. There's no good reason to put up a fight, but then there are some people who just can't help themselves. That's when these deals go bad.

Two of the men walked through the crowd, one with a rifle and another carrying the bag. Sienna and I gave up what we had easily. We didn't have what they were after. People were frightened but compliant. They emptied their pockets, stripped their wrists, necks, and ears. I added in my head. These people had come to the desert with seven figures in baubles under the security of a single park ranger. Even fenced this score would stay up in the sevens. I was in awe but also nagged by fear of what Derek would do. It ratcheted up the closer they got to him.

The nearer they crept to Derek, the more obvious it became that he was going to make a move, and I kept hoping this crew would read his body language and profile that haircut before they got there. Because they weren't looking for a confrontation, they were looking for a score. The last thing they wanted was a shootout.

This crew had some blind spots because nobody picked up on the obvious. Sure enough, as the man with the bag held it out to Derek's date, Derek came up from his ankle with a handgun, spun the bagman and had his arm around his neck and the gun to his head, and shouted, "Drop the guns!"

The man with the bagman looked unsure. He lowered his rifle. All of the gunmen looked unsure except one. The guy in the green shirt raised his rifle and was sighting Derek in.

Derek shouted again, "Drop 'em or this guy's dead! Somebody get a phone and call the cops."

He made two critical mistakes at the same time. First, he assumed that anyone else in the crew truly cared about the life of the man he held. Chances were, they didn't. Second, he tried to keep an eye on every one of the gunmen, so he was shifting, and he eventually hung his head out and gave the one in the green shirt a clean shot at it, and Derek's head exploded just like that. The blast reverberated against the rocks.

The man with the bag who Derek was threatening to shoot stumbled backward as Derek dropped. Everything around him was splashed in red. I was surprised he had the presence of mind to pick up Derek's gun. The small crowd was in hysterics. The man with the green shirt who fired the shot said, "Goddamn it, let's go." This was a bad outcome for everyone. Then, it somehow got worse.

Before I could do anything, Sienna was up and running down the amphitheater and headed for the man in green, screaming. As she approached, her arm drawn, he pivoted, and drove the stock of his gun into her chin, and she was down and out and bleeding, and now I was pissed. Fire ran from my heels to my crown in an instant. He could've rag-dolled her all day. He didn't have to do what he did. All that said, I was self-possessed enough not to act immediately.

The four gunmen scrambled to the UTV, crammed in, and sped away without looking back. As quickly as they did, I was up and ran to Derek's body. There was another gun on him, and as I suspected, it was at his waist. I got it and was gone with a bunch of rich guys shouting at my back that I was going to get us all killed.

I understood two things they didn't. First, those guys didn't want to kill anybody, and they definitely didn't want to kill anyone else. Derek had forced their hand. Nothing I did would bring those guys back to the wedding. Second, they had to ditch those phones, because keeping them was like taking trackers along. They should've made us power them down but maybe they wanted them out of our hands faster, I don't know. They also should've put them in a separate bag. Either way, I wasn't counting on them taking the time to sort them out before they went very far because taking them even a mile was a bread-crumb to their whereabouts.

I sprinted through the scrub and brushed hard against some needles I'd feel later. Once I cleared the rocks, I found what I hoped to see. The UTV was stopped and two of the men were out. The bloodied bagman held it open and green shirt was fling-ing our phones. At thirty yards, I went to a knee with a little cov-er from a Joshua tree. I took a moment to control my breathing. I would get one shot. I only needed one shot. I drew a bead on the center mass of the lousy bastard who knocked out my girl.

I fired my shot and immediately was up and blazing my way

toward the campground. I saw the body go down out of my peripheral vision. It was a good five seconds before anyone returned fire, but by the time they did, I was lost among the RVs. The echo of their shots had scarcely faded before I heard the whine of the UTV speeding away.

Once I was sure they were gone, I approached. It was immediately clear they'd left green shirt behind. I was wary of him, but as I drew closer, I confirmed I had landed a chest shot. His rifle and his life were both gone. I had an impulse to raise his mask but it was a dumb one and I didn't do it.

After I'd gathered what there was to see, I wanted to go back and check on Sienna. I'm not saying I loved her just yet, but I felt something. I also felt something else.

Among the discarded phones I spotted an Alfa Romeo key fob. I picked it up, pressed it, heard a chirp, and saw a flash. I pulled my shirt over my head and held it over my hands so I wouldn't leave prints in the car. I'd park it a few blocks from Sienna's, get my car, and head home.

I just had to hope Sienna would forgive me. Because I knew for sure that my PO wouldn't.

PRESIDENT-ELECT

Désirée Zamorano

Gloria stood with a cluster of her colleagues, her peers, even, some new friends, a glass of wine in her hand. The Educational Leaders of California conference in San Diego was always a pleasure. She had met Ana Arreola, a leader of great classroom innovations on a statewide level, and Belen Escobedo, the famed San Diego superintendent whose community-building steps she had long admired. She had felt, like so many others, defeated by the challenges of the past few years, but the faces of her friendly, energetic, and motivated peers filled her with enthusiasm and optimism. Maybe there were some things they could get done, maybe they could even get a few of them done right. After all, she was the president-elect of ELC.

Gloria noticed a young woman with an unusual expression on her face—a cross between star-struck and hunger—hovering at the edges of her group's conversation. Unlike the rest of the convention attendees, she was not wearing her name tag. Gloria leaned across the conversation and said to her, "I'm Gloria Herrera. Introduce yourself, we won't bite!"

The young woman blinked rapidly, then fled.

"She's got your number," ribbed her friend, Patti. "Two minutes with you and she'd be on a committee!" Patti was a few years older than Gloria, a few shades lighter. She, like Gloria, carried the presence of a professional woman who'd raged a few battles.

Gloria said, "Quiet Latinas are the ones that worry me the most."

"Personally, I don't trust them," Patti said, pointedly. "When we first met here, nearly fifteen years ago, I couldn't get you to say two words!"

Patti worked in the Lennox school district at the time, and Gloria, in San Bernardino. They clicked as friends—young, ambitious, idealistic. As colleagues, they shared war stories and strategies. Neither of them would be where they were in their career without the other: Gloria, vice superintendent at Fresno, and Patti, superintendent in Ventura. Idealism and ambition still burned, tempered by pragmatism.

Gloria made a face at her. "I've grown out of that. Some of them, I swear they've had their personality beaten out of them."

"Even better reason for me to dislike them," Patti teased.

Gloria scowled at her friend. "We can do a lot of good, we two," Gloria said. "If she meets her people, she can, too. Maybe we can help her find her voice." This organization had helped her so much. Once she had president of ELC on her resume, she would be the strongest candidate for Fresno's next superintendent.

The social hour moved into the Thursday night dinner, with speakers and speeches. As the tired attendees disbursed, Gloria spotted the young woman near the fireplace, staring into the fire, ignoring the rush of guests that passed her.

Gloria felt a twinge. She pointed her out to Patti, who shrugged, shook her head.

"I'll leave her to you. I'm beat."

Gloria settled into the couch across from the girl who stared into the fire.

"These events can be so overwhelming!" Gloria said. "I remember the first one I attended. I didn't know what to do, where to go, or, when I saw someone I wanted to talk to, even what to say."

The young woman turned from the fire and faced her. She had dark hair to her chin that was cut choppily at the ends, dark-framed glasses, brown freckles on pale skin. "I'm sorry, were you talking to me?"

"Yes? The fire looked so inviting I thought I would join you. What's your name?"

"Maribel," she said.

Gloria nodded encouragingly, but there was no surname forthcoming. "How is your conference so far?"

"Oh," Maribel said, smiling, "it's been amazing!"

Pleased, Gloria said, "I'll be sure to let the planning committee know. Of course, you can always let them know at the end—in the survey. What district are you from?"

"Lassen," she said.

Gloria said, "I don't think I know anyone from Lassen. You all are so far north you rarely make it down to the Central Valley."

Maribel said, "That's where I grew up. Right now, I live in Sacramento. I'm a state intern. Educational policy."

"That's wonderful, Maribel. I look forward to seeing you tomorrow, now I must go to my room, I am positively fading."

They exchanged good nights.

Gloria woke a few hours before the panels began, opened her laptop to check her email, then dressed for her brisk walk.

She relished her walk swiftly through the cool September air of the sea, the San Diego skyline ahead of her all inspiring and delightful. The gulls swooped, young mothers or nannies pushed their babies ahead of them; other morning walkers or joggers trotted past and exchanged greetings.

Other conference attendees also were out, taking advantage of the San Diego climate. Patti swam in the hotel pool each morning, which made Gloria shiver to even consider it. The current president of ELC cycled past her, smiling and bobbing his head.

A glorious morning, a wonderful morning! A dramatic change of scenery from her Fresno office.

She passed the Portuguese fisherman statue, made the tour of the peninsula in twenty minutes, then walked past the boat repair shops, the restaurants closed until happy hour or dinner. A few blocks later and she sat at a slightly grubby plastic table and inhaled the chile verde, beans, and rice. This was heaven.

Back in her room, she showered and dressed for the day ahead. She prepared herself for the presentation on cross-cultural intentional collaboration she would be leading that afternoon.

The hotel was set at the far end of the peninsula, with a parking lot on the street side, and a small sandy beach facing the boats. On the beach was a swing set. From Gloria's room she could see the tiny beach, the hotel, the pool, and the inland hill of Point Loma. She sat on the balcony to enjoy the view (a conference perk of the president-elect, and a large double queen with a view room!) before applying that last bit of lipstick.

Was that Maribel on the swing?

The girl on the swing swayed slowly from side to side.

Was she wearing the same clothes as last night? Gloria couldn't tell, couldn't remember.

Down the steps she went.

"Maribel?" Yes, it was her, the same wan, freckled face turned toward her.

"Are you all right?" It was with a pang that Gloria noticed she was a bit grubby. This was not the way to present yourself at a professional conference. Gloria herself was always protesting the poor portrayals of Mexican Americans in media, and Latinas in general. Maribel needed to realize she was a face of a maligned demographic and wake up and prove them wrong!

"What's going on?" Gloria asked, modulating her voice to a tone of tenderness to mask the ferocity that had just been triggered.

Maribel shook her head. "They lost my conference registration. That's why I didn't have a name tag last night. I can't afford to pay it again, so." She looked up at Gloria then glumly away. "This was a bad idea," Maribel muttered.

This pained Gloria. It was, like Patti, the quiet, demur, doormat Latinas that always vexed her. As if they had been bred to be abused and crushed by life. But what was the point of being president-elect of ELC if you couldn't exert your influence in a positive way? "No," Gloria said. "No. We can sort this out. Come with me."

Gloria led Maribel to the registration table. Patti sat schmoozing with Alan, a stalwart who could run the conference on his own, blindfolded, if he had to. He had backed the other ELC candidate, working their colleagues behind the scenes, but Gloria smiled at him, confident in the knowledge she had won, despite him.

"Hey, your presentation's up soon," Patti said.

"Yes, I know," Gloria said, always amused by her friend's gentle nagging. "Look, Alan, Maribel here—what's your last name, dear?"

"Soto," Maribel nearly whispered.

"Maribel Soto is out of funds to attend the conference. I know we had a couple of scholarship registrations."

Alan, with dark hair brushed back, wire-rimmed glasses, and a tweed jacket over a casually unbuttoned shirt, barely glanced at Gloria and smiled at Maribel. He asked, "Are you a student? Graduate student, intern?"

Maribel mumbled, "Graduate intern at Chico State."

Irritated by her awkwardness, Gloria wondered how this girl would ever survive a classroom, much less her master's program. "Alan," Gloria said, "we got any of those left?"

Alan tapped on his screen, looked up at Maribel with a smile. "As a matter of fact, we do. We'll have your name tag printed out in a jiffy. I can even throw in a few drink tickets, for the first-timer." He winked.

Oh God, Gloria groaned. This old-timer wasn't going to hit on Maribel, was he? She'd have to have a talk with her.

Maribel's expression had changed from dull worry to dull enthusiasm. But her clothing was still a mess.

Alan disappeared, then returned with a lanyard and name-tag. "All the meal and drink tickets are included."

Gloria nodded, then steered Maribel by the elbow. "Look, you may want to freshen up a bit." At the counter, she asked the clerk for another room key. "Go ahead and use my room. I don't know where you're staying."

Maribel appeared frozen.

She peered at Maribel. "Do you have a room?"

Maribel shook her head.

Gloria considered. Then, "Please stay with me. I've got an entire queen bed I haven't touched." Gloria paused. There was no tactful way of doing this. She said, "Do me a favor, buy some clean clothes, will you? Just charge it to the room. Keep it under—" What was reasonable? "Two hundred dollars. You can get a couple of tops or a dress or something that suits you. Does that work?"

"Are you sure?" Maribel said. Not exactly gushing, but not as flat as before either. It was hard to gauge this girl. Was Gloria hoping for some kind of burst of approval and appreciation?

"Yes, I'm sure. People helped me along my way. I hope one day in the future you will do the same."

She had little time to dwell on that before her presentation. She had tested her laptop previously to ensure the technology was seamless. The PowerPoint of images went spectacularly well, as she was accustomed to. She enjoyed answering questions, sparking debate, dissent, and the occasional joke. It wasn't until she sat and sipped her iced tea at her reserved seat in the conference room that she wondered what had gotten into her with this odd duck Maribel, with her *sangre de leche*, as her mother referred to flatliners. What bizarre maternal instincts had kicked in? As if she were some kind of daughter figure. If she were her daughter—well, if she were her daughter, Gloria would have had a very different life, now, wouldn't she?

On the other hand, she had done this before. Part of her instincts, first as a teacher, then as a principal, and now, as a vice superintendent, was to of course build a community, not just a team. And in doing so, you had to include the outsiders until they became part of the community. Not only that, Gloria, nibbled on her roll as she waited impatiently for the lifeless salad to be cleared, but the ones that you considered an "outsider" always had something to teach you.

Patti sat down on the chair Gloria had reserved for her.

Gloria asked Patti, "Is Alan still annoyed with me for winning?"

Patti said, "I don't think so, but if he is, fuck him." She adjusted her chair noisily. "So, what is up with you with that girl?"

"What do you mean?"

"Why are you going all Mary Poppins on her?"

Gloria considered. She fortified her refreshed iced tea with more Splenda. "Because I can? Look, we've both mentored people—this one looks completely lost."

"Mmmhhhmm." Patti used half the butter on her roll. "That's what I mean. Either there's nothing going on or they're hiding what's going on—I'm always super suspicious about the quiet ones."

Gloria pointed. "Look." There was Maribel, in a clean and becoming outfit, a sleek turquoise blouse over gray slacks that made her look competent and professional. She sat at a table of young people, and appeared, Gloria scrutinized to be sure, happy. "That's why." Maybe Maribel would fall in with a group of people that would help her with her career, if that was what she wanted. And if not, it wasn't that big an investment, that large a loss.

Indeed, Gloria, despite sharing her room with the girl, rarely saw her. She saw a dirty backpack on the second queen bed, toiletries in the bathroom, and then, late at night, her quiet steps into bed, followed by her even breathing. By morning she was gone.

Admittedly, she hadn't done it for praise, but it would be nice to thanked. It would be civilized.

She supposed that, too, was a social skill she'd have to teach directly to this young lady. She shook her head in annoyance at both Maribel and herself. This was silly. Why had she taken this project on? To be gushed over? To be admired? To be appreciated? That had certainly failed. It hardly mattered; she'd be out tomorrow afternoon and it would all be in the past.

Saturday night was the poster session, Sunday morning the awards brunch. Gloria had already verified she'd have a late, leisurely checkout before her flight to Fresno Sunday evening.

Most of the conference attendees showed up at the poster session, enjoying the complimentary drinks and snacks. Gloria milled around, glass in hand, peering at presentations titled "Promoting Social Justice in Anti-racism Education in Policy Through a Statewide Integrated Alliance," and "Using a Disability Studies Lens to Examine Teacher Perspectives for On-the-Spectrum Students" and "Having the Courage to Advocate for Equity." She recognized so many people and loved introducing herself to new faces. She was, after all, president-elect, and if she could harness all the energy these people brought, what good things they could all achieve, together.

She clocked Maribel, whom she spied deep in conversation with Alan. Well, she was a consenting adult. The girl wore black pants and a silky cream blouse tucked at the front, as was the current fashion. Looked flattering on her. Gloria waved. Maribel turned away.

Now Gloria was annoyed, but she batted it aside. She'd have to have a few words with that one.

Patti came up to her. "We still gonna do poster sessions when you're the prez?"

"Why wouldn't we?"

"Do you think anyone ever reads the damn posters?"

Gloria snorted. "You are such a cynic."

"It helps me thrive and survive," she said.

Over dinner at their favorite Italian restaurant in Point Loma, Gloria confessed to Patti that she felt a bit stupid. "I mean, the girl hasn't said two words to me!"

Patti inhaled her ziti. "What'd you expect, Pygmalion?"

"Some sort of appreciation, I guess?"

"An engraved plaque commemorating it?"

"Maybe?" Gloria laughed at her outsized expectations.

That night they joined other friends on another balcony, sharing glasses of wine until Gloria was too tired to continue.

This time when she entered her room, Maribel was a lump on her bed, covered in blankets and pillows. Gloria didn't even try to move quietly. It was her damn room, after all!

She removed her makeup, brushed her teeth, decided on her wardrobe for the morning awards ceremony. She had some remarks she'd already prepared for the formal introduction as ELC's next president.

Maribel's breathing was even. Gloria spotted a new and pristine leather backpack, as well as a flashy jacket slung over a chair. Nice, she thought. Then she was filled with misgivings and irritation, the source of which was Maribel, of course, but she was too fuzzy headed to sort out the reason for this sudden intensity.

The next morning the squalling of gulls burst through her sleep and headache and woke her. Ugh, hungover, she couldn't drink like she used to! She checked the time; she had a couple of hours. Plenty of time to take a walk, shake it off, ready herself.

Maribel was already up and out.

Fine, those "words" would have to wait until later.

Gloria was headed for her quick jaunt around the peninsula when Alan spotted her in the lobby. He looked shaken, as he signaled her.

"Gloria. Gloria. I don't understand. Who are you?"

"What, what do you mean?"

They stood near the hotel's fireplace, which appeared to burn twenty-four seven whether it was sixty degrees or ninety degrees.

"Maribel told me what happened."

Gloria was confused. "What happened?" Alan glared at her with such intensity she was taken aback. "What are you talking about?"

"You roofied her," he said. "You assaulted her. She told me

how bruised and tender she is in certain spots." He made a face, then returned his glare to her. "How could you? Who are you?"

All of the blood drained to Gloria's feet. She stumbled into a seat. The lobby disappeared. All that remained were Alan's glare and the implications of his words. What had Shakespeare said, steal my purse but not my good name? That quote swirled sickeningly in her head, along with the phrase, "you can't prove a negative."

"Alan, I promise you—"

"I've already contacted the board. We're announcing your withdrawal. Don't be at the awards ceremony," he continued as he walked away. "We can do this quietly, Gloria, or we can go full volume."

Every part of her body shook. People she recognized wandered past, she wanted to shrink, she wanted to be invisible, she stared at the fire, willing people away, until the lobby was relatively empty. She approached the counter to check out. She'd go back to her room to regroup.

She didn't even know what a roofie looked like.

The clerk handed her the bill.

"There must be some mistake," she said.

The clerk reexamined the bill. "No, these charges were billed to your room—$1346 at our apparel store, $236 at the bar and restaurant."

Gloria had no words. She signed the invoice. She stumbled to her room. If Maribel were there...

Maribel was not there. Nor were any of her things, the new clothes, the chic backpack.

As she processed the now-emptied room, her phone blew up with texts.

Stepping down? Why???

WTF?!?!

What happened?

And from Patti, *Where r u?*

Clearly, the board had already made the announcement. She

lay across her unmade bed. Every cell in her body felt sick. She had been hungry, and now she felt nauseated. She retched uselessly into the toilet. All the plans she had had, the goals for superintendent, the changes she had hoped to make in Fresno Unified. Would she even have a job when she got back home?

There was a knock at the door. She ignored it.

Another knock.

"It's me!" came Patti's familiar voice. Was she there to scold her? To turn on her? To interrogate her?

The knocking turned into pounding. "Let me in, Gloria. I know you. You're my friend."

Gloria did not want to move. She wanted to seep through the floor, disappear, and miraculously reappear in Fresno where this was all a bad dream. Patti continued to pound. Might as well get the worst over. If Patti now hated her, everything was over.

"I'm coming."

She opened the door. Patti stood there, her blue eyes soft and understanding, her arms spread wide for a hug. Gloria pulled her in, closed the door, and hugged her back. Then she began to sob.

"I got you," Patti said, gently patting her back. Gloria sobbed as she recounted her meeting with Alan, the hotel bill. "That bitch," Patti said.

"What am I going to do?" Gloria sat down on the bed and covered her face with her hands.

Patti took a deep breath. "Right now, you're going to pack up and go home. You and I are still friends, this accusation never happened. But you can bet your ass I'm gonna find you a defamation attorney, and, depending on what they say, we can sue for defamation, reinstatement, or assassination of character."

Gloria looked at her, impressed. "Are you making this up as you go along?"

"Of course," Patti said. Gloria laughed. "We need to get you through now, today, and home safe and sound, and then we'll sort out your next steps."

Each part of her still shook, but with less intensity. She could breathe. She'd sort this out, with Patti's help, somehow. She inhaled and exhaled. She began to pack up her things. She examined the burgundy Tahari suit she had planned on wearing today, then laid it across her open carry-on.

"I should get a gold star," Gloria said.

Patti looked up from her phone. "What? Why?"

"I just realized I really did 'help her find her voice.' Jesus."

"I told you," Patti said, looking back at her phone. "Never trust the quiet ones."

CASUALTIES OF WAR
James Thorpe

San Diego, 1944

I woke up as the train lurched, shunting onto a new siding, slowing as we neared the city limits. My headache was gone. But I didn't kid myself. That sneaky son of a bitch would be back. It was only playing possum, waiting for its next chance to pounce from the shadows and snatch my brain in its talons.

But for now, at least, I felt good. Free. Outside my window, Mission Bay rolled by, and just beyond, cloudless sunlight forged the ocean into a sea of diamonds. A far cry from the cold, gray Atlantic that had always found a way to seep into my boots, soaking my pant legs, turning my uniform into a damp, freezing, khaki shroud.

The kid beside me roused. He blinked blearily at the glare of the ocean.

"Coming home, Ensign?" I asked.

He rubbed the sleep from his eyes. "Yes, sir. Got a four-day furlough from Fort Cronkhite." That was a training and defense camp up north in the Bay area. Right on the coast in case the Japanese tried another Pearl Harbor here on the mainland. Cronkhite was a cushy posting. That explained why his uniform still looked brand new. Whereas mine bore the scrapes and scuffs of a more harrowing history. With that one stubborn bloodstain on my jacket that would not come out, no matter how hard I scrubbed. The blood had dulled to a faded rust brown you couldn't really see unless you looked for it. But I knew it was there.

He asked, "How long were you over for, Sergeant?"

"'Bout a year."

"I'm shipping out next week. Finally." I heard the eagerness in his voice. Like a horse pawing the ground at the starting gate. I'd met guys like him before. Barely eighteen, already trained to kill, eager to do their part. In fact, I used to be one of them myself. Too young and too stupid to know the newsreel battle scenes were a load of malarkey. All Hollywood. Not what really happened... in the fields, the trenches... all the sights and sounds that, like the bloodstain, you could never erase.

But I didn't tell him any of that. He wouldn't have believed me anyway. So I just said, "Good for you."

The rest of the soldiers in the car began to stir. Eager to avoid the mad rush, I stood. "Enjoy your furlough and stay safe over there." I headed down the aisle for the rear door. A couple of servicemen were already there waiting, ready to be the first off. The sailor, a seaman first class, had one arm in a sling. With his free hand, he ran a comb through his hair, checking his reflection in the window. Not much point, really, with just a crew cut, but he was probably getting ready to meet his girl.

I recognized the other guy, a marine. "Didn't I see you get on in San Francisco?"

He grinned at me. "I'm going to kill you."

The train wheels squealed as we banked into a turn.

I blinked. What the...? "Come again," I said.

He nodded. "Yeah, wish I'd had time to ride one of those cable cars. Man, the hills in that town."

Okay. False alarm. It was hard to hear over the grinding wheels.

He said, "But I bought a few postcards to write while I'm laid up."

The guy looked intact, but then again, so did I. Since he wasn't from my car, he must have come from the one behind—the ward car, complete with doctor and nurse on duty. That's where the real wounded were.

"You headed to the Naval Hospital, too?" I asked.

In answer, he lifted his trouser cuff to reveal a wooden leg. He knocked on his thigh. It sounded hollow. "Delayed land mine."

"Damn."

"Coulda been worse, I guess. This hunk of kindling's just temporary. The docs are gonna fit me with a custom job. I was hoping for a fancy aluminum model, but with the scrap drive, probably not."

The sailor at the window elbowed him in the ribs. "Better stay away from woodpeckers."

The marine laughed, but I don't think his heart was in it. He stepped closer to me. "You weren't with us in the ward car. What's your deal?"

I pointed to my head. "One concussion too many. I get these headaches sometimes, vision goes blurry. I tell them it's getting better but they want to run some tests."

"Better safe than sorry." He glanced out the window as we pulled into San Diego Union Station.

"Somebody meeting you?" I asked.

"Nah. Folks are in Chicago. And I haven't told my girl I'm back yet." He knocked on his leg again. "She don't know about this."

That was rough. How does a guy tell his fiancée he left his leg six thousand miles away in a country he'll never see again?

"Are you two serious?"

"Engaged. Said we'd get married when I got back." He chewed on his lower lip, suddenly looked ten years younger. "Now, I dunno."

"It'll be okay." What the hell could I say? "She loves you, right? It'll be okay."

He gave me his best shot at a cocky grin, but I could see the fear behind his eyes. "Hope you're right."

I hoped I was, too. For him, and the couple hundred other

poor bastards in the hospital cars on this train. Guys like Duke, after he got Humpty-Dumptyed by that five-pound chunk of shrapnel. No amount of plastic surgery is ever going to put him back together again. Or Sammy, who lost both hands thanks to a bum grenade. I guess he can go back to selling real estate, as long as people don't mind buying a house from a guy with hooks for hands. Hell, if they take pity on him, he might even sell more.

Most of the boys on board were headed for Naval Hospital San Diego. And most of them dreading the day their wife, or children, or parents came to visit. The telegrams would have spared the gory details. And sure, the visitors will try to be brave and hide the shock when they first see their beloved husband, or father, or son with half his face blown off. But they won't be fooling anybody. Sometimes I think the families we leave behind are the real casualties of the war.

Sailor Boy had gone back to combing his crew cut in the window. I changed the subject. "You ever been to San Diego before?"

The marine leaned into me and whispered, "You're dead meat, you fucking piece of shit."

My hand shot out, grabbed him by the collar. "What did you say?"

His eyes bulged. "What!? I just said—no, this is my first time."

Sailor Boy wedged his good arm between us. "Ixnay." He jerked his thumb toward the window. "MPs are on the platform."

I let go of the marine's collar. Sweat popped on his forehead. He took a couple of steps back, shifting his weight to his good leg, bracing for a fight if he had to. "Jesus, man... what the hell's wrong with you?"

My face burned hot. My ears pounded. "Shit, sorry. I'm sorry. I thought—" What did I think? I glanced at Sailor Boy, didn't seem like he'd heard anything strange. Was I cracking up? Had those headaches done something to my brain?

I tried to smile. "I don't know what I thought. Guess I could use some rest after all."

Outside, a station conductor opened the door, dropped the steps down. The marine watched me warily, afraid of another explosion. Like that delayed-action land mine that had already altered the course of his life forever.

Sailor Boy bounced down the steps onto the platform and into the eager arms of a young redhead who burst into tears at the sight of his busted wing.

The marine still hadn't taken his eyes off me. With a curt, "Best of luck," he grasped the handrail and hobbled down the steps, dragging his wooden leg with him, a stiff and alien hitchhiker.

The crush of eager bodies behind me and cries of "Gangway!" and "Get the lead out!" launched me onto the platform. I looked around for the marine. Maybe I should apologize again, offer to buy him a drink or something. But he was already lost in a sea of laughing, crying, kissing.

Somewhere in the back of my head, a tiny pinpoint of pain flared to life. Like a light blooming at the far end of a dark tunnel. Getting brighter. Moving closer. Goddamnit. That son of a bitch was back.

"Good morning, sleepyhead."

I looked up into the prettiest pair of jade-green eyes I'd ever seen. For a moment, I couldn't figure out where I was. She must've seen my confusion. "You're at Naval Hospital San Diego, remember? You came in yesterday afternoon."

The name tag on her nurse's uniform read: Linda.

I said, "I don't remember you."

She smiled. "They moved you to a different ward. Smaller, less commotion." She checked my chart on her clipboard. "You were a little agitated when they brought you in. Bad headache. So they gave you something to help you sleep. How do you feel now?"

I did a quick inventory. I felt a little dopey, but no pain. The bastard had retreated again. "Better." My stomach growled. "A little hungry, I guess."

"I shouldn't wonder. Let's get you sitting up, and I'll fetch your tray." She helped scooch me up in bed, stuck an extra pillow behind my back. Leaning over me, she smelled like jasmine blossoms. And Ivory soap. She wore a silver, heart-shaped locket around her neck, and I saw a thin gold wedding ring on her left hand. "After breakfast, you can shower and shave. You'll feel a hundred percent better."

"Thanks, Linda." I noticed a screened divider separating the room in half.

"Oh, I almost forgot." She hurried around my bed, pushed back the divider.

The only other bed in the room was occupied by the marine from the train. He waved. "Surprise."

Linda beamed. "Isn't it nice to see a familiar face when you wake up?"

The marine said, "Can you believe we lucked out getting this private room? And the prettiest nurse in the hospital."

Linda blushed. "Happily married nurse." She turned to me. "I'll get your breakfast tray while you two catch up." She headed out, leaving a jasmine-scented trail in her wake.

The marine let out with a low whistle. "Even smells as pretty as she looks."

I felt like an asshole. Embarrassed. "Look—"

"Forget it." He swung his wooden leg out of bed, and the rest of his body followed. He wore a hospital gown, just like me. His shoeless wooden foot clomped across the tiled floor as he made his way over.

I said, "But I want to apologize... back on the train—"

He shrugged. "No hard feelings." He offered his hand. "The name's Harry."

I shook it. "I'm Ben."

"So, Ben, feeling better?"

"Yeah, thank God. Never had a spell like that before. I don't know what happened."

"Forget it. We're all here to get help. Scuttlebutt is, the sawbones in this joint are a class act. Only the best for Uncle Sam's boys." He lifted the hem of his gown, showed me his new leg strapped to a stump of flesh mid-thigh. "Brand-new model." Harry might have been talking about his new car. But he wasn't. "It's still just wood. But if that aluminum they saved builds the B-17 that bombs Adolf's ass, I don't mind."

I laughed. "That's the spirit."

"Still got a few days' rehab before I'm sprung. You?"

"I don't know. It's up to the doctors."

"You must be thirsty." Harry poured some water from a carafe on my bedside table, handed me the glass. "Sorry it's not whisky."

"You and me both." I drank the cool water. It felt good. But then... I noticed something off. "The water. Tastes strange."

"You mean, like kinda metallic?"

"Yeah. How'd you know?"

"'Cause I just poisoned you."

I stared at him. What the hell?

Harry took the glass from me. Set it back on the table. "There were two hundred and fifty milligrams of arsenic dissolved in that water."

No. This couldn't be happening again.

I shut my eyes. Was I dreaming? Please, God. But when I opened them again, Harry was leaning in closer. His warm breath reeked of cigarettes. "Your muscles will cramp up soon. Then you'll start puking and shitting yourself. A guy your size, you might only end up in a coma, but I'm hoping you drank enough to kill you."

I threw my blankets aside, leaped out of bed. "Nurse!" The tiled floor chilled my bare feet as I rushed to the door. "Help!" I collided with Nurse Linda on her way in.

She said, "Sergeant, what's the matter?"

I pointed back toward my bed. "He poisoned me!"

As she looked over my shoulder, I saw Harry was now back in his bed reading a *Liberty* magazine. He stared at me, concern and confusion etched on his face. "Ben? What's going on?"

I grabbed the water glass and carafe from my bedside table. "He put arsenic in my water."

Harry said, "What? I'm just sitting here reading. Next thing I know, you're screaming your head off."

"You're a fucking liar."

Something shadowed his face. Pity. "Ben, listen to yourself. Where the hell would I get arsenic? And why would I want to poison you?"

"Enough," Linda said. She marched over and took the glass from me.

"Smell it," I said.

"Arsenic has no smell."

I sniffed the carafe. Nothing. "But it tasted very metallic."

She shook her head. "Arsenic doesn't have any taste either."

"So he lied. Maybe it wasn't arsenic. But I've been poisoned! My heart's pounding. My throat's tightening. You've got to do something!"

She laid the back of her hand on my forehead. "You are a little warm."

The door flew open. A doctor and an MP burst in. The doctor said, "Nurse, we heard shouting."

Linda said, "This patient says he's been poisoned."

I pointed to Harry. "By him. He said it was arsenic, but it could be anything."

The doctor said to Linda, "Let's get his stomach pumped and run a blood panel. Bring the water glass and carafe." He turned to the MP, jerked his thumb toward Harry. "Don't let him out of your sight."

Linda grabbed the water carafe. The doctor took me by the arm and we rushed out of the room.

Two hours later, I lay in the recovery ward. The doctor was

still in scrubs when he stopped by and said my stomach was clean. Just water. No arsenic, no poison of any kind. Ditto for the carafe. "Sometimes water can have a high mineral content, like iron. That might account for the metallic taste you mentioned." He signed my chart and left.

High mineral content. I guess that made sense. It had to. Because the alternative was that I was going off the deep end.

Just then, the hospital chaplain passed by. The padre tossed me a warm smile and a wave. "Soldier." Making his rounds, checking in with patients fresh from surgery, he headed for a kid at the far end of the ward who was bawling his eyes out from pain or loneliness. Or both.

A whiff of jasmine tickled my nostrils. I turned to see Nurse Linda approaching with a wheelchair. She said my throat would be a little sore from where they stuck the tube down, so no hot drinks for a couple of days. She helped me into the chair, and I signed a form releasing me from the recovery ward.

When Linda wheeled me back into my room, I noticed the other bed lay empty, sheets freshly made up.

"He's been moved to another ward," she said. "We didn't want him to upset you again. I didn't know about the incident on the train—"

My cheeks flared. "I feel like such an idiot."

"Hush." She eased me back into bed. "Nobody thinks that. You boys go through hell over there. Some wounds are easy to see, some are not." She fluffed my pillow. "I'll get you some cool lemonade. That'll help soothe your throat."

After she left, I closed my eyes. My chest relaxed. So I had not been poisoned. Whatever happened, whatever I thought Harry had said or done—on the train, or here—none of it was true. But of course, if I believed that, I also had to admit something was really wrong with me. Maybe that last concussion knocked something loose in my brain, like a short circuit. That could explain the headaches and these... whatever they were. They weren't blackouts because I remembered everything that happened. Or everything I thought had happened. More like nightmares, except I was wide awake.

But maybe that's what insanity is. One long, waking nightmare.

I must have drifted off because when I opened my eyes, it was dark outside my window. Night had turned the glass into a mirror, reflecting a face staring back at me. After a moment, I realized it was my face. So on the outside, I still looked the same. But on the inside...

A figure in white appeared over my shoulder, and with it, the soft scent of jasmine. I turned over, sat up in bed.

Linda said, "See, you did need your rest."

"How long was I out?"

"Just a few hours. Any headache?"

My head felt clear. The beast slumbered. "Uh uh."

Linda shook out a thermometer, placed it under my tongue.

I mumbled, "You still on the clock?"

"No talking." Her warm fingers found my wrist, took the tempo of my pulse. "We've almost got a full house, so a lot of the girls are pulling doubles. I don't mind. We've all got to do our part."

Her locket glinted in the glow of my bedside lamp, swinging like a silver pendulum on her throat. It was a lovely white throat leading down to what, even in that prim, buttoned-up uniform, promised to be some very respectable cleavage.

She took the thermometer out of my mouth. "Temp normal. Pulse... slightly elevated."

I raised my eyes to her face. "Wonder why."

She laughed. "Amazing what a few hours' sleep will do for a guy's morale."

She pulled a syringe from her pocket and stuck the needle into a vial of clear fluid.

"What's that?"

She tapped my forearm. "You've got nice veins. Easy to see." She dabbed an alcohol-soaked cotton ball in the nape of my elbow, and I felt the tiny prick of the needle. "Some patients, it takes forever to find a good vein."

Her thumb depressed the plunger.

"If that's penicillin, don't bother. I was much too busy killing Germans to fool around with any French mademoiselles."

The syringe emptied itself into me. Linda pressed a dry cotton ball to the puncture point. "Just hold that for a few seconds," she said.

I nodded toward the needle. "What was that?"

"Heroin," she said simply.

A chill shot up my spine. Christ, no.

She giggled. Like a little girl caught doing something naughty.

First, Harry. Now, Linda?

"I just gave you a massive overdose," she said.

The beast began to stir, rumbling in my head.

"No... please." I screwed my eyes shut tight. This couldn't be happening again.

But then, her breath hot on my face, she spit her venom. "You piece of shit." She slapped me across the cheek. "Look at me, you fucking coward."

I opened my eyes. The corners of her mouth foamed white. "You don't deserve to live."

My heart jackhammered. The beast howled in its lair, bellowing for blood.

I shouted above its roars. "Please, make it stop!" I shouted loud enough so God himself would hear me. "This isn't real!"

Her face transformed into a mask of pure hatred. "Fuck you!" Those cool green eyes now blazed with fury. "What's it feel like to die?"

I cracked. Right then and there.

I screamed. In rage this was happening again. In terror for my sanity. My throat still raw from the stomach pump, the muscles and tissue and cartilage rupturing in agony, still I kept screaming.

And the beast exploded out of the shadows. Hideous. Slavering. Talons sliced the air. Pain leaped triumphantly in my brain. The victor and the vanquished.

The door to my room flew open, slamming back against the wall. Two MPs burst in, guns drawn. They took in the scene.

Linda lay on the floor, her hair tousled, her uniform torn open down to her navel. Trembling, she pointed up at me. "He attacked—" Her chest heaved with sobs. She gathered her uniform to cover herself.

"No!" I bolted up in bed. "I swear!"

One MP crossed to my bed, pushed me back. The other bent to help Linda.

I stared up into the stone face of the guy holding me down. "This isn't real!" Did I even know what was real anymore?

He called over his shoulder to his comrade. "Get a doctor." The MP hurried out of the room with Linda, who shook with fear.

"I didn't touch her."

"Shut up." His firm hand held me pinned.

A doctor hurried in. "What the hell—"

The MP said, "He attacked the nurse."

"I didn't!" I nodded to the only evidence of my story, the hypodermic and vial. "She said it was heroin."

The doctor read the label on the vial. "Sodium amytal. A mild sedative. Nothing more."

Pain arced across my brain like lightning.

"Oh, God... no."

The doc and the MP shared a look. Another head case. That's what they were thinking. Step right up to the rubber room, folks, and behold the gibbering idiot.

The MP's granite hand crushed my chest, pushing me down, down through the mattress, through the floor, into the ground... the grave.

I couldn't keep my eyes open.

As if from somewhere far off, a voice said, "He'll sleep now..."

And the beast chuckled softly.

* * *

When I woke up, I was paralyzed. I couldn't move my arms. Then I saw why.

Thick leather straps bound my wrists tightly to the sides of the bed. Another strap across my chest kept me pinned down.

A footfall beside me. I turned to see the chaplain standing there. He smiled warmly. "Hello, Ben."

I struggled against the restraints. "These straps—"

"I'm sorry about that. They didn't want you to hurt yourself." Then, more softly, "Or anyone else."

It all came flooding back. The hypodermic, Nurse Linda crying on the floor, her uniform torn.

"Is she okay?" I asked.

He nodded. "A little shaken up, but otherwise—"

"I can't believe I—" Even saying the words might make it more real. "I don't know what to believe."

The chaplain pulled up a chair beside my bed, sat down. "I talk to many men who come back. Some of them injured in body, some injured in soul. The things they saw, the things they did. Moments of great courage. But also fear. And sometimes... cowardice, or shame."

I looked for judgment in his eyes, but all I saw was kindness. "Father, do you believe in hell?"

"Only the one we make ourselves."

His fingers brushed a tear from my cheek. I hadn't even realized I was crying. "I wonder sometimes if this pain in my head... the things I think... the things I do—"

He said, "You know, God forgives all. He sees us at our best and our worst, and He never stops loving us."

Before I knew what I was doing, I said, "I killed a man."

He didn't flinch, didn't even blink. "But son, you're a soldier."

"You don't understand."

He took my hand in his. It felt warm, safe. "Would you like to tell me?"

I hesitated, poised on the brink. "Do you think it would help me... heal me?"

"I'm not a doctor. I can't set a broken arm or stitch up a wound. But I do know some injuries are more than skin deep."

I'd never told anyone before. How could I? But maybe confession could be my ticket out of this nightmare. In which case, the padre was a safe bet. I took a deep breath and plunged. "Northern France. In a field outside Arras. Most of the guys in our trench had already moved forward. A young private and I were gathering up the spare ammo, ready to follow."

My voice rasped, my throat still ached. But the trickle of words had forced a crack in the dam. It burst. "There weren't supposed to be any more Germans behind the line. Suddenly, out of nowhere, up pops one with a rifle. His first shot missed. My gun was on the ground. If I dove for it, I was a dead man. Hearing the shot, the private beside me spun around. Caught by surprise, shell boxes dropping from his hands. I yanked him in front of me and grabbed his sidearm. The German shot again, hit the private in the chest. I fired his gun, nailed the Nazi dead. Then the ground exploded. We were being shelled again, driven back. Blood pumped from the young private's chest wound. I couldn't help him. So I left him. And I ran. More shelling all around me. Dirt falling like rain. I ran and ran and didn't stop until I found cover in some trees. I was still holding the private's gun. And a spot of his blood stained my jacket."

I paused, breathless.

The chaplain's eyes had never left mine. But now I thought I saw something flicker behind them. Just for a split second, like a lightning flash. He said, "And you feel guilt for your actions."

I nodded mutely, my throat ravaged from the effort of confession. "I wasn't thinking. I panicked." A hacking sob rattled up from my chest. "I killed a man. A boy." My lips trembled. "I don't even know his name."

"Here... don't strain yourself." He grabbed the water carafe from my beside table, poured some, held the glass to my lips.

I gulped the water.

He smiled. "I said, God forgives us all."

Then the smell of it hit me. Acrid. Stinging.

He stopped smiling. "But I don't."

I tried to spit it out, but it was too late. My throat burst into flame. Like I'd drunk gasoline and swallowed a lit match. No! I must be insane. Do I scream? Truly insane. But I can't scream. This pain is unbearable. Why can't I scream? Oh my God, the pain.

I gaped at the chaplain. He watched me calmly.

He said, "His name was Private Charles Warren."

I gagged. Each breath a razor blade.

He stood up, crossed to the door of my room, and unlocked it. Nurse Linda and the marine, Harry, came in. They looked at the chaplain. He nodded. "It's him."

Harry and Linda approached my bed while the chaplain locked the door behind them.

My body shook all over. I couldn't feel my legs.

Linda took a small brown bottle from her uniform. "Mercury bichloride," she said. "Used externally to treat syphilis sores. But if taken internally results in multiple organ failure, blindness, coma, and finally, death. If your vocal cords weren't already paralyzed, you'd be screaming in agony."

My throat combusted.

She put the bottle in my hand, pressed my fingers around it. "That should give them some clean prints if they decide to check."

My brain shrieked NO NO NO!

I. Am. Insane.

This isn't really happening!

Harry said, "That glass of water I gave you yesterday just had zinc in it. That's why it tasted metallic. But this time, the poison is real."

My head pounded. The beast thundered its fury.

Harry pulled a sheet of paper from his pocket. "When you signed those release forms in the recovery ward, you also signed this."

The room tilted, rocking on invisible waves. My eyes scanned the typewritten page. Words lurched in and out of focus... *losing my mind... afraid... hurting others... deserve to die...* and at the bottom, my signature.

Harry said, "Your suicide note."

My bowels emptied. The stench of shit and piss crawled up my nostrils.

The chaplain said, "Harry and his men were forced back by heavy fire. He saw the wounded private lying in the trench. And even under constant bombardment, he hauled him out and over his shoulders, ran for cover."

Harry nodded. "That's when the shell hit. Shrapnel cut my leg in half, I went down. And with his last breath, the private told me what happened. How you traded his life for your own."

Harry began removing the straps from my body. But even free of those restraints, I still couldn't move.

The room faded slowly, the corners dimming. And with it, the pain in my body ebbed. Even the beast grew quiet, sullen.

The chaplain said, "Private Charles Warren was my baby brother."

A distant fragment of what was left of my rational mind suddenly realized... I'd been set up. I wasn't crazy. Never had been. I looked up into their faces. My tribunal. Judge, jury, executioner.

Linda bent over me. But I couldn't smell any jasmine this time. I couldn't even smell my own shit anymore. And just before everything went black, I watched Linda's fingers pluck the locket from around her neck, flip open the tiny clasp. The silver heart parted. Tucked inside one half was a photo of a young man in uniform. A private. I'd already recognized his face before she said in a soft voice that sounded very, very far away, "Charlie was my husband."

BUSINESS OF DEATH
Kim Keeline

As I crawled into bed late Saturday night, my cell phone buzzed. With a heavy sigh, I reached over and checked the caller ID. Two funerals in one day had left me drained.

I sat up and cleared my throat. Veronica Osura had been a demanding client all week, but we'd buried her father that afternoon. What could she possibly need now? There was nothing more to do than to send my final invoice. I always waited a respectful couple of days after the funeral to allow people to grieve before dealing with the bills.

The woman didn't let me get past hello. "I'm most displeased with you."

"What happened?"

The only flaw at the graveside service occurred when Mrs. Osura confronted some of the attendees as they were leaving. Everything I'd planned had gone smoothly.

"Quite a bit." Veronica Osura had sat at her father's graveside, a modern Japanese empress chiseled from marble and covered in gilt, wearing a tailored black dress and four large gold chains. Her shoulder-length black hair, pulled tightly and secured with a black bow at her neck, smoothed out wrinkles as effectively as Botox. The voice on the phone was tense but as imperious as ever. "We were robbed."

My heart began racing. "I advised you to hire a house sitter for the service." Even if it didn't happen often, everyone in my industry knew of the possibility of robbers using obituaries to discover when homes would be vacant. Hadn't she listened to me?

"Our house wasn't hit. Three others were."

That was a new twist. "Have they notified the police?"

"My dear friend Lucille called me as soon as she finished with the police." Her clipped tone indicated she felt completely justified to have then turned around and called me, even though it was late. Lovely.

"I'm not sure what you expect from me." I wanted to point out that I didn't control the world but bit my tongue instead.

"You said there would be nothing to worry about. Well, I'm worried."

She clearly expected me to do something—but what? "Let's talk about this in a day or two after the police have investigated."

"Fine, but don't expect your final payment until this is resolved satisfactorily." The line went dead.

Just great. I needed that paycheck. Most of my clients came by word of mouth through San Diego's South Bay Latino community. I thought my advertising had finally paid off when I landed this gig for a rich La Jolla family. They were, as my Tía would say, *estar forrado*, absolutely loaded. But did any amount of money make up for dealing with a woman like Veronica Osura?

"A death doula?"

The officer across the neat, institutional-style metal desk peered suspiciously at my business card labeled "Nilda Santos—Death Doula."

I'd faced this attitude about my work before, but I still flushed. "A doula is a midwife, but I help the dying and their families."

I still couldn't believe Mrs. Osura asked Officer Bradshaw to question me about this robbery when she knew I had nothing to do with it.

The Osura family obviously had pull at the Northern Division. Bradshaw made it clear when he called early that morning that he wanted me to come in with no delay. Luckily, there wasn't much traffic on the 5 freeway on a Sunday morning, and I made it from San Ysidro to his little office near UCSD in La Jolla in record time.

At least he hadn't stuck me in some interrogation room like on TV. Several police officers milled around the crowded office, presumably talking to witnesses and suspects. Only two people were in handcuffs.

Bradshaw stared at me like I had grown a third eye in the middle of my forehead.

"Think of me as an event planner specializing in funerals." I didn't want to explain the Hispanic heritage of the role or any of its history. Nor all the different things I could do for the dying or their families. I simply wanted to get out of there quickly.

From the rigid lines of his military haircut to the solid cut of his chin, Officer Bradshaw appeared more rock than man. He sat, unmoving, looking from my card to me. "A bit morbid."

I gave him my sweetest smile. "Death comes for everyone. Is it morbid to acknowledge that?"

Bradshaw shook his head and then looked at his notes. "You organized the Osura funeral."

A statement of fact and then a stare. Okay, I'd bite. "I coordinated the graveside service and notified his close friends of the arrangements."

One eyebrow raised. "Mrs. Osura says you warned her burglaries happened during funerals." The boulder of bureaucracy waited for my reaction.

"It's an old story. Were there really three break-ins during the funeral?"

"We've had several recently." He flicked my card in his hand. "We'll need a list of your clients for the past three months."

My throat tightened. "I don't see why it would be relevant. Do I need a lawyer?"

"You're welcome to a lawyer." His tone made it sound otherwise. "We're just trying to rule you out."

Everything inside me screamed that it was never good to talk to the police. As a DREAMer, brought to the US by my parents when I was a small child (with no idea that we would be called illegal), I have a right to remain in this country, for now at least. Still, authority figures brought to mind immigration offices, ICE, and everything involved. Plus, the Latino community didn't always have the best relationship with police.

I couldn't afford a lawyer. And I was innocent. Maybe I still had some faith that the system wasn't completely broken. *Maybe I'm a dreamer in more ways than one.* "I'll have to get back to you."

He tossed my card on his desk and began taking notes. "And list vendors you recommend to clients."

"If you really think it necessary."

He covered the same questions about the funeral plans for the next half hour, but eventually, I asked if I could go. After a brief pause, he said yes.

Maybe I would need a lawyer. My head hurt too much to think straight.

After his interrogation, even the punishing blast of San Diego's Santa Ana heatwave felt welcome as I walked out of the police station.

I poked around the cut flower displays in the florist shop for several minutes, waiting for Becca to wrap a dozen pink roses for a young man.

The heavy air-conditioning cooled the sweat off the back of my neck. I pushed aside all the negative thoughts circling in my head since I left the interview with Bradshaw. I had work to do now.

When the young man finally left, Becca wiped her hands on her red apron. "Nilda, another funeral or something personal?

Maybe a boyfriend?"

Becca always teased me about my almost nonexistent love life. With blue and purple highlights in her hair and floral tattoos up her arms, Becca was literally the most colorful person I did business with. And a friend.

"Death flowers—for next Saturday."

She faked a sad face then smiled. "Remember, it's not only women who need flowers in a relationship."

"I'll keep that in mind, but a bit of a dry spell on the dating front still."

Becca laughed. "Me too." I had helped plan her husband's funeral two years ago and knew she was just starting to consider dating again.

I flipped through the sample book on the counter until I selected one of my favorite funeral arrangements, a tasteful mid-range display of roses and stargazer lilies. One of the reasons I recommended her shop to clients was the number of options she listed—not just the traditional white lilies but many tasteful (or even wild hobby or sports-themed) funeral arrangements. Becca slipped me the order form and I filled out the delivery details. As I finished, the door swung open behind me.

"Gary, you're back fast," Becca said. "Come meet Nilda. One of our regulars."

"Nice to meet you." Gary's dazzling smile almost took my breath away. Curly blond hair and deep tan—and stunning. The "Surf's Up" wave tattoo on his lower arm said Southern California surfer dude as much as the laid-back drawl of his baritone voice.

"You, too." I barely got the words out. Maybe it had been too long since I'd dated, to react so strongly to being greeted by a handsome guy my age.

"You an event planner?"

Looking into Gary's deep blue eyes, I wasn't up for the awkward response my profession always inspired. "That's right."

"Cool." Gary slouched against the counter next to me. "Becca, do I have a few minutes to grab a soda before the next deliveries?"

"Gotta finish one more bouquet."

He turned his killer smile on me again. "See you around?"

I nodded. As soon as Gary left, Becca laughed. "He's a looker, isn't he?"

Oh, yes. But I wasn't giving her any ammunition. "How long has he worked here?"

"Started a few weeks ago when Bobby left for college. Would've introduced you sooner, but he's out on delivery a lot." She grinned, leaning on the counter. "He doesn't have a girlfriend. Too young for me, but you…"

My cheeks burned. "You're incorrigible."

Becca pushed the receipt across the counter. "You can't be all about death. Live a little too."

"I'm really sorry about my mother." Janine had already stuttered out three apologies since I'd arrived at the tiny coffee shop in Bonita.

Dark circles under Janine's eyes, plus her slightly shaky hands, spoke of a great deal of strain. She'd been very emotional at the funeral, asking me to sit beside her for comfort and clutching my hand as she tried to hold in her sobs.

Her mother had sat on her other side, ignoring her. Mrs. Osura wouldn't even give Janine a few moments alone at her grandfather's graveside. Instead, she'd whisked the young woman away to the waiting limo, pausing only to express displeasure with some people in the back row.

I sipped my iced mocha and watched the young woman carefully, concerned about her, but also curious why she'd begged me to meet. "She's very upset about the thefts, naturally."

Janine's coffee cup sat untouched on the blue and white checked tablecloth as she scanned the room, fiddling with the strap of her oversized Dolce & Gabbana bag. "I know you didn't have anything to do with it."

She could have said all this over the phone. "Is this why you wanted to meet?"

Instead of answering me, Janine jumped to her feet. A young man in a blue button-down shirt and jeans approached the table. He looked vaguely familiar to me, but I couldn't place why.

Janine touched the newcomer's arm like she feared he might disappear in a puff of smoke. "You're late."

"Traffic." He bent down to kiss her, then turned to me. "You must be the funeral planner."

Janine then introduced me to Peter, her fiancé. He pulled a chair up close to hers, and she leaned against him.

"Nice to meet you." I studied Janine's fiancé, wondering why he'd not been at her side for the service.

He must have read my mind. "My parents and I sat in the back row at the cemetery."

Janine's eyes filled with tears. "My mother doesn't approve of our engagement. Grandfather's funeral didn't feel like the place to push it."

Peter grimaced. "Mrs. Osura made a scene with my parents as we were leaving. They've never gotten along."

That must have been when I'd seen him before.

Janine clutched Peter's hand. "Then he found his apartment had been broken into while he was gone."

A bad day all around. "Did they take much?"

Peter shrugged, but his eyebrows creased with worry. "Computers, mostly."

"Peter and his family run an environmental nonprofit. He works from home, so losing work computers is a big problem."

"Who else was robbed?"

"His parents." Janine's voice was strained, breaking. "It's awful—more computers, some jewelry, and cash."

Peter took a sip of Janine's coffee and cleared his throat. "The other burglary victim was Lucille, an 'old money' friend of Janine's mom. That's what has Veronica Osura in such an uproar.

She doesn't care about us, of course."

That sounded like her. "The police said several other funerals were targeted," I said, savoring the last sips of my coffee.

Janine gave a wan smile. "We heard that too. I also learned Mother gave your name to the police. That's why Peter and I wanted to apologize in person. And I'll make sure your invoice is paid in full. Mother's just venting, like always."

Peter's expression seemed to disagree with Janine about the "venting," and I had to agree. Mrs. Osura moved beyond venting when she called Officer Bradshaw.

That must've been all they wanted because, now that I'd finished my drink, Peter walked me to the shop's door and shook my hand in parting. "Janine's never been good at standing up to her mother. She tries to tell herself that it's nothing, but her mother is controlling and vicious when she doesn't get her way."

I nodded. There wasn't anything more to say about Janine's mother.

As I opened the door, Peter added, "Thank you for your support during the funeral. She said you've been wonderful."

As I drove home, I began to get angry. I hated that this was happening, that it involved me, and that it was causing problems for Janine. She'd clearly loved her grandfather. Funerals were hard enough without thieves preying on the grieving.

"Word's been going around." Eduardo slapped the top of his mortuary office's front counter. Twenty years older than me, twice-divorced, constantly on the make, and a real pain whenever I had to work with him. At least today, the gossip about the break-ins kept him from immediately asking me on a date. "Any of your clients hit?"

"My last funeral—three of the mourners." I sighed. "Can I get the paperwork, *por favor?*"

"Sure, sure." He rummaged around in his desk. How he kept

things organized with so many precariously stacked files, I never knew.

I glanced around his office. "Any of yours?"

"Mine? Oh, the break-ins. Not so far. They seem to mostly hit coastal areas or South Bay. Still, I'm warning people. Vultures." Eduardo practically spat the word.

"Exactly."

"Here." Eduardo threw the paperwork I needed for my next client onto his counter. "I appreciate the business."

I responded truthfully. "You do quality work for a reasonable fee." Eduardo ran the best North County mortuary, despite his obvious flaws. The things I went through for my clients.

"And there's my good looks, of course." Again, that leer I'd come to dread. "Have dinner with me tonight."

"Sorry. Not available. See you later." As I headed out the door, I wished I could tell him to knock it off. You can't always do what you want in life.

Despite my discomfort with the police, the next day, I again sat in a crowded station.

"You could've emailed." Officer Bradshaw's voice held only a hint of annoyance as he looked over my paperwork.

"I want to help. Do you have a list of the robberies and what funerals they are connected to?"

He hummed slightly, looking over my printout. "Of course."

I waited, hoping he'd offer without my asking, but no luck. "May I have a copy?"

Now he looked up. "Why?"

"I'm in the industry. I may notice a connection you wouldn't see."

Another hum. He scanned the second page. "This is everyone who attended the funeral?"

"And all vendors I regularly use or recommend, by category."

No response. He sat there looking over my lists.

Fine. I stood up. "If there isn't anything else you need, I'll head out."

Still no response. I started to walk away.

"Ms. Santos."

Perhaps the boulder cracked a little? I turned back, trying not to smile.

Bradshaw held out a sheet of paper. "Do you recognize anything here?"

The offered page detailed almost a dozen funerals with locations, victims' names, and their relationship to the deceased.

Eduardo had been right—the break-ins were limited to certain areas of the county. The Osuras' funeral had been held at Miramar National Cemetery because Janine's grandfather was a veteran. Another military one was held at Fort Rosecrans in Point Loma. All the others were south and not far inland. Nothing at all in the East County.

Nothing looked familiar as I tried to memorize names. "If I think of anything, I'll let you know."

Bradshaw took the sheet back with a look of disappointment. "You do that."

"Nilda, Nilda!" Eight-year-old Juan and six-year-old Graciela screamed and laughed as they ran around the crowded kitchen, ducking between adults. My little cousins tended to make the evenings a little crazy.

After my father's death, my heartbroken mother had left for Mexico City to stay with her sister, but I'd spent almost my entire life north of the border. My father's family in San Ysidro had taken me in. *Mi familia.* Noise and all.

I finished helping Tía Graciela with the dishes and sat at the small desk next to the kitchen with my laptop, notepad, and the Osura funeral file. As soon as I opened the computer, my cousins were hanging on the back of the chair.

Juan prodded my left side. "*Bruja,* what are you doing?"

I sighed with exasperation, wrapped my arms around him, then gave him a small slap on the butt as I let him go. "Rascal!" I had once made the mistake of telling them that death doulas were historically considered witches—*brujas*—by some people. "I'm not going to tell you if you're going to be rude."

Graciela pushed against my right leg. "*¿Puedes venir a jugar?*"

I took her hand. "I promise I'll come play in a little bit. Go ask your papa to let you watch TV for a half hour."

They scampered off, and a few seconds later, I could hear them pleading with my Tío Marco in the other room.

I'd already entered every name I could remember from Bradshaw's list into my spreadsheet. Now I added every vendor likely to be involved in the process. Then I read the obits to see if they listed surviving family in case these were the victims.

As expected, the robbers mostly targeted the house of the deceased or the immediately bereaved, info anyone could figure out by reading the obits. The Osura funeral was the only one with multiple break-ins—and none of them listed close family in the obit. Did that mean the robbers were getting bolder?

Why was I wasting what little free time I had? The police, trained in this sort of thing, had been investigating for days and hadn't gotten anywhere.

I began to close the computer when I saw my list of flowers sent to the Osura funeral. All three robbery victims had sent flower arrangements.

Scanning my photos from the cemetery, I quickly found the three displays. Becca's work, if I had to guess. I *had* recommended her to the family, so it wasn't that odd. Becca couldn't be involved. I could rule out this idea without mentioning it to the police.

For now, the giggles in the living room needed attention, so I went to play hide and seek.

"These tacos are great." Becca and I'd enjoyed many lunch hours in the florist's back room, so this had been easy to arrange.

I grabbed my napkin to keep the filling from falling out of the shell. "I have a favor to ask. Can I look through your order book for the last couple months?"

Becca tilted her head. "Is there a problem?"

Hopefully not. "Call it market research on flower trends."

The bell rang, indicating a customer out front. Becca put down the second half of her taco. "Darn, always in the middle of eating. Be right back." She shoved a black folder at me. "Here. Last four months."

She went through the curtain to the front as I flipped through the invoices, taking a quick photo with my phone of every recent funeral order. A few minutes later, I heard Becca thanking her customer, so I closed the folder as she parted the curtain and came back.

Becca picked up her taco and nudged the closed folder on the table with her elbow. "See anything interesting?"

I shrugged. "Not really, but thanks."

We chatted for a bit, but I found it hard to concentrate. Maybe it was nothing, but I believe several of her invoices matched funerals on Bradshaw's list. I couldn't rule her out.

The boulder sounded unimpressed when I shared my concerns. As I thought, all the funerals from Bradshaw's list matched at least one receipt from Becca's store. And every funeral was within her delivery zone.

"Probably a coincidence." Officer Bradshaw's bored voice as he ended the conversation told me all I needed to know.

A coincidence? *Posiblemente*, but what if it wasn't? But I couldn't believe it was actually Becca.

Becca wasn't surprised when I came over the next day. I'd called earlier to ask when her handsome delivery guy would be around.

She'd teased me but suggested a good time to drop by.

"So good to see you, Nilda." Becca beamed at me from behind the counter. She gave a jerk of her head toward the back and winked. "Gary, come out and say hi."

A blond head peeked out from the curtain. Gary smiled when he saw me. "Event planner, right?"

"Yep. How are you?"

"Busy with deliveries but taking my break in the back."

Becca raised an eyebrow. "Want to join us for an iced tea?"

As planned. "I'd love to."

We headed into the back, and Becca poured two glasses of iced tea. I sat at the small table where Gary's California Burrito and soda lay half-finished. He plopped down in his seat and took a bite out of his lunch. Becca sat across from us and gave me a sly grin as she passed me the cool drink.

I smiled at Gary. "I'm planning a doozy of a funeral this week."

"Really?" Gary continued to eat but at least pretended interest.

"Filthy rich client but really skimping on the funeral, barely putting an obit out. Eccentric as only the really rich can be, you know how it is."

Gary let out a low whistle. "I guess you meet all sorts."

I laughed and shared a few stories—attendees who overacted their grief to be the center of attention and mistresses or secret families causing fights. Anyone in the business heard about or even witnessed some of these events.

Becca looked like she'd swallowed a canary the whole time, obviously playing matchmaker in her head.

Before I left, I filled out a form for a small funeral wreath. Gary leaned on the counter as I filled in the client's address and the funeral date and location.

"It's been nice talking with you." Gary's smile still dazzled.

I tried to be my most charming. "Hope to see you again soon."

* * *

"I'm glad you could borrow your friend's house." I reclined in a luxurious tufted armchair across from Janine, who shifted nervously on the arm of a leather couch.

Janine shrugged. "She's off for the summer at an Adirondack resort. She offered it as an escape from Mother. As long as her stuff isn't actually stolen."

The house, a mansion really, in an exclusive La Jolla community with a view of the ocean, was perfect for our purposes. The living room looked like the cover of one of those architectural magazines. Imagine living like this all the time. Then again, Janine did.

I checked the time on my phone. "The funeral starts in a half hour. If something is going to happen, I think it'll be soon."

Janine tapped on her phone. "Peter says nobody followed him when he left. He's hiding around back."

If I'm wrong, it's a wasted afternoon. If I'm right...

The sound of a vehicle pulling into the driveway brought Janine to her feet. The engine went silent.

"Did you hear that?" Janine hissed as she moved toward the window.

"Don't let them spot you."

She backed up rapidly. "I'm nervous."

I was too. Car doors slammed. I stayed frozen on the edge of the armchair.

Janine tapped on her phone, telling Peter of the arrival.

I strained to listen for any noise. All was silent—until the sound of breaking glass at the back door. Janine and I stared at each other in shock. I had half hoped I was wrong. She probably had too. Now we had thieves coming in the back door just two rooms away.

The whoop of a siren split the air. Janine and I ran to the front window as the private security officers got out of their car. A van marked with a magnetic sign claiming they were from San Diego Gas & Electric was now blocked in on the large cobblestone driveway. The security officers were looking in the van's windows.

"Stay here and watch, Janine. I'm going to the back door."

I hurried toward the back. The partially open door had a broken windowpane, but there was no sign of thieves. I stepped cautiously over the shards of glass on the tile and onto the large deck. Two men in overalls were running down the sloping garden path below. Suddenly they darted to the side fence and began to scramble over it.

The security guards appeared around the side of the house and followed them a few seconds later.

By now, the police were on their way. The thieves wouldn't get far.

"You were of *some* help." Officer Bradshaw's voice sounded reluctant but perhaps a little admiring.

I'd take it. "Glad to be of service."

"We recovered some jewelry and other items of value from earlier break-ins, but no luck on easier-to-move items, like electronics."

There wasn't much else to say, so, after I thanked Bradshaw for letting me know, I hung up.

The two thieves gave up their accomplice, Gary, after they were caught. At least Becca wasn't directly involved.

Leaning back in my desk chair in the kitchen, I closed my laptop and gave a big stretch to relieve the knot in my shoulders.

Los Niños were running around somewhere in the house. I could hear them singing one of their favorite songs from *Sesame Street*, "One of these things is not like the others, one of these things just doesn't belong," at the top of their lungs. They sang it in English and then repeated it in Spanish, over and over. A typical day in the Santos household.

Before I called Janine, I deleted the photos of Becca's invoices. The police could get the info directly from the flower shop.

As I flipped through the images to delete them, Juan and

Graciela's song struck me. Two of these robberies were different from the others. Why?

Each of Becca's receipts showed who ordered the flowers, including their billing address, and then the date, time, and location for the funeral. Except the invoices for Peter and his parents. On those Becca had scrawled "In person—Cash" and their phone number. How had Gary known where to send his accomplices?

Puzzled, I dialed Janine. "Good news. Gary and his accomplices have all been arrested and charged. Some of the stuff they stole has been recovered from Gary's apartment."

"Thank goodness. Peter really needs those computers."

"Unfortunately, the police say the computers are gone. Probably easier to fence."

"Oh no. He had some backups, but there are all sorts of important info on those he can't afford to lose."

"Did Peter and his parents order the flowers for your grandfather's funeral in person?"

"Yes," Janine sounded confused. "That place you recommended was on Peter's way home, so he stopped in."

"That's what has me worried. You see, the florist didn't have their home addresses. Gary wouldn't have known where to break in. I'm not sure Peter and his family were robbed by the same gang as the others."

Silence.

"Are you still there?"

"Just thinking." Janine was barely audible. "I can't be sure, but it's clear to me now." Janine sounded shaky. "This is my mother's fault."

That was a real leap in logic. "What do you mean?"

"I bet she hired some goons to steal his computers because she wanted info on them. Or maybe to cause them trouble. She wants to stop our marriage." Janine's voice was hard. "Since there had been other robberies, I didn't put it together."

Could her mother really be that devious? "What are you

going to do?"

"What I should have done a long time ago." Janine's voice had a new ring to it. "Peter's the best thing that's ever happened to me. I'm not letting mother's paranoia and controlling nature ruin this."

"I wish you all the luck." With her mother, she'd need it.

"You'll be invited to the wedding. I can't thank you enough." Janine hung up.

Just in time, too, because *Los Niños* came running down the hall toward me. "Nilda, ice cream, now!" Juan yanked on my arm as Graciela skipped around me.

I slipped my phone into my pocket and allowed myself to be led to the kitchen. "*Sí, sí, niños*, let's eat lots of ice cream!"

It's always good to be surrounded by life and love. Especially when your business is death.

A PEARL OF A GIRL
Victoria Weisfeld

Joe reached across the table to hold Pearlie's hand as they watched the parade of festively lit boats glide past far below. They'd worked their way along San Diego Bay toward the Coronado Bridge, on the other side of which hulked big gray ships of the Pacific Fleet. From their window seats at the Grand Hyatt's bar, forty stories up, they couldn't hear the Christmas carols blasting from the parade boats, but they could see movement on deck that Pearlie said might be dancing. Hard to say these days, Joe thought.

"Christmas spirit," she said. The holiday was only two weeks away.

"Yep," Joe said and sighed.

Pearlie's eyebrows lifted, a sign she knew he was troubled by something. And since it was always the same thing, she would know what it was. Joe believed his wife was too quick to say yes when one of her uncles called, asking for her help with troublesome children or in-laws, inviting her for visits, taking her aside at family events for long chats. Of course, she was sorry this made Joe feel left out and had apologized more than once. But then she would counter that, at their age, trips to San Diego and other nice places three or four times a year, all expenses paid, were a luxury they shouldn't turn down.

This evening, in a move he guessed was intended to make him

feel better (and did), she'd worn her best dress—one she'd bought for a niece's third wedding last September. The neckline plunged daringly for a woman Pearlie's age, but it was a pretty cerulean blue, Joe's favorite color.

This trip came about because Pearlie's Uncle Max asked her to go to San Diego, where one of his six daughters was making poor life choices. Could Pearlie help? Max was Pearlie's late father's youngest brother, and the way the births of children in the family had fallen, Max and Pearlie were just about the same age. They had always been close. She called him Mad Max— "because he *is* kind of crazy," she said—and he called her a pearl of a girl.

Pearlie and Joe finished their cocktails, watching a boat drift past, loaded with Santa's sleigh and a waving mechanical St. Nick festooned in red and white lights.

"Would you like another?" The waiter came alongside, moving as silently as the boats.

"That sounds nice." Pearlie smiled. "Joe?"

"Sure. Bourbon, rocks."

"Yes, sir. Your shrimp cocktails should be at the table soon." Before he could step away, a runner arrived with the dishes. "Very soon," the waiter amended. "I'll get that drink." He turned to Pearlie. "Wine list?"

"No, thank you. Just the old-fashioned." She looked to Joe like she had something to say, and she wouldn't want to be fussing with wine.

When the waiter was gone, she said her piece. "Joe, I know you're not happy Max asked me to come out here. But you know that, to me, there's nothing more important than family. And, not only my family—yours too." She squinted at her shrimp and exchanged her glasses for a pair of readers.

"I do know it, Pearlie." Just the previous year, she'd traveled to Atlanta to spend two weeks with his sister Helen, post-surgery. Pearlie cooked and cleaned. She organized Helen's nursing visits and medications. And Helen wasn't the easiest person in the world to get along with. "It's more Max," Joe said. "I don't like him. Or Jake. I don't like the business they're in."

"Max and Jake? They're harmless. Don't be put off by those old rumors. If they were as bad as people say, they'd be in jail for sure. They run a legitimate business, and they've always been very considerate of us—and our kids. Both Max and Uncle Jake."

"I know that too. Believe me, I'm grateful they helped pay for our girls' college. But that doesn't make me feel better. In fact, I feel worse knowing that, despite their generosity, I still can't bring myself to like them." Across the table, his wife was carefully eating her shrimp in the deliberate way she did everything, laying the tails neatly to one side. Her gray hair was arranged in a conservative style, and she could stand to lose a few pounds, but he loved the aging Pearlie as much as he'd loved his young bride, forty years earlier, when he was sure she was the prettiest girl in Brookline.

"Too bad the girls didn't pick state schools," she said. "We could have swung it then."

"But they didn't. So, you're going to spend some time with Rachel?"

"Yes, tomorrow. She's taking Monday off for my visit. I'm looking forward to it. Always such a sweet girl."

"What's Max worried about, exactly?"

"I'll have to find out from her, if I can. It's kind of vague to me. I think Max doesn't approve of her boyfriend. And some kind of money issue."

"You think she'll listen to you?"

Pearlie looked up and caught his eye. "All I can do is try."

The next afternoon, Joe met her as she disembarked the ferry. "Welcome to San Diego!" He wore a big grin. "Thanks for texting me you were on the next ferry," he said, taking an armload of shopping bags.

She laughed. "I didn't expect such a dramatic reception."

"I missed you. Let's have a drink." He steered her to the patio of a beachside bar.

When they sat down, she said, "I'm bushed!" She fished her sun hat out of one of the bags.

"No wonder. How many shopping bags were you carrying?"

"Stuff for the grandkids. So many cute shops on Coronado Island. You should have come with me—it's beautiful."

He lifted his baseball cap and rubbed his forehead. When he and Pearlie visited California, he always wore the navy-blue cap embroidered with *USS Coral Sea* and the years of his Vietnam service. He'd picked it up at a veterans' reunion, and in a big Navy town like San Diego, it was a sure-fire icebreaker.

He fingered the shopping bags by his feet.

"Oh, no you don't. Keep your hands off." She pulled the bags closer to her side of the table.

"So, how is Rachel?"

"We had a really nice visit. We talked for a couple of hours in her kitchen, then walked into town for lunch and a little shopping. Then we had a coffee at an outdoor restaurant and talked some more. I think she's going to be okay. Max blew a few things up out of proportion. She's ditching the boyfriend, she said, or has already. She came to the same conclusion about him that Max had. It just took her a while longer."

"He local?"

"No. That's the good part. He lives in Los Angeles, so it will be harder for them to get together again out of inertia. I'm satisfied. But I should call Max. He's a worrier." She fumbled in her handbag for her phone.

"Before you do that, why don't we go back to the hotel and order dinner from room service? You can't beat the view."

"Oh, that's a lovely idea! Order something good. Anyway, I'll be glad to change out of these shoes."

Joe knew it wasn't a great act of faith for Pearlie to let him order their dinner. She wasn't a fussy eater. After consulting the room service menu, he ordered coconut mussels, seafood paella, and a bottle of Sancerre. About the time he hung up the phone, Pearlie came out of the bathroom in one of the hotel's voluminous terry cloth robes.

"Feels so good to relax," she said. "I'll call Max now, then we'll have the evening to ourselves."

Pearlie wasn't a nonstop talker like some of the other women in Joe's family, but her concise conversations with her uncles amazed him. Brief comments, followed by long pauses, as now. "Hi, Max. I saw Rachel today." Then one of those long pauses. "It went well. You won't be hearing more from Mr. Wrong." Pause. "We had a nice lunch, did some shopping. And thank you for this lovely room for Joe and me." She looked at her husband and winked. "Thank you for asking. He's fine. What a special hotel!" Pause. "All right, Max. Talk to you soon. Hugs to Susan."

On Tuesday, Pearlie and Joe lounged by the pool in the early morning, then took the ferry across the bay to Coronado Island. "I want to show it to you," Pearlie insisted. The downtown offered enticing window shopping, as Pearlie led them along. Soon they reached one of the spokes of Star Park. Joe thought they were just ambling along and that Pearlie didn't have any particular destination in mind, so he wasn't really paying much attention to their route, until they rounded a corner and—"Wow! I didn't know that was here!" It was his first view of the Hotel Del Coronado. "My favorite movie!"

"Don't I know it. How many times have we watched it? And *Some Like It Hot* wasn't the only movie filmed here. Also *The Stunt Man*, you know, Peter O'Toole, *My Blue Heaven*—we loved that one."

"Wow." They walked all around the hotel, taking in its exuberant details. Joe couldn't get enough of the Victorian design, the pristine exterior, the red roofs. "Just wow."

"It's our lunch spot."

He pulled her close and planted a kiss on her forehead.

After lunch, they joined a hotel tour, and though Joe wasn't usually interested in ghost stories, a hotel with a 135-year history had some good ones: Kate Morgan, who apparently visited guests more often than room service; her maid, whose room the guide called "a paranormal bazaar" (spell that any way you want to, Joe thought). Was Kate's death an unsolved murder, or was it suicide? Joe didn't really care, but he couldn't deny the shiver down his spine as the guide told the dramatic tale. Much more to his taste, she also pointed out where classic movie scenes had been shot, and he grinned ear-to-ear as he recalled them.

After the tour, Joe and Pearlie refreshed with iced tea and started a leisurely walk back to the Ferry Center. Rather than take the main street leading to the bridge, Pearlie wove them through a residential area, "to see how the other half lives," she said. The neighborhood was a mix of brilliantly white stucco houses and low-rise apartment buildings. They strolled alongside Spreckels Park, watching college kids with dogs throwing frisbees, and admiring the park's impressive variety of trees and palms. Not until they reached the park's far corner did they notice that the next block was clogged with emergency vehicles.

"What's that about?" Joe asked, not expecting an answer.

Pearlie shook her head and tucked her hand under Joe's elbow. As they approached, a policeman gestured for them to stay on their side of the street. The house that was the obvious center of attention was on the opposite side, with police in uniform, men wearing suits, and an EMT or two standing in the yard, hands on hips. Two more EMTs awkwardly maneuvered a gurney loaded with what Joe guessed was a black body bag out the front door. At the end of the driveway, an ambulance waited.

"Doesn't look good," Joe commented and, to the policeman, "Trouble in Paradise?"

"Always." The man laughed. "Less now, though. Guy who lived there was a big-time drug dealer. We never could get to him, but somebody did."

"Terrible," Pearlie whispered. Joe felt her trembling.

"We're tourists from back east, so everything around here looks perfect to us," Joe said, gesturing broadly to indicate the entire neighborhood, the crystal-clear sky.

"Don't kid yourself." A car turned into the block behind them. The policeman stepped toward the car and motioned for it to turn around. "Street's closed," he called.

Pearlie averted her eyes from the sight of the body being loaded into the ambulance, and they walked on. Joe sighed. "It's everywhere, I guess."

"I guess so."

That brush with unpleasantness was soon forgotten, as they crossed the Bay, sparkling in the late afternoon sun. It would be their last evening in the "Birthplace of California," and they had dinner reservations in the Gaslamp District. After consultation with the hotel concierge, Joe chose a Russian restaurant he hoped would have some of Pearlie's grandmother's dishes—you never knew. A nice treat for her, his sweet, reliable, capable wife. That was a definite benefit of Max's largesse. The free trip meant Joe could splurge on a dinner that really pleased her.

Their flight left midmorning on Wednesday, but between the distance and the three-hour time difference, they wouldn't arrive at Logan until evening. The trip back to Boston would be long and seem longer, knowing that the gray and slush of December awaited them. In the San Diego airport, Joe bought himself a crossword puzzle book and the *Union-Tribune*, hoping to forestall a nap that would have him waking up over Cleveland with a crick in his neck. Pearlie bought a paperback thriller and planned to finish it before the flight ended. Another thing Max was good for: first class.

Joe rattled the newspaper pages and nudged his wife. "Look, Pearlie. A story about the murdered guy we saw yesterday."

"Really?" She didn't sound interested.

"Drug dealer, just like the cop said. A man named Manny Ventimiglia. Even sounds like a gangster. Gunned down in his kitchen." He glanced farther down the story. "They think a rival drug gang was probably responsible. Hunh. Haven't found the weapon."

Of course not, Pearlie thought. She'd slid it off the back of the ferry on Monday. *Max, Max, when will you stop asking these favors of Little Pearlie? This was the third one this year.*

Their plane took off to the west and made a climbing turn over the Pacific before heading east. As it flew high over San Diego again, Pearlie looked down at the Bay and thought about the gun that lay down there, under forty feet of saltwater. She'd never mention it, but it was safe to think about it. Joe would never know. After all, he wasn't a mind-reader.

Yet, Joe did know the fate of the pistol. He'd watched her dispose of it. His *USS Coral Sea* cap had gotten him onto the ferry's bridge to jaw with the captain and from that vantage point, he saw exactly what Pearlie did. Another person would not have noticed a slightly dowdy middle-aged woman on the crowded upper deck, would not have seen how she worked her way to the stern or noticed her furtive actions, would not have guessed why she was staring into the ferry's wake. As the ferry neared the San Diego dock, it was an easy thing for Joe to be first off the boat and station himself at the end of the gangway to welcome Pearlie when she appeared.

Now, she was looking out the tiny airplane window at the Bay below, and he knew what she was thinking. About the gun. About the late Mr. Ventimiglia. About the unlikelihood someone like her would ever be suspected of a contract killing. None of this was a surprise to Joe. After all, he'd told Max to hire her for the job.

PALMS UP
Anne-Marie Campbell

Four swift gunshots shattered the twilight tranquility.

It was the fifth night Chelsea Navarro had heard them since she'd moved into this upscale hillside neighborhood a little over two weeks ago.

"So, that's the way it's going to be," Chelsea murmured. Her back muscles tensed against the leather cushion of her Eames lounge chair, a masterpiece of mid-century modern furniture that cradled her body like an oversized baseball mitt.

Would've been nice to know about the crazy neighbor taking potshots at harmless little animals before she'd dropped a cool 2.1 million on this place. Not counting the sixty-thousand-plus on kitchen renovations.

Like a solitary queen of her culinary castle, Chelsea savored these nights off on West Ullman Lane, a cozy pocket where the residents kept to themselves. Viewed from Google Earth, West Ullman Lane and East Ullman Lane resembled a double-pronged carving fork, with a cactus-studded ravine separating two short, narrow streets.

Neighbors notwithstanding, from the summit of Point Loma, her view of San Diego Bay was worth the hefty price, especially from her floor-to-ceiling living room window. Her fifteen-plus years of busting her back in culinary school, taking on random cooking gigs, and studying under master chefs were finally paying off big time.

Chelsea reached toward the end table and picked up her recent gift to herself, a set of high-end Swarovski binoculars valued for ergonomic black barrels, crystal-clear optics, and razor-sharp clarity. She pointed them at the window and leaned slightly forward, her eye sockets against the cool cushion at the rim of the eyepieces. Squinting slightly, she watched the lineup of planes in the distance to the left. At night, the view made her think of bright planets obediently waiting their turn to land at San Diego International Airport. During the day, the house's position on the sharply inclining street provided a clear vista showcasing Shelter Island several miles below, populated with palm trees excitedly waving their fronds to welcome aircraft carriers entering the bay.

Four more volleys knifed through the air.

"This is bullshit," Chelsea said aloud. "Squirrels and opossums have just as much a right to walk through our yards as we do." She swiveled the binoculars toward the smaller window to her right and slightly rotated the focusing ring as she searched the shadows behind her house.

The lenses zeroed in on the silhouette of a man seated on a wooden deck that overlooked the sixty-foot ravine separating her backyard from his. The tip of a cigarette glowed periodically in the darkness, like the blinking red lights of jets in the night sky.

Chelsea hadn't seen any animal carcasses when planting her organic vegetable garden the previous weekend. Dude either had an air gun or incredibly bad eyesight.

Four additional punches of gunfire.

What was that guy's problem? There was enough food to go around. She always planted extra seedlings so the critters could have their share, too.

The oven timer on her Viking 7 Series Range beeped. Chelsea put down the binoculars and checked her watch. Seven o'clock. Time to liberate the chocolate lava cakes. This batch was infused with Bailey's Irish Cream, an experiment that might eventually grace the restaurant menu.

As the embrace of the leather chair reluctantly released her, a single shot echoed across the ravine. She stopped in her tracks. Just one? Not four? That was new.

Chelsea gave herself a little shake. In her journey as a chef, she had learned to go with the flow in any kitchen, whether serving the masses in a prison or catering to the socialites at Beverly Hills parties. But she hadn't quite gotten used to this place yet.

On East Ullman Lane, directly across the ravine from Chef Chelsea Navarro's house, four pops rang out.

Short, short, short, long.

Tiffany Vanderhoof's hand remained steady as she applied perfect swoops of Black Ecstasy eyeliner, followed by topcoats of volumizing mascara.

Short, short, short, long.

"Hey, babe," called out Tiffany, her yellow diamond wedding ring set flashing in the lights framing her makeup mirror. "He's doing Beethoven's Fifth tonight."

The Real Housewives wannabe rose from her vanity table and walked into her husband's home office, the bouncy waves of her blonde ombré hair cascading halfway down the back of her sleeveless little black dress, carefully chosen to accentuate Tiffany's twenty-three-inch waist and Meghan Markle legs.

"Jeffrey. Did you hear?" she said, leaning down to scoop up the tiny fluff of a dog dancing alongside her Christian Louboutin heels.

"Hear what? Oh, that." Her husband continued to tap the keyboard of his MacBook Pro. "Yeah. Well. As long as the old man keeps the coyotes away."

Tiffany kissed her Teacup Maltese, glossy pink lipstick staining the silky white fur between the little dog's ears. "Totally agree. You know, I'd just die if something happened to Cookie. I'd just die."

Four staccato shots punctuated her words.

"Hang on, Tiff. I'm almost done with this document for the systems engineer. One of the key deliverables to NASA for that Jupiter project I told you about."

"No rush," said Tiffany. "Nobody arrives on time to these cocktail parties." Cookie in her lap, Tiffany sat in front of the telescope in Jeffrey's office, lowered it a few degrees, and peered through the finder scope toward the house next door.

Jeffrey's eyes left the screen. "Ah, geez. Babe, I set that up to see Jupiter's moons later tonight." He lowered his stubbled jaw and stared at his wife over the rims of his Ray-Ban glasses, looking handsomely bookish. "Tiff. You really got to stop spying on people."

"Relax," said Tiffany, turning and briefly lifting her hands, as if surrendering. "I never see the faces. I just like to stay on top of the goings-on next door." She caressed Cookie's fur. "And Sheree has a lot to stay on top of, if you know what I mean."

"You have a dirty mind," said Jeffrey, closing the laptop.

"You wish. Maybe when we get home tonight, you and I can..." Tiffany ran her tongue over her lips.

"Sounds good," Jeffrey said, approaching his wife. Eight years into their marriage and they still kept things spicy.

Another loud pop sounded from the ravine, but Jeffrey and Tiffany didn't notice it.

Several minutes later, Tiffany reapplied lipstick while Jeffrey straightened his tie.

"I'll bring the Jag around to the front," he said.

"Good. The sooner we get this fundraiser over with, the sooner we can come back for dessert," said Tiffany with a long-lashed wink.

As usual, the sets of four muffled little explosions began about an hour after Lolita Wilson's nighttime shift started at six and lasted anywhere from a half hour to two hours.

The gunfire from across the ravine always quickened Lolita's heart rate. But it didn't bother her enough to quit. No, God had blessed her with this job in this beautiful home on West Ullman Lane, tucked between two quiet houses, and diagonally across from a couple who always seemed to be wearing fancy clothes and heading out in their fancy car. But most of all, Lolita loved having an easy patient. Mrs. Lundy was docile and relatively continent for an eighty-six-year-old.

Even better, Mrs. Lundy was hard of hearing, so she never complained about noise. But Lolita had grown up in south central Los Angeles, where the shots she heard at night were frightening reminders of rival gangs proving whatever they thought they needed to prove to each other. Here, where homes cost upwards of two million dollars, she figured the nightly gunfire was probably from an air gun handled by some bored teenager with rich absentee parents, entertaining himself to get some target practice between video games.

Lolita bustled into the expansive bedroom, a cheery smile on her face and a singsong spin on her voice. "Good evening, good evening, Mrs. Lundy. It's time for your pill. Pill time, pill time. Open, open."

Her patient sat up straighter in bed, obediently opened her mouth like a baby bird, and downed the tiny capsule with a few sips of water.

In an attempt to mute the next set of four shots, Lolita closed the burgundy velvet curtains, their frayed gold tassels languishing on the trim. She then adjusted Mrs. Lundy's pillows, reached for the remote, and turned on the nightly television ritual. *Jeopardy! Wheel of Fortune.* Then whatever cable nature show was on until Mrs. Lundy's bedtime at ten o'clock. That's when Lolita began her nighttime vigil in the recliner chair next to the bed, which ended when Miriam arrived at six the next morning for the daytime shift.

Even though the television volume was cranked up, Lolita heard another flurry of four shots emanating from the little ravine behind the house. A couple of minutes later, as the third

Jeopardy! contestant was introduced, Lolita's sharp ears distinguished a sharp crack—just one, instead of the usual grouping of four. A trained nurse practitioner, adept at noticing anything out of the ordinary, Lolita sat up straight. "Did you hear that?" she asked.

"What, dear?" Mrs. Lundy's watery-blue eyes rested fondly on Lolita.

"Oh, nothing, nothing," said Lolita.

Mrs. Lundy settled into her pillows, smiling at the spinning image of the Daily Double.

But Lolita got up to check the back, front, and side doors of the house, making extra sure that everything was locked. Hadn't Miriam told her that there had been some robberies in the area?

A familiar series of popping noises peppered the air.

On West Ullman Lane, at the tip of the double-pronged fork and approaching Chef Chelsea Navarro's place, Freyda Gordon slowed and stopped.

"Hear that, Max? Our neighbors should thank Sergeant Heider. Our guardian angel."

The dachshund lifted his leg at the base of the pygmy palms at the sidewalk's edge, unfazed by the noise. As he relieved himself, he stared blissfully up into the dusky tinge of the late July sky.

Four more pops.

While Max sniffed a smorgasbord of canine pheromones sprinkled over low-growing succulents, Freyda inhaled the aroma of chocolate wafting down the steep street. The Point Loma Association website had posted an article describing her new neighbor, Chelsea Navarro, as a vibrant and innovative culinary talent who had recently topped the list of America's Best New Chefs of the Year. Evidently, she was the genius behind the success of a new restaurant in the Gaslamp District—one of those places that charged over twenty-five dollars for a Caesar salad.

The Ring camera installed at Freyda's back door validated the gist of the article, alerting Freyda to every movement the construction workers had made over the past several weeks as they gutted Chef Navarro's kitchen and installed top-of-the-line cooking equipment.

After kicking up dirt with his hind paws as if washing his hands, Max happily trotted toward Freyda as they neared the end of their nightly walk. The lights of Shelter Harbor started to wink with the approaching twilight. The dachshund gently pulled on the leash, leading Freyda homeward.

Four more faint pops reverberated through the balmy breeze as they neared old Mrs. Lundy's short driveway, where the nighttime caregiver's car was parked. Freyda peeked over the cement block wall and saw Lolita putting dishes away in the kitchen.

Seemed that caregivers did a lot more these days—cooking, cleaning, and even doing light housework, if you were lucky. Mrs. Henry Lundy had been lucky indeed: married, widowed, and made a mega-millionaire. Her late husband had been one of the founders of the intrastate airline California Southwest Airlines, known as CSA, "the world's happiest airline" until its merger with a larger, unhappier commercial airline in the late '90s.

Another Ring camera, this one installed at Freyda's front door, recorded Mrs. Lundy's slow but steady morning walks with Miriam, the daytime caregiver, every Monday, Wednesday, and Friday. The grand old dame never ventured out in public without gloriously coiffed white hair, chunky gold chains, sparkling jewelry, and a cherry-red lipstick smile reminiscent of the black smile that used to be painted on the nose of each CSA aircraft.

Max's short legs hustled as they neared home. Freyda scooped him up and stroked his sleek black fur as she walked through her front door. "Good walk, sweetie. No coyote sightings tonight. Time for a snack."

She set Max on the floor. The dachshund pranced on the tiles, tail swishing like windshield wipers in a downpour as he awaited the nighttime ritual of treats and then cuddles in front of the television until Freyda's husband Eric came home.

For Freyda, the months of July and August were golden. Students didn't realize their professors looked forward to summers off as much as they did. In fact, Freyda could hardly wait to take an early retirement next year after twenty-two years teaching in the School of Psychology at San Diego State.

Freyda held a strip of organic chicken jerky over Max's quivering nose. "Speak, Max. Speak!"

Max's sharp bark drowned out the sound of a single shot that echoed in the ravine behind Sheree Carpenter's house on East Ullman Lane.

After a day hidden away resting or sleeping in camouflaged crannies in the ravine separating the lineup of homes on West Ullman Lane and East Ullman Lane, the opossums always ventured out at about six thirty or seven in the evening.

Sergeant Michael Heider, retired marine, sat in his wheelchair on the redwood deck that overlooked the ravine directly opposite Freyda's place. He'd built the deck himself forty years prior and still defended it like a fortress. His mission? To protect all the neighboring decks and homes on stilts from the enemy. Damn opossums could chew through wood, drywall, and wiring like hungry soldiers in a mess hall.

Every night Sergeant Heider recharged his air gun, donned his night-vision goggles, and defended his territory. Neighbors probably thought he was just taking random potshots at the opossums. No, sir. Sergeant Heider's pinpoint accuracy was legendary in his tours of duty and even in retirement decades later. His strategy was not to kill the creatures but to simply beat them into a retreat. Whether opossum, squirrel, or coyote, four quick pops of the air gun and the rush of pellets mere centimeters from their fur kept them away for the rest of the night.

In the past five minutes or so, he'd already scared a team of opossums, plus a couple of partners in crime: bushy-tailed squirrels attempting to feed on the navel oranges that looked like bright buttons in the tree by Freyda's back steps.

More intruders. He raised the air gun and instinctively performed the next maneuver. A satisfied smile cracked through Sergeant Heider's grizzled face as another squad of opossums scurried away.

A few minutes later, the night-vision goggles targeted another movement. Something had emerged from the shadows underneath Sheree Carpenter's deck.

The sergeant's eyes narrowed. This one was a big bastard he'd seen many times before. He paused. *Set the sight picture. Focus on breath control. Steady the scope. Adjust for the breeze. Squeeze the trigger.*

The solitary shot cut through the air.

As usual, Sergeant Heider's aim was one hundred percent accurate, the pellet precisely hitting its intended target.

The figure staggered, tripped, and fell behind a thickly speared agave plant. Only his tassel loafers showed, unmoving.

The sirens had faded into the distance hours before, but Sheree Carpenter still couldn't sleep. For the past three hours and twenty-five minutes, she had been huddled in a fetal position on top of her bed covers, staring at the digital display of her alarm clock, which had just morphed to 03:15 a.m.

How could she have known that the crazy old-timer would finally hit something, let alone kill someone? People around here should've put a stop to his behavior before an accident like this happened.

Her mind replayed the events of the previous seven hours.

The cops had interviewed the neighboring residents on West Ullman and East Ullman, well aware that three home invasions had recently hit the news, with one just a mile away. The cops had concluded that a concerned neighbor had used an air gun to scare away a suspicious-looking man lurking in the shadowy ravine. It was a fluke, a one-in-a-million chance that an air gun pellet would rip into the "T-Box," evidently the official name for a lethal head shot.

She reluctantly thought of Freyda, Eric's wife and now, widow. Sheree buried a pang of guilt. Hey, it wasn't her fault that Freyda and Eric had a crappy marriage. Why else do guys go to strip clubs? Eric had been one of her regular customers at Jazz Hands Gentleman's Club on Rosecrans, where experienced dancers like herself earned very generous tips and took advantage of other opportunities to score some nontaxable income. When Eric realized Sheree lived across the ravine, he regularly ditched Freyda for some one-on-one at the house on East Ullman.

Of course, Sheree wouldn't admit that to anybody. No way. Keeping secrets was the name of the game in her line of work.

The next morning, Max sat comfortably in his mom's lap as she sipped her tea on the big guy's wooden deck. Max leaned into her hand as she stroked his sweet spot, right behind his left ear. He felt her fingers slow down as she spoke to the big guy sitting opposite them in the chair with big wheels.

"Uncle Mike, I can't believe you did that for me. You could've gone to prison."

Max nuzzled his mom's hand, and she resumed his massage.

"Freyda, hon," said the big guy. "I had to. Your husband was a cheating, self-absorbed scumbag."

"I wanted to leave, but I felt trapped. Eric was so controlling, so demeaning."

The big guy shook his head. "Nobody deserves that kind of treatment."

Max sat up straight in his mom's lap. *Treat? Did someone say treat?*

His mom tore off the edge of a bran muffin and offered a chunk to Max. "You know, Eric had all nine traits of narcissistic personality disorder. My psychology students had no idea that their own professor was the victim of a narcissistic abuser. You saved my life, Uncle Mike. I was so beaten down. I wasn't strong enough to walk away."

Max nudged his mom. *Walk? Did someone say walk?*

"But Freyda, now you're free," said the big guy. "As to what really happened in the ravine last night... we'll just keep it between you and me."

"You and me... and Max," said his mom, holding up her hand in front of Max. "High five! Who's a good boy, huh, Max? Who's a good boy?"

Max lifted his paw and touched his mom's palm. *I'm a good boy! Just like the big guy. Always ready to protect us from varmints.*

A BAYSIDE MURDER

Jennifer Berg

Coronado Island, 1954

The doctor pulled a white sheet over the body. The men lifted the gurney and carried Stella down the wooden stairs, through the fishing shop below, and out onto the narrow street. Jean looked but she couldn't see the bay, or the palm trees, or the sandy beach, all she could see was the van—a white van with a bold red cross.

Jean forced herself to look away. The boats in the little marina swayed and the morning sunshine danced and flickered off the waves. She closed her eyes and listened to the palm trees rustling in the wind and the seagulls squawking. But then she heard the doctor whispering something to the policeman. Then the doctor went downstairs too. Seven people heard the ambulance doors close. Then the engine started, the van drove away, and Stella was gone.

The policeman stood in the middle of the little café and took out a notepad. The old man at the lunch counter adjusted his cap and focused on his coffee. Behind the counter, a young man had been drying the same plate for several minutes while his middle-aged mother arranged and rearranged the salt and pepper shakers.

By the window, Jean, Barry, and Charles had sat back down. There were four coffee cups, four hats, and four chairs around the table. No, there were only three chairs—the fourth chair was overturned and lying on its side.

The policeman took a pencil from his suit pocket and checked his notepad. "So her name was Stella Waters, she was thirty-seven years old and worked as a secretary, is that right?"

Jean glanced at Barry, and he nodded.

"How did it happen?" the policeman asked.

Jean pointed to the small medicine tin in the middle of the table. The tiny, unfolded tissues that had held the headache powder, Stella's empty coffee cup, and Stella's diamond bracelet. Jean tried to clear her throat. "I don't know what happened. She had a headache."

The policeman picked up the tin with a handkerchief. Godfrey's Headache Powders, he muttered quietly. He sniffed it carefully, turned it over, then he gathered the tissue squares. He put the empty tissues back into the tin and dropped it all into a paper bag. Then he looked at Jean. "And you are?"

"Jean Waters, Stella is—" Jean took a deep breath. "Stella was my cousin. We shared an apartment by Balboa Park." As Jean gave the address, she thought of returning to that apartment and she felt a pang of loneliness.

The policeman marked his notepad. "Okay, Miss Waters, so your cousin deliberately took the stuff that killed her?"

"No!" Barry looked up sharply. His knuckles were pale from gripping the brim of his straw Stetson. His colorful Hawaiian shirt seemed as inappropriate as Stella's glitzy bracelet. "Stella suffered from headaches," he stammered. "She didn't deliberately..."

The policeman's tone softened. "Stella was your wife?"

"My fiancée." Barry frowned. "We were going to get married in September."

"Do you live on Coronado Island?"

Barry shook his head as he indicated the man sitting beside him. "We were meeting Charles. We were all going to sail to Baja or Catalina for the weekend."

Jean looked at Charles, with his broad shoulders and strong

jawline. He was the vice president of a bank in Los Angeles, but at the moment, he didn't look like a banker. He was sporting a white skipper's blazer, complete with brass buttons, and a matching captain's hat. The policeman's gaze lingered briefly on the red gemstone in Charles's signet ring, then he took down their full names: Miss Jean Waters—Stella's cousin and roommate, Barry Blackwell—Stella's fiancé, and Charles Craig—Stella's friend.

Jean looked down at the handbag and red sun hat that were still lying beside the toppled chair. The honeycomb yellow handbag was embroidered with bold pink flowers and red dots. Jean gathered up her cousin's treasures. She set the sun hat on the table, but she held onto the colorful handbag. It was extravagant and Stella had paid nearly four dollars for it. The center of each flower was sewn with a cluster of shimmering crystal beads. It had matched Stella's bold pink sundress; it had matched everything about Stella.

Holding out his hand, the policeman said something, and Jean surrendered the handbag.

He rummaged through her cousin's personal belongings. Two lipsticks, a cigarette case, face powder, gum, mints, a compact mirror, a pen. The policeman extracted a slip of paper; it was a handwritten receipt from the local drugstore.

He turned to the middle-aged woman behind the lunch counter. "Darlene, would you please telephone Chester down at the drugstore and tell him not to sell any more Godfrey's Headache Powder."

Darlene picked up the telephone and asked the operator to connect her. They all listened as she relayed the policeman's message. She glanced awkwardly at Jean and Barry as she avoided telling Chester exactly what had happened. The old man at the lunch counter tried to light his pipe, but his match wouldn't strike. The younger man handed him a box of matches.

As soon as Darlene hung up, the policeman turned to the young man. "Tom, when did you get here this morning?"

Tom took a deep breath. "I opened the tackle shop down-stairs at six o'clock for the early birds. Mother opened the café at half past seven and I've been up here since then, taking inventory and packing for a fishing trip."

"Herman, what about you? When did you get here?"

The old man rubbed his whiskered chin and took his pipe out of his mouth. "I reckon I come here 'bout fifteen minutes after Darlene. The coffee were just ready." He put the pipe back in his mouth and bit down on it.

The policeman turned to Jean, Barry, and Charles. "And how about you folks? When did you get here?"

Barry ungripped his Stetson and set it on the table. "I left Hill-crest around eight o'clock. I picked up Stella and Jean at their apartment. We must have arrived here about twenty minutes lat-er. Stella had a headache coming on, but she didn't want to keep us waiting, so she dropped Jean and I off here, then she drove my car to the chemist's."

The policeman looked at Charles and raised his eyebrow.

"I sailed the *Sea Diamond* down from L.A. last night." Charles pointed to the pristine yacht. It was easily twice as large as every other boat in the marina. "She's the seventy-five-foot beauty docked at the end. Last night, I slept on board and came to the café at nine o'clock to meet my friends."

The policeman looked around. "So all six of you were al-ready here when Stella arrived?"

Everyone agreed. Jean, Barry, and Charles had been sitting by the window, drinking coffee and waiting for Stella. Herman had been sitting at the counter, smoking his pipe. Darlene was talking to him from behind the counter, and Darlene's son, Tom, had been counting inventory and packing for a fishing trip.

"Stella got here about fifteen minutes after nine," Charles explained as he adjusted his ring.

Charles had been talking about his other boat, the twenty-six-foot *California Mirage*, and he had just invited them to join him at his ski lodge that winter. The invitation had been for all of them, but he'd been smiling at Jean when he said it. Some things were better left unsaid. "We were talking about the holidays," Jean explained. "I saw Stella pull up in the Bel Aire, and I said she was back from the chemist's, then someone said that we would start out after she'd had her coffee."

The policeman walked to the window and looked down at the red and white Bel Aire with its shiny chrome trim. "So, Miss Waters bought the headache powder from the chemist, parked on the street, and joined you all up here."

"That's right." Barry was fidgeting with his cigarette case. "Charles and Jean were facing the door so they saw her come in. I stood up, and she kissed me and sat down."

The policeman turned to the locals. "Did you three see Miss Waters come in?"

"Sure did." Herman took his pipe from his mouth. "Darlene and I were talking 'bout which fishin' boats might be for sale and Tom here was mostly packin' for his trip. And in comes this pretty lady with a big red hat and sunglasses. She was a real friendly gal. And she says 'Mornin', Darlene,' and she asked for some coffee and then she sits down at the table there, and starts talkin' with her friends."

The policeman turned to Darlene. "You knew Miss Waters?"

"I didn't know her name," Darlene explained. "But she and this fella, Charles, came by several times last year with another lady, a pretty redhead lady, and I think there were usually some other folks with them too. But I didn't know any of them well. I actually thought Stella and this fellow were a couple." She looked apologetically at Barry. "Of course, now I know that wasn't so because she was engaged to you."

Jean glanced at Barry. He was staring at the diamond bracelet he'd given Stella last week. Barry was a successful accountant, but he wasn't nearly as rich or as handsome as Charles. And unlike most of Stella's friends, Barry was thoroughly sensible. According to Stella, he purchased government bonds instead of stocks, he had already paid for their honeymoon, and he had preemptively purchased life insurance policies for both of them.

"An understandable mistake." Charles smiled. "But the pretty redhead was my wife. Stella was just a friend."

Just a friend.

Stella had never admitted pursuing Charles, not even to Jean. After all, until recently, Charles had been married. But Charles was one of the few men around with a bank account large enough to capture Stella's interests. In any event, Stella had moved on last spring. She'd announced that she was going to marry sensible Barry and Jean had always wondered if Barry knew that he had been her cousin's backup plan.

"And where was the medicine tin?" the policeman asked.

Jean remembered her cousin bursting into the café. Stella announced that it was a perfect day for boating; she wanted the sun on her face and wind in her hair. She flattered Charles by saying that his yacht was the biggest in the marina. Charles had beamed proudly. "Go big or go home, I always say." Barry had stood up. Stella had kissed him and then she bent over and folded back the brim of her sun hat so she could kiss Charles's cheek.

"The tin was in Stella's pocket," Jean explained. "She tossed her handbag and sunglasses on the table, and she sat down and turned her coffee mug right side up."

"And Darlene was right behind her with the coffee," Charles added. He turned to Darlene and added with a smile, "I remember you telling Herman there that the *Seagull* was twenty feet when you poured it, and he said something about the *Baja Baby*."

"*Baja Baby's* a good boat," Herman muttered. I used to go fishing on it back when—"

"Wait," the policeman interrupted. "Was Miss Waters the only one who drank that coffee?"

"Oh, no!" Darlene snapped. "You're not suggesting that my coffee had anything to do with that poor woman's death?"

"It's my job to get answers," the policeman said.

But Darlene's hands were on her hips and her face was flushed. "I've got a clean kitchen, homemade jam, and the best coffee on

Coronado Island! If you start spreading rumors, you can be damn sure—"

"The coffee was fine," Charles interjected. "It was a fresh pot. And Miss Darlene re-filled all of our cups at the same time as Stella's. We all drank the same coffee."

Darlene huffed and the policeman nodded and cleared his throat. "And did Miss Waters seem upset or bothered in any way?"

"She was perfectly happy," Barry stated. "Our wedding was coming up and we had our honeymoon booked in Rome. Stella was happy. She wanted to buy a boat. I've been reluctant and this weekend was supposed to get me hooked."

The policeman picked up Stella's bracelet, inspected it closely, and set it back down. "Were all these things on the table?"

"Let me see," Charles said. "Before Stella arrived, we had our three coffee cups, my hat, Barry's hat, and…Jean's handbag." He looked over at Jean. "Is that right?"

Jean nodded. "And when Stella joined us, she set her sunglasses, her sun hat, and her handbag on the table. Darlene poured the coffee, then Stella took the medicine tin from her dress pocket and set it on the table."

"So the tin was sitting on the table." The policeman considered. "Did anyone touch it?"

No one had. The policeman frowned and asked if they were absolutely sure.

"Of course we are," Darlene said. "There were only six of us here, plus Stella. No one else came or went until the doc arrived with the ambulance."

"Except me," Tom said from behind the counter. "I went downstairs for the spare can opener." He turned to his mother. "You remember, don't you? You and Herman were talking about the *Rambler*."

"That's right," his mother said, "but that was after I poured Stella's coffee."

"Did you go anywhere near the table?" the policeman asked.

Tom shook his head. The policeman looked back at the table

and frowned. "And the coffee cups were already on the table when you arrived, they were all the same?" Everyone agreed and he nodded and wrote something on his notepad.

Herman took his pipe out of his mouth and said quietly, "Tom, if you're gonna be out for a few days, you ought to drop a lobster cage."

The policeman looked up and raised an eyebrow. "Does your boat have a sleeping berth?"

"My twenty-two-footer has a small cabin," Tom said as he put a couple cans of baked beans into his bag. "It's not grand, but it's enough."

Charles cleared his throat irritably. "I believe we were discussing—"

"Of course," Tom said apologetically. "My mother poured the coffee; I went downstairs for the can opener. I think you folks were talking about a penthouse at the time."

Barry blushed. He owned a charming house in the suburbs, but Stella had wanted a penthouse in the city. She had pushed the point until Barry was forced to admit that he couldn't possibly afford both a yacht and a penthouse. That's when Stella had removed her bracelet, declaring rather loudly, that surely her future husband could afford a modern apartment and at least a small yacht, if it was less than forty-five or fifty feet.

"That was when Stella took off her bracelet," Jean added vaguely. "Then the clock struck nine thirty, and we decided it was time to set off. Stella said she wasn't going to let a headache ruin her perfect day. She grabbed the tin, opened it up, and..."

Jean's voice faltered. Barry was still staring at the bracelet, so Charles continued the story. "Stella opened up two packets of headache powder and poured them into her coffee. Her cup was nearly empty and she had to swirl it around a bit." He lowered his voice. "Then, she drank it all in one go."

"Stella always used Godfrey's for her headaches," Barry said. "It never gave her any problems before."

Not until this time. This time, when Stella took the powder, everything went wrong. She grimaced. Then she touched her stomach and her face convulsed. She tried to stand up but she collapsed, and a few minutes later, she was dead. Those horrible minutes. The shouting, the rushing, the panic. Darlene telephoning the doctor, Barry trying to get water, Jean trying not to cry.

The policeman put his notepad in his pocket and picked up Stella's chair, setting it upright. "I need to telephone the station."

Charles sighed and patted Barry's shoulder. "Stella was a beautiful woman," he said quietly. "I can't tell you both how sorry I am. Under the circumstances, I understand if you need to change your plans for the weekend." He looked over at Jean. "Of course you're still welcome to join me, even if Barry chooses not to. The fresh air would be good for you."

Stella had warned her cousin about the handsome banker. "He's a playboy," Stella had said. "That's why his wife is leaving him. But he's absolutely irresistible and stinking rich. If you're not the jealous sort, you could try being the next Mrs. Charles Craig."

Barry's brow furrowed. "But it's an overnight trip."

Jean didn't need Barry's chivalry. What she needed was a way to stop thinking about Stella. Stella's fabulous life, Stella's unbelievable death, and the fact that sooner or later, Jean would have to go back to their shared apartment, alone.

The policemen hung up the telephone and turned to them. "You're free to go."

"So that's it?" Jean asked. "What about Stella?"

"A terrible accident," the policeman said. "Naturally, we'll check the rest of the chemist's supply, but I think we'll find that it's just regular Godfrey's powder," the policeman said.

"Then what caused her death?" Jean demanded.

The policeman shook his head and shrugged. "It could have been an allergic reaction, or maybe it was her heart. The doctor will be able to tell us more later. It's rare, but unfortunately, sometimes these things just happen." He patted Jean's shoulder and took out his notepad.

Jean sat down beside Barry. After a few minutes, he squeezed her hand gently and went to the telephone to make some calls. Dear, heartbroken, Barry.

Jean looked out the window. The boats were still swaying in their slips. The seagulls were still squawking, the palms were rustling in the wind, and the waves were splashing on the sand. Charles sat down beside her and rested his hand on hers. Jean could smell his heady cologne. He was an attractive man, and single, but he had an ego, and two ex-wives, and Lord-only-knows how many ex-secretaries. Under normal circumstances, Jean would never... She tried not to think about it.

Charles leaned closer. "Jean, are you all right?"

She looked out at the bay. Charles must have thought she was admiring his yacht, because he said, "The *Sea Diamond* is seventy-five feet from bow to stern; she has three roomy cabins, a modern galley, and all the comforts of home." He gently swept a lock of Jean's hair from her cheek. "Everyone will understand if you'd rather not go back to your apartment. After all, you've been through a shock. We could sail down to Mexico for a few days. You'd be able to relax and forget all of this. And when we get back, I can help you find another apartment; a nice new place, maybe closer to the beach, someplace without the memories."

Charles rested his large hand on hers. She knew what she wanted but Barry was still on the telephone. The policeman was talking to Darlene. Herman lit his pipe again and Tom added a couple bottles of beer to his paper bag. Jean found it appalling, and heart-wrenching, and reasonable all at the same time. As soon as Barry was off the telephone...

Herman puffed smoke from his pipe. "Maybe Doc will sell me the *Yellow Rose*."

"But your *Rambler* is a fine boat." Darlene topped up his coffee. "It's big enough for catching tuna. Why do you want another one?"

"Well, like your boy, here, I'd like to be able to go down to Baja or out to Catalina. The *Rambler's* only big enough for a day trip. Tom, how long can you stay out on the *Salty Dog*?"

Tom glanced up and smiled. "I sold the *Salty Dog* to Miller. My new boat is the *Seagull*. Now I can go down to Ensenada or further, if I want to."

Herman nodded. "That's right, the *Seagull*. She's a good boat."

Jean turned and looked at Charles. He smiled and squeezed her hand. Charles was rich, and good-looking, and he was certainly proud of his boat.

An icy shudder swept up Jean's spine.

His boat.

Jean let go of Charles's hands and stood so abruptly that she knocked her chair over. It hit the floor with a thud.

"It wasn't bad luck!" she shouted. "And it wasn't an accident. Stella was murdered."

"What?" Charles frowned.

Barry hung up the telephone receiver. Everyone looked at Jean.

"Don't you see?" Jean's face was hot but the words kept coming. "Stella always used Godfrey's Headache Powder for her headaches. We all knew that. Everyone knew that. Someone wanted to kill Stella, so they poisoned a tin of headache powder and then switched the tins."

"I understand that you're upset," Barry said slowly, "but what you're saying just isn't possible. Stella had just bought a new tin of powder and no one had touched that tin except her."

"Barry is right," Charles said gently. "Stella took the tin from her pocket and set it in the middle of the table. It was in plain sight. If anyone had touched it, we would have seen them."

"I finished my coffee." Jean closed her eyes. "Barry and Charles were talking. From the window, I saw the Bel Aire turning onto the street and I said that Stella was back from the chemist."

Barry pointed toward the staircase. "Yes, and a minute later, Stella came through the doorway. We were all here."

"No." Jean opened her eyes and slowly shook her head. "Tom wasn't here because Tom had left as soon as I announced that Stella was back."

"That's not right, miss," Herman said gently. "Tom went

downstairs for the can opener, that's true, but that was after your cousin was already sittin' down and drinking coffee with you."

Jean shook her head. "We remember it that way because that's how Tom retold it, but at the time, none of us were really paying any attention. And Tom had been moving around and taking inventory and packing for his trip. He must have left the room twice. The first time, no one noticed because as soon as Stella entered, everyone's attention was on her. Darlene poured the coffee, and while we were drinking it, a few minutes later, Tom went downstairs a second time."

Darlene spoke softly. "My dear, I can assure you that my son was here the whole time; he and Herman and I were all talking together."

"That's just it," Jean explained. "You and Herman were talking about boats, and just before you poured Stella's coffee, you told Herman the *Seagull* was twenty feet long."

"Yes." Darlene frowned. "But why does that matter?"

"Because the *Seagull* is twenty-two feet," Jean explained. "Tom just said so; the *Seagull* is his new boat and it's twenty-two feet. You got it wrong, and if Tom had been in the room when you said it was twenty feet, he would have corrected you. But he didn't say anything because he wasn't here. He was still on the staircase where he'd gone to meet Stella."

Darlene's brow furrowed and she slowly looked toward her son. "But why would you do such a thing?"

Everyone looked at him.

"Because I loved her," Tom said quietly. He took a deep breath. "We started seeing each other last summer when the *Sea Diamond* first came to San Diego. She said she loved me but that we had to keep it a secret until her divorce was final. Then last April, she admitted that she never had been married, but that she was going to get married, and she was going to marry someone else. That was the last time I saw her, but when the *Sea Diamond* sailed in last night..." Tom took a tin of Godfrey's Headache

Powder from the pocket of his jeans and set it on the counter.

Everyone was silent.

"My old man's heart medicine," Tom explained. "I got the powder ready this morning. I could have given her the tin any time but I knew she'd just come from the chemist, and that made it easy. She stopped on the stairs long enough to say hello, and that was all the time I needed. It was easier than unhooking a sand shark." He grinned and leaned against the bar.

Jean stood by the Bel Aire as the policeman put Tom into the black and white car. The palms swayed overhead and the waves washed up on the beach. At the end of the dock, the *Sea Diamond* gleamed invitingly in the bright sun. Charles was onboard, arranging the deck chairs.

"I don't know what to say," Jean said as she took a deep breath of salty sea air.

Barry sighed. "Did you know she had dated that man?"

"No," Jean said. "But when he said that the *Seagull* was his boat, I realized that if he'd left the room when I said Stella was here, he could have met her on the stairs before she joined us."

Jean was holding Stella's things. She handed the bracelet to Barry, and he looked at it with a sad, grateful smile. "I don't know that it would have worked out," he whispered. "Stella and me."

Jean took a deep breath and looked out over the marina. Some things are better left unsaid.

BIDDING WAR

Tim P. Walker

Keir could tell right away that he didn't want the guy anywhere near him. With pasty skin, a scraggly patch of stubble on his chin, dirty jeans, and a canary yellow windbreaker sporting more moth bites than zipper teeth, the guy certainly didn't look like someone he'd have any business with. Worse, the narrow set of eyes peering out from beneath the lid of the faded red cap told him the guy probably had his own idea of business, and the fact he was walking his way didn't bode well either.

The guy slid into the spot across from Keir in the corner booth of Kessler's Harborview Tavern. The squeak of the padded umber vinyl soiled the comfortable silence, and his foul, catch-of-the-day stench slimed the air. Keir greeted him with a stony glare over the rim of his glass of beer.

"Hey, bud," the guy said, hand extended across the table. "Name's Dobie."

Keir waved the guy's hand away with a twitch of his lip.

Dobie pulled his cap off and scrunched it in his hands. "Look, some guys—" he started to say. "Actually, no, see, what I got is a business proposition for you. How'd you like to make ten bucks?"

Keir answered with a long cold sigh.

"Okay, so some guys..." Dobie looked briefly over his shoulder, but Keir knew who he was talking about—the well-heeled pair sitting at the far end of the bar who looked like they stepped

243

out of one of those sunny magazine ads for shitty mentholated cigarettes. These guys with their bronzed skin, molded windproof hair, and Ray-Ban sunglasses clipped to collars of their brightly colored golf shirts—it seemed like they had eyes on every other part of the tavern but Keir's booth, as if they were pretending not to pay him any mind. The smirks splashed across both their faces like rancid, overpriced cologne suggested otherwise.

"Okay," Dobie said, "these guys offered me fifty bucks if I came over here and tugged your ponytail one good time, so I—"

"Fifty bucks?" Keir cut in as he threw a look to the grimacing pricks at the bar. "And you thought I'd be jazzed to let you touch my hair for a measly ten?"

"Well, I—" Dobie sputtered. "I ain't gotta cut you in on anything. All I gotta do is tug your hair and I get the money. But you see, I figured, you know, I'd do you a favor 'n' stuff."

"A favor?" Keir felt a whiff of steam rising from his creased forehead. "Pulling my hair is doing me a favor?"

A picture of his own hand reaching across the table, grabbing a tuft of the bum's own greasy brown hair, and smashing his face into the metallic tabletop popped into his head. But the word *BUSINESS* flashed across that fantasy in big red letters. Any moment a man was supposed to be joining Keir in his booth. From what Keir heard about him, just a whiff of Dobie's lingering smell would've set him on edge. Add a few drops of blood from a busted nose and that would've been it—meeting canceled.

Keir swallowed whatever bit of ire he was swishing in his mouth and forged a grin as he reached into the left breast pocket of his black sports jacket and pulled out a thick wad of green paper bundled together with a shiny gold-plated clip. He unclipped the wad and peeled off two bills marked a hundred a piece. Dobie's eyes lit up.

"Tell you what," Keir said. "Two hundred if you go back there and slap both those motherfuckers in the face." He looked past Dobie and fixed his eyes on the two as he slid the bills across the table. "I mean it. Cut them in if you like. Do *them* a favor."

Dobie gazed at the bills for a moment, then he swept them into his hand as he glanced over his shoulder.

"Both," Keir said as Dobie stood up and stuffed the cash into his pocket. "I'll be watching." But as soon as Dobie shuffled off, Keir slid around the curved bench until he wasn't facing any of those bozos. Maybe the bum would go through with it; maybe he'd take the bills and scram. Either way.

He ran his fingers through the sweat-dampened strands of hair tied together in the back, then grabbed his glass of beer and took a sip. The moisture on the glass felt cooler than the beer and wetter as well. He must've been sitting there for half an hour because that's how long it takes for beer to grow bored waiting for someone to kill it. Keir knew he'd likely have another one before the man showed and another after he arrived, but as he took a big swig, it dawned on him that he could wind up downing three more waiting for anyone to show.

Past the bar, the tavern's tall and wide windows looked out on a small armada of docked sailboats whose masts traced lines in the blue sky as they rocked in the gentle harbor waves. The sound of yacht motors humming filled the air while their exhaust fumes ambled through the door and mingled with the lingering cigarette smoke. If Kessler's was the type of place with a clock on the wall, Keir would've spent every minute watching it, waiting for the hands to cross themselves like scissor blades.

Dobie crept into view as he sidled up to Keir's table with his hat crumpled in his hands.

"Yeah?" Keir grunted. He hadn't heard a slap or a scuffle, so it went without saying that the guy didn't earn his pay.

Dobie planted himself in the same spot, "I meant to ask— any them boats out there yours? Those guys there—one got himself a Four Winns—"

"And you didn't slap the motherfucker?" Keir cut in.

"Well," Dobie said, wincing as he scratched the back of his neck, "I told them about what you were gonna pay me—"

"*Paid*," Keir cut in again, his tongue sharper. "I already paid you. Sounds like you didn't do your job, pal."

Dobie's face lit up a shade of red brighter than his hat. "Well, that's what I'm getting to. See, they went and said they'd give me more'n what you would."

Keir sighed. "They countered? How much?"

"Three hundred," Dobie answered. "But now they want me to punch you."

"*Punch* me?" Keir laughed. "Really? Where?"

"Like, in the cheek." Dobie illustrated by tapping his own face with his knuckles.

"And how much were you planning on cutting me in on?" Keir threw the guy a sharp look and added, "You know, on top of the two hundred you were already giving me back."

"Hold on." Dobie held up his hands, and his claw-like fingers seemed to stretch half the way to the ceiling. "See, I was thinking, you having that roll and all—"

"This roll?" Keir pulled out the clip from his left breast pocket again.

Dobie nodded, eyes wide.

"Oh, you thought you were gonna milk me for every last bill this afternoon. I bet you don't even really have a counteroffer from those pricks. You're just trying to pull a fast one, aren't you?"

Dobie shrank back in his seat. "Whoa, bud, it ain't like that."

Keir whipped a finger at him. "No, you want play it like that? Fine, let's play it like that." He peeled off another three bills and threw them on the table. "On top of the two hundred I already gave you, that's five hundred bucks right there. Here's what I want you to do—I don't want you to punch them. What I want you to do is go over there and kick those smarmy fucks right in their dicks."

Dobie's jaw dropped as he glanced back over his shoulder.

"Kick them hard, too," Keir added. "I mean it. I want see their balls flying out of their fucking mouths."

"They're both sitting down though. How do I—?"

"Tell them to stand up. Show some initiative. What am I paying you to do?"

"So what do I tell 'em, then?" Dobie asked as he stood.

"Tell 'em they can still jerk each other off, they just have to do it with ointment for a while."

Keir brushed his hand at Dobie like he was a gnat. Still, the man hovered, hesitant.

"Go before I take my cash back and kick you in the dick myself."

As soon as he was out of sight again, Keir leaned back and fished a Parliament from the pack sitting on the table. *Yuppie pricks probably smoke those shitty menthols, too*, he thought as he started to strike a match, but then he caught a glimpse of the five butts in the ashtray, all his.

A cigarette every six minutes? No, he would've had to have been there longer than half an hour. He tossed the match and slid the cigarette back in its pack. There was half a swig left in his beer glass. No bubbles—it died waiting. He grabbed the glass and slid out of the booth.

He stepped up to the bar, fished two crumpled ones from the front pocket of his pleated black Cavaricci pants, and laid them both flat on the counter.

"Another Michelob?" the woman behind the bar asked. She was short, with long stringy hair struggling to hold onto every last shade of blonde color. She wore a white shirt with the top buttons undone to show off her cleavage.

Keir winked and pushed the two singles toward her. Her face beamed as she winked back at him. She grabbed the empty glass with one hand and the dollars with the other, all while she pressed her body against the counter, which gave her chest some extra oomph. Keir felt that wad thump in his breast pocket and he briefly considered reaching for it. It would've made her day, sure, but what else would it have made for her? As it was, a dollar tip on a dollar draft wasn't too shabby.

He'd be reaching for that wad again soon enough. Out of the corner of his eye, he spied Dobie waving his hands and two heads of molded hair nodding along and sliding an occasional eye down the counter to Keir's end of the bar. If he tuned out the whirring ceiling fan and the dull murmur of other people's conversations, he'd be able to hear the three of them scheming, negotiating—anything but Dobie talking the other two off their barstools so he could deliver the agreed-upon kick to each of their groins. This fucking bum.

Keir leaned over the bar and thought about asking the bartender what the deal was with Dobie, but guys like that were all the same. They hung around places like Kessler's all day, shaking down tourists and locals for booze, money, cigarettes, or some combination of all three. No matter where they were, nobody was tasked with putting up with their antics more than the person behind the bar. He didn't need to imagine what the girl thought of him. So Keir asked her where the phone was, then he pointed at the corner booth where he was seated and told her that if anyone came looking for him in that particular spot to tell them that he stepped out for a moment and he'd be back shortly. He pulled another crumpled one from his pants pocket and slid it across the bar top. Before he stepped out, he grabbed a paper coaster and placed it on top of his glass of beer, which he left on the table.

The pay phone clung to the wall out front near the side entrance, fifty feet from where Keir parked his Datsun 280ZX and a hundred from the nearest palm tree or awning or cover of any kind from the late afternoon sun. The phone's black receiver had soaked up enough rays to nearly scald Keir's palm as he picked it up, and he had to juggle it in one hand as he plugged some coins into the slot and dialed.

"Potts, it's Keir," he said as soon as the line clicked over. "Where is this guy? I've been waiting for an hour now."

The man on the other end of the line hemmed and hawed for a full minute as trickles of sweat ran down the back of Keir's silk paisley-patterned shirt. "An hour, you say?" Potts said, smacking his lips as he spoke.

"Hell, probably longer. I thought you said this guy was really anal about punctuality and whatnot."

"I don't know what to tell you, Keir. I mean, from what I know about him—and let me tell you again, I don't know this cat very well at all—but from what I do know, he's anal about a lot of things. There isn't anything down there that might've spooked him, is there? Any shady characters hanging around, giving off strange vibes?"

Dobie's scruffy mug flashed in Keir's mind. Pesky as he was, there was no way a guy like that would spook anyone. Still, a trace of red tinted his image of the bum.

"No," Keir said. "Joint's pretty quiet, actually. Just like you said it would be."

"Okay, well..." Potts smacked his lips some more. "How about the merch? How's it looking?"

"Fine. Good as it ever was."

"You holding samples? Mind reading off one of the serial numbers?"

Keir sighed and held the receiver between his shoulder and his ear as he reached into his jacket's breast pocket. The phone had cooled somewhat, but still he could almost hear the sizzle as the heat bit into his lobe.

"Ready?" he said as he briefly glimpsed the sequence printed in bright green above the number 100 on one of the bills. "It's N-Five—"

"Eight-Six and so on and so forth," Potts jumped in. "Same numbers as every other batch, right?"

Keir slid the wad back in his pocket and sighed again. "Look, I keep telling him that he's gotta change the numbers up. I don't know, he thinks he's some kind of artist like Rembrandt or something. You know what he tells me? He tells me those numbers—they're like his signature."

"Keir, I don't care," Potts cut in again with his tongue firmly pressed on the gas pedal, "Not my problem. Could be a problem with Mister Anal, maybe? I don't know. I'm just talking here. I got nothing to do with any of this. Okay?"

Keir listened as Potts drew quick breath and shifted gears. "But hey, here's to fixing all that on the new bills, right? You guys getting new presses or what?"

Keir held the phone away so Potts couldn't hear him mutter curses. Just a month before, the Federal Reserve rolled out the new series, and it took a full week for Keir to talk Rembrandt out of his one-bedroom apartment in San Pedro. The man's breath reeked of a week's worth of cheap tequila and his eyes were half-sealed from the reddened puffiness around them. The only light turned on in the apartment was a desk lamp on the kitchen table which was leaning over a microscope. Laid out beneath the lens—one of those crisp new hundred-dollar bills. Keir figured the guy must've run the lens over the oval border around Benjamin Franklin's portrait in the center thousands of times. The words microscopically printed in the border must've looked tinier with each glance.

Keir swallowed his bitter tongue and told Potts, "We're not up on the new style yet. Matter of fact, I can't imagine anybody who would have something that can print like that yet. How about you? You know anyone?"

"Whoa," Potts said, "I don't know nothing about the intricacies of nobody's businesses. I'm just a guy who kinda sorta knows people."

"Just nobody closer to L.A. though, huh?" Keir added as he looked around the parking lot and street and palm trees off in the distance. Several more beads of sweat dripped down his back. He was only a hundred miles from home, but it felt much hotter.

Potts hemmed and hawed some more and reminded Keir that the guy he only kinda sorta knows—a supposedly anal-retentive contractor looking to cut costs by paying all his Mexican day laborers with Keir's product—was the only client he could swing in a moment's notice, and he'd already told Keir that he couldn't make any guarantees about the client either.

"Who knows, buddy. Maybe you should cut and run. Come

back around when you and Mister Rembrandt got a fix on the new style. Count your blessings. Know what I mean?"

"Count my blessings?" Keir said. "The fuck do you—?"

But Potts sped on. "Eh, forget it. I don't even know what I mean. Good luck, buddy."

The high-pitched buzz of a dead line filled Keir's ear, and since it wasn't going to answer his questions any more than Potts could, he hung up the phone.

Blessings—Keir counted two thousand of them that he'd stuffed into the back of his Datsun. And *the new style* wasn't something Rembrandt could ever comprehend. When Keir last dropped him off at his apartment and said good riddance, he was wearing the same brown velour sweater and flared trousers he'd been wearing since the Carter administration. An hour and a half before that, Keir found him naked on his back in a pile of freshly minted hundreds at the Moulton Avenue shop where the press was kept. The guy was dragging the dull blade of a hunting knife across his wrist like he was playing a sad violin song. Keir thought about finding him a sharper blade. By the time Rembrandt would have new plates ready, the Fed would have already rolled out the next series. Who had that kind of time? So after Keir dropped him off, he doubled back to the shop and swept up as much of the latest batch as he could count and took off south on the I-5. The whole ride down, the thought itched: *What if I keep driving straight to the border? Pass those bills around myself?* They would've carried him a lot further in Mexico than in California. For a few months anyway.

Instead, he steered the Datsun to Kessler's, where he made it for his scheduled appointment on the dime. Now it was an hour later, and walking in from the blinding sunlight, the tavern was nearly as bright from the glare pouring through the windows. If that California sun could find Keir anywhere he went, he hoped it at least caught that jagged sneer he threw at the two yuppies still seated at the bar as he passed them, because something needed to catch it if those guys were going to keep pretending not to notice him. Keir figured without their middleman around, they wouldn't have the means to pay him any mind anyway.

And where did that—?

Shit.

A figure occupied the corner booth with their back to the windows, and unless the man he was supposed to meet also wore a yellow windbreaker with a red cap—

"Motherfucker," Keir said in a low growl as he approached the booth, "there's dozens of other empty spots here. Find one."

"Hey bud, take it easy," Dobie said, half-standing as he took his hat off. "That girl there," he muttered and gestured to the empty bar. "Well, she said you'd be right back and for me to just go ahead and wait."

"She didn't mean you, shithead. Now scram."

Keir eyed his glass of beer and noticed the paper coaster that he'd put on top had fallen to the side. "You touch my beer?"

Dobie waved his hands as he backed out of the booth. "Keir, c'mon, I wouldn't mess with your beer like that."

"Wouldn't you? You really seem to enjoy messing with me, don't you?" Keir fixed a stare on the man who in turn shrank where he stood and wrung his cap in his hands. It didn't actually matter to Keir if he touched it or not. The beer would've been tainted from sitting unguarded in close proximity to him anyway, so Keir nudged it aside as he slid into the booth. "Your friends there don't look like they've had their dicks kicked in. Why not?"

"Oh, you know, I got to thinking and, well, I figured any man's dick wasn't worth kicking for any kind—"

"I don't care," Keir cut in as he dug into his breast pocket again. "I got somebody I'm supposed to meet here. What's it gonna take to get you to fuck off?"

Dobie threw his hat back on and waved away Keir's wad. "Sorry, bud, I don't think your money's any good."

Keir tightened his stare as he laid the wad on the table. "Fuck you mean it's not any good?"

Dobie checked over his shoulder and slid back into the booth across from Keir. "Okay, you see," he quietly said as leaned in, "those guys I've been talking to—I told 'em about your offers and that you paid me up front and they asked to see the money. So I showed them, and you know what they say? They say your money's bullshit. Like funny, you know? And they show me one of their hundreds, and it's got, like, teeny little words around Ben Franklin's picture." He pointed at the half portrait of the founding father peeking up from Keir's fold. "Plus, there's those little strips they now got in 'em. I've never seen nothing like it myself, but these strips—threads they're called—they're just like those strips you pull when you're opening a pack of smokes."

"I know that. Those are the new bills." Keir tapped his wad. "These are the old bills. They're phasing 'em out, sure, but that don't make 'em worth any fucking less."

"Well..." Dobie shrugged. "That's the other thing. See, they told me these look like you just got them from a bank. They say banks ain't giving out those old hundreds anymore. Plus, the ones you got all got the same number on them."

A tinge of red clouded Keir's vision as the guy reached across the table to tap the serial number with his greasy finger. Fucking bum. Fucking yuppies. They must've torpedoed his deal while he wasn't looking. All three of them. Mister Anal must've arrived and walked right out the moment he saw them all poking and prodding his product. And if the bills couldn't fool this bum and the other two pricks...

Keir tasted blood boiling in his throat. He leaned across the table, inches from Dobie's face, and as he spoke a fleck of spittle flew from his lip to the bum's nose. "Just tell me what the fuck it is you want already."

Dobie let the spit linger and drip down his nose as he leaned forward, wide-eyed, and patted the table as he laid it out: "Okay, so here's a brand-new deal—one thousand dollars right down the middle. Five hundred for both of us. They're cutting you in on it now, too."

Keir leaned back, arms crossed. Five hundred bucks was five hundred more than he'd probably see from Mister Anal. It wasn't much, but if he split for the border, it would carry him for at least a few days. Mix in some of Rembrandt's paper and it might float him a good distance down the coast. It would've been more than enough to cover the shots of tequila needed to help forget whatever embarrassment these assholes had in mind. "All right, motherfucker," he sneered. "Let's hear it."

"Okay, so what they want you to do is pull your pants down and walk outta this place with them around your ankles. Easy five hundred."

Keir forced a wide, gnarly grin. "Really?" he hissed through his teeth. "Tell me, where the fuck do you come in?"

Dobie held up a finger. "Okay, so all's I gotta do is slap your nut sack a few good times."

The fake grin vanished from Keir's face as he fired a piercing glare across the table.

Dobie held up his hands to block it. "Look, I don't even have to do it *that* good. I just gotta give 'em some little taps is all."

"*Little* taps? How many?"

Dobie shrugged. "However many it takes to get to the door, I guess."

Keir tasted a full geyser of blood percolating in his throat. If he raised his voice above a whisper, it was sure to erupt all over the table and half the tavern. "All the way to the fucking door?" he hissed.

"Well, if you run fast enough—"

"If?" Keir shut his eyes so tight that red was the only thing he saw, and he had to choke the air with his hands to keep from wrapping them around Dobie's throat. "What makes any of you think I'd go for this?"

"Well, at first they weren't gonna cut you in on anything. With those hundreds being funny and all, they said it'd be enough for you to get away without them calling in the Secret Service."

Keir's eyes flew open as the grin returned with a vengeance.

"Oh, so they were gonna call the—?" he snarled. "Oh, I see."

He slapped the table several times as he stood. The fake grin still screwed to his face, he told Dobie not to move and that he'd be right back. The word *BUSINESS* flashed briefly in his mind then melted to a thin red puddle that reflected the faces of those two yuppies, neither of whom threw him a single glance as he passed them rounding the end of the bar on his way to the door. The sun gave him a hard stare as soon as he stepped out, and it stayed on him as he crossed the lot to his Datsun. As he sat in the driver's seat, the urge to stick the key in the ignition, turn the engine, and gun it the hell out of there struck him. Five minutes to the freeway and another twenty to the border— gone, forgotten, yesterday's news. Blessings counted. Instead, he reached into the glove box, grabbed his Detonics Pocket 9, and stuffed it in his jacket. The yuppies still didn't pay him any mind as he sidled up next to them at the bar.

"Fuck is your deal?" Keir asked with lead in his voice.

They both fed him dumbfounded looks. The blond one closest to him, the one who didn't know that he had a gun pointed at his side, spoke, "Pardon?"

"I asked what your deal is. Why don't you just tell me what you got on me instead of sending your fucking dog."

"My dog?" the blond asked. He squinted his eyes. "I'm sorry. I don't understand—"

"The fucking guy in the yellow jacket," Keir growled in a low voice as he raised the barrel slightly.

The dark-haired guy saw it first, and his eyes went wide as he gasped and pointed.

"Oh shit!" the blond blurted aloud. He jumped backwards from his stool and grabbed his partner's wrist.

"All right Keir, that's enough," he heard Dobie's voice tell him. For a moment, he thought the guy might try to broker yet another deal, but when he spoke he didn't dither or stammer, and it dawned on Keir that he never once actually told the guy his name either.

"Just put the gun on the counter and keep the hands where I can see them," Dobie told him. The cold metal that kissed the back of his neck told him that it wasn't Dobie's red cap.

The yuppies shuffled off as several mustachioed men dressed in K-Mart jeans and navy flak jackets poured in and surrounded Keir with pistols drawn. Soon out of sight, those yuppies may as well have been actual cutouts from those cigarette ads for all Keir was concerned. Turned out their conversations with Dobie—or rather Special Agent Dobbins as he reintroduced himself as—had had nothing to do with Keir. No talk of hair pulling, punching, or pants around ankles. And certainly no bids either.

"So who was it? Who fucked me?" Keir asked as a pair of handcuffs were slapped on his wrists. His mental Rolodex flipped straight to P. Potts set the meeting up. He picked the place. He even suggested where Keir should sit. Then again, there was Mister Anal. But hell, did that guy even exist? Or perhaps his partner Rembrandt...

"Does it matter?" Dobie/Dobbins said. "I mean, you practically stuffed all the evidence I needed right in my hand. And damn, you go and pull a gun on those yuppies... We don't need a warrant right now. We got all the probable cause we need to search your vehicle. You know that? Seriously, collars don't come as easy as you, bud."

Keir felt his face redden. He also felt himself sink into the earth. He pictured his pants around his ankles, and this guy—this federal agent—slapping his balls all the way to the parking lot. He also thought about jumping back behind the wheel of his Datsun and steering it north or south or any direction the hell away from Kessler's.

"I don't suppose that offer still stands," he muttered.

"What offer? You mean this one?"

Keir yelped as his head jerked back when something yanked his ponytail hard. He found himself bent over backward and staring up at that same scraggly pasty face that now towered over him.

"There," the man said, grinning wickedly. "I owe you ten bucks."

GIRL OF GOLD
Emilya Naymark

Martin hunted treasure every day, even (or maybe especially) on the day he retrieved his wife's ashes from the Chula Vista crematorium over on F Street. The ashes came in a clear plastic bag that fitted snugly into a black plastic box, and he held the box on his lap as he drove east to Mount Laguna.

He parked just as the sun began to sink. The trails closed at dusk, but no one was there to stop him, it being cold and a Tuesday. This high above sea level, snow covered the hard ground in grayish lumps, promising a difficult hike. He wanted difficult.

It'd been a week since the hit-and-run. A week of howling loneliness where there'd once been a wife and a dog. A week of nobody to touch, of the type of silence that kept him awake through the night and anywhere but home in the daytime.

His first impulse was to move Elena into the trunk while he hunted. But she always hated small, dark spaces, and after a moment's pause, he put her down on the back seat and covered her black box with the blanket they'd kept there for when Barney traveled with them. Barney, in his own tiny black plastic urn, was right now sitting on Martin's bedside table, awaiting funerary decisions.

But Martin was nowhere near any kind of shape to be deciding. Additionally, he'd spent the entirety of his paltry savings on the two cremations and couldn't afford a proper urn, much less a burial plot.

Instead, he opened his trunk and retrieved the Garret AT Pro, secured his headphones over his ears, and strapped his torch around his head. An hour's hike up a pine-bordered trail placed him on a sloping hill, all scrubby grasses and snow, the sky a murky charcoal. The metal detector pinged and cheeped at him as he walked, singing of things hidden and lost.

Some people hunted for fun, on weekends, at the beach. But ever since Martin lost his job (okay quit, he quit, couldn't hack the eighty-hour weeks anymore, felt he was dying), he hunted for practical reasons. He conducted nightly sweeps of playgrounds, parks, and beaches; sometimes walking away with twenty dollars in coins, often quite a bit more. If he found jewelry, he sold it. He had a knack. Elena used to say he had a divining rod for metal inside his skull, which he thought was terribly corny and also cute, because they met at a Slipknot concert, both of them in black clothes and black nail polish, both metal fans since forever.

The signal coming through Martin's headset told him something interesting was at his feet.

Could be gold. Could be nothing. But could be gold.

He knelt and drove his serrated shovel into the stubborn ground.

"You got something?" Martin heard the man's voice despite the headphones, so startling it took all his self-control to stay still. He turned his head, his eyebrows climbing with disbelief.

Gerry, the newest member of the San Diego Metal Detectorist Club, stood not six feet away, holding his own Garret, his headlamp making Martin's eyes water.

What the hell?

Martin resumed poking the rocks and dirt aside, his heart pounding with outrage and confusion. "Probably a pull tab," he said, which, under the circumstances, was such an inappropriate response, he stopped digging and unfolded himself to his full height. What he had was not a pull tab but fuck if he would let

Gerry see it.

He took a moment to gather himself, then asked, "What are you doing here?"

"Couldn't sleep," Gerry said. Gerry lived in a pricey San Diego neighborhood and... why was he an hour's drive away, at night, in the cold mountains? Talking to Martin?

Possibly in response to the bewilderment on Martin's face, Gerry said, "I see you finally came here to hunt." He jutted his lower lip. "Thought you'd call me, you know? Thought we could do this place together."

Martin first noticed Gerry six months ago at a metal detectorist meeting when the man expressed curiosity about all of Martin's finds. Gerry quickly began following him around, planning hunts, asking for advice.

"Fucking dilettante," Martin told his wife one night after Gerry visited and then stayed and stayed, examining whichever of Martin's treasures hadn't sold yet and drooling over pictures of those that did.

"He's just lonely," Elena said, because she believed everyone was good and right, in their own way.

Shit. Gerry had told him about Mount Laguna weeks ago, and the suggestion must have stuck, surfacing as a desire to go someplace cold and punishing and lonely. Martin figured if he broke to pieces on this hill, there'd be no one to hear, and no one to tell him idiotic things like *she's with God* and *it will get better* and *you need to find a way to move on*.

He looked away from Gerry's pouty face and returned to digging because he didn't want to leave the thing he knew was underfoot for the other man to find, and he didn't want to talk to him, and this was his goddamn hunt. Goddammit.

Despite the low temperature, Martin worked up a sweat boring his way to the mug-sized lump buried a foot deep. The instant he tugged it free and rubbed his thumb along the surface, he knew it was gold, its solid heft a giveaway.

"Whatcha got there?" Gerry hovered directly behind him.

Martin hunched over the lump, as if examining it. Of course, Gerry didn't know about Elena and Barney. Martin kept the news to close family and friends, and although the San Diego Patch mentioned the accident, it was only a blip. Nothing anyone would notice.

He said, "Eh, looks like a brass fence ornament." He kept his hands between the thing and Gerry's line of sight. "Nothing special."

"Oh yeah? Mind if I look?"

Martin rose to his feet slowly, making a show of brushing off his jeans. What surprised him most was that he still cared about something. He cared about keeping Gerry's paws off the gold lump. He cared about getting home, which was the first time he'd felt this way in days.

"Sure," he said, and handed Gerry an unidentifiable chunk he'd dug up the other day, having hidden the gold piece inside the pouch strapped around his waist.

"Why, that's just some smelt." Gerry chuckled. "That's definitely not an ornament."

Martin removed his headphones and folded them away. "I gotta be going," he said.

"Oh," Gerry studied him, his lamp making it hard for Martin to read his face. "Okay."

As Martin started down the hill, he paused and turned around. "So, like, did you follow me or something?"

Gerry flicked off his lamp, and now he was in shadow, in darkness, a hulking figure against the tree line. "Nah, man," he said after a while and shrugged, though maybe Martin's tired eyes played a trick and he never moved. "Just, you know. Great minds think alike."

"Got it," Martin said. "Okay, well." He descended, unease clotting once again into self-centered despair. Yes, Gerry was ignorant of Martin's loss. But that was not the point. The point was that Gerry's presence, and his own irritation at this fact, reminded Martin of Elena's largesse. She would have hugged the incompetent oaf and offered him tea from her own thermos.

Later, in the double-wide mobile home still redolent of Elena's shampoo and lotions, its couch and chair still furry with Barney's hair, Martin carefully scrubbed the dirt off the evening's prize, revealing a graceful gold statuette of a woman. She stood with her toes caught in a roughly hewn base, her back slightly arched and her face tilted upward as if trying to spring into the air.

He smoothed and polished her with a cloth until she shone a dull ochre. She was heavy, close to two pounds, and with gold going for fifteen hundred an ounce, the statue was worth... a lot. Also, it looked old, so probably even more than that.

He was too tired to calculate.

Martin fell asleep toward morning, his fingers wrapped around the cold metal until it warmed, Elena's black box nestled companionably next to Barney's by his bedside.

When his phone rang a couple hours later, the light in the tiny bedroom was dim, the sun not yet fully risen.

"Damn robocall," he muttered and shifted in bed.

But the phone rang again. Fully intending to turn it off, he jumped out of bed, then answered it accidentally, only to hear nobody on the other end.

Now he was wide awake. He grabbed the gold woman and brought her with him to the bathroom where he took a shower with her perched on the toilet lid, watching him.

"I know I'm not supposed to ask, but how old are you?"

The statue said nothing.

That much he expected. What he didn't expect was Gerry sitting on the edge of his bed when he walked out of the bathroom.

Martin stopped short, electrically alert, and gripped the wet towel wrapped around his waist to keep it from slipping. His right hand squeezed around the gold woman.

"I'll take that," Gerry said, pointing to the statue.

"Get the fuck out," Martin said. He wondered, oddly, how they got so immediately to the point. It usually took them hours, days to say anything of meaning to each other.

Gerry lunged for Martin, and Martin raised his hand and smashed Gerry in the left temple with a sharp, gold, lady statue edge.

Gerry crashed to the floor.

According to the large clock above the bed, the whole interaction lasted less than two minutes.

Martin peered at the statue and noticed beads of blood on her head.

Interesting, he thought. She's bleeding. I should clean her up.

As he washed her, the shock-induced calm evaporated, and by the time he came out of the bathroom the second time, his heart was slamming so hard against his ribs that it hurt.

The phone rang.

He didn't answer. It rang again, and this time he picked it up with fingers shaking so hard he almost dropped it.

A man's voice asked for Gerry.

"Who's this?" Martin asked.

"His brother," said the man after the briefest hesitation.

"He's not here." This was, existentially, true, but an even truer truth was that fear finally grabbed hold of Martin's gullet and pressed. He swallowed.

"Are you sure?"

Martin sat down on his bed and stared at the very dead Gerry wedged sideways between his bed and his closet.

"Yeah," he said. "I'm sure."

As soon as he hung up, he called the police. But when the dispatcher answered, he ended the call, his bowels turning liquid with sudden terror, sending him staggering to the bathroom.

After he washed his hands and his face and his hands again, he returned to the bedroom.

"Elena!" he said into the quiet house, because for just that second, and despite Elena's ashes sitting silently by his knee, he believed his need would conquer reality and she'd appear.

She didn't, and he nodded, pressing his lips tight to keep from blubbering.

"I don't want to go to jail," he said to the statue.

She said nothing.

"But it's not like I can bury him in the backyard, right?" Martin wiped his face. "No, of course not." He bent forward, placing his elbows on his knees and hanging his head. "Fuck."

He dressed, stepping carefully over the large body on his floor, then gathered the two urns and the statue and got into his car.

The cop at the front desk heard him out, waved over the desk sergeant, who in turn called a couple of detectives, the result being Martin in an interview room with a cup of cold coffee by his elbow and two detectives across from him.

At some point they read him his rights.

At some other point they left him alone in the room.

And six hours later they let him go.

"Sir," the older detective said, "is there anyone you'd like us to call?"

"What do you mean?"

"It might be better if you weren't alone tonight, sir."

"But... at home?"

"Sir, there's no body in your house."

Martin's mouth opened and stayed that way.

"We did a very thorough search. Your house is all good."

"What?"

"We found no evidence of a forced entry or a struggle."

When Martin still didn't move, the detective elaborated. "Or a body."—and, because even that was not enough to get Martin to his feet—"Your neighbors had nothing to report either."

Martin left the precinct, stepping out into dusk. Everything in his life now seemed to happen at twilight. Last week the sun had been setting when an SUV careened around a corner and knocked Elena into the air, poor Barney already lifeless under its wheels. The SUV dislocated her hips, but that didn't kill her. She was alive and conscious when a second vehicle, a Dodge truck, ran over her body, crushing her chest.

In Martin's memory of that evening, he experienced her death like a shove. As if her hard little fists punched his back, and he stumbled forward, burning his hand on the skillet he'd been using to fry their supper. He turned off the stove and walked out into the blue gloaming, unsure of what he expected until he heard the sirens.

Tonight, as he slipped into his car outside the precinct, he wondered if maybe he wasn't okay anymore. If his mind wasn't working right. Surely Gerry had been there this morning. He remembered braining the man, the soft "oh" sound he made as he crumpled. The burgundy blood on the beige rug.

The detective wasn't kidding when he said they'd done a thorough search. Not a single item was in its place, and most of Martin's possessions littered the floor. All the lights were on. He picked his way to the bedroom and leaned against the door-frame, too tired to support himself upright. Photographs, candles, Elena's tablet and phone lay heaped on the rug. The clean rug. The very much unbloodied rug.

Okay. Martin bent to pick up the photos and his eyes fell on the box under the bed. Elena's box of silly treasures (her words, not his). He knelt and dragged it into the light. A pin from the Combichrist show he took her to on their first date. Purple and silver beads from Mardi Gras. Her mother's gold bracelet. And at the bottom, two slightly bloated cans of Chef Boyardee meat ravioli.

He snorted and wiped his face. Among other things they had in common, they were both art school graduates. He became a video game designer while she stayed resolutely with print work. Her first job was to design a logo for a local entertainer, a clown/magician/comic named Ernest Desire, who, after paying her fee with cash, added the two cans of ravioli. "You look like you could use some fattening up," he'd said.

"My first paying gig!" She put the cans proudly on their kitchen table. "I will never open them. They're proof I'm not a starving artist."

Martin lifted the cans out of the box and carried them to the kitchen. When he used the can opener, they made a faint hissing sound, accompanied by a mildly sour odor. He emptied them into a pot and turned on the stove.

The gold statue, which had waited out the day in the glove compartment of his car, now watched him from the counter.

"I've read," he said as he stirred the red and white mass in the pot, "that there is a tribe living on the banks of the Amazon, that used to eat its dead. They believed that if they ate even a little bit of their beloved person, then that person's soul would abide inside of them and not wander the jungle forsaken and alone. It was a kindness."

Martin tapped his spoon against the pot's edge to dislodge bits of gluey ravioli and turned down the flame. He went into the bedroom and brought back the black plastic box with his wife's ashes.

As the tomato sauce and pasta burbled quietly, he used the spoon to scoop a few heaps of coarse, gray ash into the pot and stirred.

"How bad can it be, huh?" he asked the statue. "Maybe some diarrhea. Maybe I'll die." He shrugged.

The statue said nothing.

The knock came just as he reached for a bowl. He froze, one arm up, the other hovering over his phone. The second and third knocks were louder, a *rat-rattatat-rat* of insistence.

He slid the statue into the cutlery drawer, switched off the stove, and opened the door. Two men barreled inside, knocking him off his feet before closing and locking the door behind them. He sat up, and one of them, the wiry one in a blue sweatshirt, punched his face with a ring-studded fist.

After that, they made themselves comfortable on his couch and waited for him to stop spitting blood.

"So, this is what's going to happen," said the second man, the one with a soft paunch encased in a pin-striped button-down. "You're getting your metal detector and we're all going up to Mount Laguna."

Martin wiped his mouth and touched his tongue to the new, sharp chip in his upper tooth. At any other time in his life, he'd have body slammed the intruders with the full impact of his two hundred pounds, but the past thirty-six hours had been so surreal, and he'd slept and eaten so little, that all he had the strength for was a sneer. This response was pathetic and feeling pathetic on top of battered made him weepy, but he clenched his throbbing jaw and swallowed back the tears.

"I'm waiting," Wiry Guy said.

"Why are we going to Mount Laguna?" Martin said through the chipped tooth, lisping. Crap. He couldn't afford to fix it.

"Where's my thanks?" Wiry Guy asked.

Martin stared in confusion.

"Dude, we got rid of the body," Wiry Guy stage whispered.

Clarity brought back fear, and Martin squared his shoulders, unconsciously readying his muscles for whatever was coming.

"Actually," Paunchy one said, "you made it easy for us. Killing him. Gerry was an idiot."

He couldn't argue with that. Although he never wanted to kill anyone, Gerry attacked him first, and somehow the men facing him made that act seem acceptable.

"Hey, whatever that is, smells real good." Paunchy sniffed and got to his feet, wandering over to the stove. "Oh wow, look at that! Chef Boyardee! I used to eat this all the time as a kid."

"Yeah, you know? That does smell good. I didn't eat dinner yet." Wiry glanced at his partner, then back at Martin. "You mind?"

Martin tried to say something, he really did. He coughed and swallowed and made a gurgling noise, but none of it stopped Paunchy from rooting around the drawers until he paused and brought out the gold statue. He weighed it in his hand and glanced at his friend, who grinned, his eyes narrowing. Paunchy tucked the statue into his pocket, where it bulged comically, and excavated two spoons from the same drawer.

As Martin watched two men eat his wife's ashes mixed with

(possibly) botulism-laden ravioli straight out of the pot, he wondered how exactly his life got him to this moment. And then put his head down and began to cry, because even this, even giving his wife a loving body to inhabit after death was apparently beyond him.

"Oh, geez, come on, don't CRY," Wiry said between spoonfuls of Elena. "We're not gonna HURT you. Hey, you want some of this? Are we eating your dinner?"

Martin shook his head and rubbed his eyes with his already bloodied and snotty sleeve.

"You know what this needs?" Paunchy got up again and headed toward the kitchen. "Tabasco."

"Right on." Wiry held out the pot as Paunchy shook a solid dose of hot sauce into it, then stirred, and tasted a dollop. "Man, that did it. Perfect now."

They ate in comfortable silence for a while, scooping the pasta with their spoons until they scraped metal.

"So, here's the deal." Wiry burped discreetly into his fist and patted his chest. "Gerry, the moron you so conveniently dispatched for us, had a job."

Paunchy shook his head. "One job!"

"Right, and he fucked it. That pretty statue you had in your drawer? That's part of a whole stash. We won't go into how we came about to have it, but I'll tell you what."

Paunchy said, "Moron lost it."

Wiry rolled his eyes. "He let someone steal it. Which is WORSE."

Paunchy nodded.

Wiry said, "So we found the guy who stole it."

Paunchy shook his head again.

Wiry threw his hands in the air. "And all he told us was that he buried it on Mount Laguna. And then you know what he does?"

It was Martin's turn to shake his head since both of them were looking at him, waiting.

Paunchy (disgusted), "Has a heart attack."

Wiry banged his bowl on the coffee table. "A HEART attack!" He sighed. "So Gerry—"

Paunchy (grim), "The moron."

Wiry, agreeing, "The moron decides he will buy a metal detector and go look for this stuff. Like he's hunting buried treasure. Like it's a GAME."

Paunchy pointed at Martin with a spoon. "That's where you come in."

Wiry grinned. "He couldn't stop talking about you. How you always found something."

They smiled at him.

Martin closed his eyes. An hour ago, he'd invited death into his kitchen. A grand gesture. A spin on the wheel of fortune. But fortune had other ideas. He felt Elena's cold little hand on the back of his neck. Or maybe it was the ceiling fan.

He said, "Okay. Fine. Let's go." Because, really, come to think of it, how long did it take for food poisoning to take effect? "Can we listen to music? I hunt better after listening to music."

They drove in Wiry's car, Martin's phone blaring Rob Zombie through the speakers as the road climbed higher and a gaseous effluvium permeated the interior.

Wiry burped. "Dude, the Tabasco is really killing me tonight. I knew I shouldn't have ate it."

Paunchy rubbed his belly and grimaced. "I'm usually okay with it, but yeah, might have been expired or something."

Wiry rolled down the window and spat into the night. "Hey, what the hell are we listening to?"

Martin pressed his hot forehead against the cool window in the back-passenger seat. "Rob Zombie. My wife loved this guy."

"It's not bad." Paunchy belched loudly. "Excuse me."

Once Wiry parked and Martin reclaimed his Garret from the trunk, they began their trek. The moon was out, and the night was clear, the stars like ash dusting the endless sky. Martin took them up a different trail, bypassing the location where he found the statue last night.

Was it really only last night?

"You know the story behind that statue, right?" Paunchy wheezed as they walked up the mild elevation toward Garnet Peak. Wiry had been spitting, hiccuping, and belching ever since they got out of the car, so he said nothing.

"No," Martin said.

"So, back in the Gold Rush days, a guy came out and struck it rich. I mean, like a millionaire many times over by today's standards." He stopped and bent down, hands on knees. "Fuck, that Tabasco is burning a hole right through me." After a minute he straightened, and they continued the climb. "So, he builds a beautiful house overlooking the ocean and he marries. He's old, but his bride is a teenager. So, as you can tell, happy marriage." He halted again, opened his mouth, and spewed a dark stream of lumpy matter onto the rocks. "Jesus. Excuse me."

Walking again, he said, "But they only have one kid, a daughter. And, you know, she's cute and smart and eventually becomes a teenager herself, at which point he's a real geezer. And then she gets sick and dies." Paunchy snapped his fingers. "Just like that. Dead. And the geezer loses his mind. He doesn't care about his money anymore, so he gets a solid gold statue made of his daughter."

Wiry grabbed his stomach and veered off into a nearby sugarbush where he quickly unbuckled his belt, dropped his jeans, squatted, and let loose.

"Nice," said Paunchy, though even in the moonlight it was obvious he wasn't doing great himself.

Wiry moaned but assembled his clothes again and tottered up the rocky trail without a word.

"Where the hell did you find the statue, anyway? Much farther?" Paunchy was slowing down, having to stop every five paces or so.

"No, not far," Martin said. Garnet Peak via the Pacific Coast Trail was Elena's favorite hike, and they'd done it dozens of times in the last few years. As he led the two men up the incline, the sky wheeling above them and the rocks like black cutouts in the fabric of space, he promised himself he'd never dig up the lost treasure for Wiry and Paunchy. Not because they broke his tooth and bruised his face. Not because they ate Elena when he was supposed to. Not even because they stole the treasure to begin with. The simple and awful truth was he wasn't sure they would ever leave that mountain, and he thought the last thing they saw should be something grand. Something breathtaking. After all, Elena was a part of them now.

The two men were on their hands and knees by the time they reached the peak, expelling bodily fluids from both ends, but still, somehow, asking how far to the treasure.

"Very close," Martin said, sitting cross-legged on a rock, the canyons and valleys below shadows upon shadows.

Paunchy lay down, curled into a fetal position, and Wiry lay down next to him, their heads touching like those of conjoined twins.

"I think I'm dying," Paunchy said.

"Dude," Wiry said.

Martin slid off his rock and started down the hill. When he got to the tree where he'd dug up the statue, he turned on the Garret and swept it side to side. The signal this time was high and pure, and he thrust his shovel into the rocky ground.

It took nearly three hours of digging, moving the coins, gold pieces, and jewelry into his bag, and then filling in the holes. He made sure the spot looked as neat as if nobody walked on it, never mind dug ten-inch-deep pits throughout. After he came down the mountain, he walked past Wiry's car and continued down Sunrise Highway. Then he called 911 and said he thought there might be two lost and very sick hikers up on Garnet Peak.

And after that, he called an Uber.

At the trailer, he packed, threw his detectors and the loot into his car, then placed what was left of Elena on the passenger seat. He secured her box with the seatbelt, then added Barney's box and tucked Barney's hairy blanket around them for good measure.

Then he drove. He drove east through the city, the canyons, and then the desert. Gas station coffee and donuts kept him fueled and he didn't stop until signs for Phoenix shimmered above the highway, and he pulled into a motel, handed over the credit card he hoped still worked, and collapsed into bed.

And after that, he drove some more until he found a place that was not so small he'd draw attention, but not big either. A nondescript town in the middle of nothing where no one knew, nor cared to know, him.

He scoured the internet for news of two hikers dying on Garnet Peak but found none.

Some nights, he stood at the edge of an overpass, talking his feet into plunging onto the highway below. Some nights he walked into the canyon, willing himself off a ledge. Some nights he held a razor blade to his wrist.

But most nights he watched Netflix.

He sold, discreetly, portions of the hoard.

He visited a chapel and lit candles for Elena and the two unlucky thugs. Then, because Elena would have wanted it, a candle for Gerry.

One late afternoon, six months after he fed his wife to strangers, he parked in the lot of Mount Laguna campground, slung a backpack over one shoulder, and wandered toward the sloping hills. Wildflowers and sun tinted his pale skin a warm rose. When he reached the top of Garnet Peak, he sat down and waited. Hikers came and went, said hello, and he said hello back. The sun set, the moon rose, the Milky Way shifted.

Martin withdrew a telescoping shovel from his backpack and pushed it into the ground underneath a clump of sagebrush. Once the hole was large enough, he removed a black plastic box, a smaller box, and a gold statue from his backpack and stacked them in the hole, the statue on the bottom.

He knelt in the dirt and smoothed the earth on top of the little grave with his filthy, bleeding hands. He stayed like that for a while, sometimes patting the ground, sometimes wiping his face.

As the sun's first light warmed the air, he felt the rays like a touch, like a finger grazing his neck. Chickadees rustled and sang. The birdsong, he thought, sounded very much like two girls laughing. Like a dog yapping at dragonflies.

And although the world was not right for Martin, and never would be, a part of him settled; the small fist squeezing his heart loosened its grip.

Elena would not wander the jungle alone.

THE CELESTIAL

Naomi Hirahara

Tokio, Washington. 1891

I don't remember the day or month, but I know something about the night I first met him. It was a full moon, glorious and bright, even blinding, in fact. Back home, they would say that a white rabbit would be pounding rice cakes in that moon, but there was nothing innocent and playful about its appearance. It reminded me that I had been here too long, working under Marudome-san in the hotel.

I had my regulars. Most of the other Japanese girls only had Japanese customers, usually the age of their fathers. My customers, on the other hand, included *hakujin* men, who often stank of drink, old sweat, and tobacco, which stained their white hands yellow. Many of them only washed once a week in the summer and early autumn; in the winter, even less. It was September, still warm enough for them to take a dip in a neighboring stream. I tried to feel fortunate. Over the last two years, I'd learned to take pleasure in simple things—green tea with rice, a new pair of underwear. Otherwise, the older women tell me, you will go insane.

He came that night after all the others left. About the only thing that I liked about my second-floor room—and it wasn't

275

even the room where I slept—was the window that faced east. I'd gaze at the moon and wonder if my parents were looking at it across the sea at the same time. Of course, that would be impossible because they were so far away. But it was still a comfort.

I saw him approach the house through that window. He was wearing a hat, so I couldn't see his face. But when he turned toward the door, I noticed his long single braid down his back. His hair was longer than mine. He was not hakujin. My door was still ajar and I heard the women down the hall. "No, no celestials for me. You know that, Maru."

Maggie had been there the longest and wasn't afraid to talk straight to Marudome-san: She would not service men from China or hakujin men either. She preferred, for reasons known only to her, men from Japan. She was the only hakujin woman among us; she apparently had angered all the other brothel owners within a fifty-mile radius. It probably helped that she couldn't speak a lick of Japanese and Marudome-san didn't know much English. Their communication gap would be her salvation: Marudome-san wouldn't be able to understand the insults she sometimes spewed at him. She had fiery red hair on her head and *chin-chin*, which she religiously dyed once a month.

"I don't service them either," Ne-san said about celestials. Ne-san was three years older than I, and I considered her like an older sister.

I got up from the bed and went to the door. I nodded to Marudome-san, who had appeared from downstairs. I did not mind servicing celestials, as they were cleaner than the hakujin men who so often came to me.

I took off my robe and got under the covers. I liked to start off naked because it usually was faster that way. I kept the room brightly lit with lamps so I could keep watch of my customers' actions. Marudome-san didn't mind the extra cost of oil because he just charged the men extra.

The Celestial was clean and nicely groomed, not one hair

loose from his braid. As he rubbed my neck I could smell onions, garlic, and ginger on his fingertips. *He must be a cook,* I thought, *maybe from one of the neighboring mining camps.* The height of the Gold Rush was over, but we still heard of men collecting gold dust through dry washing from time to time.

I was used to the hakujin men bulging their blue eyes at me as they climaxed. But the Celestial closed his eyes, as if he were someplace else.

After he finished, he slowly drew himself away from me. He turned from me as he dressed, even though we had both been naked in the same bed. I watched him as he pulled on his long johns, pants, and suspenders and finally covered his head with his hat.

He leaned forward on the dresser on the other side of the room. I couldn't see what he was doing, but when he left, I noticed the glint of a coin on the top of the dresser. Marudome-san warned us not to accept any tips; one girl had been forced out when she was caught pocketing some extra cash. I couldn't take that risk. Marudome-san's place was at least clean and safe. I ran to my dresser and picked up the coin. Before I could return it, I noticed that the Celestial had drawn a smiling face in my lipstick on the face of the coin.

The Celestial returned a week later. Apparently, he had asked for me. I wondered what he had said, how he had described me. He didn't know my name as I didn't know his. I never used my real name, anyhow. None of us Japanese girls did. We never revealed the names of our hometowns for fear that our situation would be communicated to our families. My parents thought I was still married. Even though they had been the ones to send me off to this fate, lying was easier for everyone concerned.

The Celestial became one of my weekly regulars, always

visiting at the end of my work night. A smiling coin was always left on my dresser. I sewed each coin separately in the hem of my dress. The fabric was getting worn, and I decided to go into town with Marudome-san on his weekly trek to get supplies.

At the house, we had one horse, an old mare, which was connected to a worn wagon. I knew a little about horses and farms as I lived on one for a short time before I learned about Marudome-san's place and journeyed here. As a result, Marudome-san always had me take the reins. He said the mare always went faster when I was in the driver's seat.

There was only one dry-goods store in our little town. It was next to the post office and across from a brothel and gambling den. The store was more like a shack than anything else. Boxes of nails were placed next to bags of sugar, which were next to bars of soap. The shopkeeper always had a special item that he displayed on a barrel right next to the cash register. Today's special was a revolver. It was double-action, which meant that you didn't have to cock the hammer every time you shot the gun. I knew this much from my husband.

I actually wasn't sure if we had officially married. I had left all those details to him and my parents. The boat ride was choppy, taking two weeks. I got sick every day, and only another girl from the next town over was willing to nurse me. I thought that I had been abandoned when I arrived in Seattle because he had been so late to pick me up. He looked nothing like the photo my parents had presented to me. In the photo, he had hair and wore a suit and tie. The man in front of me was balding and his clothes were almost soiled black and smelling of cow dung.

Apparently, he was even less impressed with me. "You'll do," he said to me in Japanese.

We rode on a train to Spokane. It was a long, arduous trip, and compared to the majestic mountains closer to the coast, the land there was flat and grim. I did not think that America could be more remote than my village, but it was. His house had dirt floors, and our only neighbors in walking distance were one couple from Japan. As a result, he pretty much could do whatever he wanted with me, which he did on a regular basis.

My only respite was taking care of the horses. And then every Sunday evening, we sat at the table and cleaned his guns with special oil. Everything around our house was covered in dirt and dust except those guns. It actually gave me great pleasure to learn how to take them apart and clean the chambers.

I guess that my technical skill had impressed him, because he took me shooting one time. Rabbits were damaging our crops, and we needed to be rid of them. He gave me the double-action revolver and ordered me to shoot them as soon I spied them coming out of their homes in the woods. BANG-BANG-BANG. Three lay dead in an instant.

My husband tried to cover up his surprise. "You're a good shot," he said, practically the only compliment he ever paid me. He had me gut the rabbits and take the meat with us for a stew. "I guess I should be worried." He then laughed, as if he were telling a joke. Only he wasn't because he stopped letting me touch his guns after that.

The one thing my husband wanted was a child. In particular, a son. I could not produce either, no matter how many times he came to me, which sometimes was a couple times an evening, especially on his day of rest from the fields.

He would yell and scream that he had been deceived. How was *he* deceived, I wondered. My family had been told of fine china, polished wooden furniture, and beautiful dresses in the State of Washington. But the only dress I had was made from the fabric of the kimono that I wore coming over here. He had taken the fifty dollars that I was required to travel with. What he had done with that money, I never knew.

One day, he came home in a particularly good mood. He wore a lopsided grin so big and wide that I thought it would slide off his face. "I know now that it was all your barrenness," he said. "I am to be a father." The one giving him a baby was our neighbor's wife.

The next day, he was gone, along with the neighbor woman. Days later, I found out that our house was actually owned by the neighbor man. He claimed that all of this was my fault and literally threw me out of the house. And that is how Marudome-san's house became my new home.

Marudome-san didn't keep any firearms in the house, so I hadn't been in front of a revolver for more than two years. I gingerly traced my finger on the gun barrel in the store. It was smooth, but I could have made it shine even more with some oil.

"Careful, little girl, you're bound to blow your head off playing with that thing," the shopkeeper said and then laughed. We both knew that the gun wasn't loaded.

Just then, three large hakujin men filled the store's doorway. Their smell stung my nostrils, and I bent my head and covered my nose with the collar of my coat.

"We hit the jackpot!" they announced, panting like dogs. One of them opened a small leather bag, which he'd extracted from his jacket pocket.

I hid behind some bolts of fabric and snuck a look. The shine of gold sparkled on the shopkeeper's table.

"Thought that the Chinamen were the only ones able to do anything with dry washing," the shopkeeper said, wearing a special pair of glasses to look at the gold dust.

"Well, you thought wrong."

The heavy men wore boots, and their weight strained the wood floorboards. Their excitement over their good fortune pulsed throughout the small place. They bought bottles of whiskey, a new set of spurs, and then the youngest one, with matted hair the color of burlap, took hold of the revolver. "I'll take this. Today's special."

Apparently, the men didn't own any guns because they took turns holding the revolver awkwardly. The young one then spotted me and aimed his new purchase toward my forehead. He tugged the trigger, causing the hammer to go back and click. He then lifted his head back and howled, as if he told a joke, but I did not laugh back.

A couple of days later it was New Year's Day, and the moon was ready to disappear soon. We had all gathered to pound rice cakes with a baseball bat, as was tradition back in Japan. Marudome-san was good and drunk, which made us all happy because we could pick and choose our customers. Maggie also had her share of drink and collapsed next to the wooden mortar, rice flour all over her red hair.

I asked Ne-san if it would be all right if I went to bed early. Filling herself with soft white rice cakes, she nodded. New Year's always made her feel nostalgic for the family that she left behind.

I went into our sleeping room, the room that I shared with Ne-san and three other girls. The other girls stayed downstairs, talking about I don't know what. I slept in a bed with Ne-san, while the others had a big mattress on the floor stuffed with hay.

He came into the room without any warning. How he found me here was beyond me. The Celestial seemed to have a sixth sense like a cat's. He put his finger to his lips, but I never said anything to him, anyway.

I heard the banging of feet against our wood floors below. Men's voices echoed to the upstairs rooms.

"Have you seen a Chinaman around here?"

I listened for Marudome-san's voice, but he must have passed out alongside Maggie.

A faint murmur, a woman's voice.

"Speak up, girl."

"No understand." It was Ne-san, who always pretended she didn't know English at the most convenient times.

"She may be one of them."

"She's a Jap, you fool. When have you seen a Chinawoman? They don't have them over here."

"Anyway, if you see a Chinaman, you let us know. Our camp is along Cow Creek just west of Ritzville."

Footsteps sounded from our parlor onto the porch. The door burst open. Ne-san's face was flushed, pressed into a frown. "Get him out. Now."

We heard the following morning. Ten celestials in a camp near Cow Creek were shot and scalped. Their fortune taken. Maggie damned the Indians, who had apparently killed her second husband, but Ne-san and I exchanged looks. Somehow the men who visited the brothel last night were involved. I hoped that the Celestial was now far, far away.

Most everyone didn't want to eat much breakfast, choosing some dark black coffee instead. Before I knew it, only Marudome-san and I were left in the dining room.

I began to clear the table, but Marudome-san stopped me, telling me to pour us some green tea instead. "And get out the nice cups," he added.

We had just used them to usher in the new year and I figured that Marudome-san wanted to continue the celebratory mood.

Green tea was special; it didn't come from our local dry-goods store but either via post or a traveling Japanese salesman who went from camp to camp with rice and dried bonito for sale in his wagon.

I savored the bitterness of the tea with my tongue.

"I have great hopes for this year," Marudome-san said. "I plan on moving into labor contracting."

I didn't know why Marudome-san was telling me these things.

"I'll need a partner in life. My parents want to send a wife to me."

It seemed strange to think that Marudome-san had a mother and father back in Japan. I wondered what kind of story he had made up for their benefit.

"I was thinking that it would be better to marry someone

here. Someone who understood."

Marudome-san then stared at me, and I took in the roundness of his face, his odd eyebrows that drooped like dying leaves.

It wouldn't be a bad life. Marudome-san never lifted a hand against us. And he never seemed to want relations with us.

"You could still work," he said. "Maybe just with select customers. Think about it."

He drained the rest of the tea into his mouth and rose from the table.

My cup was empty, but the bitterness stayed in my mouth. *You could still work.* Just what did he think of me?

That night hakujin men came to the hotel. They were the same ones I had encountered at the dry-goods store, and I believed I recognized their voices from last night.

"I want me a Jap girl, too," I heard one of them say. "I saw a young, pretty one at the store."

Marudome-san must have directed him to my room, because the stinky one with the burlap-colored hair stumbled in, dropping his pants even before he closed the door behind him. Something hard hit the floor, and then he grabbed me on top of the bed, as if I were a swine ready to escape.

I, however, wasn't going to put up a fight. Some of our customers wanted us to play games, fight back, so they could pinch or even slap us. No one would dare to actually disfigure or seriously harm us—they would have Marudome-san to answer to.

The hakujin man ripped off my robe and dove into my breasts. The whiskers on his chin felt like sandpaper, and his hair was oily. Nausea almost overcame me, but I swallowed any vomit that crept up my throat.

Before he pushed his *chin-chin* into me, his friend barged in. "C'mon, we've heard word that the Chinaman is out by the creek."

He quickly put on his pants and hat and stumbled out the door.

I checked under the bed. It was as I had suspected. He had forgotten his revolver.

I dug my heels into the mare's side, but she wouldn't be rushed. I searched for a sign of the moon, but fog had descended over the sky.

I felt as though we'd been traveling for at least an hour, next to the trickle of the creek, when I smelled smoke. Soon I saw flames lick the end of a torch held by the tallest one, standing in a clearing.

I watched as they surrounded the Celestial, placing a noose around his head.

My mare stepped on some dead leaves, and the sound scared a sparrow into some bushes.

The youngest one turned, his hands ready to fight. When he saw me, his face immediately softened. "Lookee, it's my little Jap girl, bringin' me my re—"

Before he could complete his sentence, I squeezed the trigger, aiming six inches below his wide-brimmed hat. The other two men shrieked, and I stilled their voices by squeezing the trigger again, again, again, and again.

It was as if I didn't have to think. My body reacted as if it were a revolver itself, built to destroy the destroyer.

The torch had been dropped; it glowed bright orange for a few seconds before burning out completely.

The Celestial acted as if he'd known I was coming to save him. He pulled the noose from his neck. He didn't say anything to me and I nothing to him. I picked his hat up off the ground and handed it to him, but instead of putting it on, he slipped it on my head instead. I didn't know if it was meant to be a memento or a disguise, but I was touched either way.

He got on one of the men's horses. I pulled the coat off the burlap-haired dead man and placed it on the back of my mare. I had been riding bareback and could use some padding going home. We then headed in opposite directions. I knew that I would never see the Celestial again.

The next night all everyone could talk about were the three hakujin men who were found dead near Cow Creek.

"Godawful Injuns," Maggie murmured. "Savages."

The other girls chattered about how dangerous our region had become.

"You feeling orai?" Ne-san asked me. She said that my face was as white as snow. "Is it the monthly time?"

I nodded. Ne-san knew my monthly flow had been heavy over the past year. I could not work under such conditions.

"Go upstairs," she said. "I'll explain to Marudome-san."

Once I was in my room, I changed out of my dress and ripped open the hem. I had fifty dollars in coins, about the same amount I brought over to this country. I could do a lot with fifty dollars. I had hidden some of Marudome-san's old clothes while doing the laundry that week and put them on. His shirt lay loose on my body, perfect for concealing my breasts, which weren't that big anyway. I'd woven rope from my kimono, which I used as a belt around the pants. My hair, I plaited quickly into a singular braid. With the Celestial's hat on my head, I looked like a younger version of him, perhaps a younger brother. I then put on the dead man's coat and slid open the eastern-facing window. I could barely fit through, but I did fit. I climbed down the drainpipe and, once my feet hit the ground, I raced for the mare.

The crescent moon was barely visible. A storm must have been on its way, based on how fast the clouds were moving. As they traveled over the slip of the moon, the crescent seemed to wink at me knowingly.

Traveling on the mare, I wondered what the girls and Marudome-san would say when they discovered I was missing.

Maggie may blame the Indians, say that I was kidnapped. Marudome-san would assume that it had to do with his marriage proposal. Ne-san would secretly suspect that I had escaped with the Celestial, chasing a future that we girls could only dream of. And she would be halfway right.

"The Celestial" was originally published in Gary Phillips's Asian Pulp *(Pro Se Productions, 2015). Barbara Goffman edited it further for her* Black Cat *curated e-book series for Wildside Press in 2021. The author thanks both Gary and Barbara for their editorial contributions to this story.*

ABOUT THE CONTRIBUTORS

KATHLEEN L. ASAY is a California native and a mystery writer and editor currently residing in Northern California. In her reading and writing, she particularly enjoys the beauty—and quirks—of her home state. Sacramento inspired her first novel, *Flint House*; a sequel is in revisions. Kathleen was an early member of Sisters in Crime and is a long-time member of the Sacramento chapter, Capitol Crimes. She has had stories in and edited three Capitol Crimes anthologies.

JENNIFER BERG writes traditional mysteries set in the mid-twentieth century. Her 1950s Elliott Bay Mystery series is published by Level Best Books and includes *The Charlatan Murders, The Blue Pearl Murders,* and *The Hatbox Murders.* Jennifer is currently working on a new whodunit series set in San Diego during the 1940s. Her short story, "Schemes in the Dark," was published in Bouchercon's 2020 Anthology, *California Schemin'.* A native of Seattle, Jennifer now lives in a small village in Bavaria, Germany.

C.W. BLACKWELL is an American author from the Central Coast of California. His recent short stories have appeared in *Reckon Review, Shotgun Honey, Tough Magazine, Rock and a Hard Place Magazine*, and Fahrenheit Press. He is a 2021 Derringer award winner and 2022 finalist. His fiction novellas *Song of the Red Squire* and *Hard Mountain Clay* are available wherever books are sold.

C.J. BOX is the #1 *New York Times* bestselling author of thirty novels, including the Joe Pickett series. He won the Edgar Allan

Poe Award for Best Novel (*Blue Heaven*, 2009) as well as the Anthony Award, Prix Calibre 38 (France), the Maltese Falcon Award (Japan), the Macavity Award, the Gumshoe Award, two Barry Awards, and the 2010 Mountains & Plains Independent Booksellers Association Award for fiction. He was recently awarded the 2016 Western Heritage Award for Literature by the National Cowboy Museum and the Spur Award for Best Contemporary Novel by the Western Writers of America in 2017. Over ten million copies of his books have been sold in the US and abroad, and they've been translated into twenty-seven languages. Two television series based on his novels are in production (*Big Sky* on ABC and *Joe Pickett* on Spectrum Originals).

WESLEY BROWNE is an author, attorney, and restaurant owner. He lives with his wife and two sons in Madison County, Kentucky. His debut novel, *Hillbilly Hustle*, was named one of *Merriam-Webster's* seventeen recommended pandemic reads.

ANNE-MARIE CAMPBELL is a writer and former French professor who lives in Southern California with two very fluffy dogs. She is a member of Mystery Writers of America and Sisters in Crime. A love for language inspired Anne-Marie to achieve a PhD in French, which led to years of teaching and countless trips to France. Anne-Marie currently writes mysteries set in Paris, with locations ranging from skull-packed catacombs to feather-filled dressing rooms at the Moulin Rouge. Anne-Marie loves flavoring her novels with French wine, cheese, and pastries... and oh là là, you might learn some French swear words, too.

ANN CLEEVES celebrated publishing thirty books in thirty years in 2016 and just keeps going. Her books have been translated into twenty languages. *Raven Black* was shortlisted for the Martin Beck award for best translated crime novel in Sweden in 2007. It has been adapted for radio in Germany and the UK, where it was a *Radio Times* pick of the day when it was first broadcast. Ten series of *Vera*, the ITV adaptation starring Brenda Blethyn, have been shown in the UK and worldwide, and series eleven is currently in progress; there have also been five series of *Shetland*, based on the characters and settings of her Shetland novels, with a sixth currently airing. A television adaptation of *The Long Call*, the first in Ann's new series set in North Devon, was also broadcast in October 2021.

L.H. DILLMAN writes mainly crime fiction. Previously, she practiced law. A lifelong Californian, she's at work on a novel about the murder of a powerful landowner and the fight over his water rights in the Central Valley. One novel manuscript now living in a drawer is set in The San Francisco Bay Area in the late 1960s/early 1970s and deals with the FBI's war against the Black Panther Party. Her short stories can be found in the anthologies *Entertainment to Die For*, *Last Exit to Murder*, *Ladies Night*, *Last Resort*, *Avenging Angelenos*, The Bould Short Story Awards 2021, and online at KingsRiverLife.com. Her nonfiction has appeared in the *Mystery Readers Journal*.

JOHN M. FLOYD is the author of more than a thousand short stories in publications like *Alfred Hitchcock's Mystery Magazine*, *Ellery Queen's Mystery Magazine*, *Strand Magazine*, *The Saturday Evening Post*, *Best American Mystery Stories* (2015, 2018, 2020), *Best Mystery Stories of the Year 2021*, and *Best Crime Stories of the Year 2021*. A former Air Force captain and IBM systems engineer, John is an Edgar finalist, a Shamus Award winner, a five-time Derringer Award winner, a three-time Pushcart Prize nominee, and the author of nine books. He is also the 2018 recipient of the Edward D. Hoch Memorial Golden Derringer Award for lifetime achievement.

NAOMI HIRAHARA is an Edgar Award-winning author of multiple traditional mystery series and noir short stories. Her Mas Arai mysteries, which have been published in Japanese,

Korean, and French, feature a Los Angeles gardener and Hiroshima survivor who solves crimes. The seventh and final Mas Arai mystery is *Hiroshima Boy*, which was nominated for an Edgar Award for best paperback original. Her first historical mystery is *Clark and Division*, which follows a Japanese American family's move to Chicago in 1944 after being released from a California wartime detention center. Her second Leilani Santiago Hawai'i mystery, *An Eternal Lei*, was published in 2022. A former journalist with *The Rafu Shimpo* newspaper, Naomi has also written numerous nonfiction history books and curated exhibitions. She has also written a middle-grade novel, *1001 Cranes*.

KIM KEELINE, when not running a 1907 steam locomotive or lecturing on Shakespeare, is active in the mystery community, especially with Sisters in Crime. Her first published story, "The Crossing" (*Crossing Borders*, San Diego Sisters in Crime anthology, 2020), was a 2021 Derringer Award finalist. Nilda Santos is also seen in the anthology *Hook, Line, and Sinker* (January 2023), where she dealt with a con artist. This is Kim's sixth published short story since 2020. Check kimkeeline.com for information on her short stories, novels in progress, and freelance work for authors in marketing and web designing.

MARY KEENAN is a longtime resident of Toronto. Several of her short mysteries have been included in anthologies, most recently *Entertainment to Die For*, published in 2023 by Sisters in Crime's Los Angeles chapter. Her longer fiction has been named as a finalist for both the Daphne du Maurier and Claymore awards. Mary is fascinated by social history. She regularly attempts to produce recognizable flowers in watercolor, and she maintains a blog, hugsforyourhead.com.

RICHIE NARVAEZ is the Agatha and Anthony Award-winning author of the books *Roachkiller & Other Stories*, *Hipster Death*

Rattle, Holly Hernandez and the Death of Disco, and, most recently, *Noiryorican*.

EMILYA NAYMARK is the author of the novels *Hide in Place* and *Behind the Lie*. Her short stories appear in *A Stranger Comes to Town*, edited by Michael Koryta, *Secrets in the Water, After Midnight: Tales from the Graveyard Shift, River River Journal, Snowbound: Best New England Crime Stories 2017*, and *1+30: The Best of MyStory*. When not writing, Emilya works as a visual artist and reads massive quantities of psychological thrillers, suspense, and crime fiction. She lives in the Hudson Valley with her family.

KATHY A. NORRIS writes fiction featuring people of color in settings ranging from the Great Depression to the current Covid-19 pandemic. Two of her short stories are included in Sisters in Crime anthologies. She is currently working on a detective series featuring an African American Vietnam War veteran battling PTSD. Kathy lives in Los Angeles but loves to wander. Next up: an expedition to Southeast Asia to gather the sights, smells, tastes, and sounds that make fiction sing.

J.R. SANDERS is a native Midwesterner and a longtime denizen of the Los Angeles suburbs. He's an award-winning author of both historical fiction and nonfiction. *Stardust Trail*—a detective story set among the B-Western film productions of 1930s Hollywood—was his first novel featuring L.A. private investigator Nate Ross and was a 2021 Spur Award Finalist (for Best Western Historical Novel) and a 2021 Silver Falchion Award Finalist (for Best Investigator). J.R. lives in Southern California with his wife, Rose, and rescue dogs, Ruby and Marlowe.

JAMES THORPE's father was a mortician, and his mother played the accordion, so even at a tender young age, James realized he was destined to become either a serial killer or a writer. Splitting the difference, he began his Emmy Award-winning career in advertising, eventually leading him to Hollywood, where he now writes and produces for film and television. James is a proud member of Mystery Writers of America, International Thriller Writers, Crime Writers' Association, and Sisters in Crime and rarely wakes up screaming anymore.

TIM P. WALKER lives in Baltimore, Maryland. He already knows who you think he looks like, but if you're willing to buy him a drink, he can try to recite that bartender joke from the film *Desperado* the way the other guy told it. You can find his (not the other guy's) brand of pulp fiction in many fine publications such as *Rock and a Hard Place*, *Out of the Gutter*, *Pulp Modern*, the late great *Baltimore City Paper*, and such anthologies as the Anthony Award-nominated *Under the Thumb: Stories of Police Oppression*.

VICTORIA WEISFELD's short stories have appeared in *Ellery Queen's Mystery Magazine*, *Mystery Magazine*, and *Black Cat Mystery Magazine*, among others, and in numerous anthologies, including: *Busted: Arresting Stories from the Beat*, *Seascapes: Best New England Crime Stories*, and *Sherlock Holmes: A Year of Mystery 1884*. They've won awards from the Short Mystery Fiction Society and Public Safety Writers Association. She's a member of those groups, plus Sisters in Crime and Mystery Writers of America. Her first novel-length crime thriller, *Architect of Courage*, was published in June 2022. She blogs regularly at vweisfeld.com and reviews books for the UK website CrimeFictionLover.com.

HOLLY WEST is the Anthony Award-nominated author of the Mistress of Fortune historical mystery series and the editor of *Murder-A-Go-Go's: Crime Fiction Inspired by the Music of the Go-Go's*. Her novella, *The Money Block*, is out now from Down & Out Books. Holly lives in Folsom, California with her husband and two spoiled dogs.

DÉSIRÉE ZAMORANO is the author of the highly acclaimed literary novel, *The Amado Women*. Her novel *Human Cargo* was Latinidad's mystery pick of the year. An award-winning and Pushcart prize nominee short story writer, her work is often an exploration of issues of invisibility, injustice, or inequity. A selection of her writing can be found at *Catapult, Cultural Weekly, The Kenyon Review Online*, and in Akashic's *South Central Noir*. "Caperucita Roja" was chosen as a distinguished short story in *Best of American Mystery and Suspense 2022*. Her historical novel *Dispossessed* is forthcoming from Rize.

On the following pages are a few
more great titles from the
Down & Out Books publishing family.

For a complete list of books and to
sign up for our newsletter,
go to DownAndOutBooks.com.

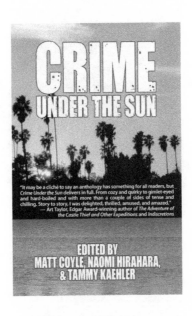

Crime Under the Sun
A Sisters in Crime Anthology
Edited by Matt Coyle, Naomi Hirahara
and Tammy Kaehler

Down & Out Books
July 2023
978-1-64396-322-8

In *Crime Under the Sun*, the second anthology offered by Partners in Crime, the San Diego chapter of Sisters in Crime, fifteen stories capture the hopes and dreams of characters trying to live the idyllic SoCal life. Instead, they bump up against greed, treachery, corruption, and murder.

These stories will thrill readers with unexpected twists and turns and surprise endings.

Psycho Therapy
A Diamond Mystery
TG Wolff

Down & Out Books
July 2023
978-1-64396-323-5

An intervention puts Diamond on a therapist's couch, dropping her in a high-stakes game of blackmail, kidnapping, and murder.

From a video gaming Beastmaster in Michigan, to a suicide bomber in Virginia, to a psychiatric conference in France, Diamond jumps in with her usual flair for chaos and destruction.

Just as she is about to win, Fate rears up, inserting a knife and twisting.

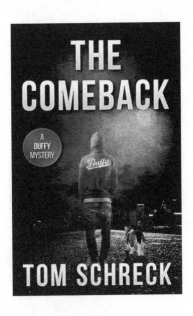

The Comeback
A Duffy Mystery
Tom Schreck

Down & Out Books
August 2023
978-1-64396-326-6

After almost a decade, our social-working, pro-boxing, Schlitz-drinking, basset hound-loving, bleeding heart tough guy, Duffy, has no idea what he's in for. His world literally blows up with a new gig, a career shift, another hound and, though he's still spending most of the time in AJ's, now it is from the other side of the bar.

On the trail to get even for a friend, he's up against the Chicago Mob, the city's toughest street gang and a crooked doctor preying on the addicted.

Loud Water
Robby Henson

Down & Out Books
August 2023
978-1-64396-327-3

Eight years into a 15-year sentence, Crit Poppwell finally discovered something he was good at, besides destroying his family and abusing drugs. He found art. The solitary act of drawing, painting and creating brings a calmness to his chaos.

Crit returns to his hometown where his brother is the reigning crystal meth kingpin and his ex-wife wants him dead. Can Crit flush the past from his blood and bones? Or die trying?

"A brilliant noir debut with a bittersweet ending."
 —Jim Winter, author of the Holland Bay series